BODIES AND SOULS

BODIES AND SOULS

Nancy Thayer

HODDER AND STOUGHTON
LONDON SYDNEY AUCKLAND TORONTO

*All of the characters in this book are fictitious
and any resemblance to persons, living or dead,
is purely coincidental.*

British Library Cataloguing in Publication Data

Thayer, Nancy
   Bodies and souls.
   I. Title
   813'.54[F]   PS3570.H3475

   ISBN 0-340-33007-4

Hodder and Stoughton Editorial Office: 47 Bedford Square, London, WC1B 3DP

For Joshua and Jessica

*With special thanks to Kate Medina, Bob Buckwalter,
and Bill Peck*

BODIES AND SOULS

Here is the church,
Here is the steeple,
Open the door
And see all the people. . . .

PART ONE

Sunday morning
October 18, 1981

PETER TAYLOR

This Sunday morning the first chill of fall had risen from the land like the delicate silver frost on a plum. The grass was etched with rime; the sky foamed. It seemed the sun had moved a crucial degree all at once, overnight, and there was a change in the air.

The Reverend Peter Taylor knelt alone in his church office to ask the Lord to give him the wisdom and strength to minister well to his congregation. Over the years he had established a ritual. In his mind's eye he envisioned the vast arc of space, the churning galaxies, that most beautiful of planets, the blue earth, the continent of North America, this New England town with its white colonial and collegiate stone buildings, and finally, his own modest white Congregational church with its storybook steeple. In this way, he supposed he was using magical thinking: by funneling his view of the world in toward himself and his church, perhaps he could also help God focus toward this minute segment of the cosmos. "Look, God, right down here—here we are."

His knees hurt; he wasn't used to kneeling. No one knelt in church anymore, and he thought it a pity, another sign of the continual division between mind and body. He was old-fashioned and believed that it would do his congregation good to compose their bodies in an attitude of worship and supplication, if only for a few minutes a week. Heaven only knew what positions those bodies got up, down, and into the rest of the week. He believed that it was man's spirit that made him Godlike, but there was no getting around the fact that as long as men and women inhabited corporeal bodies, it would be those bodies, that flesh, which told them what was important to the spirit.

Beauty was not abstract; it was in a concerto by Bach, and came to humans through the delicate organs of the ear; it was in the sight of a naked body or the New England hills in autumn, and came to humans through the fastidious complexities of the eye; it was in water after thirst, laughter after loneliness, embrace after absence. Messages came to the human spirit through the body. Peter Taylor believed that a few minutes of kneeling would do more to convince his congregation of God's supremacy than all the words of his sermon.

But he was old-fashioned, and his congregation, for the most part, was not. Most of his parishioners were attractive and educated and affluent; many were chic, facile, even lecherous. Life was too easy for some of them. Sometimes he wanted to ship them all off to live for a year in Harlem or India. But mostly he loved them, and he knew they had their share of sorrows, and more than their share of sins. They were a continual challenge to him: there was always something going on, even in this small and comfortable town, which brought him to a full test of his intellectual and ecclesiastic abilities. For he was a modern minister, and he knew there were seldom simple answers to human questions.

The bells were tolling; it was time to begin. He rose, brushed his knees, and crossed the room to glance at himself in the mirror. He had been told, often and with varying degrees of subtlety, that he was a handsome man, and although he tried to fight vanity, it was a help to him to know just how he looked before he faced his congregation. He was tall, broad-shouldered, and if he had put on weight here and there, the general effect was to make him seem massive, influential. His black hair was graying at the temples, and the lines his face had gained with age were a help. When he was younger, his blue eyes and symmetrical English features had made him seem too young, too untested, for such a position. But he had gained some wisdom with his forty-eight years, and this showed. He looked like a minister, and this gave him the confidence to take on the complicated crew who awaited him now. He left his office and walked down the hall and into the chancel.

Through the years the exterior of the First Congregational Church of Londonton had graced as many calendars as Marilyn Monroe because of its simple architecture, its classic steeple spiring toward the sky. But Peter preferred the interior of the church. He believed no one on earth could enter this sanctuary without feeling an exultation of spirits, and an attending leap of faith, if not in the reality of God, at least in the reality of grace. The walls of the church rose up around him for sixty feet, and were crowned by an oval ring of ceiling that was slightly vaulted to make the most subtle of domes. The walls and ceiling were soft white in color, simply ornamented by a rim of wood painted gold. The sanctuary was slightly longer than it was wide, with six long, high, narrow windows on each side. These windows were matched by six columns with composite capitals which were set in the semicircle of the chancel itself. The pews were hardwood painted white; the floor was covered with a deep red carpet that spoke more of old and dignified elegance than of expense. The beauty of this church was not in any superficial decorations but in the basic architecture itself. It rose up and curved into itself with complete simplicity, as if it had been built by men with peaceful hearts.

The building was situated so that on cloudless days the sun streamed into the first three windows on the right-hand side, making the burled cherry wood of the altar and the flowers on either side of it lustrous with light. Many members of Peter's congregation complimented him on the beauty of that delineated radiance, as if he were personally responsible for the focused beam of light. But he knew how they felt; bright sunlight came through those windows with the benevolent force of a blessing. Still, Peter preferred the church on cloudy Sundays. Then all the windows were equally illuminated by a silvery-white glow, and Peter felt that they were all at one together, drawn together and encompassed by that gentler light.

Today was so cool and cloudy that for the first time in months, Peter's congregation sat before him arrayed in sweaters, wool blazers, and heavy coats. Liza Howard was already wearing a fur coat, though she was probably wearing it more for the effect it had on others than for the warmth. People would just have to get used to sitting through church with their coats on, Peter thought, for with the rising cost of fuel it would be impossible to keep the church really warm. Perhaps the slight chill in the air would provide that edge of discomfort which kept people alert and awake. He gazed out at the congregation a moment, counting the house, then bowed his head in prayer.

This prayer was the same as always: Dear Lord, now that they were all actually here, let what he had to say make sense to someone.

A man came up the four steps to sit across the chancel from him, and Peter raised his head and nodded. It was Reynolds Houston, the lay reader for today. Reynolds would read the Call to Worship, and later, the scripture lesson, and he would do it beautifully. In fact, no one in the world looked more like a minister than Reynolds Houston, who was so tall and slim he would have seemed ascetic, were it not for the sensuality of his hair. Few men in their fifties have beautiful hair, but Reynolds did, and although he wore it cut fairly short, there was no mistaking its abundance.

Reynolds was a conundrum of a man to Peter. His long stringy body seemed mismatched with his voluptuously handsome face; and it was unusual that a man with his cold, intellectual competence should speak with such a sonorous and soothing voice. Reynolds taught Latin and Greek at the local college and served on many committees for both the college and the town. One could often see his lanky body stalking across the grounds on one mission or another. He was seldom accompanied; he was the sort of man who preferred his own company. Peter knew very little about Reynolds' private life, and so he had been surprised, earlier this morning, when Reynolds had asked if he could speak with him after church regarding "a matter of grave concern." Peter could not imagine what sort of problem it could be that this reserved man would want to confide. He studied Reynolds for a moment, admiring the cut of the gray flannel suit which must have been specially tailored to fit such a gawky body so elegantly. Reynolds was leaning forward in his chair, his head bowed, his arms resting on his legs, his hands folded in prayer; and Peter noticed the awkwardness of his very long fingers and hands, delicately embraced by the cuffs of an expensive cotton shirt, set with silver cuff links. Reynolds was an immaculate man, and his face was equally smooth just now; Peter could read no emotion there, no clue to his problems.

The choir began to sing the Introit, which announced that the service was beginning, and Peter's mind turned to broader contemplations.

Reynolds rose and went to the pulpit to lead the congregation in the Call to Worship, then returned to stand by his chair as Mrs. Pritchard, the organist, pounded out the introductory stanzas of the first hymn of the morning. As Peter sang "When Morning Gilds the Skies," he did not look down at his hymnbook, but out and around him at his congregation.

The church was full today. He was glad to see that the wealthy Vandersons, who were always off vacationing in some exotic place, were here today; but he was equally glad to see Norma and Wilbur Wilson in their usual place at the back of the church. The Wilsons were an older couple, neither wealthy nor sophisticated, but they had their own special prestige: they were *old* Londontoners. Their parents had been born here, and their parents before them, and Norma and Wilbur had lived in this town for over sixty-five years; they had been married in this church by another minister long ago. When Peter had moved to Londonton to take the position as pastor of this church several years back, he had been acutely aware of the Wilsons' quiet skepticism, and it was a point of pride to him that they had retained their membership in the church and continued to attend faithfully—even though Wilbur's frosty eyebrows raised defiantly now and then when Peter's liberal political beliefs showed up too blatantly in his sermons.

Well, the Wilsons were here today, and the Moyers, and the Bennetts, and all the rest of the regulars. Peter sometimes thought this was the best moment of the Sunday morning. Everything seemed fresh and new, ready to begin: his congregation gathered hopefully before him, not yet restless from sitting. His flock. Perhaps after all he could do them good. Hadn't they gone to the trouble this crisp October morning to climb out of their beds, dress, and come to church, when they could be doing any number of other things—staying by the first fire of fall, sipping hot coffee and reading the New York *Times?* Or they could be out raking leaves, or stacking wood, or hiking through the mountains— they were by and large athletic and energetic people. But here they were, like children, offering their faces up to him, willing him to say the words that would change their lives, if only by bringing a few minutes of peace into the flurry of their days. He wanted to comfort them, enlighten them, uplift them, and perhaps even bring them closer somehow to God.

Peter had become a minister in part because of his secret belief that he might be the only happy man on earth. He had been raised on a large farm in Vermont which had been handed down by three generations of Taylors to his father, John, and which was in turn handed on to Peter's older brother, John, Jr. The farm was mostly given over to apple orchards, and the beauty of those orchards in all seasons had filled Peter with a durable joy. His parents were both gone now; they had died within ten months of each other, but while they lived they had cared for each other with such steadfast affection that Peter grew up completely assured that such a thing as love existed on the earth. Against the horrors of the outside world he could hold up the example of their personal goodness, and this made it possible for him to be an optimist. He had not married until he was thirty, but he had married happily, and loved his wife not only with an enduring fondness but with an enduring lust. He was a fortunate man, and he believed in God, in the innate order and goodness which he thought must surely operate at the core of the universe, and in the ultimate perfectibility of human beings and the world they made. He really did have Faith, and his congregation was able to sense that in him. They trusted him, as one who has been blessed, to pass blessings on.

Because he was an intelligent man, he also had his share of doubts about the messages he preached. But his greatest fear was not that he was all wrong and there was no God; he was not afraid of dying into oblivion. His greatest fear was that if there really was an afterlife, and if there really was a God, at the ultimate confrontation God would accuse him of failure. He could imagine God's wrath, God's words: "You fool! I gave you everything, and you did nothing of any real value! You were no help at all!" What would Peter do then?

Peter thought ministers were, even more than average professional men, prey to crises of confidence, of faith. It wasn't a purely personal problem, either; much of it had to do with changing standards and beliefs, which in turn altered the very foundations of the Church, and the way the Bible was interpreted. Peter was now forty-eight. Things had changed drastically since he was a small boy trembling on the edge of a pew as the pastor of the North Alton, Vermont, Methodist Church threatened him with hellfire and damnation. The idea of Hell was unpopular these days, and ministers were called upon to talk about charity more than righteousness. It was an attitude Peter felt quite comfortable with, given his temperament: he would always much rather forgive than castigate. Anyway, he had been so lucky, who was he to condemn anyone else? He would prefer to bring God into his parishioners' lives through the doors of hope and wonder rather than through the doors of fear. But what if he were getting it all wrong? What if he were misinterpreting everything? What if, by his tolerance, he was committing sins of omission—and making it possible for his congregation to slip into Sin? It was passé now, he knew, the idea of Sin, yet it all the same existed, as alluring as a cool blue lake on a hot summer's day. He felt as though he were leading his flock near that lake, when he should perhaps be angrily shooing them away; that he was consciously turning his back while certain of his congregation dabbled their toes or waded in, or even went for long swims.

Liza Howard, for example. Now Peter really did worry about the state of her soul. There she sat, just three rows from the front, wrapped in her mink coat. She was one of the wealthiest members of the congregation, and one of the worst. It was not just that she gave so little of her wealth to the church—although of course that irked Peter greatly. His poor church needed so many things and Liza Howard gave so little. Also, he secretly felt that her lack of generosity was a reflection on his preaching. If someone better were in the pulpit, surely Liza would give more? But money was not the main issue. He was not angry with her or worried about her simply because of selfish reasons. He was worried for Liza herself. In his most extreme moments, he believed that if there were a Hell after death, it was to be her inescapable destiny. More often and more rationally, he simply thought that anyone as dreadful as she was must secretly be miserable.

She did not seem miserable, however. She seemed well fed, well read, highly intelligent, critical, capable, and utterly self-satisfied. And no wonder: she possessed a ripe, complete beauty of face and body unlike anything he had ever seen before, a mythic beauty. If Renoir had painted Mae West in modern dress, perhaps the result would have resembled Liza Howard: she was a blue-eyed blonde with an hourglass figure, a blooming summer garden of a woman. She usually wore her thick honey-colored hair pulled off her face and piled in soft convolutions at the back of her head, the better to display the emeralds or pearls in her ears. But the very way she restrained her hair indicated how long and wavy it would be when she released it. Everything about the woman was undulant, the gentle turn of her arms or legs, her full pink lips, her high, pillowy breasts. She was a tall, long-waisted, long-legged woman, perfectly proportioned: the sort of woman who made slimmer women look angular and ropy and tough. She was a woman of luxurious flesh.

But she was also a woman of licentious flesh. She counted on the lust of men to keep her entertained and she did more than her share of coveting neighbors' husbands and committing adultery.

Peter knew certain things from gossip, and others from occasional confessions from outwardly proper but inwardly wretched men. Still, she was going too far with her attempts to seduce Peter himself.

Peter knew he was a handsome man and that this helped him in his ministry. Other women had had crushes on him and expressed this in a number of charming, embarrassed ways: serving diligently on committees, giving him chaste, handmade presents, even asking him to help them deal with the burden of their feelings, because they knew he was a married man.

But Liza displayed no such delicacy. Once or twice he had asked her to help him with some church task, in the hopes that over the casual friendly ease of an afternoon's work, she might drop her guard and let him see the frightened child within. For there was surely a frightened child within us all, wasn't there? Peter thought so. Liza *did* attend church, and she was intelligent—she must know that she was greedy, adulterous, uncharitable, and vain. Peter believed that in her heart of hearts Liza mourned for herself, for what she had become.

Just last weekend he had asked Liza to join him in visiting three very old couples who lived on farms in the mountains around Londonton, thinking that as they drove from farm to farm Liza would reflect on the difference between her state and that of other parishioners, who were at this point all too old or crippled to make the journey into church most Sundays. He thought the sight of their withered bodies and humble homes would fill Liza with pity; she would see how lucky she was to be so wealthy and beautiful. The last old couple they visited had a nice home filled with drying apples and obliging dogs and cats. Peter expected Liza to say *something*—how she admired the old couple, how she envied them their quiet going on with life, how she was aware in the middle of dark nights that in spite of the superficial beauty of her life she was in truth more lonely and miserable than the old couples they saw who had so few material goods. Liza at thirty-five was a widow; Peter wondered if she had played a role, if only indirectly, in helping her aging husband to a heart attack.

But as Peter and Liza had ridden together through the brilliant New England day, Liza had not opened her heart to Peter. And so, finally, Peter had made a great attempt: he had reached his hand across the seat to place it gently over Liza's elegant smooth hand, which fairly blossomed with rings. Liza had not withdrawn her hand, and so for a moment they had gone along that way, hands clasped in friendship.

"You know," Peter had said, "it is what is in one's heart that really matters."

"Do you want to sleep with me?" Liza had asked in reply.

He had dropped Liza's hand and nearly run off the road in horror. That she would invite him, suspect him! The entire afternoon, the old people—none of it had meant anything to Liza. She was too self-occupied.

"Liza," he had said after a moment, "I love you in the way I love all the members of my church. And you are a lovely woman, which I'm sure you know without my saying. But I'm a married man, and a minister. I don't lust after you. I'd like to be your friend. I'd like to help you." Surely, he thought, he could not be any plainer than that.

Liza had studied Peter for one long moment with her gambler's eyes—Peter had felt the gaze upon him, and had concentrated fiercely on the winding road. Then she had looked away. "Of course," she said.

When Peter glanced over at her again, he saw that she had rearranged herself seductively, so that ostensibly she was looking out the window, but with her body positioned in such a way that her skirt, which was one of those incredible new things with a slit up the side, exposed almost the entire length of one long, sleek, expensively stockinged leg. And she had placed her arm on the armrest of the car door in such a way that her blouse curved open, exposing a touch of creamy lace and of even creamier, curving breast. Again he nearly ran off the road. He was offended, and deeply disappointed. He had attempted to minister to her, and had been affronted. Churlishly he thought: The hell with it then, there is nothing more I can do. He had to drive a good five miles before he could forgive her or himself for his anger.

They had parted pleasantly enough, as if nothing had happened, and Liza had continued to attend church, and Peter had said nothing more to her. But he was despondent at the thought of his failure, at his inability to reach her, to let her know that she was God's child and owed something both to God and to herself. How could he ever reach her? At this very moment, she was staring at him directly, with a frank come-hither look on her face, and Peter thought that if he were a different kind of minister in a different kind of church, he might stop the hymn and openly chastise her.

Of course he would never do that. It was not his style. And it wasn't done, not here in this great New England pocket of reserve and propriety. He would never be able openly to confront Liza with her wickedness; and so he would never be able to help her. Every time she came to church she stood there in front of him as a blatant sign of his inability to be a true minister. But the most he could do at the moment was to try to turn wrath away from his heart.

No. He could do more than that. While the ushers seated late-comers and the organ music carried them through the final verses of the hymn, he could use these few moments to admit the truth to himself. It was not wrath he was trying to turn away from his heart, but lust; and he wasn't sure that he wanted to turn away the lust, either. It was such a pleasurable sensation.

If he were honest with himself, he would admit that he liked having Liza in his church, that he enjoyed her presence and looked forward to it—wasn't she the first person in the congregation that his eyes went to every time? She was a beautiful, sexy young woman, and his feelings about her were complicated. When he had invited her to help him with certain church tasks, had he not been secretly hoping for something more reasonable than a religious conversion? He had been hoping that she would find him desirable, and would express that desire in some definite way. When they were riding together in his car and he reached out to touch her hand, he had done so only partly from genuine human concern: he had also quite simply wanted to touch her. It was too bad that she had been so blatant and definite in her response; if only she had been subtle and shy. Then he could have had the joy of knowing they were physically attracted to each other without the attending responsibility and moral concerns. But no, she had immediately asked him if he wanted to sleep with her, and what could he do but reply as he had? He was a minister, a married man.

But what if he had said, "Yes"? What if she had replied, "Good, because I want to sleep with you, too"? What if they had agreed to make love just that one time, and to never touch each other or speak of the occasion again? It had been a beautiful, warm October day, and the country roads had been full of isolated driveways where a car could shelter behind shrubs and trees. It would have taken only minutes for him to convert the back seat of the station wagon into a large flat space that would serve as a bed—not a very comfortable bed, but serviceable all the same. What would it have been like to stand in the hushed and dappled sunlight of the woods carefully removing the lacy coverings from Liza Howard's body? It would have been so quiet—no ticking of clocks or muffled domestic rattlings behind doors—only the sound of their quickened breath, their exhalations as they moved against each other, their bare feet rustling in the high grass, the slippery sigh of branches rubbing together above them. They would have taken their time; they would have goaded each other into leisure; he would have stood naked, a light breeze playing over his skin, and he would have seen her standing nude in the open air, the sunlight exposing the white bulbs of her breasts, the ferny growth between her legs . . . they would have been back in the Garden of Eden.

And here his imagination stopped, for now, because he was a minister and the lush imagery in his mind had triggered off too many intrusive symbols. Yes, he would have liked to be with that woman just for a while—and what would have been the consequences? For he did believe there would be consequences; he had long ago lost the ability to be a simple sinner. The worst thing that could have happened would be for someone to see them, for the tale of his infidelity with the scarlet woman of Londonton to spread among his parishioners, causing them to lose their faith in him, and to his wife, causing her pain and anger. At the least, even if no other person discovered them, even if Liza Howard didn't bruit the news around town, he would have had his own conscience to deal with. No. That sexy sin would have been too fecund; it would have grown like a swampland of weedy trees, extending its shadow and roots over his entire life. It would never have been worth it. Never the right thing to do. But he realized he had wanted to do it then, and found pleasure in imagining it now; and this revelation shook him. How could he have been so dully unaware, so oblivious of his own bodily appetite? Liza Howard had probably been no more seductive than he. This sort of thing must happen to her often, Peter thought. People must often take her sexiness personally. Bodies were always getting in the way of things. Now he looked out at her, winging a silent apology toward her, but she only stared back at him blankly.

He looked away from Liza Howard and searched through the congregation for his wife, Patricia, and finding her, he found instant consolation. He did love her. He had been terrified all during his twenties as he came to know more and more people who had had miserable childhoods—alcoholic parents, drug-addicted parents, divorced parents, hateful parents, absentminded parents—that after being gifted with loving parents, he did not deserve, he would not get, a loving wife. His childhood had been happy; was his marriage bound to fail? It was more than superstition, it was logic: who gets everything in life? So he was afraid of seriously considering marriage with any woman he met. Yet because of his religiosity and his everlasting sense of responsibility, he had trouble considering any lighter liaison. He went to graduate school for a master's in English literature, and on to seminary, and during these years he had no trouble meeting women, because he was handsome, smart, witty, and kind. But he never dated any one girl for very long out of fear that one or the other of them might tip the balance of their affections by caring more or wanting a commitment when the other didn't. Still he did not lack ever for women friends or lovers, and because he was pleasant and gentle, he often found himself comforting the young women who had been somehow hurt by friends of his. He often felt helpless in the face of their pain.

"I can't live without Bill," a young woman would cry to him. "Oh, Peter, what shall I do? I want to die."

He would gaze at the grief-stricken face of a heartbroken friend and think to himself that this was the ultimate cruelty on God's part: not death or disaster or disease, which were at least honest, but love, which was deceitful. It used irresistible beauties to lure a person into a moment of joy and then into almost intolerable pain.

He did not know how his parents had come by that happy marriage of theirs. Perhaps it had been mere luck. But he did not expect such luck in his own life.

At last a wonderful thing happened to him: a woman broke his heart. He was twenty-seven, and just starting out as a pastor of two small churches in rural Maine. Sarah was an artist. One day Peter had looked out the window of his church office to see a woman in a soft blue dress sitting cross-legged in the grass, sketching the lines of the simple Protestant church on her large white pad. She was intent on her job and did not notice when Peter came to stand by the window and stare at her. She had very long blond hair which fell over her shoulders as she moved, so that the quick certain gesture which she used to brush her hair back was an integral part of the definite rhythm with which she drew; as if her work and her self were one and the same. Peter watched the woman for a long time, and when he finally left his office to intrude himself into her presence, he felt it was the bravest thing he had yet done in his life: he knew that this was a woman he would love. And he did come to love her, and she him. They saw each other for over a year and then became engaged. But Sarah could never bring herself to set the wedding date, and it all ended with her admitting that she did not want to marry Peter.

"Tell me the truth," Peter had said to Sarah the night before she was to fly to Colorado to live with another man, a former lover. "You're afraid of marrying me because of my profession, aren't you? You don't want to be a minister's wife."

Sarah was as straightforward as she was lovely. "I know how much the truth means to you, Peter," she said. "No, I am not afraid of your profession. I'm not afraid of anything. The truth is that I don't love you enough to be married to you. I'm glad I was your lover for a while, but it's over for me now. But I'll always care for you."

When she left, Peter did not think he could bear the pain. He lay in bed for days, telling others that he had the flu, crying in a way he never dreamt a man could cry, and wondering how on this earth he could ever find a reason for getting up and out of bed. Finally other people's sorrows rescued him: someone in the parish died and he was called upon to minister to the family. And so he began to function. But he found himself dwelling on the loss of Sarah's love in the same way that a miser might cherish a rough-cut diamond, turning it and pressing it with his hands, even though the glittering edges would slice and cut him till he bled.

Later, he learned of the refinements of sorrow, the companions of grief: bitterness, cynicism, despair, apathy, anger. For a while he wished that Sarah had left him by dying, because then she would not be able to love any other mortal. Sometimes his lovesickness made his life and the very space of the room he was in seem thick and crowded;

as if sorrow were a billowing cloud. At other times his life and the room he was in would seem sucked clean of meaning, empty; as if sorrow were a vacuum. There were times when he would grip the sides of the lectern to keep from crying out to his congregation that *he hurt*: he missed Sarah's body, her sweet breath, long legs, laughter, breasts.

So he learned genuine compassion. One Sunday morning, four months after Sarah had left, Peter realized with a start that at least a third of his congregation in this rural Maine area were widows and widowers. There they sat, the kindly Christian women who had put on straw or felt or fur hats and pinned flowers or brooches at their necks, weathered older men who had put on their best suits and ties, and all not out of vanity, but in order to come out into the cold winter days alone to attend church. These were industrious, persevering people, not the type to indulge in despair—and yet surely there were nights when their bodies ached as his did for another body to hold. As he studied his congregation, he found himself thinking that there must be ways to ease their mutual pain. And so he called for Sunday-night potluck dinners, and musical performances by the young and old of the community—and for a while there was a flurry of activity in his life that used up his time and taught him the healing powers of hard work.

One day sixteen months after Sarah had left, Peter caught himself admiring the long curve of leg of a pretty young woman who was taking over the elementary Sunday school classes. She blushed; he lusted; and smiled with relief at his lust. That night he sat in his apartment alone and drank a toast to himself, pronouncing himself healed. He had survived. Furthermore, he had learned a lesson: that the human heart was not the fragile, limited organ he had thought it was; it was tough, and it could expand endlessly. It could curve with necessary grace around almost any wound.

How could this happen? How could his own fist-shaped heart close like a hand around a rock of pain only to open with a flourish to present live flowers? He did not understand, but he thought that certainly if a man could believe in his own heart he could easily believe in God.

The pretty young woman was Patricia. She taught second grade in the public schools and had been in love with Peter ever since his first sermon at that church. She had not been able to get his attention during all the weeks she had faithfully sat in the front pew of the church, and out of desperation she had agreed to teach Sunday school. If Peter's strength lay in the knowledge that he had been happy as a child, Patricia's lay in the conviction that she would be happy as an adult. Peter was so dazzled by her fearless optimism that there were times when he was amazed to realize that she was also physically beautiful. The times when her beauty was recalled to him most forcefully were the times when they were in bed together; he would lie on his side and smile at Patricia in sheer delight.

"What's so funny?" she would ask, tracing his smile with her fingertips.

"I keep forgetting how lovely you are," he would say. "It's always such a pleasant surprise."

Patricia would shake her head, pretending he was speaking nonsense, but he was speaking the truth, and at no time were his words more true than after they had made love. Then Patricia's power was transformed into content, and her determination for the future distracted by the idle pleasures of present joys.

They had been married eighteen years now. Their love had undergone the transmutations natural to a family: they had two sons and a daughter, and emotions shifted and glittered within their family with the same intact and interconnected variety of patterns as in a kaleidoscope. There were nights when Peter was glad to send his children off to bed so that he could be alone with Patricia, but there were also nights when he crept into their bedrooms to linger a moment above each sleeping child, his heart nearly breaking with love and hope and fear. If God really did look upon each human as His child, or even upon humankind as His children, then *poor God,* Peter thought, He didn't know what He was getting Himself into when He created us. Peter wanted so desperately to keep his children happy and safe, and now they were awash in the turbulent teen-age years when he could not protect them. He and Patricia had seen them through the perils of childhood, through illness and accidents; they had done the best they could to ease them into the civilized world of school and society. The early years of fatherhood had been demanding enough—but these last years! Peter's children were being confronted with cars, drugs, sex, philosophies. They would have to make choices. They would have to leave home.

Peter worried about Michael, his oldest child. Love had never been easy between him and Michael; it seemed that from Michael's birth the two of them had been engaged in a series of strange skirmishes that grew less subtle as the years went by. Black-hearted child! Peter often thought, yet he loved this first son with a desperate love that was nearly a frenzy. Michael was making it absolutely clear that he wanted nothing more than to leave home, to live his own life, and as much as Peter often longed to rage at the boy, "Just go then, you ingrate, I'll be glad to get rid of you and your wretched sulky ways!" he also was terrified for the boy's sake, terrified to have him go off on his own. What did Michael know about life? He was so young, so pigheaded. Oh, this was a terrible age, seventeen, and a terrible time for the entire family: Peter felt that Michael's approaching departure was a kind of amputation of the family, and he dreaded it.

But surely this was an unnatural response, at least an overdramatic one. Peter looked down to see Leigh and Mandy Findly standing side by side, their heads bent together over a hymnal. Mandy was a year older than Michael; at eighteen this year she had started her freshman year at a college an hour away from Londonton. Peter didn't know the Findlys well, but he did know this much: Mandy was back for a visit after only six weeks away at school; here she stood next to her mother with all apparent friendship and goodwill. How had Leigh managed to accomplish this? She was not a perfect mother, or at least she had not had the perfect circumstances: she had been divorced for years and years, and had lived her life in a sort of attractive artistic muddle. She was a potter of some renown but apparently little ambition, the bohemian of Londonton. Peter knew from Patricia and other committee chairpersons that Leigh Findly could never be counted on to help with church or community projects; she was always too busy with her pots. She probably made a decent living from her work, for she and Mandy lived in an attractive old Cape Cod house in one of the better sections of town, but it was possible that the house was an inheritance from her divorce. At any rate, while she never seemed to be poor, she never seemed rich, either, and was always drifting around in turquoise or magenta batik cotton skirts. She wore the skirts even in the winter, with high-heeled, fleece-lined leather boots. She was around forty, a pretty woman, even a sexy one, although her sexual attraction was different from Liza Howard's: Liza's was pure, a chemical, a beam, powerful in its simplicity and directness. Leigh's sexuality seemed more tied up in

her intelligence and her sense of humor. Probably she would never be
able to seduce men as completely as Liza did because Leigh wasn't able
to take sex so seriously. Still it was known that she had had her
share of lovers through the years. Sometimes, when a man had moved
in with her, she had brought him to church with her, with her and
Mandy. No man ever lasted very long, not more than a year or two,
but Leigh did not seem to suffer from this. She seemed quite happy on
her own, and was in fact a likable woman, a nice woman. Still she had
not provided what could be called an ideal environment for a child.
What textbook would say that the best environment for a child was
that provided by a flaky, divorced, absentminded, fornicating mother?
Yet Mandy was a lovely and well-adjusted girl. Peter did not know her
well, but it was obvious to him that the young woman liked herself—
and that she liked her mother.

How had Leigh managed this conjuring trick? Peter wondered.
Was it sheer luck or force of personality? How had she managed to
have her daughter standing next to her, happily sharing a hymnal,
when Peter's son was standing at the back of the church, making
no pretense of singing, undoubtedly snapping his gum in irritation and
boredom?

Which made the better minister, Peter sometimes wondered: the
solitary priest who had no children of his own to pull his affections and
attentions from the congregation and who thus could work undistracted
by personal hopes and worries, or the minister who learned only too
well from having his own family just what a frightful obstacle course
life was, and thus was able to understand and help his congregation,
because their fears and needs were his own? There could probably be
no one certain answer to this question, but the very presence of the
question gave Peter comfort when he found himself neglecting his congregation in his thoughts because of personal worries.

He thought, for example, as he surveyed those gathered before
him this morning, that he could sympathize more completely with a
woman like Suzanna Blair than he could have had he been childless.
His glance rested on her again and again, because of all the people
standing before him, Suzanna Blair seemed the most troubled. Yet this
was only a hunch on his part, only a guess; she had never come to
confide in him, had never asked for his help. Still there were moments
when he caught her looking down at her two small children with such

sorrow on her face that he longed to interrupt the service, to call out to her, to ask what was wrong and whether he could somehow help.

He knew very little about Suzanna. He had first met her when she was still married, about three years ago, at a cocktail party at the Moyers'. Actually it was her husband that he remembered meeting. Tom Blair considered himself a memorable personage, and he *was* one of those characters who manage to seem just a little bit bigger than life. That year he had chosen to attire himself and his life as a college professor in a lumberjack-naturalist style. He wore plaid wool shirts and tweed jackets and leather boots which came up over his jeans to his knees. He smoked a pipe and was hearty, and if it was with an air of self-congratulatory heartiness that he moved through the world, as if announcing, "Look at me! Aren't I a big, powerful, Hemingwayesque fellow, and isn't it amazing that I can teach Milton's poetry and split my own firewood!"—still he was a likable enough man. Of Suzanna at that particular party, Peter remembered only that she had been so gentle-looking that he had been surprised to discover from her conversation that she had a quick and witty turn of mind.

From time to time afterward he had come across the Blairs, and they had seemed another normal, agreeable young couple. When he heard about their divorce, he was surprised: *why?* he had asked, and no one seemed to know. Many divorces in the community took place with the elaborateness of a full-scale movie production, complete with a cast of hundreds and a script full of tears and ravings that would have driven a soap opera director to fits of envy. But the Blairs, as far as Peter could tell, had just sort of slid into divorce. One day they were, at least superficially, happily married, and the next Tom Blair was showing up at parties with various adoring young women at his side. After a while, Tom moved away, and a few months later Suzanna began attending Peter's church with her two young children. The first Sunday Peter had noticed her sitting there, he had felt expansive with anticipation; perhaps soon he would know something more about her.

But as the months passed, she not only remained a mystery to him but grew even more mysterious. When she first started attending church, Peter had considered her really just a pretty, pleasant woman. Suzanna taught first grade in the public school, and to his mind she looked the way a first-grade teacher should look. She had short, curly brown hair, pink cheeks, blue eyes, and a slightly plump, good-natured figure; her attractiveness made no demands. Then one morning about two years ago, Peter had looked down into the congregation to see Suzanna sitting there looking absolutely disheveled, even though her clothes were perfectly tidy. She had been grinning at her hymnal; then she had blushed, then covered her mouth with her hand, and finally shaken herself a little, as if trying to settle her body back down. Well, Peter thought, perhaps she's fallen in love. But the months passed, and Suzanna came to church and parties and meetings alone, and Peter had heard no rumors of any love affairs. But surely something was going on.

Every Sunday morning, Suzanna brought the children to church, and they sat together in the pew, whispering to each other, a normal, family group. After the Children's Story, when her son and daughter and all the other children left the main sanctuary for their various Sunday school rooms in the basement of the church, Suzanna Blair would recompose herself in her pew in such a way that she gathered in the very space around her and made it private. Peter had gotten pretty good at judging whether a parishioner was listening to his sermon or daydreaming, and Suzanna seemed almost always to be daydreaming. In the midst of a most serious sermon, Peter would see an absolutely beatific smile pass over her face. To her credit, she immediately covered her mouth with her hand and shook her head slightly to reprove herself. Peter did not know just what aroused his curiosity more: those smiles of Suzanna's or the equally intense expressions of sorrow which often during the hour overcame her so completely that her body seemed to sag under the weight. In spite of her daydreaming, she was the person who more than anyone else looked up at him during the course of a sermon as if beseeching, as if searching, as if asking him for an answer. Clearly something was wrong in her life; she was harboring some secret that caused her both joy and pain. But how could he help her when he did not know the cause? It had something to do with the children; of that much he was certain, because of the way she watched them walk away as they left the main congregation for Sunday school. It seemed as though each Sunday she were watching them leave her forever.

But how could he help her? She would not come to him. Now Peter stared down at Suzanna Blair's unassuming head as she bent over her hymnbook, singing her "Amen" with the others, and for one still moment he felt a cold metallic shaft of anger rise within him, as if a sword had struck his heart. For he had to look down upon her each Sunday in her suffering and fail to give her aid, because no matter how he spoke to her, she did not seem to hear, and no matter how he placed himself before her, she did not seem to see. And he wanted to smite her down, because she made him feel he was a failure and she lured him to despair.

The air was filled with shuffling, rustling noises and then expectant silence as the congregation settled back into their pews. As a body, they looked up at him, waiting for him to begin the unison reading of the Common Prayer of Adoration and Confession. Necessary stage presence brought Peter's thoughts away from the troubled woman, and he began to read aloud, leading them all.

"Most merciful Lord, in whose kingdom the lion and the lamb lie down together—"

Now he was working: performing, teaching. He thought no more about individual members of his church, but only of leading everyone through the sturdily constructed phrases of prayer. The intermingling of human voices, female and male, young and old, strong and meek, made a chant which was pleasing to the ears. Peter thought as he often had before how odd it was that such an artificial gathering of people should produce a genuine and legitimate sound, as if people were by nature meant to read aloud together no less than birds were meant to sing in unison. This weekly harmony, contrived as it was, reaffirmed his congregation's faith in God, and Peter's faith in them.

At the end of the prayer, Peter asked, "Would all the children like to join me at the front of the church for the Children's Story?" He walked to the steps and sat on the second one, and the children from the ages of four to ten gathered in a circle on the floor around him. Each week, for four or five minutes, Peter told a Children's Story—always an easy lesson with a catchy beginning and an obvious moral. Today he talked about the signs of changing seasons: the moral was to welcome each thing in its time. The Children's Story provided a break in the formality of the service. This morning, as always, there was one child who interrupted to ask an irrelevant question and another who pointed out a new pair of shoes, and the adults laughed and glanced knowingly at each other, pleased with themselves for being grownup. At the end of the Children's Story, the congregation rose to sing a hymn while the children filed out. Then Peter settled back in his chair as Reynolds Houston went to the pulpit to read from the Bible.

Part of the scripture lesson for the morning came from Mark, the old familiar words: "And thou shalt love the Lord thy God with all thy heart, and with all thy soul, and with all thy mind, and with all thy strength: this is the first commandment. And the second is like, namely this, Thou shalt love thy neighbor as thyself. There is none other commandment greater than these."

Well, of course, Peter suddenly thought: there's the answer. If *he* couldn't help Suzanna Blair, perhaps someone else could. They were a congregation. He scanned the group before him. Who could best help Suzanna Blair? Possibly Pam Moyer, who was always kind; but no, not quite right, Peter thought, not now. Pam had become very active in civic and political affairs, almost aggressively so; she would be too busy to focus on such a small, personal matter. There was always Norma Wilson, who was kind, too, but she was in her sixties, and Leigh Findly, who was closer to Suzanna's age, but as adamantly liberal in her views as Norma was conservative. Peter continued to look around.

When his glance fell on Judy Bennett, he smiled involuntarily and knew his search had come to an end. In fact, he was surprised that he had not thought of Judy immediately. She would be the perfect person to help Suzanna—she would be the perfect person to help anyone.

When Peter and Patricia and their three children had first moved to Londonton, it had been the hospitality of Judy Bennett that had made that move bearable. The Taylors and their moving van had arrived from Maine in August. The day of their arrival had been scheduled for months, but it had rained in Londonton for an entire week, and the roof of the parsonage had sprung a leak. Because no one was living there at the time to notice it, it had widened and opened, so that the walls and ceilings and floors of the bedroom and the living room below it were stained and marred, and the living-room ceiling had collapsed in places. Judy Bennett had gone to the house early, to open it up for the Taylors, and she had met them at the door with the bad news: workmen had come, and were working as fast as they could, but it would be a good week before the house was livable. Before they could gather their wits together to despair, she hurried on: the Taylors would stay at her house for the week—there was plenty of room since her two children were off at prep school, and she'd enjoy having the Taylor family around.

So the moving company had piled the furniture and boxes into the rooms that were not damaged, and Judy had welcomed all five Taylors into her home. Not only had she made them feel totally at ease in her large and beautiful house, not only did she serve them delicious meals rich with homemade breads and desserts, but she also had contrived to introduce them to the community, and the community to them, with a deft and graceful hand. She had small social gatherings that week and the week that followed. There were morning coffees for the older ladies of the church, and evening cocktail parties, and a buffet dinner for a few of the more prestigious members of the congregation. People were presented to the Taylors in small and manageable groups, so that Peter and Patricia could learn the names and faces of at least fifty people with relative ease.

Their second week in Londonton, when they had been in their own house for only two days, Patricia had had to return to Maine to take care of some necessary legal matters. She had taken their youngest child with her, leaving the two older ones and Peter in the newly repaired parsonage. Within hours of her leaving, Peter was flat on his back with a powerful flu that made him stunned with exhaustion, and he was furious with himself for getting ill at such a crucial point in his family's life. He felt that it was a terrible failure on his part that his two older children had to scavenge around in cardboard boxes to find clean towels and clothes; and as he heard them rummaging through the kitchen to find bowls for their cereal, he vowed that by that afternoon he would be up and around, preparing a decent meal. Instead, he fell into a profound invalid's sleep, and did not awaken until eight o'clock that night. He walked into the living room on weak legs to find his two children cross-legged on the floor, eating more dry cereal.

"I think you should call Mrs. Bennett," he said, and collapsed back into bed. When he woke again, it was morning, and he could hear Judy Bennett in the kitchen with the children, laughing. He could smell eggs and bacon frying, and he felt all was right with the world.

For three days Peter remained too drugged by the flu and the medicine Judy brought him to keep hold of consciousness for long; but

he was aware from time to time that she was in the other room, un-
packing boxes and arranging dishes on a shelf, or towels in a closet.
She made him tea, and when he could take it, milk toast, and she sat
with him as he ate, reassuring him that his children were well and
happy, that Patricia had called and would be back soon. When Peter
had finished eating what he could, Judy would rise and smile and bend
to take the tray away, and Peter would lapse back into sleep. So the
events of that week slid by, dreamlike; and he slept and woke in wrinkled pajamas, unshaved and shaky, vulnerable to Judy Bennett's scrutiny and judgment. He thought he had never been in a relationship of
such intimacy with any woman other than his mother or his wife, and
he marveled later at Judy Bennett's fastidious compassion, because
never once in her intimate serving did she graze that invisible, delicate
screen of propriety which separated a man and his family from the rest
of the world.

She had her own family, of course, but they seemed to find it only
natural that she would be so involved in helping others. Ron Bennett,
her husband, was a tall, handsome, confident man with great charm;
he worked as a contractor and over the years had built many private
homes and small buildings in Londonton. He was respected, admired,
and he was rich. But both he and Judy seemed not to have been
affected by his wealth, for they continued to devote much personal
time and energy to their community. And Judy remained as innocent-
looking as a bride. She kept her slim face scrubbed of makeup, and her
brown hair was always pulled straight back from her head and braided
into one thick braid which fell down her back or over her shoulder. So
she looked as wholesome and winsome as a farm girl, and she was
forty-five.

"For heaven's sakes," Patricia had told Peter once, "*you* know
nothing about women and their wiles. Judy Bennett knows exactly
what she's doing. She just happens to have the kind of face that shows
well without makeup—she's got high color. She'd look like a clown
with makeup and she knows it. Don't think she's never experimented
with rouge and eye shadow! And her hair is really too pretentious; it's
as obvious as a costume—can't you *see* that?"

Patricia's outburst had surprised Peter. He knew that Patricia
liked Judy, and he could not understand why she would criticize her appearance in such detail. He did not think that Judy Bennett was dan-

gerously attractive—Liza Howard was dangerously attractive! He simply found Judy refreshing, lovely, and capable. In point of fact, he found her perfect, and he supposed that was what irritated Patricia so.

But who could find fault with Judy Bennett? She was able to tune herself with exquisite perception to just the right emotional current needed in a gathering. She was inexhaustible. She filled her own house with the fragrances of cut flowers and homemade bread; she performed endless duties for the community and church with a carriage of body and expression of face that indicated she was doing exactly what she pleased. She was intelligent and clever and had a good sense of humor.

She even had managed to get her twenty-three-year-old son to attend church, and that was nearly a miracle these days. Peter looked down at the Bennett family seated before him in a middle pew; how good-looking they all were. John Bennett had gone to a nearby prep school and on to a first-class college in the South. Recently he had returned to work in his father's business, and he would do well, because like his father he was handsome, and like his mother he was unassuming; so he seemed wonderfully charming in the most natural way. Perhaps he was not all that bright, but that didn't matter so much. He was so fine-looking and easygoing and likable that people would not let him fail. He was the sort of person that other people conspire to keep happy; Peter could envision clients buying property from John simply to please him.

In the past year, John had accomplished what many people in town considered a real coup: he had become engaged to the daughter of the president of the local college. Sarah Stafford had just graduated from Mount Holyoke, and at twenty-two she was a slim and pleasant-looking woman, not given to frivolity. Her family could trace its lineage back to the American Revolution, her uncles and grandparents were all judges or scholars, and her own personality was so sensible that no one could believe that she had only been enchanted by John Bennett's marvelous looks. So the community thought—the community thought—well, the community *did* think, and observe, and judge, and when the engagement had been announced, the social atmosphere of Londonton had been tremulous with the wonder of such a perfect match. The wedding between John Bennett and Sarah Stafford would provide the community with a nearly allegorical marriage between commerce and learning. Gossips of all ages and both sexes seemed at a loss as to whom to envy most—Sarah for acquiring this most handsome of men, or John for winning the most prestigious of women.

They were to be married on Christmas Day, in the Congregational church. They could have been married, such was Sarah's position, in the college chapel, but it was too small to hold the number of guests who would be invited to the occasion. So both the college chaplain and Peter would officiate at the wedding, which would be the most elaborate and magnificent ceremony ever performed within the church's plain white walls. When Ron Bennett discussed his son's marriage, he took on the look of a man about to sit down at a seven-course meal. Judy Bennett was less ostentatious in her pride, but Peter could see how her eyes shone in spite of herself. Now the Bennetts would have it all! This would be a transformation as much as a marriage, and the Bennetts would become part of the royalty of Londonton.

Now Peter noticed Liza Howard looking right at John Bennett with an expression very much like that of a fat cat stalking a mouse. No. It was a much more smug expression than that, it was more the expression of a fat cat who sees a bowl of rich cream within easy reach. Did Liza know something about John; was she having an affair with him? Peter could understand certainly why the two would be attracted to each other, but it would surely be a shame if John jeopardized his future with Sarah Stafford for a foolish fling with Liza Howard. Peter wondered if Judy had any idea about it all—whether something was going on. Liza looked so very pleased.

After the service, during coffee hour, Peter would take Judy aside for a few moments, he decided. He would ask her how things were with Johnny, and he would ask her if she could do anything to help Suzanna Blair. He was pleased with this decision, pleased to think how the members of his congregation interacted with each other. Now he smiled, and rose to give his sermon.

JUDY BENNETT

Judy Bennett felt Peter Taylor's eyes resting on her, and she involuntarily straightened her back and stared with a more thoughtful expression at Reynolds Houston, who was reading the scripture lesson. She liked Peter Taylor, and thought that he admired her, but when she felt him studying her at length, as he was doing now, she went cold with terror, fearing that because he was a spiritual man, he might be able to see into her soul. And she did not want him seeing into her soul—she did not want anyone seeing into her soul. So she began energetically to envision the apparent facts of her life, as if by summoning them up in her mind she could build a force field of pleasing, safe ideas that would protect her from Peter Taylor's scrutiny.

She was Judith Bennett, married to Ronald Bennett, mother of John and Cynthia Bennett. Her husband was an intelligent and well-educated man who was much admired by the town. Ron was an independent contractor; he also spent a great deal of time in community endeavors. He served on boards, he headed fund-raising campaigns, he worked tirelessly for certain charity groups. At the present time he was involved in a huge and important task: he was building the Londonton Recreation Center. He had never been in charge of such a large construction before, but when the town raised the money for the youth center, the managing committee had decided unanimously that Ron should be the contractor. They had even gone to the trouble of forming a private charitable organization so that they could appoint Ron without the hassle of putting the job out to bid, something they would have had to do if they had been a public organization. Ron was living up to their expectations. He worked day and night. He was obsessed with the center, devoted to it; he wanted it to be perfect. They were paying him well for the job, but financial payments could never equal the time, energy, and concern he had invested in the rec center. Judy did not mind his commitment to the project; she knew this would only enhance his position in the community.

Judy was also proud of her children. Cynthia, her eighteen-year-old daughter, was a freshman at Smith, and making straight A's as she always had. She was not as physically attractive as her older brother, but she was smarter, and she had her father's determination and ability to work, and she would make a name for herself someday. And Johnny —well, she was so proud of him and so grateful to him that if she could take years off her life to give to Johnny, she would gladly do it. It seemed to Judy that she had never looked at her son once in all his life without amazement on her part: he was that beautiful. He was six feet two inches tall, with long legs, a long torso, broad shoulders, slim hips. He had perfect white teeth and enormous green eyes, thick blond hair that held glints of gold in the summer. Where had he come from, this beautiful man—out of her body? It was amazing. She was so proud of him. Ever since he was a toddler, girls had swarmed around him, and Judy had wondered how in the world he'd ever choose among them, there were so many, such an endless supply. She could imagine how eagerly all those girls offered themselves up to him once he was virile; she had been afraid that he'd make a mistake and get some little fool pregnant. But he had come through his youth into such a triumph Judy was still reeling with the pleasure of it: he had gotten himself engaged to Sarah Stafford, the daughter of the president of one of New England's most prestigious colleges. If anyone judges me, Judy Bennett thought, let them judge me by my son. She carried him before her like a shield.

It did not occur to her to think at any moment in her life that people were only seeing her rather than judging her, for she was always judging other people, and she knew precisely how much her charitable actions were a cover for the lack of charity in her heart. Judy judged everyone, herself included, severely and without clemency. It was a habit that had come to her too early and forcefully in her life ever to be changed. Its twin was a devotion to appearances that was obsessive—and she knew it was obsessive and did not care. There were worse obsessions one could have; she knew that, too.

This Sunday morning Judy had awakened at six-thirty without the aid of an alarm clock. It was a deal she had with her body; she would say to herself before going to bed at night: "It is now ten-thirty. Wake up at six-thirty." It always worked. She was pleased with her body's complicity, and her silent waking enabled her to rise from the bed without the noise of an alarm clock waking everyone else in the house. She had wrapped her fleecy robe around her body and gone into the bathroom to brush her long brown hair; she tied it back with a yellow ribbon, knowing that it was a cheerful thing for her son and husband to see a yellow ribbon at breakfast time. Very quietly she had padded down the stairs of the enormous old farmhouse, and through the long hall into the kitchen.

Which room was the most beautiful room in her house? She believed it would be hard for anyone to say. The front rooms were elegant and a bit formal, but the kitchen was in its own way the most luxurious. It was a large bright room with a fireplace at one end and many windows along the long left wall. Judy had decorated the kitchen in a colonial country style; instead of cabinets she had armoires and pine cupboards, and at the cooking end of the kitchen stood a long pine table. She worked at this table, mixing up cakes or kneading bread, and was still a part of whatever was going on at the other end of the room, where a multicolored braided rug lay before the fireplace and rocking chairs covered with patchwork cushions sat on either side. This morning Bruce, the black Lab, was stretched in the very middle of the rug; Rags and Flapper, the cats, each occupied a rocking chair. The scene was as symmetrical and cozy as if Judy had arranged it herself.

"Out you go," she said to them all, opening the kitchen door to the side yard. "Go on now. You'll get your breakfast in a while." She did not especially care for the animals except as they decorated her life —she was well aware that people considered animal lovers to be kind-hearted and warm-spirited; in short, morally superior to other human beings. Quite often, as Judy washed the floor of muddy tracks or vacuumed up the ubiquitous balls of hair, she thought that the animals' charm did not quite make up for their bother. But she was committed to appearing to be an animal lover, and she did not want to change.

This morning the braided rug was still fairly clean, so Judy kicked off her slippers and laid her robe over an armchair and stood in the middle of the rug to do her exercises. At forty-five, her body was not voluptuous—it had never been that—but it was slim and firm and tight. It was *neat*. Like everything else in her life, this body of hers was kept up to her standards by discipline and energy. Even though the rest of her family were continually engaged in jogging or lifting weights or working out, and the house was often filled with the rhythmic thumps and thuds necessary to the maintenance of physical excellence, it would have discomposed her to have her husband and children know that she, too, exercised, because she needed to have them believe she was effortlessly perfect. So she waited until her husband and son had gone off to the office for the day, then locked herself in her bedroom on the second floor where no passerby could glance in, and went through her exercise routine to the accompaniment of radio music. But on Saturday and Sunday, when her family was at home all day, she found it necessary to run through her routine in quiet secrecy in the kitchen. If anyone woke and came downstairs, she could hear immediately and be in her robe and at the kitchen sink before they caught her. But this had never happened; her family liked to sleep late.

Now she bent frontward, touching her toes with her fingers, then stretched upward. For twenty minutes, she exercised her body to a routine she had established years ago. Her goal was not beauty. She did not want to have a body that drew attention; quite the opposite. She was determined to have a body so clean and trim that no one would think to notice it at all.

When she had finished her exercises, she sat for a moment, catching her breath, then slipped back into her robe and slippers. She would shower later, when the others were up. Now she opened the damper of the fireplace and laid kindling across the arms of the brass andirons and lit a fire. She went outside to gather up logs from the woodpile, and stood for a few moments to consider the day. It was cool and overcast, winter was coming: and on Christmas Day her son would marry the daughter of a college president.

After the fire was going, Judy went into the working part of the kitchen. She had several things to accomplish this morning before going to church, because they would be having guests today. Ron had recently finished building a home for a new young doctor in town, and it was his custom to invite the more prosperous of his clients to dinner. Judy never minded fixing these dinners or spending the time telling newcomers about the town. She was always glad to give them the names of the best plumbers, electricians, clothing stores, and supermarkets. She was more than pleased to linger over a homemade chocolate cake in the dining room, telling her guests about families in town who had children the same age or similar sports and hobbies. By doing this, she received exactly what she wanted: people's admiration and gratitude. In fact, almost nothing pleased her more than the sight of a new young couple staring with envy at the sight of her copper pots, silver bowls, crystal chandeliers, casually packed bookcases, well-trodden antique rugs. They yearned immediately to live here, to *be* her: to have a life as graciously arranged as her own.

Today the couple coming to dinner were relatively young and as yet childless, so the entertaining would be easy. They would sit on the porch, if it did not rain, drinking cocktails, then have an early country dinner. There would be beef stew in wine, and Judy's homemade wholewheat bread, and applesauce Judy had made from apples fallen from trees in the old orchard, and a pie made from raspberries Judy had picked and frozen this summer and set out to thaw last night. Now she put a white paper filter in the glass coffeepot and set the water to boil. As she turned to the antique glass canister that held the flour, she remembered that Reynolds Houston had called yesterday afternoon and asked if he could stop by tonight. He said he would come around eight; the newcomers would have gone by then, and Reynolds would surely have had dinner. There would be enough berry pie left from the afternoon to offer him. She looked in the refrigerator: yes, she had remembered to buy enough whipping cream.

She measured flour into a red crockery bowl and began to cut in the butter she had let soften in the cupboard overnight. The room began to fill with an agreeable brightening warmth from the fireplace. She was aware of how the scene she made would look to anyone coming in: a slender woman with a yellow ribbon in her long brown hair, rolling out piecrust dough on an antique pine table while at one end of the room the fire crackled and nearby on the stove coffee brewed. How warm and attractive her room was, her family was, and perhaps this was why Reynolds Houston wanted to visit.

She did not know him well. He lived alone and kept to himself and was polite at cocktail and dinner parties, but he was not the sort of man Judy felt comfortable with. There was something chilling about such an immaculate man, Judy thought, and as she lay the dough in the pie pan and carefully crimped the edges into patterned scallops, she felt that old familiar monster, anxiety, stir and wake inside her, in the pit of her stomach, where it always lay in wait. She could not breathe. Why had Reynolds Houston asked to come tonight?

It could not be because of a simple desire for the company of his fellow man. He had almost nothing in common with Ron, except for the few committees they served on. Perhaps something was wrong. But what could possibly be wrong? Reynolds Houston had no connection with her life that she could think of. Still the anxiety was now fully aroused within her, and greedy and powerful in its arousal. It bloomed inside her, like a malevolent cloud, filling the cavity of her stomach and chest relentlessly, pushing her breath away. There was no room left inside her for air. Something was wrong. She knew it, and could not get her breath. She gripped the edge of the pine table with both hands and shoved her chin down into her chest to stifle a scream. She gasped, trying to pull air into her lungs, but the anxiety had mushroomed within her and was billowing upward now, blocking her throat. She could not let her son and husband see her like this.

"It's okay," she whispered to herself. "Judy, it's okay. Just give yourself a minute. You'll be okay."

It was only a matter of steps from the kitchen to the half-bath off the hall. She kept the Valium in the linen closet in here, with sanitary napkins and tampons and other things the men in her family would find, if not embarrassing, at least not of interest. She kept the Valium in an old Midol bottle next to a small brown prescription bottle which also contained Valium: if anyone cared to check, it seemed the Valium bottle was seldom opened. She took two blue pills out of the Midol bottle and swallowed them immediately—long ago she had taught herself to swallow pills without water. Oh, Valium, dear, sweet, *blessed* Valium, how she loved it. She knew the drug was a crutch, but the important thing to keep in mind was just that: that *she knew* she was using it in just that way. She was in control of it. She believed quite firmly that in this case self-knowledge provided sufficient exoneration. She did not believe she was addicted to Valium—she would only be truly addicted if she were not aware of her addiction. As long as she was aware of the frequency of usage, she had the usage under control.

Besides, she had been using the drug for years under the supervision of a highly qualified and respected psychiatrist. She saw him only once every few months now, but she had been going to him regularly for seven years. He knew almost everything about her there was to know, and he agreed with her that until both her children were grown and gone away, a moderate, controlled use of Valium was sensible and even necessary. He did not know what he did not need to know—that Judy also had a prescription for it from a local doctor for her bad back. And another source—an old school friend.

Even at eighteen, Judy had been sophisticated enough to realize the possibilities inherent in forming an alliance with such a shy, homely, lonely girl as Katrina Brouwer, who lived down the hall in Judy's dorm at college. Judy had made it a point to be kind to Katrina, and if her friendship was premeditated, calculated, it was still the best Katrina was to get. Katrina went through life with an attitude that put people off—she was too modest and shy. When she graduated from college, she went back to the poor New England city she had come from, lived with her mother, and worked as a receptionist in a doctor's office. So it was easy for her to call in prescriptions to the local pharmacy for a nonexistent patient, pick up the prescriptions herself, and mail them to Judy. Judy always reimbursed Katrina for the cost of the postage as well as the medicine, and she also remembered to send her gifts and cards on the appropriate holidays. In addition, Katrina had the pleasure of receiving the intimate confidences of another living human being.

"Oh, Katrina, you are so kind," Judy would say during one of her phone calls. "I don't know what I'd do without you. Londonton is so small, and I know all the doctors personally, and the pharmacists— well, if I took one Valium, everyone in town would know it and would wonder about my private life. It would be such a strain. This way, no one knows but you—and we are too close to judge one another."

Perhaps Katrina would have judged Judy had she not been under the illusion that the Valium she supplied Judy was the only Valium Judy ever took. But what did it matter what Katrina didn't know; in this case the illusion did everyone nothing but good. Katrina had a friend and the satisfaction of knowing she was helping a friend; and Judy had her Valium.

Judy had her Valium, and in the evenings she had her vodka-and-tonics or scotch-and-waters, and sometimes at lunch she had her wine.

Still she did not think of herself as addicted. She never, ever lost control. The alcohol, like the drugs, helped her *keep* control. And in a life with a façade as flawless as Judy's, control was essential.

And control was flowing back into her body, she could feel it in her blood. That blessed calm. She slumped against the bathroom wall, closing her eyes a moment, taking deep breaths, shaking her head in wonder at herself: How could she continue to let such insignificant things upset her? How silly she was! Reynolds Houston was alone and winter was approaching, and he was probably only feeling that human need to reaffirm human contact against the coming darkness. She checked her face in the mirror: she looked normal, quite pretty and composed. She went back out to the kitchen to finish the pie.

Now, here she sat in the sanctuary of the church, studying Reynolds as he read the scripture lesson. She had known she would see Reynolds at church, and so had fortified herself with another Valium before leaving the house this morning. By now the drug did not so much flow through her as appear to flow around her, screening her from anything that could cause pain. She felt wrapped around by a gauze as clear as air, as impenetrable as iron. She felt beautiful, in a sturdy and respectable way. It pleased her to think how she must appear to the other people around her: a slim, strong, perfect woman, with a family that anyone would envy. She knew that no one could have been a better mother, wife, woman. And what did it cost her? Nothing. She did not drink so much that her health was impaired, and although the gloomy newsmongers, looking for something sensational, occasionally claimed that Valium might cause cancer, she knew better than to take them seriously. If Valium were harmful to human beings, why, it would be taken off the market. No one else in the world knew that she indulged in her helpful little habits, and she looked upon the drugs with gratitude. They helped her make life pretty, and what could possibly be wrong with that? Life was difficult; life was hard; the world needed people like Judy to move through it with serenity and generosity and grace. Actually, she could think of any number of people in this very church who would do well to start improving their lives by taking matters into their own hands.

If she turned her head ever so slightly to the left or right, she could see someone who was anxious, disorganized, not pretty, someone whose spirit was cramped by the hardships of life; it showed in the person's face. Such a person would be much better off for the use of drugs, and would certainly be more presentable.

For example, Leigh Findly. Sometimes it wrenched Judy's heart to see Leigh come into the church with her daughter. Judy felt no special sympathy for Leigh—as far as Judy could see, Leigh was a silly woman who had managed to get herself divorced from a charming and intelligent man. But Leigh considered herself an artist, or so the story went, or as much of the story as Judy had been told by mutual acquaintances. Leigh considered herself an artist, and her husband had been too demanding, expecting her to do such monumental tasks as cooking regular meals and doing the laundry, and so she had asked him to share the housework, and naturally he had gotten a divorce. After all, he worked at a real job and brought home the money and while some people might call the pots Leigh made valuable, they didn't, as far as Judy knew, bring in real money. Judy felt sorry for the husband—or *had* felt sorry for him; it had all happened years ago. He had quickly remarried and moved away. She felt even sorrier for the child, an eighteen-year-old girl named Mandy.

In the first place, *Mandy*—what a name! Judy had read in the church directory that Mandy's real name was Amanda, and she wondered why on earth Leigh didn't call her daughter *that* instead of using such a tacky nickname which conjured up images of servant girls. Mandy was a pretty girl, with long thick blond hair that Judy would have loved to see put up in a classy French twist. But from the looks of it, Leigh Findly never reminded her daughter to put her hair up, or even to comb it. How many times they had come rushing into the church at the last minute, their clothes aflutter, Leigh's face uncomposed, her eyes darting here and there, looking for a place to sit, and then breaking into a grin when an usher approached to seat them. What a way to enter church! Then Leigh and Mandy would sit, whispering and grinning and shuffling, taking off their coats or sweaters and turning to the right page in the hymnal, or looking for a tissue in Leigh's purse—whatever they were doing, they did it in such an obvious way, as if they were a pair of birds settling into a nest. Judy always studied Mandy and owned that the girl did not look unhappy. But she did look unkempt, and that was never necessary. Perhaps Leigh thought that wearing such shabby clothes gave her an artistic air, but that was no reason to let her daughter dress that way. Sometimes when Mandy entered the church in sneakers of all things, or a sweater that was missing a button, Judy wanted to rush to the girl, snatch her from her mother's side, close Mandy up in a protective embrace, and say, "It's all right. I'll take care of you. I know how you're suffering!" For if Judy could know anything, it was how a teen-age girl could suffer.

But this line of thinking was courting disaster, and Judy looked away from Leigh Findly's oblivious fluffy head. It would not do to think of mothers and daughters today. She needed the tranquilizing sight of familiar, like-minded people whose lives reaffirmed her own.

Discreetly, so that she would not insult Reynolds by not appearing to attend to his reading, she gazed around at the heads in front of her, searching for consolation. The heads that were white or gray or bald she dismissed—nice enough people, but old: they did not count.

The Vandersons kept her attention for some time; she studied Mrs. Vanderson especially, and was torn between admiration and disgust. They were such snobs, the Vandersons, true old-New-England-family snobs, the worst kind. Jake Vanderson was president of a paper-manufacturing company that had been in his family for generations; as president he really worked very little. He didn't need to work, because the wealth that had been handed down to him by his ancestors was more than any one family could spend in a lifetime. He spent his time traveling—"for the company"—to places such as Bermuda and St. Tropez and Geneva, and his wife Lillian accompanied him. When they were in Londonton for any length of time, Lillian headed up charity committees and gave elaborate parties for their friends. Everyone talked about these parties—they were so clever and lavish. Judy and Ron had never been invited to one of these parties, and this was a source of irritation and even grief in Judy's life. Oh, the Bennetts had been in the Vandersons' house, but only for the charity parties—and those did not count socially. It was to one of the frivolous theme parties —the disco party, the F. Scott Fitzgerald party, the Halloween masquerade party—that Judy wanted to be invited; she didn't hope to be included in one of the intimate dinner parties. Lillian Vanderson always greeted Judy and Ron with perfect friendliness: "It's so nice to see you," she would say, "and how is that handsome son of yours these days?" But she never invited the Bennetts to any of her parties—and Lillian and Jake had never attended any of the Bennetts' parties in spite of Judy's consistent invitations. The Vandersons' excuses were al-

ways impeccable and given with the utmost kindness, but Judy would
still take their refusals as yet another private defeat. What were they
doing wrong? she wondered. Sometimes she dreamed of asking: *Why*
don't you like us? Why won't you include us? What can we do? Every
time she heard from another couple about one of the Vandersons' parties, her mouth went sour with bitterness. Who did they think they
were, to snub the Bennetts? She and Ron had gone to the right
schools, they had enough money, they wore the right clothes, they sent
their children to the right schools, they attended the right church and
gave to the right charities. They ran with the right social set, shopped
at the right stores, read the right magazines and newspapers, voted for
the right party. They were attractive, affluent, pleasant, genial, responsible, and well-liked members of the community. Why did the Vandersons leave them out?

Well, Judy thought, with a flash of inspiration that made her
nearly explode with laughter, *well*, she thought with a pleasure of discovery and justification so violent she felt a shiver pass through her
body: *Well!* She would be sure that the Vandersons were not invited
to the Wedding!

This could prove tricky—for undoubtedly Sarah's parents were acquaintances, if not friends, of the Vandersons. Since Jake Vanderson
was an alumnus of the college, he always donated a satisfactory sum to
the college each year. But Judy would manage it somehow. She would
ask to help mail the invitations, and then lose the one to the Vandersons. Or she could ask the Staffords not to invite the Vandersons—
although that would take a lot of thought in order to come up with a
proper excuse. Still, she would manage it, and the idea of excluding
this family who rankled in her heart provided her with the greatest satisfaction she had experienced in days.

Now Judy felt benevolent, and as her gaze slid away from the
backs of the Vandersons, she saw Pam Moyer and thought: I must do
something nice for Pam. Pam and Gary Moyer were old, close friends
of Ron and Judy's; they had known each other for almost twenty years.
Pam and Gary had three children, and Judy and Pam had seen each
other through diapers and teething and Little League and ballet lessons
and school trips and legs broken while skiing and the agony of waiting
for acceptance into the right college. They had so much in common.
The men also had a lot in common: Gary had started his law practice

the same year Ron had opened up his own contracting business. They
weren't as close as Pam and Judy were—men never were—but they
played tennis regularly once a week, and were comfortable enough
with each other, so that the two families had even taken vacations together. They had spent Christmas Day dinners together; the Bennetts
and the Moyers were an integral part of each other's lives.

Recently it had seemed to Judy that Pam was overdoing it with
her community service and political work: Pam was becoming so serious, so involved. Judy appreciated the energy Pam was dedicating to
the various social issues in the world, but wished that Pam could be a
little *lighter*—her earnestness was getting to be a bore. It must certainly be hard on Gary, Judy thought, to have someone so dreary
around; it couldn't be good for the marriage. Judy wondered if she
should speak to Pam about this, out of friendship. But no, probably she
shouldn't, for Pam had been prickly lately, and it seemed whenever
they bumped into each other in the grocery store or post office, Judy
could see a mote of anger floating like an unwanted shard of light in
Pam's dark brown eyes. Why should Pam be angry with her, though;
what had Judy possibly done?

Judy smiled: of course. Pam was undoubtedly jealous of the marriage between Johnny and the Stafford girl. If only she would just
come right on out with it and admit it. It would be such a relief to
both of them. Pam's children were all doing well. One was in law
school, one was in med school, and the youngest boy was finishing his
senior year at Londonton High School. Still, none of the Moyers' children's accomplishments could come close to equaling John's marriage to
the daughter of the president of one of New England's finest colleges.
Judy could understand Pam's jealousy—she would certainly feel exactly the same way if she were in Pam's shoes. Yet she thought that
Pam was being rather silly about it. She ought to be grateful that her
three children were alive, healthy, and happy. Not everyone could
marry the child of a college president. It would be just so much nicer
if Pam would go ahead and admit how she felt. But she could not
think how to approach the subject gracefully without somehow further
injuring Pam. She would have to be oblique.

She would send Pam flowers. Or buy her a book—she had seen a
new coffee table sort of book on needlepoint in the local bookstore. She
could get that for Pam. In the past she and Pam had often surprised

each other with just such gifts, spontaneously thanking the other for her friendship, or simply giving the other woman some one thing that she would want. Women tended to do that sort of thing more than men, Judy had discovered; men just didn't think that way. She and Pam were lucky to have each other.

She especially was lucky, Judy thought, and as she carefully glanced around the church, looking at the other people, she smiled a small secret smile to herself: for she felt superior to every person there. Just in her line of vision, on the side, sat Suzanna Blair, who hadn't been able to keep her husband and was now struggling along trying to raise two small children herself. Judy pitied Suzanna, but couldn't develop very much interest in the woman, for Suzanna was younger, and didn't have much money, didn't run with Judy's group, would never be of any use to Judy. In front of Suzanna sat Jean and Harry Pratt—what a time they had had of it, when Harry lost his executive position at the mill. It had been so embarrassing for everyone; no one knew what to say. One couldn't say, "I'm so sorry that you're suddenly poor." It wasn't the same in Londonton as in other less wealthy towns; wives couldn't rush over to the Pratts' house with casseroles and cakes, and no one could pass the hat to help them make it through a month's mortgage. Instead, everyone in town had simply left the Pratts alone, which seemed the kindest thing to do. To his credit, Harry had rallied, and now was a manager of one of the local clothing stores. Once more the Pratts were a central part of the Londonton social life. But what a strain they had caused the community for a while!

Near the Pratts sat Liza Howard, who was just a whore. Judy couldn't imagine why she was allowed in the church; everyone knew she had the morals of an alley cat. Judy made it a point to snub her, cut her dead, at every occasion. Liza was beautiful, that was a simple fact, but it still was a puzzle to Judy that Liza could attract men so easily. Only a fool would want to get involved with someone who was so cheap.

Judy felt valuable and smug by contrast. Here she sat in the sanctuary of the church, with her handsome husband on one side and her handsome son on the other. She was wearing a light gray houndstooth-check suit with a melon-colored silk shirt and gray suede pumps. Her hair hung in a rich, competent, braided rope down her back. Once, years ago, a little old lady named Dotty Dinkman had accosted Judy after church. Laying her wrinkled hand on Judy's arm, she had said, "Dear, I just want to tell you what beautiful hair you have. I sat staring at your nice braid all through the sermon, and it gave me the greatest pleasure—your hair is such a pretty color, and that braid is so —well—*satisfying!* I hope I'm not embarrassing you by telling you this." But Judy was not embarrassed, and she thanked Dotty Dinkman with real gratitude. That was just the sort of remark that Judy rearranged her life by, and since that day she had not entered the church without that agreeable memory returning to her mind. She, too, found the neat interweaving of substance greatly satisfying; and she found herself fancying from time to time what a pleasure it must be to God, who could look down with His magical eye to see the way the lives of the people of this town interwove with each other in intricate and congenial designs.

Everyone had problems, yet life was good. Judy was devoted to the idea of a good life, and determined to have one. No one could ever say that she did not work hard to bring this about. And she liked to work at it, at life; she was not afraid of work. If only fear were not such an intimate part of her life. If only God would speak to her with the same sweeping authority that Carlos Aranguren had.

Carlos Aranguren taught French and Spanish at the local college; his wife taught German. They were a marvelous couple, always in demand for parties and occasions because they were so majestically entertaining. Now, in church, they sat slightly out of Judy's sight; she would have to turn her head rudely in order to see that pair of elegant heads: the serenely blond Ursula, the dramatically brunet Carlos. They were certainly the most glamorous couple at the college, if not in the entire town. They had reached Ron and Judy's age without ever having children, and this did not seem to be an absence in their lives— they were always traveling here and there, and adding on unusual sections to their house, and having dinner parties replete with exotic foods, and they went about in such romantic clothes: tunics, caftans, ponchos, capes. Still they were respectable—no one taught at the college who was not respectable—and while this couple more than any other held the promise of doing something adventurous, outside the social pale, they had as yet done nothing outrageous. They were the town's darlings, consistently whetting the social appetite for scandal, and as consistently keeping just within the bounds of custom. It was quite a trick, and Judy imagined that the Arangurens gave the energy to this that they would have had to give to raising children. Judy was slightly leery of the couple, and knew it, as if she were a house cat occasionally required to occupy the same territory as a pair of flamingos. Yet Carlos had once said something to her that had touched her deeply.

It had been almost exactly a year ago, around Halloween, that time of year when night fell early and the woods around Judy's house were full of rustling and she wished her children were still at home, young enough to dress up in costumes which established the idea of ghosts and witches as childish human fancies. The Sloans had had a dinner party, a casual buffet affair with hot chili and cornbread and green salad and beer. The Sloans' house was a modern, architect-designed oddity with a family room floored with red tiles and a black metal fireplace in the center encircled by a sort of dry moat. This was called "the conversation pit" and everyone exclaimed in admiration of it, but Judy thought it looked like a setup in a bad restaurant. And in spite of the thick red carpet that covered steps down into it, she found it terribly uncomfortable to sit there. But Nina Sloan was a good hostess, and she placed fruits and little chocolate cakes and trays with a variety of unusual liqueurs at the four sections of the pit that were left uncarpeted to serve as tables. Her guests arranged themselves around the blazing fire, seeming happy enough. Everyone found themselves, of necessity, divided into intimate groups—it was difficult to hear someone on the other side of the fire, and almost impossible to see anyone without kneeling uncomfortably so as to peer above the flames but below the vast cast-iron hood.

Judy found herself seated next to Carlos, and his proximity just slightly alarmed her. She wondered what on earth they would find to talk about. She was aware of how she must look to him: the All-American Housewife in her long plaid skirt, Shetland sweater, and gold chains. Few people discomfited her as Carlos did. He was so brazenly masculine—and he was such a flirt! Tonight he was wearing —of all things—a floor-length caftan which a student from South Africa had given him. It was quite beautiful, a silky deep blue with the neck and cuffs and hem embroidered in gold. Most men would have looked like fools in it, but Carlos wore it with ease. In fact, it suited him, and he knew it. He was tall, with a burnished look to his skin, and thick black hair, startling black eyes. He was vain, careful of his appearance, but his masculinity had never been called into question —he was such a womanizer.

"Oh, my darling," he would say to whatever woman happened to be near, "I haven't seen you for so long. Let me hold your hand. How delicious you smell. That scent reminds me of the white flowers that bloomed outside my bedroom when I was a boy in Spain."

In spite of all his years in the United States, he still spoke with a Spanish accent, which added the thrill of foreign possibilities to his words. Men were never angered to hear Carlos romancing their wives, for Carlos was so democratic in his compliments, and so obvious. No woman at any party escaped his extravagant Spanish praise, and he did love women so much that he never found one he could not somehow admire. His blond German wife went about her own conversations quite naturally, with no more sign of jealousy than if her husband had been playing a game of tennis. She was beautiful and clever and did not need to worry.

It had been a long time since Judy had seen Carlos, however, and as she attempted to arrange herself on the carpeted steps around the fireplace, she felt that quick flash of fear she always felt when privately encountering Carlos: what if he could not think of anything about her to praise? But Carlos immediately took up her long braid of hair and held it against his face with such tenderness that it almost seemed to become as sentient as a limb of her body.

"Ah, your beautiful hair, Judith," he said to her. "So thick, so rich. It must be so long that unbraided it would cover your breasts."

"Oh, Carlos," Judy laughed—which was usually the most she could muster when he went on like this.

As Carlos spoke, he ran his hand gently along Judy's face and down her thick braid, which fortunately had fallen down her back. Carlos' hand slid from the end of her braid to her sweater-covered lower back, and rested there a moment.

Judy shivered. She really did not like to be touched like this. She was always delighted to receive compliments from Carlos, because he managed to compliment her on something she was in fact proud of. But tonight his words—his hands—bordered on being openly sexual, and it annoyed her. If she thought of sex at all, she saw it as a sort of personal Loch Ness monster, and she did not understand why grown-

ups kept trying to entice the creature up from the murky depths
when after all these years they should have finally placated and subdued it. She had worked this out a long time ago with her psychiatrist,
and she knew that different people had different sexual needs at
different times. Men were more demanding than women. She did not
mind having sex with Ron once or twice a week, because it provided
relief for him. She imagined it did for him more or less what Valium
did for her. Ron was a sensitive and considerate lover. He did not expect Judy to throw herself about as if she were a teen-ager in the
throes of a hormonal assault. They had come to an implicit, sensible arrangement: he would not pester her, and she would not ignore him.
She did not think they were the only couple who had worked out
their marriage this way. She did not like it when Carlos slipped from
the verbal into the tactile, and she found the sensations he teased up to
the surface of her skin irritating. He might as well have sat on her
back and tickled her; it was the same sort of thing. She had outgrown
all that.

But Carlos removed his hand before she could speak, and studied
her a moment in silence. Then he took her right hand in both of his.

Oh, no, not more of the same, Judy thought, and said aloud,
"What courses are you teaching this semester, Carlos?"

But he did not answer her question. He spoke as if he hadn't
heard. "I am going to read your palm," he said.

"Well!" Judy exclaimed, startled. "Can you actually do it? I didn't
know you were so talented. Oh, yes, of course, now I remember—you
did it last spring at the fair for the hospital. But I thought it was all a
joke."

"Not at all," Carlos said. "You would be amazed at all the talents I
possess." He paused to let the innuendo settle, then went on. "But it is
true, I can read palms. I have been trained, I have studied, and it is in
my blood from gypsy ancestors."

"That's so interesting, Carlos, but you know I'd really rather not—"
Judy tried subtly to withdraw her hand from his.

"What's the matter?" he asked, smiling, not releasing her hand.
"Are you afraid that I'll reveal some secret?"

"Of course not!" Judy declared. She was trapped. She could not
bear to let him think she had anything to hide, and she didn't really
believe in what he was doing.

"Good," Carlos said. "Then I will read your palm. The question is
—how honest shall I be?"

Judy smiled. "Be perfectly honest, Carlos, of course."

Carlos turned her hand slowly in his, studying it all around.
Then, with a little flourish, he took the four fingers and laid them back
flat in his right hand, exposing her palm with an air so triumphant that
Judy quickly glanced at her hand as if expecting to see something
amazing there. But it was only her familiar palm, crosshatched with
two sets of parallel lines that ran like avenues, one horizontally, one
diagonally, across it. Between one avenue and her thumb a smaller and
more intricate network of lines lay; it all made her think of the map of
a very small suburb.

"Ah, yes," Carlos said. "I see. You have a strong, good life line,
and you are excellent at handling money. But—this is very interesting.
You have an astonishing private life. You have secrets, hidden deep
within you. There are obvious things here, too—you are generous,
kind, loving, immensely capable—"

"Is Carlos reading your hand?" It was Nina Sloan, calling to
Judy from the other side of the fireplace. Without waiting for Judy's
reply, she turned to the couple sitting near her and said, laughing,
"That Carlos. He can find more ways to compliment a woman than
there are stars in the sky!"

Nina's comment distracted Judy, and for the next few minutes she
listened with impatience as Carlos peered into what she suddenly felt
to be an embarrassingly ordinary hand. He was saying pleasant enough
things—but then he had known her for *years* now, and there was nothing he was telling her that he hadn't already discovered by simply living in the same town with her. She almost snatched her hand back,
but then he spoke with sudden authority, almost sharply.

"Judy. Listen to me. You think I am a charlatan, I know. But I
see something here I want to tell you. Something you should know."

Judy glanced around quickly to be certain that no one else was listening. "Well, what?" she asked, hoping by her smile to let Carlos
know just what a joke she thought all this was.

"I am only an amateur at this, and yet the lines are so clear. They
show that something happened to you when you were a child. I can't
see what. Perhaps a death, an accident, a siege of misery. But some-

thing happened to you before you were eighteen, and nothing that bad will ever happen to you again in your life."

"Carlos, are you sure?" Judy cried. She was completely entranced. She stared in surprise at her hand, feeling gratitude. "Please tell me all that again."

Carlos repeated it: something terrible had happened to her when she was young; nothing that bad would ever happen to her again.

"God, how I wish you had told me this years ago!" she whispered, then sat back quietly for a moment, stunned. All the nights she had spent worrying about her children—their illnesses when they were small, their lateness when they were teen-agers riding in other teen-agers' cars—and yet, here they both were, safe and sound. If only she had known! When she thought about it, she supposed it was not too much to expect from Fate, because something terrible *had* happened to her as a child.

"You look rattled, Judy," said another guest, a woman. "Has Carlos struck a nerve?"

"No, no," Judy said, moving from the internal to the social with only a slight shiver at the change. "It's just that Carlos really seems to know what he's doing."

"Oh, how exciting! Carlos, come share your talents—come read *my* palm."

And Carlos left Judy's side. But Judy didn't mind, she had suddenly become very tired. She made the effort to talk politely with the other guests, but over and over in her mind she was thinking: Oh, dear Lord, what if Carlos is right? What a relief it would be to live out her life, knowing that the worst had already happened!

After that night, Judy had seen Carlos read other people's hands at parties, but she had avoided him. She was aware that he was more entertainer than seer, and she did not want to be disillusioned by having him read her hand again only to give her a completely different interpretation of what he had seen, or claimed to have seen.

Judy knew that very few people have perfectly happy childhoods, but there are degrees of happiness and misery, so that looking back, a person can say: Well, after all, I was fortunate.

When Judy summed up her childhood, she thought: Well, after all, I did not die of misery, and it did test my mettle and strengthen my character and show me what is important in life.

Money was what was important in life. Money was the most important thing. If she could have changed anything, she would have chosen to lose her father or her mother or her brother rather than to lose what her family had so stupidly, *stupidly* lost—their money.

When she had been a little girl, there had been plenty of money, and all the nice things it could buy: a canopy bed for her room, candy after school for her and her brother, bikes and roller skates, trips to the ocean, Easter outfits complete with white gloves and white patent-leather shoes. All of Judy's friends and Judy's parents' friends had more or less the same amount of money, and it seemed in fact that everyone in their small New England town had the same amount of money, so for Judy as a child, life spread around her like the prosperous green fields which surrounded the town: as far as her eye could see, abundance was the rule.

When she was ten, Judy had her first epiphany. She sat in church, not listening to the minister (he droned; he was boring). Instead, she moved her wrist in and out of the block of sunshine that fell across her lap so that she could see the way her silver (real sterling silver) charm bracelet caught the light. And she realized why people came to church. It couldn't be because they wanted to hear the minister's sermon—he really was often boring! It was to see other people, to show off new clothes, to say thank you to God. She was not an especially spiritual child, but she did always remember to say thank you to God.

So it seemed a personal slap in the face by God when Judy's family lost their money. It was even worse because they lost their money because they followed their Christian beliefs. What fools they had been, Judy thought, what *fools!* And she could never forgive them for their stupidity or God for His treachery.

After her thirteenth birthday, life began to unravel with the determined rhythm of a pavan. Each step her parents took moved them further along in the ritual of their undoing. They went bankrupt with unswerving grace.

"Did you have a chance to ask Rupert about that bill?" Judy's mother would ask Judy's father as they drove home from church.

"I saw him, but I didn't mention the money," Judy's father would reply. "I don't suppose church is the proper place to discuss business."

"No, you're right," Judy's mother would agree, and then there would be a silence between the two grownups that was so powerful and sad that Judy and her brother, sitting in the back seat of the car, felt it chill their skins like rain.

Later that year, Judy became aware that her parents spent less and less time entertaining people and going out with friends and more and more time sitting together in the living room, talking in low voices. The grownups did not like the children to hear their conversations, but of course Judy eavesdropped, as did her older brother; and they realized that a mysterious sorrow was taking over their family and they needed to know the cause.

The cause was simple and crass. Their father owned a large wallpaper and paint store, the only one in their small town. Individuals came to the store to buy three rolls of this or a quart of that, but most of the business was with contractors doing major jobs for building developers. These men were her father's friends; some even attended the same church. So when they asked for credit on their purchases, it seemed only right to give it to them, and then long-term credit, because of extenuating circumstances. . . . Judy was too young to understand it all, and her parents did not think to call the children into the living room to explain it to them. But what developed over the course of the year was that Judy's father continued to give the men their wallpaper and paint in spite of the fact that these men did not pay him; and he continued to pay the conglomerates from which he ordered the paint and wallpaper, in spite of the fact that he had to take it out of his own pocket, because he believed that his friends would pay him back when they could. But they did not pay him back. Some eventually took bankruptcy, some left town, and Judy's father finally had to declare bankruptcy, too.

Bankruptcy. The ugliest of words. Judy heard the word over and over again as she listened at the living-room door, which by this time was always closed when her parents were in there, as if they wanted to protect the rest of the house from a growing, pervasive contamination. Judy heard this ugly word, bankruptcy, and could envision it exactly: the rupturing of their lives, a mortal wound, a horrid tear that let all the money that made their lives beautiful spill out into the void, leaving them empty and desolate. Judy thought she would rather be dead than so suddenly poor.

And the worst of it was that her parents had been such fools about it, such saps! She would never, ever, forgive them for their irresponsible set of values. They actually tried to live a life that conformed to the teachings of the Bible!

Hiding at the crack in the living-room door, Judy would hear her mother speak: "Listen, Will, I've found the passage the minister read in church this morning.

" 'Jesus said unto him, If thou wilt be perfect, go and sell what thou hast, and give to the poor, and thou shalt have treasure in heaven: and come and follow me. But when the young man heard that saying, he went away sorrowful: for he had great possessions.

" 'Then said Jesus unto his disciples, Verily I say unto you, that a rich man shall hardly enter into the kingdom of heaven.

" 'And again I say unto you, It is easier for a camel to go through the eye of the needle, than for a rich man to enter into the kingdom of God.' "

"But Mr. Watson is not POOR!" Judy would want to scream through the door. "Why can't you see that? You're not helping a poor man, you're helping a rich man, and you're hurting your own family!"

But there was nothing she could do. She was only thirteen, and it was all so complicated, and it all happened so fast. In one year she witnessed a regular flowing away of all she loved, while her parents cried gently and reread the parable of the Good Samaritan. Then, with a fluid continuity, things began to disappear from their lives: the silver, antiques, and finally the house were all sold. The vacations disappeared—and then so did the work.

Judy's father started off optimistically enough each day of that long bruised time. As she dressed for school, she would hear him whistling, and see him, clean and shaved and dapper, going out the front door. But when she returned from school in the afternoons, she would find her father lying on the living-room sofa, dressed in old slacks and a sweater, a newspaper hiding his face; he had sagged into the sofa with all the heavy passivity of a bum on a park bench.

Judy could no longer bring friends home. And she was no longer invited to the homes of former friends. She had moved away from the gracious section of town where her life had begun, and she was learning with cruel sharpness that life was not a stretch of prosperous pastures for everyone. Her friends were not mean to her. They did not taunt her. They just forgot her. They would swish by her in the halls at school, in their full skirts with cancan petticoats trimmed in matching material, and they would hardly take time to flash a quick smile and say hello. Judy felt stranded, estranged, diseased. She did not like the people her age in her new neighborhood; she had nothing in common with them, coming from such dissimilar backgrounds. Generally the kids in her new neighborhood were the dummies, the wise guys in her class. As the years went by, those kids grew tough and insolent and bold, fortified by their own company; *they* were the ones who taunted Judy. As the months passed and she showed no sign of wanting to become one of them, the taunts changed in tone. At first they only called her "snob" and "creep," but she quickly gained the labels "bitch" and "whore." She was smart enough to know that these taunts did not mean they thought she was actually a whore, but simply that they hated her, and were discomfited by having her intrude into their lives. Still, that her own superiority was the only refuge she had in life was a cold knowledge.

In the beginning, when the drastic changes in her family's life had just begun, Judy had been naïve enough to assume that God would reach down an invisible remunerative hand and reward her parents for living a truly Christian life. But this did not happen. In fact, it seemed that almost the reverse happened, for at church the people who had greeted Judy's family with such warmth now greeted them with condescension. Judy learned that even in church there was one cardinal rule: A rich man is loved more than a poor man. A church, after all, is a business, too. Not one person in the church thought that Judy's father had been virtuous and kind; they all thought he had been a fool, or so it seemed from their treatment of him. Friends flowed away from the family's life as if they were being carried away on the current of rapidly vanishing money.

Judy's mother got a job as a secretary. Judy's father spent more time each day lying on the living-room sofa. Soon the very lineaments of the furniture in that room seemed tainted and shaped by despair. Judy had to do the dishes, ironing, and cleaning. There was no longer someone to do the housecleaning, and her mother, who worked all day, could not do it herself. Her father, being a man, did not do such things. So it all fell to Judy. Her brother, who was three years older than she, was also exempt from household chores due to masculinity, so he filled his time by getting into trouble. He was finally sent away to boarding school for his last two years of high school; and though it was Judy's mother's engagement ring that paid for most of that particular cost, it drained their pallid financial life even more. There was nothing left for Judy at all.

Finally this dark period had ended. Judy's father got a job with a large chain of paint companies, and although he had to travel quite often, still it was a profitable job. Judy's mother continued to work as a secretary, and by the time Judy was eighteen, they were able to send her to a decent state university. The pleasure of knowing she could attend a university was offset by the realization that all her friends from her former neighborhood were going off to small private colleges. So she felt she had been cast out and away forever: her parents would never be able to earn enough money to buy away the misery she had learned.

Religion, Judy decided, was nonsense, and those who practiced it were fools. She realized that her parents had gained some perverse satisfaction from their struggles, but all their patient virtue could not ease the pain, or buy her a dress to wear to the Senior Prom—although she was not asked to her Senior Prom, because by her senior year, Judy lived almost in complete isolation. She felt scorned by half the school, and she scorned the other half. She spent hours in libraries, poring over ladies' and society magazines; she was determined not to let poverty affect her taste. She worked hard in school, and although she was not innately brighter than others, her hard work paid off. Gradually, a plan for her life took shape. She knew she had to defend herself. The religious and financial crisis that had beset her family proved only one thing: money was all-important. She felt betrayed by her parents; she turned her back on them with cold finality. For the rest of her life she saw them as she felt they were: cruel fools.

This hurt. The worst thing that can happen to a person, the most scarring knowledge, Judy came to believe, is to realize that one's parents are fools.

At first there were fights.

"Judy," her mother would say, "it's time for church. You aren't even dressed."

"I'm not going."

"Oh, Judy—"

"Why should I go to church? How can you expect me to go to

church? How can you and Dad bear to go? How can you stand to go to church and see Mr. Lawton driving up in his brand-new Cadillac, when he cheated you out of so much money that we lost our nice house? How can you keep from standing up in church and screaming? Half the people in that church are hypocrites! They're thieves! Liars! How can you go to a church that lets people like that in? How can the church let people like that enter the doors?"

Judy's mother, shaking her head, would sink onto a chair. "Judy," she would say, when Judy had calmed down enough to listen, "you've got it all wrong. Where did you ever get the idea that church was for good people? Haven't you been paying attention? Church is for *all* people—and we're *all* hypocrites and sinners, Judy, every one of us. No person on earth is perfect, and we all know it in our heart of hearts. Church is the place where we are forgiven, where we are reminded of what we are striving to attain. Heavens, darling, if sinners and hypocrites weren't allowed in church, the churches all over the world would be empty!"

"But, *Mother*," Judy would cry, her fists clenched with anger, "how can *you* stand to be in church, in *that* church, wearing your old shabby coat, while Mr. Lawton's wife wears a brand-new *fur* coat? She's wearing a fur coat, and Mr. Lawton said he was in debt, and we lost our house. I don't understand how you can be in the same room with that man!"

"Judy, in the Bible, Jesus says to forgive the brother who sinned against you seventy times seven. We must forgive others just as we expect God to forgive us. We—"

"Oh, *stop it!*" Judy would scream, and would cover her ears and throw herself on the bed, knowing she was acting like a much younger child. "That thief Lawton first cheated you, and now he snubs you, and *you* quote the stupid Bible! Well, don't talk to me about it anymore, because I don't want to hear it. It's all a bunch of rubbish made up to help the rich keep power over gullible people like you and Dad!"

"Judy," her mother said, "I'm worried about you. I think you are losing your religion."

This made Judy laugh. "Oh, Mother," she said. "No. I'm not losing religion. Religion is losing me!"

The worst fights happened at the beginning of Judy's senior year,

when she was terrified that she wouldn't be accepted into a university.
By then she had convinced her parents that she would not go to
church, and they went off on Sunday mornings by themselves, after
softly tapping on her bedroom door to say that they were on their way
and would be home around noon. Judy would wait until their car had
pulled out of the driveway and had disappeared. Then she would slip
out of bed and go into the kitchen to make herself breakfast. With her
brother away at boarding school and her parents off at church, Judy
found herself alone in the house for a definite period of time. Sunday
mornings, she discovered, were luxurious. What fools people were to
give up this lazy stretch of time to sit with hypocrites and thieves in
buildings built to the glory of a God that didn't exist. After eating her
breakfast, Judy would go back to bed, and read romantic novels or
magazines. If there was any time during her senior year when she
could rely on being happy, it was on Sunday mornings when she
didn't have to go to church.

One Sunday her mother came home, came into her bedroom, and
sat on the edge of her bed, as she did so often.

"I want to read you the parable that the minister talked about in
church today," she began. She had the black family Bible in her hand.

But Judy had been looking at the new spring issue of *Mademoi-
selle,* and as she studied it, she had realized that she wouldn't be able
to afford those dresses, espadrilles, clever costume jewelry, purses, lipsticks, eye shadow, and perfumes. Her spring wardrobe would come
from Black's basement, where the sale rack was. Her mother would
pull out a dank ruffled shirt and suggest that she buy it for both of
them to wear, herself for work and Judy for dress.

And so Judy screamed, "Goddamn you and your goddamned para-
bles and the goddamned Bible and stupid fucking lying goddamned
God!" She wrenched the Bible from her mother's hand and threw it
across the room; it smacked into the wall and thudded to the floor. "*I
do not believe in God!*" she yelled, shaking with rage. "*I do not believe
in the Bible! And I do not believe in you!*"

Judy's mother had only sighed, "Oh, my poor little Judy," and she
rose, picked up the Bible, and walked out of the room. After that, there
were no more invitations to church, and no more discussions about
religion. Judy found a job at an ice-cream parlor and worked there all
day Saturday and Sunday and evenings after school. She lived out her

senior year in a rapture of frugality, saving all the money she made from her job to buy books and clothes for her new university life. What did her high school matter, she decided, or the creeps she saw there—soon it would all be behind her.

At the end of her senior year in high school, the fights with her parents stopped after one final confrontation. The minister of the church had called Judy to ask if he could meet privately with her, but she had been adamant in her refusal. That evening, both her parents had questioned her over dinner.

"There's no reason for me to talk to Reverend Thompson," Judy had said. "I do not believe in God or in the Church, and frankly, the whole subject bores me to tears. I'm sick of discussing it."

"You're getting arrogant, young lady," her father said. "It doesn't become you."

"Poverty doesn't become me, either," Judy replied.

"Judy," her mother intervened, "how can we explain it to you? You are such a child. When you are grownup, perhaps you'll understand how necessary it is to live by your chosen values. Otherwise, life is meaningless."

"Your precious values ruined my life," Judy said.

Judy's mother stared at her for a while, then lifted both hands gently, palms open to Judy, as if holding out an invisible gift. "I think when you have children of your own, you'll discover that life doesn't always turn out the way you intend for it to. You can't control everything, and so you do your best to control your own actions. Even your own children don't turn out as you intend them to." She smiled at Judy, her gentle Christian smile that both moved and infuriated her daughter. It was the closest she would come to stating that she was just as dissatisfied with her daughter as her daughter was with her.

The fights ended. A cold peace reigned. There began to be more money in the family. For her graduation present, and as a sort of unadmitted apology, her parents gave Judy a car. It was a used, dented, clunker of a car, but it was a car, and it made Judy's life much easier. Still, her harsh judgment on her parents remained, and her second thought after seeing the car was: I bet they really got taken on this, the fools. They probably paid twice what anyone else would have.

When she got to college, her life was a mixture of pleasure and pain. Pleasure because she was finally away from her parents, controlling her own life, purchases, and activities, working as hard as she could to get ahead. Pain, because no matter how fiercely she controlled and worked, there were others so far ahead of her. It took all her energy not to collapse in despair, because she had fallen into the seductive habit of selective envy. She envied this person her brilliant mind, that person her wealth, another person her social skills, and another her figure. Rarely did she stop to consider the entire person, or when she did it was only to consider someone who possessed all the enviable qualities. Judy became adept at envy. Still, she did not quite let it rule her life; she kept her life charted toward goals.

First, she decided to major in education. Really, what else was there for her to do? She had to be prepared to support herself, and she wasn't interested in abstract ideas. By her junior year, she discovered one definite talent: she was an excellent committee member. She *liked* committees. She enjoyed the structure, hierarchy, the sense of assembly, the shared achievement. She was either secretary or treasurer of several clubs. When she was sitting at an oval table, taking down the minutes of a meeting with earnest scrupulousness, the touch of the pen to paper provided her with a physical pleasure. There was more reality and worth to her in the details of a projected car wash for the French Club than in the academic substance of many of her courses. However, one could not get a university degree in committees, so she plodded through her education courses dutifully.

Her junior year she met a girl named Sharon Lake in an education course, and they quickly became close friends. They double-dated, studied together, did favors for each other, and soon Judy came to wonder how she had ever enjoyed life without Sharon's friendship. But one night, as they sat in the student union drinking coffee and quizzing each other on a test for the next day, Sharon said to Judy, "You really don't remember me, do you?"

"What?" Judy said. "Remember you? What are you talking about? I just met you."

"No, you didn't," Sharon said. "You've seen me lots of times. I used to go to the same high school you did. I used to pass you all the time in the hall. And I lived two blocks away from you—well, my family still lives two blocks away from your family."

"On Whitton Drive or Green Street?"

"Green Street. Well, I mean your family lives on Green Street, of course. My family lives on Drake. You had to pass it on the way to school. The white house with thirty-seven bikes in the front yard."

"How strange," Judy said. "I can't believe we lived so close and never got to know each other."

"Well, you always sort of kept to yourself, you know. In fact—to be honest, I always thought you were stuck-up."

"Oh, no!" Judy protested. "I was just shy. Well, thank heavens we finally met."

How cruel Fate was, Judy thought, to have let her live so close to such a perfect friend for so long without somehow causing them to meet. It drove yet another peg into her scoreboard against God.

Her friendship with Sharon continued through their senior year. Judy was devastated when Sharon accepted a graduate fellowship at a university in Oregon. At the end of her senior year, Judy's determination almost foundered; she could not think how she would live without the gratifying structure of Sharon's friendship and college life. She was offered a teaching position in a high school near Boston, and although she spent the summer nearly sick with fear, in the end it turned out to be the best thing that could have happened to her. It was there that she met Ron.

The years of the past have a way of melding together; memories flow past the mind's eye in a great flood. Judy felt she had little control over which events and people tumbled to the surface of her memory; and even so, the ones that did emerge floated on past too rapidly, visions beckoning from boats or the tops of unanchored garages, visions seen at best briefly and indistinctly before they were swept from sight. Judy married Ron, moved to Londonton with him, had two children, decorated their home, but these happy events did not stand out with the precise integrity of the scenes of her adolescence. Perhaps contentment is not as easily remembered as misery.

And now, after so many years of being safe, Judy shied away from remembering the pain of her childhood. She kept far away from all that, as if it existed on the other side of a chasm. And she looked back only now and then in order to remind herself that she must protect her own children and herself. She did not like memories; she liked the present, and planning for the future.

She and Ron were in this regard well matched. They were hard workers; they were both embarrassed by their families. Ron's parents came from wealthy, establishment Bostonian stock, and they were handsome people. But Ron's father was an alcoholic, and gradually he declined in life, taking the family pride and possessions with him. If Ron's maternal grandmother had not had the foresight to establish a trust for her grandson, Ron would have been penniless. But the trust saw him through college and helped him set up his business. After that, it was just a matter of work—and Ron and Judy were both glad to work. Their pleasure, even, was their work, because they shared a common goal; they measured their progression up the social scale of Londonton with the same sort of pride with which they marked the ascending heights of their children on the kitchen doorjamb.

John and Cynthia were healthy, intelligent, graceful children, well liked by everyone. They had the normal childhood illnesses, an occasional broken leg from skiing or a sprained arm from playing tennis, but they were never seriously ill. Ron's business flourished. Judy organized and ran her days with the efficiency of possessive love.

Ron and the children left the house at eight-thirty, and by nine-thirty Judy had cleaned the bathroom sinks, made all the beds, done the breakfast dishes, and vacuumed the front hall. She then had plenty of time to devote to charities and committees, and the years went by just this way. Because it is in the nature of the human creature to be continually amazed at the trials with which life besets him—no matter how fortunate he may seem to others—Judy always assumed that she had a lot to cope with. It was not until the fortuitous gathering by the fireplace at the Sloans' house, when Carlos made his startling pronouncement, that Judy stopped to think that she had lived her adult life with really unusual ease. She did not attribute any of this good fortune to the intervention of God. She had joined the Londonton church for the same reason she had joined every other socially prominent organization in town; and she did not plan to be taken in by anything the ministers or hymns or scripture readings said. Still, she enjoyed the rituals, and it was nice to see the children, when they were little, dressed in white robes and singing Easter songs. Over the years she had become friends with Jews and atheists and Catholics, and she knew beyond a shadow of a doubt that one's fortune in life had absolutely no connection with one's belief in God. She did not believe in God; and yet for the past twenty-five years of her life she had been fortunate.

Why, then, was she always afraid? It really had nothing to do with religion—she probably would have led an even more anxious life if she had believed in God, because she knew so well what that belief could do. Not until Carlos had spoken with her at the party had she realized that in a way she had come through it; through much of life, unscathed. She decided, as she sat in church listening to Reynolds Houston finish the scripture reading, that it was probably not fear that she felt after all. It was just that she was so vividly aware of the possibilities of each moment, and she wanted desperately for each of those moments to be as perfect as possible. What else was life about? She was proud of the standards she set herself, and if fear provided the necessary energy, so be it: look what she was accomplishing. Look at all she had: her intelligent daughter, her admirable husband, her handsome, devoted son.

LIZA HOWARD

I saw the look you gave me just now, Judy Bennett, that quick judgmental glance. I am familiar with that look. You have never looked at me any other way, you have never given me a chance. Every time I stood at the entrance to your life, you have judged and dismissed me swiftly and harshly; it is always as if you were slamming a door in my face. But it's done you no good, Judy Bennett, for I am in your house.

How women like you tire and anger me with your pretensions, your cold superficialities. You really do believe you are better than I am, and you've consistently tried to impress this fact upon me. Well, your husband liked me well enough—and your son, your precious son, loves me.

If one can call it love.

It was in Londonton's most elegant, expensive gift shop that we first saw each other, just two months ago. Johnny was there, sort of hulking around looking foolish, while Sarah showed him place mats and pottery bowls. I was standing by a high table covered with black velvet which displayed a variety of old-fashioned glass paperweights. I was looking for a gift for one of my midwestern friends who was soon to have a birthday, and I was so surprised to find the paperweights that I would not have looked up and seen Johnny if it had not been for Sarah's voice. If he never thanks me for anything else, Johnny should thank me for sparing him a lifetime of listening to that voice—high, whiny, nasal. Sarah speaks as if she's trying not to move her lips.

"John, please," she said. "I want to get some of these things down for the bridal registry. Do you like the place mats with the jelly-bean print or the butterfly print?" It was obvious that she was trying to show

him off, but was irritated because he wasn't suitably involved in the se-
lection of wedding gifts.

"Well," Johnny said, trying to please, "they both seem kind of
young to me. I like the plaid."

Oh, how exasperated she became! "Johnny, *we have plaid* already," she hissed. Hadn't he been paying attention?

"Oh, Sarah, you have such good taste, and it's sort of a woman's
thing to do. Why don't you just decide."

"But it's a *new world*," Sarah said, nearly in tears now. "You're
supposed to take an interest in the home if our marriage is going to
last. I want you to like our place mats."

"Well—the jelly beans. Yeah, the jelly-bean place mats are good. I
really like them. All those different colors."

"Well, why didn't you say so?" Sarah said, and immediately she
perked right up. "They are cheerful, aren't they? I wonder how many
we should ask for. I mean, they aren't right for a formal dinner. But if
we have friends stay the night and for breakfast—"

"Six. Or eight. Get eight to be sure," John said.

Sarah searched around in her handbag for her notebook and pencil, and called out brightly to the saleslady, "I'm just adding a few
more things to our list here."

"Dear, if you like those jelly-bean place mats, you might want to
see these," the saleslady said, spotting an easy sale.

Sarah tripped off to talk with the saleslady, and Johnny looked up
and saw me staring at him.

Looking at Johnny was like looking at a thick sable coat. All my
instincts said: Touch. Feel. Stroke. Rub. It had been a while since
I'd paid serious attention to any man, but even so, Johnny would
have stopped me in my tracks any day. Six feet two inches tall, with
big shoulders, a wide chest that tapers down to a smooth slim stomach,
and such lovely long long slim legs. He was wearing a green and blue
striped sweater, and oxford-cloth button-down blue shirt, jeans, and cow-
boy boots. I just stared and stared. He has such thick blond hair—none
of that thinning stuff that other men (like his father) have, but real
thick, vibrant hair, falling down over his forehead. His eyes are green
and his lashes are long. *Honey child,* I thought. I smiled at him. He
smiled at me, a slow, easy, confident swagger of a smile. In a flash I
saw that life had always been good to him, that he had never lacked

for the love of family or women, that he had always had his own way. You great big baby, I thought. I'd like to play with your toys.

"I wonder if you could help me a moment," I said, still smiling. "I'm buying a gift for a friend of mine—a man—and I'm not sure just which paperweight a *man* would like best. Men's tastes are so different from women's. Could you come give me your opinion?"

He was so obviously delighted to be reassured of his masculinity after standing there choosing jelly-bean place mats that he just grinned all over.

"Sure," he said, and ambled over to the black velvet table.

"I'm Liza Howard," I said, and gave him my hand.

"John Bennett."

"Oh, yes, I can see the resemblance. I know your parents— slightly." (I've been in bed with your father—twice.) "Well, now, I really would be grateful for your help. I tend to like this one, with the flower, but I suppose a man might like the spiral?"

We were standing close enough to smell each other. He picked up a paperweight full of red and white and green geometric designs that made me think of Christmas candy in a crystal bowl.

"This is the one I'd like," he said. "It's beautiful." He turned it over in his huge long-fingered hand. "God, it's two hundred and fifty dollars. Imagine spending that much on a paperweight. You must really love this friend."

So I knew immediately just how to make that first subtle but definite invitation.

"No," I said, and took the paperweight from him and placed it carefully back on the black velvet. "Actually that man doesn't mean that much to me. I guess I'll look for something else. But thank you so much for your help."

Sarah, in the meantime, had been on the other side of the shop, too engrossed in her bridal registry choices to have the sense to be jealous. He moved off from me, and I felt the reluctance in his blood.

"John," Sarah said, "what do you think of this solid-brass rooster-shaped napkin holder? Don't you think it would be real cute on the table at breakfast?"

I quickly went out the door, thinking: Sarah, you dummy, you're paying attention to the wrong cock.

Later that afternoon I went back to the gift shop and bought the

Christmas-candy paperweight. I had it beautifully gift-wrapped, and I sent it to Johnny with a plain white card on which I wrote: "I hope you like this. I can think of lots of things you might like. Please call."

He called the day the paperweight arrived, and came to my house that night. I led him into the living room and gave him a drink of brandy, which I could tell he badly needed, because he was almost white with fear.

"Listen," he said, "I'm not sure what I'm doing here. I mean—well, I'm engaged to Sarah Stafford, and her father's president of the college, and she's a real nice girl, and I'd hate to hurt her feelings. And my mother—"

I could see through Johnny as easily as through the glass of the paperweight. The only part of his body that's ever been broken in his life is his leg, from a skiing accident. In high school and college he only had to smile for girls to pull up their skirts and lie down for him. He has a pale blue MG his parents bought for him, with condoms in the glove compartment and Bourbon in the trunk. I don't suppose he's genetically dumb, but life has never called upon him to exercise his intelligence in any way that would sharpen it—but an easy luscious charm steams off him like the scent of lilacs on a hot May day, and that takes care of everything. He doesn't *need* to think, so he's never really bothered.

I lured and snared him with such obvious intent that I was embarrassed for us both. Sweet huge delicious animal, he watched me construct my trap, and then he cheerfully plunged right into it.

I let him talk. I assured him of his moral strength and selflessness; here he was, thinking of his fiancée, mother, father, friends, community, before thinking of himself. And all he was possibly intending to do, after all, was to have one last pleasant fling before settling down to years and years of fidelity with Sarah Stafford. I wanted nothing of him but to look at him—and maybe hold him—poor lonely widow that I was. I was planning to move from this town as soon as the house was sold, and I had no friends to gossip with anyway; all his secrets were safe with me.

"Well," he said at last, weakening, grinning that lovely grin, "lots of guys do have stag parties . . ."

"That's right," I said. "I could be your own private stag party."

He kissed me then. We were standing in the living room, with brandy snifters in our hands, and that first kiss grew so intense that I nearly let the glass just drop to the floor. Instead, I pulled away from him, and led him up the winding stairs to my bedroom. We were both nervous. I can't even remember how we got out of our clothes; in the past few weeks I've managed to do some rather drawn-out striptease routines when undressing in front of Johnny, but that first time we just got out of our clothes and into the bed as fast as we could.

"My God," Johnny said as we lay together. "You are so beautiful. I didn't know real women could be like this, so—curvy . . ."

He ran his hands over my breasts and stomach, he kissed my neck and breasts, he made some attempt to be a good lover. It was obvious that he was experienced, for he did know what to do, where to touch, but suddenly he just lost control, forgot himself, forgot the new etiquette of lovemaking that even the youngest men are learning these days. He stopped being gentle and considerate: he grabbed me, held me down, and entered me with all the finesse of a rapist.

"My God, you're so beautiful, you're so soft," he said. "My God."

They were sweet words, but he was hardly articulate, he was breathing so hard, and he was moving against me with the speed and sensitivity of a jackrabbit. I wanted him to realize whom he was with; I wanted him there with me. So I slid my hands between our stomachs to slow him down. I pressed, palms upward, against his flat stomach, so that each time he fell against me he felt the pressure of my palms, the teasing cut of my fingernails against the skin between his crotch and legs. I thwarted his rhythm. I slowed him down. Johnny raised his head from where he had buried it in the pillow and looked at me.

"Johnny," I said, "hey."

Then I began to move my hips, slowly. I wrapped my legs around his legs and brought my hands around to press down gently on his backbone.

"Slow down, Johnny, there's no hurry," I said, and smiled.

He looked at me. He did not smile. He saw who I was. He said, "Liza."

He wanted to heave against me. But I stayed in control, I stayed slow. I arched and sank away, tightening and pulling, taunting Johnny's body into a different mood. I remained deliberate, controlling the cadence of our colliding bodies until I could sense just how he ached, how he yearned; we were both trembling, and our stomachs were slick with sweat. Then I too lost control and just held on, the rhythm quickened, and finally we both came, not in one quick explosion, but with the prolonged shuddering power of a rocket leaving earth. We rose, and flared, and flared.

I had concentrated him; I had won. He collapsed against me, grimacing, rubbing his head against my neck, the pillow, gasping. I stroked his back. Ha, darling Johnny, I thought, you're mine now. And I was right.

Didn't you warn your son about older women, Judy? No, I don't think you did. You don't have the imagination. And you obviously have all the sexuality of a straight pin. All the times that your son has come home to you from my bed, and you've never once suspected: it makes me laugh, makes me want to laugh out loud in this church right now. God, how I despise you, you and this town, with its placid, rotten people with their smug and plastic smiles. I can't wait till Friday comes. Then I will crack their foolish complacency, and especially yours, Judy Bennett. I will have to use my entire life as a hammer, and I'll cause only a minute hairline crack, but that crack, that fracture, will be crucial in the dam of their lives. Once Johnny and I break free, who knows what else will follow?

It will be marvelous for this town, our little escapade; it will wake them up. I sit here, looking around me, and I want to stand and scream: How passionless you are, every one of you! I burn to think how all the roiling ages of conquering disease, ignorance, and poverty have come down to this: this congregation of tidy people simpering through the service of this mealy-mouthed minister. Does even one person here actually believe there *was* an Annunciation? An angel appeared in Mary's room to tell her she was pregnant, and all the space and air in the room was broken into shafts of gold that glittered like the sound of bells. Brilliance flamed from the angel's hair and body like a fire, and his great beating wings whirred the air. No diamond I possess can flash like that angel's voice. *He* was magnificent.

Why does the Bible cheat us so of all the details? I want to know if the wings of that angel were made of soft feathers attached to his back with a horn-like shaft in the manner of birds or if his wings were made of mist and light. Or if, as some pictures show, they were made from molded gold. I want to know if Mary ran out into the streets after the angel appeared, calling to the neighbors, touching the

walls of houses, the dirt of the road, the rough bark of trees, to assure
herself that the earth was real, that she had not gone mad. What did
people say to her when she told them an angel had appeared to her? I
think I know: the worst people mocked and scoffed, and the kindest
feared for her mental stability. *She* probably feared for her mental stability herself: although the vision of that angel was undoubtedly
burned into her mind, how could she be sure it had not been a hallucination? If only the angel had left her something tangible to hold in her
hand as proof. Well, there was the baby in her womb—but that's not
exactly what I mean.

I do not think anyone in this church is prepared to deal with what
the Bible teaches. Do we believe a transparent human being slipped
through plaster walls and levitated a few feet off the ground? No, we
don't, not really. We are so scientific these days; spaceships and Mar-
tians are the miracles we're expecting, and the vision of Captain Kirk
and Mr. Spock beaming on and off the starship *Enterprise* has more
validity for us than the appearance of an angel. We doubt God and
yearn for UFOs. Never mind. We doubt, because we are too lazy for
the burden of belief.

Religion is by nature passionate, or should be to be real. But
here in this prissy place it's been subdued. It's been perverted. It's become a lie.

Look at the Reverend Peter Taylor, the prig, staring out at me
with his collection-plate eyes. All the other women in this church sniff
around him like bitches, hoping to leave their scent accidentally on his
robe so he'll come search them out. How surprised they would be to
know that he searched *me* out—and then could not even follow
through with his pathetic little seduction.

It was a surprise last week when Peter asked me to go with him
on his mission of mercy to those little boxes in the woods. What a parody that afternoon was—didn't he realize he was only doing a bad imi-
tation of every adolescent first date? The trip to the countryside, the
sinuous approach, the timid attempt to hold hands; I've seen it all a
million times. The oblique attack: muttering about our hearts, for
heaven's sake! "It's what lies in our hearts that really matters." Meaning if our hearts were pure we could commit adultery and still be good
Christians. At first I thought he was being subtle from some gallantry,
but then I realized he was only scared. As a minister he could not

come right out and say, "Liza, I'd like to fuck you." He probably doesn't even let himself *think* such things. No, he had to camouflage his words, but he was surprised to find that I'm a hunter as much as he is, not ever the prey, and while he finds sneaking necessary because of his profession, *I* can spring and pounce.

"Do you want to sleep with me?" I asked, because his flaccid courtship was so transparent. He responded exactly as I had expected —he withdrew his ardor and his hand and scuttled back to the safety of his profession. Ministers are just as macho as the next man; they can't stand to have a woman make the advance, and they don't like to have the truth spoken clearly. Peter Taylor would gladly have screwed me in the back seat of his car—as long as I never said aloud, "Do you want to screw me in the back seat of your car?" But I spoke.

Oh, it's a shame that he was such a coward, because I would have liked to make love to that man. He is vain, and has kept his body trim and muscular. His profession would have brought guilt and naïveté to heighten the excitement—guilt is such a strong aphrodisiac. The skin of his body would have slid sucking against mine. Once at a picnic I saw a woman slice a ripe watermelon in half, and her son, intrigued by the exposed pink fruit, immediately stabbed his forefinger into the fruit's juicy depths. Juice and seeds spurted out. His mother scolded him, but the boy looked so pleased, and withdrew his finger in the manner of one who has achieved an unexpected triumph. Just so would Peter Taylor have entered me, with fears of all kinds—jealous wives, outraged parishioners—making his blood pound all the harder. All his knowledge and beliefs would have caused him to taste my body like a good man biting into sinner's fruit; and it would have been the most savory feast of his life. But instead he drew his hand away from mine.

Now he stands in the pulpit looking as pious as a saint, but he seldom looks my way. He is afraid, I know, that if his eyes meet mine, a recognition of lust will ignite for all the world to see. The coward. He does not really interest me. I don't want to fan his skittish flames.

No, I don't want a tepid, timid, ministerial lust. Even if I were able to involve Peter Taylor in a flirtation, it would be a bore: he is so well known and loved that people would forgive him instantly, or not believe their eyes and ears. I am not sorry that I didn't screw Peter Taylor, though it would have been amusing; I've never been to bed with a minister. But I am quite content with Johnny, for our lust swells daily, like a music beating in our blood. He makes me weak, dazed, damp, ecstatic. He gives me fever. He makes me flame.

And he is my antidote to this town. People here are so boring, so settled, so safe—zombies. Just look at the women in this church, how they dress. Count how many have plaid fabric stretched across their bottoms. Fat or lean, the women in this town wear plaids. Is it because the harsh bars and blocks in the fabric mirror the workings of their minds and hearts? Certainly there is no pattern more perfectly designed to deny desire. People here want to be seen as sexless, as emotion-free as furniture. Perhaps that is one reason why they've always hated me. I flow in silk. I reek of sex. The patterns of my life are soft and coiling. My hair is long and thick; I brush it constantly, and I know just how to put it up in a twist so that at a crucial moment before making love I can release it and let it fall about my naked shoulders. I have walls of mirrors, and I know just which angle of my body is the most alluring—and just which positions to avoid. I am thirty-five now, but I can look innocent, with the aid of practice and knowledge. And I am beautiful and wealthy; I have learned to wear my jewelry like skin and my skin like a jewel.

This may be why they hate me. When Mitchell was still alive, when he brought me to this town, I sensed the coolness of the women. But I thought: Well, what can one expect from women who wear plaids and hide their breasts? Mitchell had warned me that New Englanders keep aloof, so I was prepared for it, and while he was alive there was enough socializing. The people of this town courted him as they would court any wealthy man, but I did not figure out soon enough just how jealously they guarded him for themselves. They hovered around me in those early days, trying with their self-serving smiles to pry secrets from me. They were hoping to discover some great unforgivable error in my past which would let them bar me with a righteous flourish from their lives—and which would win Mitchell away from me and back to them. Because I am beautiful and love luxury, they labeled me as bad. They only had to look at me to decide that.

Back in the Midwest, they judge people just as harshly, but there they say so. Finally, there, some indignant soul puts her hands on her hips and says, "Liza, I think you ought to know we just don't approve of the way you dress. To be honest, there's something cheap about you and we think you ought to do something about it." In their most cruel criticisms is a kind of frank friendliness, and after all, that flat frontier land has had too many outcasts tame it for anyone to be called a stranger there. But here in New England, people judge you once, then turn their backs. Or if they must face you, it is with averted eyes. That's how they faced me when Mitchell was alive. They held me off with remote courtesy, but because Mitchell was my husband, they had to let me into their midst.

But when Mitchell died, so did every bit of their pretense to friendship. The whole town came to his funeral, expressing frigid sympathy to me, and then turning away, stood in groups as far away from me as possible, staring at me with accusatory eyes.

"Your husband died of a heart attack, and you caused that heart attack." Everyone was longing to say that, but no one did.

What do they think I did? Do they think I fucked him to death? Perhaps they think I'm a witch, these old New Englanders; perhaps they think I put a curse on him. For they do think I'm responsible.

They are right to suspect that I have powers, but they are all directed toward exciting the human heart, not toward stopping it. And though not one person in this town would believe it, I loved Mitchell and wanted him to live forever. I've been married to a richer man, and I could have married richer men the day I married Mitchell. I did not marry him for his money, although that is what everyone here thinks.

It's called projection. The whole town wooed Mitchell because he was wealthy, and so it never occurred to them that anyone could love Mitchell for any other reason.

It was in Bermuda that we met. I was there with friends—well, with what passed for friends in that time of my life—and I wanted nothing more than to get a good tan and lots of sleep. In the past twenty-five months I had gone through a divorce, an abortion, and a screwed-up love affair, and the only thing that kept me from committing suicide was the absence of energy for such an event. I spent that early October day lying on the beach, then went to my room in the late afternoon, drugged by the sun into one of those wonderful helpless sleeps. I showered, oiled my skin, and slid naked between cool sheets. When I awoke it was nine o'clock at night, and someone was knocking at my door.

"Go away," I said, furious at having been awakened.

"Darling, it's *me!*" It was Bea Dolton, an acquaintance of mine who functioned in our group as a sort of anorexic, Waspish Dolly Levitz. "I have someone I want you to meet."

"I don't want to meet anyone," I said. "I'm tired. Go away."

There was a murmuring, then silence, and I drifted back into my stupor. But before I was completely asleep, I heard another noise at my door. Clever Bea, she had managed to weasel the room key from the desk clerk. In she swept, all svelte and fragrant, pulling poor old frowning Mitchell with her.

"Wake up, Liza, don't be rude," she said. "This is Mitchell Howard. He's been wanting to meet you. We've been waiting for hours for you to come down for a drink. And he's leaving tomorrow. Liza, sit up."

Bea had owed me a favor for a long time and I could tell by the tone of her voice that this was it. This was something—someone—important. So I sat up, trying to struggle up away from the tug of sleep, holding the sheet against my breasts. And I stared at Mitchell Howard.

I liked him that second. I thought he looked like Napoleon—short, stocky, powerful, bold. He had blue eyes, and they were judging me. Any other night I would have reached for my dressing gown in such a way that a slide of hip or a bit of breast would be accidentally, invitingly revealed. I'm not a whore, but neither am I a prude, and I find there's usually nothing as pleasurable as sex. But that night I was just so tired, from the sun and from my whole life, and so I only sat there, and didn't even smile.

"Hello, Mitchell," I said.

"Hello, Liza," said Mitchell.

"I'll leave you two," Bea said, and disappeared as gracefully as she had come, closing the door behind her gently but firmly so that the lock clicked.

I lay back down, pulled the sheet up over my shoulder, and went instantly back to sleep.

Later I was to wonder at what I had done: who goes back to sleep when a strange man has just come into her room? But the need for sleep had sucked my eyelids tight against my eyes. I had no energy and no desire to stay awake. And Mitchell's presence in my room meant nothing to me one way or the other.

When I awoke, it was seven-thirty the next morning. I stretched, feeling wonderfully hungry, and rolled over and stretched again, and saw a strange man in a gray suit asleep on the double bed next to mine. For just a moment I was perplexed, and then I remembered Bea's late-evening introduction, and then I laughed. Mitchell opened his eyes, yawned, looked at me, and smiled.

"Good morning," he said.

God, he was a gentleman. He said, "Would you like to use the bathroom first?" And he closed his eyes while I got up and put on my robe.

I've made love with enough men to fill this church. What fun it would be to have them sitting here, all lined up in pews. I could stand at the pulpit and judge them: the schoolboys, the professors, the pilot, the banker, the sailor, the dentist, the carpenter, the Boy Scout leader, the tennis coaches, the congressman, the scientist, the businessmen. My good parents provided me with almost more money and good looks than I can use in one lifetime, so I've never needed to use sex to pay my mortgage or to buy me the company of men. And the company of men has been the greatest pleasure in my life. Many times I've sat here in this very church, trying not to topple off the pew with boredom, entertaining myself with the age-old question: which is most enjoyable, the courtship or the act? I love those early moments, when both people are breathless with lust and anxiety and indecision, when a man gently helps me into my coat and lets his hands linger just a few seconds too long on my shoulders, so that his fingers seem to touch accidentally the rise of my breasts. I love the dance of it all. I love seeing a man's face when I walk into the room for the evening, and it dawns on him that under my silky dress my breasts are free. On the other hand, that sort of pleasure, while perhaps the more exquisite, is also the more delicate and subtle—and rather precious. I suppose I do prefer the actual act. In spite of the number of lovers I've had, I find each penetration a great physical surprise: my mind and the rest of my body goes numb and quiet, and all my senses become focused on that one sweet intrusion, as if my nerves were a crowd who rushed to gather around a dramatic scene. I love all the vulgar thrashing, the groaning barnyard sounds. I love the focused, tense, desperate climb to orgasm, and then the helpless arch of release, when the fork of the body pumps like a machine. I love it when I come, and when a man comes, pulsing. After making love, the feeling flows back again from my crotch into my limbs and extremities, and I feel like a tree must feel when in the spring the sap forces itself up and out through tight vein-like channels so that each twig pushes out a leaf.

Am I depraved? Perhaps. Or perhaps only honest. There was a time when I thought it would be best to give all that up. I decided that I should settle down, get married, be monogamous, have children, and run charities—that's what people do with their lives. I had a friend named Grady whose father owned a local insurance company. Grady was as pretty a man as I am a woman, and he was bored, too, and we thought what fun it would be to have a big lovely wedding. Sexually we were beautifully matched; we'd both had our share of experiences, and knew what we liked. Our making love was a form of eating on the order of starved rats with Swiss cheese: we bit and burrowed. And as the months went by, after the wedding, we constructed ourselves the most lovely maze: a large sun-filled modern house with blond parquet floors and dhurrie rugs and silver cigarette cases on the glass-topped table. For four months we played this game called marriage: Grady went off to work at his father's business, and I stayed in that lovely house that curled about me as aromatically and luxuriously as a fresh wood shaving. I unpacked wedding presents and tried to decide in just which perfect spot to place them. I hollowed out cherry tomatoes and stuffed them with crab meat and mayonnaise and capers. I left the house each Monday to swim at the country club, or just drink, so that I wouldn't inhibit the maid while she cleaned the house. Some nights we entertained envious friends; other nights, Grady and I took our wineglasses to bed and screwed our minds out, then watched television, like any other normal American couple.

But one morning, four months after our wedding, Grady came down to breakfast looking strange. I thought perhaps he was sick to his stomach. His expression was that of a man who has food poisoning but hasn't figured that out yet. He sat down across from me at our blond butcher-block kitchen table, which I had set with quilted place mats and Wedgwood china, and at first he just drank his coffee. I waited.

Finally he said, "Liza, I think I'm going mad."

"Grady. What's wrong?" I asked, only slightly alarmed. Grady liked his theatrics as much as I.

"All this—*stuff*—makes me feel—*trapped*," he said. "I can't explain it. But every day when I come home from work, and every morning when I wake up in this house, I feel scared. I feel like I'm walking into some kind of cage."

"My God, Grady," I said, "that's just the way I feel. I mean, you at least get to *leave*. I'm here all alone to dust and rearrange these things. Why didn't anyone ever tell me how demanding appliances are? Just look at that kitchen counter! There they stand, all in a line, and they inspire in me the most awful sense of *duty*. Sometimes I think I hear tiny metallic voices, whining, 'Use us, use us! Blend something, toast something, fry something, open a can, sharpen a knife, crush some ice, slice an onion, grate some cheese! What do you think we're here for?' It's like having a stable of electric avocado-colored dwarves! Do you realize that it's possible to fill a house with appliances and furniture and objects, and then to think *that's what life is about?* Most people feel protected, assisted, by the objects in their homes, but I feel imprisoned."

I realized then that I had shoved my chair back from the breakfast table and was clutching my knife and fork in my hands. I dropped them on the table and leaned back in my chair.

"Oh, Grady," I said.

"Oh, Liza," he said. "No wonder we love each other so much."

"What are we going to do?" I asked.

Grady grinned. Then he reached out one long arm and snatched the toaster cord from its socket, then sent the toaster flying across the room. It slammed into the refrigerator and crashed to the floor.

"Grady!" I said.

"Where's the blender?" Grady asked.

I got up and got it from its shelf, and meant to hand it to him, but instead I threw it past him, and it thudded into the window seat.

"Let's get 'em," Grady said, and he laughed, and his laugh was full of lust.

We rampaged through the kitchen then, ripping electric cords out of sockets, smashing the ice crusher into the Cuisinart. The room filled with metallic shrieks and snaps. We could feel the angry energy from those dying machines come oscillating out of their plastic shells into the air around us. Many of the instruments we had to throw several times, because they had been so sturdily built, those insidious jailer-robots. Grady finally took a porcelain-handled ladle and banged savagely at the can opener, but though the plastic can opener body split open, it was the porcelain ladle that broke first—it cracked in half. And that was too bad, because the ladle was pretty and delicate and had asked nothing of us but admiration.

"I think we killed them," Grady said at last. By then we were standing together in the kitchen, panting from exertion, surrounded by shattered appliances. They lay all about us on the Eternal Shine vinyl kitchen floor, their plastic cases cracked open, exposing their metallic innards, wheels, and chunks and shards, and their cords trailed away from them like broken tails. The room was silent, except for the self-defrosting freezer, which let a trickle of water slip down its back, with a sound like a sigh of relief.

I looked at Grady and he looked at me, and we hugged. I don't know when we were ever more delighted with each other. We went back to bed and made love, growling and rolling about and biting, still full of that eerie triumphant energy that had been released down in the kitchen. Afterward, we lay in bed, sweating and holding hands.

"Do you want me to destroy the dresser?" Grady asked.

I looked at the dresser. It was an old mahogany thing that had been in my grandparents' house, and the burled boards looked more like fabric than wood. It just sat there, not doing anything.

"I don't think so," I said. "Actually, it's not the furniture that bothers me. It's just those appliances. And the houseplants. When you're gone and I'm alone in the house, they rub their leaves together and whisper, 'Water us, water us. Get me out of the sun, I can't take this heat. Feed me, feed me, pluck me!'"

"We'll kill them tonight," Grady said. "I'd better get to work. I'm late."

So Grady showered and put on his gray pin-striped three-piece suit, and I showered and put on slacks and a shirt and got out of the house as fast as I could. I wasn't going to sit in there all day with a kitchen full of dead appliances and a bunch of pleading plants. I went to the country club that has the good golf course and played a few holes of golf with a friend who was hanging around there waiting for someone to drink with. The kid who caddied for us was so cute I regretted being married. Whatever else marriage means to me, it means monogamy. I ate lunch and had a few drinks with my friend, and watched

TV in the club lounge all afternoon, thinking to myself: This is no way to live a life.

I went home around six, when I expected Grady to arrive, and he was already there, in the kitchen, wading around through jagged plastic and metal, trying to fix drinks.

"Don't come in," he said. "It's dangerous in here. You might cut your ankles."

He brought the drinks into the living room, and we sat there, sipping them slowly. They were unattractive drinks, because with the demise of the ice crusher, Grady had had to resort to dropping in plain cubes of ice.

"Shall we kill the plants now?" he said after a while.

I looked around the room. "No," I said, "I don't think so. They don't seem as threatening—as militant—as those appliances. Besides, no matter how you pull off their little green fingers and arms and pinch their little pink heads, they've still got those creepy roots sneaking around down under the soil. I can just hear them *growing*. No, you can't kill plants by ripping them apart."

"Well," Grady said, "then let's just not water them. If we stop watering them, they'll die eventually, won't they?"

"That's brilliant, Grady," I said. "God, you're smart. And sexy. I love you."

Grady and I went out to dinner that night, and for the next week we managed to struggle along without ever going into the kitchen. It was hard getting out the door in the morning without coffee, but we had smashed the coffeepot, and kicked the stomach out of the tea kettle, so we couldn't even boil water. Every night for a week we went out to dinner. It was just too depressing living in that house with those dead metal things and those dying plants. I tried not to look at them, but they seemed to stretch their limp brown arms out to me in supplication. I had to call the housecleaning lady to tell her not to come, because I couldn't think of a reasonable explanation for the way the house looked. Housecleaning ladies impose their own sense of duty, and I just wasn't up to it.

One morning about ten days after we'd destroyed the kitchen, just as I was going out the door a friend of my mother's came up the walk with a coffee cake in her hand.

"What are you doing here at this hour of the morning?" I asked in alarm.

"Liza, have you forgotten?" the woman asked. "I was afraid that you had. I've been calling you all week, but there's been no answer. The Ladies' Hospital Auxiliary is meeting at your house this month. Don't you remember? We arranged it last month. I told you I'd be here early to help you set up the coffee. You newlyweds, I can't imagine what's on your mind!" She laughed, pleased with her wit, and tried to elbow past me into the house.

"You can't go in there," I said.

"Whyever not?" she asked.

It was that very Thursday morning, standing on the slate sidewalk of my luscious well-groomed front lawn in a suburb of a wealthy city in the middle of the United States, that I realized that I could never be what I had intended. I could never be a housewife. No matter how much you guard against it, people will come into your house. The thought of having to live out the rest of my life explaining myself to people like this dear charitable lady was enough to make something in me snap.

"Everything's in a dreadful mess in there," I said. "Grady and I got in a fight and threw things at each other. I'm just on my way to a lawyer now to start divorce proceedings. You'll have to have your meeting elsewhere."

I burst into tears and ran down the walk and got into my car. But as I looked up at that poor bewildered woman, I felt no sense of guilt. I might have inconvenienced her by refusing to let her have the meeting in my house, but I had given her the most marvelous new piece of gossip! And she was the first to have it. An exclusive. "Imagine," she would say to all the Hospital Auxiliary ladies, "Grady and Liza are getting divorced, and they've been married only four months. I wonder what's happened." Oh, how happy all those women would be!

I drove down to Grady's office and asked if we could talk privately. We went out to a little bar and sat in a padded booth and talked. We felt we had given it a good try. But neither of us was cut out for marriage. We could still be friends and lovers, of course. We felt so tender toward each other that we went to a hotel and made love. We ended up living there for three weeks, while we went to a lawyer and started the divorce. We shared a lawyer—we each kept our own money, and agreed to split down the middle the proceeds from the sale of the house. Grady packed his clothes and silver cigarette box and moved into a men's club; I packed my clothes and silver cigarette box and went to France. My only regret, as I slipped out the door of that house for the last time, was that I hadn't thought to take a knife to the sagging belly of the vacuum cleaner.

In France, after a time, I realized I was pregnant. It's funny how babies are made: I don't think the system is very sensible. I can understand the nine months of growing the baby, because that's necessary to make a whole child, and to help the mother come to terms with the fact of this new life. It's the bit about conception that's so ridiculous, because there seems to be no connection between the act and its consequence. No woman ever gets a choice at the actual time; it's always a sort of ambush. I often think of the Virgin Mary—how it must have happened, if it really happened. If Mary was a flesh-and-blood person, not a religious fiction, and if that angel was real and not a hallucination, well, *poor* Mary. I don't think she knelt before that angel and said, "Well, tell God thanks." I think she got up and stomped around the room and cried. I think she said, "Look, I don't even know if you are *real*, fluttering around up on my ceiling like some kind of science-fiction moth, but if you are, and if what you are saying is true, well, I don't like it. Listen, I just got engaged to this real nice man, and if you're an angel, you know how this society is, it's a righteous, vengeful place we're living in these days. Women are supposed to be pure and chaste. Well, hell, I *am* pure and chaste. Now you come along and tell me I'm pregnant? That's not fair! Why can't you wait till after I get married? I like kids, I'll be glad to have children, but I need to be married first, or I'll be ostracized. Do you think anyone's going to believe me when I say, 'God put a baby in my stomach but I'm still a virgin'? I'll sound like a fool and no one will believe me. Joseph will probably leave me, and I'll be disgraced. It's just not fair that I don't get any choice in this matter."

It still isn't fair that women get no choice in the matter. Mary was lucky, apparently, because Joseph stuck by her, and she had the baby, and some other children, too, and a more or less normal life, considering her connections. I envision her as a pretty, young, rather flaky woman, who walked around muttering to herself a lot. I can just see her in some wheat field, beating out the chaff, and stopping to catch her breath, to look up at the bland sky. "No angel this time, huh, God?" she'd ask the sky, and the other women in the field would look at each other and smile: there goes Mary, talking to herself again. But poor Mary would have to talk to herself to stay sane. It's God who's insane—He's perverse. I can't figure it out. Here He gave human beings this delightful, fun thing they can do with each other, something as necessary to life as breathing or eating, something that is so much more *impressive* than breathing or eating. Sex. Then He attaches this sneaky, underhanded consequence, and says: If you have sex, you might make a baby, and you won't know you're making a baby while you're having sex, but if you do make a baby while you're having sex and you don't want to be making a baby then, you're bad.

I've seen women walking around town with slogans on their T-shirts indicating they believe God is a woman. I've never believed that for a minute, and I don't know how anyone else can, either. If there's anything real that people can observe on this earth, it is that women have the raw deal in reproduction: they're the ones who get pregnant, who ruin their reputations, who bear the pain, who end up with skin that looks like a plow's passed over it, and who get blamed for everything the child ever does that's bad. Sex for men is like some wad of bubble gum they can casually chew and blow and pop; but for women sex is always some kind of seed; once they conceive, they've got to carry a baby, or a grief, or a burden of guilt, all their lives.

When I married Grady, I thought in an optimistic, offhanded way that I might have children. I would have a house, an electric can opener, and some children. But never once when we were in bed together, rubbing our bodies like two giant matches, wanting our friction to provide that sudden wild flare of pleasure, did we think: Now we're making a child. No. We didn't think at all. I chose to leave that house, that can opener, even that delicious man, and it was not fair—I will never think it was fair!—that when I left I inadvertently carried a child within me. Grady left, too, and carried nothing with him. Why should he have gone away more free than I?

Oh, poor baby, your body was jelly and twigs, but your new spirit I think of as trembling white wisps which I blew away like a dandelion puff. I swear that the moment the doctor shoveled into me, I felt *something*—your human spirit—escape from me with the ease of a dandelion seed spinning off into a spring night. Life is lighter-hearted than we like to think. I knew you were only miffed, and would float off to land and burrow into someone else's life. I could almost hear you laughing, chiding, teasing, as you spun away. I'm sure someone else has gotten you by now, you happy-hearted child, and anyone else in the world would be a better mother than I. I'm meant to be a tramp in many senses of the word. If I did not have the money my parents had left me, I would still ramble about the world, and I'd make my way as a prostitute, and I'd be just as happy as can be. The way I live is not a mistake I made, but a philosophical choice. I do not want children cramming themselves into my body and my life; men can, because their entrance and residence is transient.

After my divorce from Grady and my seed-baby, I went back home to my generous midwestern city, intending to have some fun. Instead I almost fell in love.

What a grim, heartless business love is, provoking so much need. Love has no decency. When I was younger, I used to be puzzled by the section in Corinthians that goes: "And now abideth faith, hope, charity, these three; but the greatest of these is charity." What about *love,* for heaven's sake! I used to think. But now I know that what is extended to another person when a marriage is made is not love, but charity. Love is too fickle; it changes shapes, like a devil. It is that agreement to be charitable all of one's life to one other person that provides the real bond we call marriage. I found that "being in love" was just like being in a crowded disco with throbbing music and flickering strobe lights; everything becomes distorted, exaggerated, grotesque. Lust, jealousy, possessiveness, need, desire, hunger, hurt all come thumping at you like a relentless beating of drums—it is so exhausting that it threatens life. But charity is as cleansing and renewing as a hot bath; it slows our blood and makes us mild again.

When I awoke in that hotel room in Bermuda and saw Mitchell Howard there on top of the other bed in his three-piece suit, I felt like a wanderer must feel when he stumbles through miles of jungle and discovers a Christian church. There was such a quality of kindness about him, and before we had said ten words to each other, I knew that I wanted this man to enclose his life about me like a great soft cape. How good he was. If he had been rich or poor, it would not have mattered. I would have married him. If he had lived in New Zealand or Alaska, I would have gone with him. If he had been married, I would have been his mistress, but since he was widowed, I was able to be his wife. He needed me, too, for all the things older men need younger women for—my looks, my laughter, my pretty flesh. I offered my glowing body to him like a votive candle.

And no one understood.

Society is a conspiracy with secret rules. I suppose we've learned all those devious double-binds from God. No one ever came out and openly accused me of marrying Mitchell for his money, so I could never come out and openly tell them that it was not the truth. If I've ever cared for any man—extended him charity, fidelity, and trust—I cared for Mitchell. We had fun together. We took our sex with each other as casually and sporadically as afternoon tea. We were both tired. He had three grown children, a dead first wife, a flourishing business, and a demanding community. He wanted constant civil company from me, and while that does not seem like a lot to ask for, it is actually quite rare. In the three years I was married to him, I had sex with him perhaps twenty times. Not even as often as once a month. He was so afraid for his heart, and the sputtering tumult of breath and blood and juices that sex calls up inspired in him more terror than ecstasy. I suppose I cannot expect the town to be aware of that—and I'm not sure that it would help matters any if they knew that Mitchell had not married me for whatever youthful sexual delights I could provide. Well, the town would think, if she didn't marry him for his money and he didn't marry her for sex, then why did they marry? No one would believe that we married for sheer cordiality. We liked to watch the television news and read newspapers and magazines and laugh about the gossip; we liked to eat and drink together, to travel, to plan little pleasures. We were as comfortable with each other as a pair of ten-year-olds spending the week with Grandma. He had a housekeeper at his huge home in Londonton, and a gardener, so I didn't ever have to face the threat of incarceration by any mechanical household devices. Often we traveled and lived in hotels. We read books and played golf and went to plays and concerts and galleries.

I'm not sure why I didn't miss having sex. Perhaps it was that my brush with love just before I met Mitchell had redefined the meaning of sex so harshly for me that I found the absence of it a relief. In any case, there were no temptations for me in Londonton. I hadn't met Johnny; he was still away at college. The husbands whom I met at parties were terrified of me—so many people are terrified of physical sexual beauty; that's why men and women of all ages, shapes, and sizes squeeze themselves into asexual navy blue blazers. It's the unspoken costume of the Anti-Lust League. It took me a while to come to such a drastic conclusion, but I haven't been proved wrong yet. At any rate, I lived in this town for three years without once desiring another man. I was as happy in Mitchell's company as a child with Santa Claus, and though he provided me with all the things that money could buy, those gifts were not the ones that bound me to him. He was quite simply a good and beautiful man. I had not come across that before—few people, I believe, have—and it was a constant balm. I saw the world through the filter of his presence, and for a while I believed that the world could be good.

And yet—the people in this town believe I helped him toward his death; that I did not love him, that I wanted him dead. Being good New Englanders, so proud of their reticence and reserve, they have not said aloud such things to me—but they do not call on me socially, they do not speak to me in shops, they will not meet my eyes.

After every church service, I go to Friendship Hall, with everyone else, and take a cup of coffee and walk around. Well, at first, right after Mitchell's death, I used to walk around. Now I saunter. I'm aware now of what these people expect of me, and I don't mind giving it to them. After all, it is such a boring town—honestly, they'll miss me when I'm gone. Every town needs its pariah. Still, one would think that in a *church*—well, never mind. During coffee hour after the sermon, I talk to the little old men and women who huddle at the sides of the room on folding chairs, who are too infirm to escape me. I talk to Wilbur Wilson, who is old, but not infirm, who could walk away, but does not. He at least seems to offer me genuine friendship, which is strange, because he is so unsophisticated. Why should he like me? I smile at the husbands who come over to talk to me about the weather while looking down my blouse. I am obliging now; I dress so that they have something to see. The women do not come to speak to me; but they never did. They bustle by me, pretending to be headed toward something or someone on the other side of the room. The most magnanimous throw me a brief, condescending smile. Women have no scruples at all.

I come to this church because it is the only company of humans in this town into which I am allowed.

I learned long ago, even before I came here, the most important lesson of my life: being a whore is a way of being a nun. It is a way of taking on the social trappings of isolation and exemption from human responsibility. No one can really touch you; and you can hurt no one, being bound to vows of self-chosen ostracism. My mistake was to make myself vulnerable to society. For a few weeks I suffered: I lost Mitchell, whom I had in my way loved, and I undeservedly gained the hostility of this town. I spent a few weeks—twenty-two days, to be exact—lying in that huge house, in one small bedroom, crying; pain stretched himself out beside me like a lover and embraced me with his poison arms and pierced me with relentless energy—pain has constant strength.

But one morning I awoke and thought: Where's my sense of humor? What am I doing here? If I'm to have a lover so soon after Mitchell's death, it might as well be a living man! If I'm to be judged and sentenced, I might as well commit the crime. I got out of my bed of self-pity and bathed and perfumed myself and as I dressed I wondered just how long it would take me to get one of Londonton's pompous fathers into my bed.

It took three days. Ron Bennett was the first. I went to his office to discuss some papers Mitchell had left regarding his trust to the Londonton Recreation Center. I cried; Ron took me home; I said I was so sad and lonely. I said I would soon be leaving town. I pressed myself against him, and said, "Please hold me. Help me. I'm so frightened and alone."

That's all it took. I was not the first affair for him; he was certainly not the only one for me. It must make the men sitting around me in this church nervous to have me sitting here. I often think, as I sit in church, of jumping to my feet and shouting out that one man has a scar on his left thigh, and one man has an odd tail-like swirl of hair at the base of his spine, and one man cries out "NO!" when he comes, and another prefers to turn me on my stomach so that he can pretend I am a boy. When I stand to sing the hymns, I gaze around the room, and visions of bellies and testicles dance in my head. But I will return them like for like: if these good New Englanders insulted me with silence, I'll do the same. I'll let these men I've slept with stew in their own guilty knowledge until the skin of their spirit pops open and the truth spurts out. The most I will do is to walk toward them during coffee hour in such a way that the sensitive wives read a message in the movement of my hips.

And I will take their golden boy away.

Johnny, you are my just dessert. Your nipples are strawberries, your testicles are plums, and your penis is lovely, big, and firm; I bruise and crush it in the mouth of my pelvis until sweet white thick juice oozes out. You like me to eat you. Any boy as handsome as you are has had many women, but no one has had you with the skill I have. It's fortunate for me that during this period of time when I need someone like you, you are engaged to Sarah Stafford. Your vocabulary, Johnny, is not as varied as mine, but you did amuse me once by telling me that making love with Sarah was like fucking a hole in a tree. That was a pretty artistic metaphor for you, Johnny, and apt, I imagine. I've only seen Sarah twice, but she is as upright and rigid as an ash tree; she's hard and rooted and barky. Her limbs are muscular from playing field hockey and soccer. I can envision her passion as a rather athletic en- thusiasm: she must huff and puff and thrust and bounce. She probably cheers when you come, or maybe she just pats you on the back, jock style, and says, "Well done." I'm sure her attitude toward sex is healthy, clean, and sportsmanlike. And you're such a pretty boy; she must think of you as a kind of trophy. Well, so do I.

I'm sure you and Sarah have similar bedrooms in your homes: framed photos of you as children skiing or jumping horses on the wall, plaid bedspreads on your beds. You've had many women, but never one like me, whose house spreads rippling around us like a moat against the world. Weeks before, I had dismissed the housekeeper, and the gardener and housecleaning people came only twice a week, and never when you were around. We had my huge house all to ourselves, and we drifted through it naked, and as unseen as ghosts. My phone never rings, uninvited guests never arrive, and the mailbox is at the bottom of the long winding drive, so there is not even the delicate in- trusion of a postman into our world. What freedom. It was a delicious pleasure for both of us suddenly to be able to roam up and down the three floors of Mitchell Howard's mansion, through all the rooms, casu- ally drawing the curtains against the outside world, leaving electric lights burning all day long. What did you finally tell your parents and

Sarah? That you were off to spend a week with a friend on an island off the coast of Maine, and the friend had no telephone—some appropriate story. And your family and fiancée believed you, and you did spend that week on an island, after all. Our pleasure isle. I stocked the cupboards and refrigerator with every conceivable treat: thin-sliced rare roast beef, French mustards, scallions and melons, expensive champagnes, Godiva chocolates. It was the end of May, but still cool enough for fires, and we often fell asleep in front of the fireplace, into those deep, sated, dark sleeps caused by sensual exhaustion.

Johnny, you are so young and inexperienced. At twenty-three, you had never stopped to consider how every aspect of your life was dominated by social concerns. From the clothes you wear to the books you read to the women you bed and brag about to friends, to the woman you planned to marry and live out your life with—it is all fiercely, relentlessly, subtly, insidiously controlled by the affluence and snobbish society into which you were born. Your mother pulls your strings with the authority of a puppeteer. I was the first choice you ever made on your own; well, your first major choice. You have been allowed for some time to choose the colors of the sweaters you buy, and which foreign country to go to for winter break—all the little illusions of freedom your mama fed you like bits of bread to keep you feeling like a real boy instead of Pinocchio. That sweet week we spent together in my house with no other human being terrified you. You had never been so alone, without reassurance from your peers. Who were you? Suddenly you were not the good Bennett boy who pleases his parents so, not the big popular jock, Londonton's favorite son, not the fiancé of a social prize with a cardboard soul. No. You were just Johnny, alone with me. At first I know you missed it, wanted it—wanted to pull on your clothes and rush down the main street of Londonton so that all the shopkeepers could nod and smile and sell you something and thus restore your identity. But you were drugged with sex and could never quite manage to get out of bed. Then, in a rusty, amateurish fashion, you began to think. You talked aloud. You began to examine your life.

Mostly you spoke about your mother. How horrified and heartbroken she would be if she knew what you were doing. How family-proud she is, how much she cares, how hard she works, how good she is. I listened and did not comment. You were on your way, and there was no need to rush you. I felt no guilt as I listened to you talk, because with each word it became more and more clear that you are not suffering from a social conscience. You do not want to be a dancer or an artist or a liberal politician or a Peace Corps volunteer; there is not that kind of tension of dissent. You are just, in your spoiled child's way, unhappy with the necessary duties of your life. You do not want to marry Sarah. You do not mind going to work for your father, because one way of making a living is as good as another when money is not really the object. You like the idea of remaining in Londonton— that is, your imagination is not sufficient to cause you to think you could be happier anyplace else. You don't even really mind the idea of getting married. Getting married is something everyone does, something you would have to do sooner or later, you've known that all your life. But marrying Sarah— Well now, there's the problem.

You do not love Sarah, although that does not really matter, because you can't always expect to love the woman you have to marry. You do not even particularly *like* Sarah. You find her shallow—and if *you* find her shallow, well, my God, Johnny, *I* think she must have a thimble for a soul. You find her rigid and bossy and silly and vexatious. You have little in common, you think, which comes down to the fact that she likes to ride and you like to sail, and you prefer casual get-togethers with friends and she prefers formal parties. In fact, the more you talked, the more you wondered why on earth you were engaged to this woman. You remembered how your mother's face glowed with pleasure when you first said, a year ago, "I took Sarah Stafford home from the Dorans' party last night." You remembered that more than the initial meeting with Sarah. Although you cannot articulate it, you are beginning to see that courting Sarah was a way of wooing your mother. And not to marry Sarah now will be to disoblige your entire family, and the whole town, greatly. But to marry Sarah, to actually stand in front of God and your community and take her for your life-long wife—you are frightened at the thought. You are confused. You do not love Sarah; you do not want to marry her.

Your arrogance dazzles me. You think *you* suffer.

What presumption. You have lived twenty-three years in a world as carefully constructed as one of those plastic shells which shield hyperallergic people from real air. You have had everything: money, beauty, loving parents, perfect health, unlimited possibilities, and yet you dare to think you suffer. I let you. I help you. I help you indulge in self-pity, in the luxurious sensation of thinking yourself misunderstood by your mother and the world at large; it's an emotion you weren't often aware of during your childhood, because no one ever let you lack for what you desired. Self-pity is a novelty for you, and so has a strong sensuous side to it; you become boyish and petulant and stare gloomily into the fire, absorbed in your thoughts. How gently, subtly, deftly have I nurtured your belief that you've been somehow wronged; it suited me to do so. I watched and waited while you snuggled down into your nest of self-indulgence, and oh, how self-absorbed you were then, wallowing in illusions of injustice. It thrilled me to see you there before me, your face and body sleek, handsome, strong, perfect, your spirit slack.

You lack a sense of humor, which might have saved you.

I had to be careful to step in before your mood of petulance turned into real nastiness. At that crucial moment, I would stop merely listening, holding your hand, stroking your hair, murmuring, "Poor Johnny." I would actively interrupt your thoughts by kissing your mouth, or belly, or thighs. I would push you backward on the bed or floor, wherever we happened to be, and say, "Sssh, sssh," as if you were still a little child. I would undo your shirt, if you were wearing one, and slide my wet tongue along your belly. "Never mind, never mind," I whispered, dragging my fingertips up your arms, down your back. Your body would relax, you would sigh, and your self-consciousness would slip away from you until you were helpless under my ministrations. I caressed you with expertise and pleasure; the same principle is involved in stroking cats or other handsome beasts. For great long periods of time you lay sighing and stretching under my hands as I acted upon your body with the gentle skillfulness of masseuse, geisha, nurse, and whore. You splayed yourself before me on the sheets and trusted me. Why should you not? Perhaps you felt your spirit had been aggrieved, but you knew only too well that your body could win only admiration and slavish love—every experience you had ever had with a woman proved this to you a thousandfold.

Peter Taylor, you are a fool—we are all being fooled. The Life Force is stronger than the Death Force, and the force of life is every bit as despicably evil as the force of death—and I give you Johnny Bennett's body as my proof. Against the knowledge of nihility, the black sacred space which we fear will encompass our lives and this earth, I

present you with the physical being of Johnny Bennett. Look at his
body. There is no reason for him to exist, yet here he is, and he is perfect. His back, arms, legs, and chest swell with muscles as hard and
smooth as rocks, and the skin that covers him—his veins, heart, nerves,
muscles, sacks of organs—flows flawlessly all in a piece. Who asked for
this? No one. What earthly good does it do? None. In fact, he does
evil, this spoiled would-be god; he breaks the hearts of women and does
not care, he ignores the sad, disdains the poor, gives compassion to no
one, and lusts constantly. How many women has he inadvertently im-
pregnated and forgotten? How much of the world's resources go to
keep him in his pure cotton clothes, comfortable cars, healthy foods?
What does he know, whom does he help, when does he cry for others?
Nothing, no one, never—he should offend our sight. And yet look at
him sitting ahead of me, skin and sinews and thick healthy hair, and
every inch of him beautiful. What a *trick*. Don't talk about the human
spirit and its attainments until you can first prove that most of the
women and men in this church wouldn't give up a month of their lives
to be physically loved for just a day by a human being with a body as
beautiful as this boy's. Just looking at him, feeling him, the strong,
long, lean, hard, tender substance of him, brings awe, a wonder, a delirious ecstasy. This is the path to religion. If we can believe that such
beauty exists, then surely we can believe in God! Life is sly, a cunning
cheat, Life is all evil deception: for this boy has a beauty he does not
deserve.

Sarah Stafford, that piano-legged prig, will hate me all her life.
She'll never know that what she really should feel is overwhelming
gratitude. For I am relieving her of Johnny, I am stealing him from
her, I am taking him away—and her life will be the better for it. Of
course, there will be difficulties because of the scandal. But the town
has cast me, undeserving, into the role of villainess, so I'll play my part
to the hilt. Well, he suits my purpose very well. He will help me get
my petty revenge on this petty town. And now that I'm leaving this
place, where I was happy with Mitchell, he will provide me with—en-
tertainment, if nothing else—as I throw myself back out into the void.
He will keep me from becoming complacent and dull; for as long as I
am with him, I'll always be trying to figure out the puzzle of our lust.
We do have something special when we are in bed together—but what
does that mean?

It was easy to convince him to run away with me. Of course I had to take care that there not be any worries; I had to supply a perfect plan. And I had to offer him assurances as complete and selfless as any mother's: I said that I would be there for him as long as he wanted me, but that I would never try to tie him down.

This Wednesday he will tell his parents and Sarah that he is driving to Boston to a stag party for a friend who is getting married. Instead he will drive to my house, and together we'll drive to the airport, and literally fly away. It will be difficult to trace us, because the lawyers who are handling the affairs for this Londonton house operate out of Chicago, and I will pay them enough to protect my privacy.

We'll go to Las Vegas first, I think. Johnny's never been there, and he'll be entertained and distracted by the gambling, the nightclubs, the flashy lights and lives. We'll have fun. We'll act like children and indulge ourselves. We'll go to Switzerland to visit friends in December, and a good month will pass in skiing and parties. After that, I don't know. It doesn't matter. Johnny might get tired or frightened and want to run back home. But my purpose will have been served by then. I won't be surprised if he decides to stay with me for a good long time, because without this town and his parents to tell him what to do, to provide the center and boundaries of his life, he'll be lost. He'll begin to worry after a while about living off me financially, and so sooner or later we'll go to Florida, where friends of mine can let Johnny play at selling houses and property—he'll be good at that. We'll turn him loose on the rich widows and he'll make a fortune.

It will all work out. It's foolish to look too far into the future. Maybe we'll just go to Mexico and lie in the sun. The night I fell asleep in Bermuda I had no plans or even hopes, and then Mitchell Howard entered my life and changed it forever. Now here I am. Who knows how these things happen? So why try to plan? I don't expect anything much from Johnny—not marriage, love, trust, kindness, or even friendship. I will get from him all I want the day we leave this town together. My bags are packed, and soon I will strip this town away from me like a useless skin. Already I anticipate the shiver of freedom that will come when I feel free uncensured air once more.

I sit in church, Johnny, and you know I'm watching you. When you came in with your parents today you gave me the slightest smile before glancing away; our little conspiracy makes you happy. It makes you feel powerful, independent, capable of an amazing variety of emotions; in your own mind you've become a psychological Renaissance man. Not only can you love your family, community, and friends, not only can you succeed in the proper world, you can also be wicked and adventurous. How proud you are of yourself.

And I must say that treachery becomes you. I've never seen you look more handsome. Later today you will come to my house, having told your fiancée and parents that you're going to drive around in the mountains for a few hours—you have implied that you are looking for a perfect spot on which to build a home. The moment you come in my door I will be there, wearing only a soft cotton caftan, and I will press my body against yours and cover your mouth with mine. You always take my ardor as sheer flattery, I can see you thinking: My God, she can't wait to get her hands on me! And you puff up, pleased and cocksure. You enjoy the belief that you are irresistible—and, Johnny, you almost are. I've had many pretty men, but none quite so lovely as you. I like the height, the length of you, the insistent firmness of your flesh, the dumb optimism of your perfect health. A wholesome, faintly alcoholic, earthy smell reminiscent of hops emanates from your body and your breath; it is heady and seductive and masculine, like beer. Today, before you've taken three steps into my house, I will begin to unbutton your shirt. I will keep my mouth on yours while with both hands I unzip and unbutton your jeans. There is a thick rug on the front-hall floor and I'll make love to you there, it will amuse you. Since we have not been together now for two days, you will be quick and eager. I will strip you naked, then slide my caftan from me in one smooth move. You will lie naked before me on the floor, oh sweet young silk-skinned boy, beautiful fool. My passion will be real. In all sincerity I will admire you, desire you, devour you. You will lie with me, helpless and willing, my sweet Johnny boy, and I will slither over your body like a snake, and coil about you till you come.

WILBUR WILSON

Wilbur Wilson had a pain in his chest, and more than anything else, this pain made him mad, because it distracted him from Peter Taylor's sermon. At seventy years of age, Wilbur often indulged himself in the rather crabby certainty that one of the compensations of old age was that he had heard it all before. He always looked forward to church, because Peter Taylor continually provided a challenge to that certainty; he reversed it: listening to the new minister, Wilbur thought that one of the pleasures of old age was hearing something new. Peter Taylor was full of surprises. He was unlike any pastor the First Congregational Church of Londonton had ever seen before. He was a liberal thinker who didn't shrink from mixing political issues in with religious ones, and while Wilbur didn't always agree with the man, he couldn't help but admire his courage, and the way he had with words.

Right now Peter was preaching a sermon broadly based on the old commandment "Love Thy Neighbor." It hadn't taken the minister but five minutes to get from that biblical behest onto one of his pet topics: the need for a nuclear arms freeze. On this particular point, Peter Taylor was eloquent and impassioned. He made a most handsome crusader there at the pulpit, with his dark robe, dark hair, and blazing blue eyes, and Wilbur thought it was a good thing that Peter was also intelligent and dignified, otherwise there would be a danger that he'd turn into a real rabble-rouser. He did hold the congregation's attention.

Wilbur wanted to listen to this sermon closely, for he had lived too long and through too much ever to trust the Russians, and he wondered whether or not Peter was going to deal with this portion of the issue—but the pain that flared in his chest distracted him. He thought he needed to belch, and dug his chin into his chest a moment. The pain flickered, dropped, then flashed upward again. He closed his eyes tightly, as if that would squeeze the pain away.

A moment later, he felt his wife's hand pinch his thigh. He opened his eyes and glared at her: he knew she thought he'd fallen asleep in church. She smiled at him, but he continued to glare, offended by her, offended more by this presumptuous pain in his chest. She patted his knee and removed her hand.

He shouldn't be angry with her, he knew, for he had fallen into the habit recently of dropping into little catnaps at inconvenient moments during the day, sometimes right in the middle of a conversation with her or during a TV program. It was damned annoying how sleep was treating him these days, ambushing him at the wrong times, eluding him at night. In fact, in the past few weeks, sleep made him remember Bobbeen DuPont, his childhood sweetheart, whom he hadn't thought of for years. She had played the same silly games with him that sleep played now: she had led him on and ignored him all through the year he was a freshman in high school, fifty-five years ago. Whenever he'd ask her to go for a walk down to the river with him, or to attend the church ice-cream social, she'd giggle and make excuses. If he gathered up his courage and walked right up to her house and knocked on her door to ask for her, she'd send one of her brothers to say she was busy, or that she wasn't there—and Wilbur would walk back down the sidewalk, embarrassed and kind of mad, because he knew she was there. Sometimes he could even catch a glimpse of her at the upstairs window, or hear her whispering to her brothers, "Has he gone yet?"

"So much for *her!*" he'd think. "There are lots of other fish in the sea." Then, another day, he'd be walking home from school, and she'd come right up to him and ask if he'd carry her books or come over to help her with a math problem. Once she had even walked the two blocks from her house to his and begged him to come help her get a kitten down from a tree. Why she hadn't gotten one of her brothers to get that kitten down, he didn't know, but he'd gone back to her house and climbed that tree and rescued the kitten.

"Oh, you're so *brave,*" Bobbeen had simpered. "Oh, thank you so much, Wilbur. I was so afraid my poor kitten would never be able to get down." Then she had insisted on taking him into the kitchen and washing off the scratch marks the terrified animal had made on his neck and arms. Bobbeen's light girlish hands had lingered as she applied the Mercurochrome. She had pushed him down onto a kitchen chair and leaned over him to inspect the damage the kitten had done, and her breasts in her thin cotton dress were right there at eye level. He'd been in agony, feeling his penis swelling helplessly inside his pants. He'd been terrified that one of her brothers would come in and know at a glance just what kind of feelings Wilbur was having about his little sister. He could still remember that dress—it was a blue-and-white check—and he could still remember the amazing pleasure of her hands on his skin, her breasts near his face, her breath on his hair. It was the first time in his life a girl had touched him intimately, and he wanted both to sit there forever as if in some kind of spell and to jump up and run away, frightened by what all this might mean. Bobbeen had walked him back home that day, chattering away, looking up at him through her long eyelashes. But the next day when he wanted to walk her home from school, she had surrounded herself with a cluster of girls and didn't even acknowledge him.

Two or three nights ago Wilbur had been up in the attic at three in the morning, trying to write a poem about this very thing—about how Bobbeen DuPont and sleep both played the same frustrating games. He thought there was some kind of lesson to be learned from the analogy, but he hadn't yet concluded what it was.

His wife, Norma, would be—amused?—horrified?—pleased?—to know that he had taken up writing poetry at the age of seventy. He only did it at nights, on those nights when he snapped out of sleep with the precision of a switch flicking on and found himself wide awake for no reason at all. Norma was a deep sleeper; he envied her that. He'd turn over in bed and watch her. Norma always looked as if she were enjoying her sleep. She'd be all curled up with her head bent so far down he couldn't see her face. She made him think of a bird with its head under its wing. She liked to pull the covers up over her mouth so that the edges just touched her nose, and sometimes, when insomnia first hit him, he used to ease the covers down from her face, hoping to waken her. But she would only sigh and perhaps roll over, or dig her face deeper into her pillow. Norma was such a complete

sleeper it made him jealous, as if sleep and his wife had conspired together and left him out.

So he began his own secret life, and it did give him a sly pleasure.
He'd slide out of bed and grab up his robe and tiptoe out of the room.
The first few nights he had gone down to the kitchen for a soporific, a
glass of warm milk with a little brandy in it. After he realized that
wouldn't work and that he was destined to be awake for hours, he decided, well, then, he'd make use of those hours. Maybe it was a gift
from God, those hours of consciousness while the rest of the world
slept. So he began to take his milk up to the attic with him.

At first he had only looked at old photo albums or out the window
at the night-altered world. Then, without really thinking what he was
doing, he'd begun to write down what he now thought of as his little
poems. He didn't suppose they were any good or that anyone would
ever read them, but what a satisfaction they supplied! He had often
heard his sons, who were now college professors with grown children
of their own, discuss whether or not art redeemed life, but never before
had Wilbur understood what that meant. Now he thought he knew, or
was beginning to understand. The comparison of the fickle ways of the
first love of his childhood and the first need of his old age provided
him with an oblique but definite sense of justification. There was even
a substantial, physical satisfaction about it, as if he had put together
two random pieces of wood and made a towel rack or a stool.

He wrote sitting at an antique school desk. There was a hole in
the top of the desk for an ink jar; it was a very old desk. It had been
covered with boxes and old clothes, but he had cleaned it off and
moved it over near the window so he could stare outside while he was
dreaming or thinking or writing or whatever it was called that he did
up there. He hid his poems in an old fishing tackle box because he
thought it would be the last place anyone would think to snoop around
in. He supposed he had thirty or forty poems in there by now. He
wondered if any of them were any good. From time to time he considered showing them to his sons, but each time the chance came, he let it
go by. It was not that he feared embarrassment or humiliation. It had
more to do with his awareness that right now, at this time in their
lives, his sons did not need the complication of seeing their father in a
new light, as a writer of poetry. Somehow both his sons continued into

adulthood living turbulent lives—problems with wives, mistresses, children, jobs—and Wilbur thought they needed the stability of thinking of their old father in the way they always had. They might take this poem-writing business of his as a sign of encroaching senility, and he wouldn't care for that. But because he didn't want to show the poems to his children or his wife, this strange creative activity made him feel lonely for the first time in his life, as if he were going somewhere all by himself. He really wished he could find someone to read his poems and discuss them with him.

Why? Why did he want someone to read these poems, why did he write them in the first place? Had he taken up scribbling as a means of whiling away insomniac hours? Or did the insomnia come on him because he harbored a secret desire to write poems and knew that the night hours were the only private ones he had? Since he'd sold his dry-cleaning business five years ago, he had suffered the clichéd abasements of the retired husband. He knew Norma loved him, yet in his most crotchety moods he felt he might do her a favor by dying. He seemed always to be in her way. He kept active in his clubs and organizations, and had started off five years ago with ambitious plans. He had always thought he wanted to paint; he bought an easel and a palette and paints. But after a year of serious effort, he had realized he had no knack for the visual arts. Now the easel stood forlorn in the attic, and he didn't even feel chagrined when he passed by it each night on his way to the desk.

In the warmer months he spent as much time as possible puttering around in the garden, and Norma praised his cabbages, roses, tomatoes, and zinnias. But it was a chore for him, this gardening bit; his heart wasn't in it. Still, it kept him out of the house, out from underfoot: Norma was more irritable in the winter months when the weather forced him to stay inside most of the day.

In all seasons, he took long walks. Every day for five years now—when his health was good—he had walked six miles a day, following a route around Londonton that varied according to the weather and the season. When it was cold, he moved briskly from his neighborhood out to Main Street, which was truly the main street of the town, dividing Londonton into two neat halves. Main Street was also the only highway, connecting Londonton to the rest of the world, though it had no semblance of a highway about it. It was just a two-lane road winding gracefully through a picturesque town. Tourists crowded this road during high summer or foliage season to snap pictures of the colonial mansions that lined the street, and it was only during that period of time that the Londonton residents regretted not having a stoplight on the road. Wilbur would linger, even in the coldest weather, on the iron bridge that crossed the Blue River. He would lean over the side of the bridge for a while to study the condition of the water. Then, in cold weather, he hurried on down to what everyone called "the square," but which was really a large oblong: two streets joined parenthetically around an oval green. All the shops in Londonton were here, and here Wilbur could always find one shopkeeper or another to join him for a brief chat and a cup of coffee at the local coffee shop. The only shop he never entered anymore was the dry-cleaning business he had sold to Fred Sanders. Every day he passed it, Wilbur would think that maybe soon he'd go in and see how the place looked under new management —but not just yet. In cold weather, after coffee with friends at the square, he'd hurry back to the warmth of his house.

But in warm weather, his route was different, his walk longer. Then he would climb the gentle hill at the end of the square and walk around the college grounds, luxuriating in the sight of such grand old buildings, harmonious plantings, and beautiful young students. He liked it in the spring when these students spread themselves out all over the lawns, soaking in the sun. He could remember for a moment how it was to be that way, young, sweaty, and optimistic on a sunny day, though he had never gone to college or had the leisure to consider getting a tan. When the weather was really fine, or even in the winter if there had been a good new snow, he roamed as far as Slope Road, to see how the fine big houses of the town looked enhanced by snowdrifts or blossoming trees. The Bennetts lived on this road, and the Moyers, and the Vandersons; the Howard mansion was at the very end of Slope Road, but so far away and so surrounded by acreage that Wilbur never went there. He always ended his walk by returning to his own neighborhood, which was more modest. The houses and lawns were smaller here, and more littered with children and animals and their paraphernalia. He especially liked to stop and chat with Suzanna Blair's children. Priscilla and Seth were favorites of his, and they often presented him with presents they had made for him—Play-Doh sculptures or colored pictures of Mickey Mouse which he took home and taped onto the refrigerator. These walks invariably cheered him up, for he loved his town and the people in it. He often thought that when he lay dying he would take consolation in remembering these walks: how the Blue River flowed ceaselessly under the bridge, how life flowed ceaselessly through the town, always going on.

Back at home he would try to find odd jobs to do around the house: screens to be put up or taken down, something needing to be hammered or tightened or glued, trivial masculine assignments of one sort or another. He did the same sorts of things for their various widowed lady friends. But all these things hardly provided a full-time occupation. Norma had often hinted that he should take up some kind of carpentry work; for Christmas three years ago she had given him an elaborate tool kit. And he did like carpentry. But the things he made seemed so silly and extraneous—there was actually nothing they needed that he could carve or build, and in spite of his gender he could summon up little expertise for such pursuits. He began to wonder *what* he was good at doing.

Two winters ago when Norma was sick, he had been piddling around in the kitchen and found himself making homemade bread, which had turned out, according to his palate, absolutely delicious. He had proposed to Norma that from then on he bake all the bread for their little household; Norma had assented warily. But even though she admitted that the bread was delicious, he could tell by the way her face twitched and her voice went high and tight when he was in the kitchen that she felt threatened and offended to have him rummaging around in her domain. And then it always seemed that he missed something or did something wrong when he was cleaning up. He didn't see the flour he had spilled under the table, or something. He had stopped baking. Norma regained her equanimity.

It had occurred to him about two weeks ago that if he wrote poems in the attic in the middle of the night, perhaps he could write poems in the attic in the middle of the day. If so, he thought, he could tell Norma about it, and schedule it into their daytime plans: Well, he could say, I'm going up to the attic now, and Norma would say, Good, dear, I'll be sure not to disturb you. Which would also mean that she would consider herself free from disturbances from him for two hours. That would please her, he knew.

That morning he decided to give himself a secret trial run. When

Norma went off to her church ladies' meeting, he fixed himself a glass of iced tea and climbed the attic stairs. But the attic, which seemed poetic and mysterious at night, with its shadowy corners and vagrant furniture, made him restless in the daylight. At night he could sit in the middle of that huge attic with only the light from a naked 60-watt bulb illuminating the room and the secrets it held. He could stare across the room at some hulking shape that was so disguised by the dim light and casual clutter that he could not tell for certain just what that item from his past was. And so his whole life seemed full of unusual and unlimited possibilities of interpretation. But in the day things were all too clear. He could make out the distinct outlines of each object, he could see that the outlandish shape which had aroused slightly exotic thoughts at night was by day only an old pine cupboard with one foot broken off and a set of discarded blankets tossed over it. Wilbur thought he had lived too long to be forced to see life in such a stark and pedestrian way. Surely one of the rewards the old deserved was ambiguity.

Still he had tried to write his poetry in the daytime. He put his glass of iced tea down on his desk, and arranged his paper and pen, and twisted up his mouth in a concentrating attitude. Then he just sat there and stared while the ice melted and a ring of moisture formed around the base of the glass. He couldn't think of one word he wanted to put down on paper. Finally, defeated, he went back down the stairs, and when Norma came home she found him asleep in front of the television.

That night, however, he awoke as usual, went up to the attic, and wrote what he considered to be one of his best poems. The pattern continued: he awoke and wrote at night, and fell asleep during the day. He knew his sudden escapades of sleep worried Norma, and he wanted to tell her that it was all right, he was not hitting senility so soon and quick. But he could not yet bring himself to explain to his wife just what it was he was doing. Norma was a great one for clarity, and Wilbur always found it necessary to justify his acts in detail not so much because Norma needed to judge as because she needed to understand.

He'd never fallen asleep in church yet, though, and he doubted if he ever would: Peter Taylor's sermons always kept him wide awake. Now the pastor was telling a joke—something the other ministers had seldom done—and Wilbur had to admit he liked it, found it *right,* this inclusion of levity in a religious service. There was no doubt about it: Peter Taylor was an extraordinary man, and Wilbur hoped that when he died, Peter Taylor would be the one to see his body through its last rites and to console Norma. Wilbur believed that some people just made better connections with God than other people did. Peter Taylor had such a charitable way about him and was so, well, lighthearted, that Wilbur could imagine how at his burial Peter Taylor would stand outside in the fresh air and simply lift his arms and toss Wilbur's soul up to the sky.

Wilbur spent a lot of his time anticipating death. He wanted to be prepared. He hadn't read very much in his lifetime—which made his poetry writing even more surprising to him—but he had spent a lot of time listening to ministers and thinking, and it seemed to him that the soul was the essential thing and that life was a process of building up the spirit while the body that surrounded and protected and constrained it gradually dwindled. All in all, it was not a bad system—as long as you could keep your faith in your soul, and Wilbur had managed to do that. In fact, just as much as he firmly believed in God, so did he also believe in the eternity of each individual spirit.

When his third and youngest son, Ricky, had died in a car accident at the age of seventeen, Wilbur had been caught up in a crisis of belief that had nearly destroyed him. First, of course, he had to deal with the sheer loss, the loss of his youngest, tallest, most laughter-filled child; it was an almost intolerable devastation. And with Ricky's death he had discovered that it was necessary for him to come to terms with just exactly what it was he believed about life and death and God and man, and that seemed a formidable task. He felt he was being forced to delve into the supernatural, to enter forbidden territory without the protection of host or guardian. For a long time he had been very sad and frightened. He had lost a great deal of weight, because as he had gone through the inevitable routines of daily life, he had found himself continually thinking: Ricky would have loved that joke, or I wish Ricky could have seen that home run, or if only Ricky could know that Doreen McKensie has gotten herself engaged to Ted Smith! When he had such thoughts, his whole torso would go stiff and cold with fear and sorrow, and his throat would clamp up tight inside his skin, and he wouldn't be able to swallow food or water for hours.

One day Wilbur had closed his shop in the middle of the day and walked by himself down to a spot on the bank of the Blue River where he was pretty certain of being alone—it was not an especially pretty spot, a noisy highway ran just the other side of it, at the top of a steep bank, and no one fished there because at this point the river ran so shallow. Both sides of the river were overgrown with willows and ash trees and weeds and there was no sandy beach to sit on. Wilbur had just crouched down in the middle of some tall grass and stared at the water and, finally, assured of privacy, he had cried. He had cried and cursed God and man and life and death and wondered why he shouldn't go ahead and take his own life and get it over with.

It was with perfect clarity that he suddenly heard Ricky's voice: "Hey, Dad, look at the water skaters!"

Wilbur had looked automatically at the river, where a group of bugs were skimming busily on the surface, before he realized that he had just heard Ricky's voice. He knew it was a trick of synapses, of longing and grief short-wiring his brain. Still, Ricky's voice had been so vivid. And he hadn't seen the water skaters before . . . He stopped crying, stopped thinking, and just stared at the flow of the river.

A few days later, in the shop, when he was loading up the cleaning and packets of freshly ironed shirts into the delivery truck, he heard Ricky's voice again, saying, "Dad, you'd better get that left back tire checked. It's low again." It was the sort of thing Ricky might have said, because he was the son who hung around with Wilbur and helped him in the shop. Still, it was embarrassment more than disbelief that kept Wilbur from going home to his wife and children and telling them that he had heard Ricky say he should have a tire checked. If he was going to hallucinate about his dead son, surely it should be on a more spiritual level.

But he felt continually better after that, and slowly he began to believe that all that religious claptrap he had heard all his life might be true: that Ricky might be gone from this earth, but still somehow be very much real and present, and in a way, alive. He began to feel— whenever he heard a joke and thought: Ricky would have laughed at that—that perhaps Ricky was hearing it and *was* laughing. Wilbur began to enjoy a sense of companionship as he went through life. Perhaps he was crazy and that pretense was simply the only way he could bear to continue living. Or perhaps Ricky's spirit really did accompany him, now and then.

As the years rolled by, Wilbur heard Ricky's voice less and less until now it was a rare occurrence, but certainty of Ricky's presence grew. Ricky had never been a child to hold grudges, and he didn't seem to be a bitter presence even now. Wilbur had the feeling that Ricky didn't mind being only an observer. Wilbur began to think that while life was of course usually preferable to death, the experience of daily life was just as fraught with unpleasantness, worries, fears, and griefs as it was with pleasures. Taken daily, life is harder than we like to think, and simply getting through a life requires any number of ameliorating illusions. Perhaps God had not been so unkind, after all, to take Ricky's body from him after only seventeen years. Worse things might have happened to him—he might have grown up and lost a son of his own. At any rate, Wilbur now firmly believed that Ricky's spirit still existed, and if he sorrowed over the vanishing of his son's body and smile and clear blue eyes, he felt comforted by a sense of the sturdy eternity of the boy's soul.

Wilbur found the teachings of the Church compatible with his life, or perhaps it was that he had shaped his understanding of the events of his life to be compatible with the teachings of Christianity. He believed in the definite individuality of souls. He saw Ricky's soul as hearty and adolescent, forever cheerful. Norma's soul was delicate, orderly, and elaborate, like a paper snowflake, much the same now that she was sixty-five as it had been when she was twenty. His own soul he thought of as a tough old piece of brown twine that had been put through so many convolutions by life that it now sat inside his chest all tangled in a clump of knots. Sometimes he could even feel it in there, sinewy and vigorous and triumphant in a sly way, now that it was obviously winning the game in the hare and tortoise race between body and soul. The Lord gives and the Lord takes away, and no one knows why He does what He does, but Wilbur had always thought that if you had something, well then you stood the chance of losing it. That was just the way it was. He kept trying to be grateful for what he had, for what he had not lost.

Physically, it seemed he had less and less. Long ago he'd lost most of his hair and the skin of his arms and legs hung slack in places that had once been bulky with muscles and flesh. Now even most of his teeth had decayed and been replaced. He was getting hollowed out.

On the other hand, Norma seemed to be growing. Each year there was more of her. Ten years ago, on her fifty-fifth birthday, she had come into the dining room, where Wilbur and their three children awaited her with surprises: champagne, an elaborate layered birthday cake, and piles of presents, including beribboned boxes of fancy chocolates.

"Why, how nice this is of all of you!" Norma had cried, but Wilbur could tell that somehow something was wrong. Her face had taken on that tremulous look that betrayed some secret problem. The children all pretended not to notice—later Wilbur realized that they had thought Norma was upset about growing old—and they celebrated her birthday with almost violent enthusiasm. During the birthday feast, Norma's spirits seemed to take a turn for the better and soon she was as jolly as the rest of her family, but that night when Wilbur was alone with her, he discovered her sitting on the edge of the bed in tears.

"My God, Norma, what's wrong?" he asked, alarmed.

She babbled something, but she was crying so hard he couldn't understand even a word. Finally he brought her a glass of water, and she drank it and calmed down a bit, and said, "My metabolism."

"What?" Wilbur had asked.

"*My metabolism,*" Norma repeated. "Oh, Wilbur, the older I get, the harder it is to keep my weight down. You were all so sweet to think of me and surprise me with all those delicacies, but it will take me two weeks to undo the damage I did at the party today."

"Well, for heaven's sake, Norma," Wilbur had said, "I always have thought you were silly to worry so much about your weight. You're a pretty woman. You always have been and you always will be. Twenty pounds more or less isn't going to make any difference at all."

"Twenty pounds more will make me look *fat!*" Norma declared. "Why, if I gain even five pounds more, my cheeks will swell up and my eyelids will get puffy, and I'll look like a pig!"

"You will?" Wilbur asked, and tactless in his amazement, he studied his wife's face. Norma sat glaring back at him, daring him to see how she had gotten old, how five more pounds would destroy her looks. And Wilbur did see that his wife's face had changed. She was very slim, so slim that her skin seemed stretched and taut over the bones of her face. He struggled for a moment to find the right words to say. He and Norma had lived together for so long and through so much that a necessary civility had developed in their intimacy, and this kind of vulnerability took on a crucial aspect. He wanted very much for his honesty to be kind.

"You've lost that sheen you had when you were young, when we were married," he said. "That's true. So have I. But you look—softer—now. I like softness. There's something appealing about round, soft women. I don't think anything could ever make me stop loving you, or thinking that you are the most beautiful woman in the world."

"Oh, Wilbur," Norma had said, and turned her face away. He put his arms around her, and drew her to him and kissed her hair. They made love, being very gentle with each other, without even drawing back the bedcovers, and when they were through and were lying together side by side, Norma had raised her head and studied Wilbur for a moment, then smiled.

"Okay," she said. "We'll see."

They saw. Norma relaxed her dietary standards and did gain weight; over the past ten years she had gained a good thirty pounds. Wilbur shriveled; Norma burgeoned. At last it became a joke: "Well, Mr. Sprat, shall we have some chocolate cake for dessert?" Norma would ask. As her weight grew, so did, it seemed, her sense of humor and proportion. After all, they were both helpless as various parts of their bodies became puckered and wrinkled and sagged and speckled and bent. Still they loved each other, and the realization of that was a gift of such magnitude that they considered themselves lucky. Wilbur came to believe that the sparkle in the eyes of this woman he had loved for so many years was a far prettier thing than any younger woman's more brazen blaze.

Now, looking down beside him, he could see Norma's hands folded neatly in her lap. Her wedding rings had become entrenched in the chubby finger of her chubby hand, while his gold band was forever sliding off his skinny finger and falling into the meat section in the grocery store. Now his stomach rumbled loudly and a flame of indigestion licked up in his chest and he realized his mind had wandered from the sermon. He wanted to yawn. When he clamped his jaws together, his teeth clicked. It was a hard thing, growing old, although, as the comedians said, it was better than the alternative. If old age and death signaled the triumph of the spiritual over the physical, it would be so much more appropriate if the body could simply melt or evapo-

rate or be peeled away like a husk exposing an ear of corn, in some
pure, definite, cleansing act. Instead the body rotted and grew cantan-
kerous and painful, and you were forced to spend time and precious
thought on the sheer mechanics of physical existence: food, teeth,
bowel movements, tumors, sleep. Also, it was frightening. You couldn't
help but take the deterioration of your body personally, even though it
eventually happened to everyone.

Just as hard to bear, Wilbur thought, was the gradual and subtle
deterioration of their social life. Wilbur liked people, and all of his life
he had ranged up and down the scale of ages as freely as Flora
Pritchard's fingers moved up and down the organ keys. He had
befriended, spent time with, served on committees with, gone to parties
with, people of twenty and people of seventy and every age in between.
But in the past few years, he found he had somehow gotten stuck up
at the old-age end of the spectrum. He understood the militancy of
old-age groups who demanded to be decently treated, like the real
human beings they still were, but he didn't think that younger people
were actively prejudiced against older people. Younger people just
did not stop to think—and who could blame them, they all had troubles
of their own.

Wilbur had noticed his segregation first and most sharply when he
had gone into the hospital two years ago for a bladder operation. It had
been physically painful and emotionally terrifying. He did not like
being helpless. He had spent much of his time in the hospital sick with
fury at the betrayal of his body. He had lain in the hospital bed with
his fist clenched and his jaws working, trying not to cry, trying not to
bellow out his rage and fear. The three other men in the ward with
him were even worse off; they were all in various stages of terminal dis-
eases, and one of the older men just cried and whined and called out
for people who never came. Wilbur had been miserable.

But when the nurses came into the room, squeaking on their
rubber shoes, all officious and robust, how his spirits had lifted! He enjoyed watching their capable round arms. He just liked *seeing* the
bulge and curve of breast and hip and stomach under the white cloth
of their uniforms. He liked the enthusiasm of healthy bodies. One
nurse in particular had been kind and pretty. She was a fifty-year-old
woman named Peggy, and she had recently been divorced, and she
liked to perch on the side of Wilbur's bed and discuss her life. Three

days after Wilbur had come to the hospital, she had come into his room and announced, "Well, what do you think of this!" She had gone out and had her gray hair dyed the most amazing color of red—a sort of pinkish red. She had found lipstick to match.

"Why, Peggy, you look just like a long-stemmed red rose," Wilbur had told her, and he had meant it. What an audacious and optimistic sight that head of red hair was, and from then on he had lain so that he could watch out the bedroom door to catch sight of Peggy as she flashed back and forth down the hall on her errands.

"A long-stemmed red rose!" Peggy had said, delighted with his compliment. "Just wait till I tell Joe! He'll be so jealous!" Joe was her new boyfriend, as she called him, and whenever she could, Peggy slipped into Wilbur's room to tell him about the latest development in their romance. Several of Wilbur's friends and relatives had come during visiting hours to sit and chat with him, but Peggy was always the brightest spot in his day, perhaps because she was new to him and he could not imagine her life as he could the others. She made him aware of the vastness of the world again, and the thought of the thousands and thousands of people muddling along through the hot intricacies of their lives buoyed him up tremendously. Perhaps it was just sheer impertinence that kept people going on—well, it was a contagious attitude, and after each of Peggy's visits, Wilbur found his spirit refreshed and eager, in spite of his body's dawdling.

When he got home from the hospital, a brilliant thought occurred to him, and he wrote letters to the hospital staff and the local newspapers, suggesting that the geriatric ward be placed next to the ward for the newly born, with a one-way window put in between. That way no germs would pass from the old folks to the babies, and the nurses and newborns wouldn't have to be depressed and frightened by the sight of all the old sick folks shuffling around. But the old folks would be able to sit or stand and gaze at all those bundles of brand-new life—it would do wonders for morale. Wilbur had been excited by this idea, and had offered to help raise money to rearrange the hospital in this way, but he had received only a polite, official letter from the hospital telling him that since the two areas were on different floors of the building, such a thing would be impossible.

After he came home from the hospital and found it necessary to rest so much, he began to feel like just another old bird perched out on the creaking and doomed limb of old age, peering shortsightedly as the energetic creatures in the real world scurried about their business. His children and grandchildren were thoughtful and dropped by often or sent chipper letters and humorous newspaper clippings. But Wilbur was more and more isolated. Now and then someone would drop by after work to talk, or would call him on the phone, and Norma told him each Sunday that Peter Taylor had reminded people to think of Wilbur in their prayers; after the service many people stopped her to ask her to give Wilbur their regards. So Wilbur knew that in many little ways the people of his town wished him well. That they did not show concern in an intense and desperate fashion reassured him. No one was worried, everyone thought he'd be around for years. But he realized how much he depended on parties, men's clubs, church, and his daily walks to keep him feeling in the thick of life. He tried watching television or reading, but both bored him. He needed the actual spontaneous responsive flesh. He was fortunate; after a few months he was able to go out for his walks again, and to serve on club committees and attend parties. But he feared the time when that would be a world lost to him even more than he feared death.

Of all the people in the community, four people besides Norma had been and still were the sustaining force in his days. Two were men his own age, widowers who were experiencing the same bodily defeats he was. Wilbur got together with them once or twice a week to play pinochle or canasta and to laugh over sexy jokes, which made them all feel young again for a while. Peter Taylor was also reliable. He was an easy man to be with; he'd talk with Wilbur about this and that in a casual manner, and when he left, Wilbur would realize that Peter had somehow managed to give him something to think about, or some consoling thought. It was a real gift Peter Taylor had, to give comfort in such an offhand way that the recipient was never obliged to feel indebted. Even so, Peter Taylor was a minister, and Wilbur suspected his motives: maybe the reasons he came to call were all *pro forma*.

It was Ron Bennett who had surprised Wilbur the most with his genuine friendship and thoughtfulness. Wilbur had known Ron for a long time, ever since Ron came to Londonton as a young man with a new bride and started his own contracting business. Wilbur was a good twenty-five years older than Ron, and the year of Ron's arrival, he had been president of the local Rotary Club. Ron had been as a younger man so earnest in his ambition that he verged on becoming pompous, but Wilbur had admired him because he was not afraid of hard work or new ideas. Wilbur had done a great many things to help Ron— throwing business his way, delicately apprising Ron of whom he could not afford to offend, giving him advice, and having him to dinner. It was as if Wilbur had metaphorically put his arm around Ron's shoulder and drawn him into the fold of the community.

Now, twenty-five years later, Ron's solicitude to Wilbur might have been motivated by nothing more than duty, a sort of psychological paying off of debts. Perhaps. But Wilbur did not think that was the case. In spite of the years that separated them—and the financial disparity, for Ron had gotten rich—Wilbur still counted Ron as one of his friends, and was certain that Ron returned the favor. Wilbur felt sure that Ron visited him out of friendship rather than simple consideration because of one clear fact: Ron still needed Wilbur.

Wilbur could not remember just when it was that Ron had begun to confide in him, so now it seemed that he always had. But there had been times in Ron's life when he had been troubled, and he had turned to Wilbur for guidance, and a bond had been made between them.

Ron Bennett was one of the most moral men Wilbur had ever met. If a lumber or plumbing or hardware company had a sale on some item, Ron always passed the savings along exactly to his clients, rather than paying the sale price and charging the full price and pocketing the difference. He would not try to beat the competition by giving a low estimate for a job and then surprising the customer with a much higher final bill. He had always made it a habit to give as many jobs as possible to high school and college kids, but he never tried to pass them off to his clients as accomplished professionals. He was an honest man. He had come to be much admired by the members of the community, even loved. Realtors had no trouble selling a house that Ron Bennett had built, because over the years the quality of those houses had shone through so well that "It's a Bennett house" was a phrase that inspired confidence. The people of Londonton had great affection for Ron Bennett, and in his turn he loved them back. He chaired many boards and worked tirelessly for a great number of necessary charity groups, and it was apparent that he liked doing all of this, he liked exerting himself on the behalf of the world around him.

In the past few months, Ron had been in charge of the construction of the new recreation center which was being built on a plot of land donated by Jake Vanderson. Two years ago a bill had been passed in Londonton which allowed the city fathers to raise money through donations from the townspeople to build a recreation center. Londonton was tranquil and idyllic, except for its children, especially adolescent boys from poor families who had nothing to do after school but hang around the main shopping street of town, smoking cigarettes and wisecracking. When the recreation center was completed, other activities would be possible: there was to be a large indoor gym for basketball, volleyball, gymnastics, wrestling, and other indoor sports; private rooms for music lessons and counseling; good, old movies inexpensively rented would be shown on weekend nights; there would be chess tournaments and sex education courses. Everyone in Londonton was eager for the center to be finished, and Ron Bennett was giving it all his spare time, and more. Because he was in charge of the construction, he had been given complete control of the funds, and it was apparent that he was doing everything he could to give the community the best quality for the least money. Ron was unyielding in his standards. The Londonton Recreation Center would be every bit as sound and enduring as any of Ron Bennett's houses. One had only to go over to the skeleton building and run a hand over the carefully cut and joined and sanded boards to know precisely what kind of a man Ron Bennett was.

Ron did have a flaw, however. Wilbur thought that only he and one other man—Peter Taylor—knew the complete truth about this imperfect side of Ron, and as far as Wilbur was concerned that secret could go to the grave with him. He hadn't even told Norma. Ordinarily Wilbur told his wife everything he knew—half the pleasure of knowing something was the pleasure of sharing it with Norma. But in this case the slightest indiscretion on his wife's part could do serious damage to the life of someone in the community, and Wilbur didn't want to risk that. He knew that civilization was based as much on well-chosen silence as on well-chosen words.

Ron Bennett was a womanizer. His lechery was pure and personal rather than social; he did not chase after women in order to impress other men. He had, in fact, never talked with any other human being about his escapades until four years ago, when he had gone fishing with Wilbur.

Wilbur had been cranky that day. Retirement was annoying him; he felt always at loose ends, and had quickly found the projects he had planned on filling his days with to be either boring or too quickly done. When Ron called to suggest they spend that surprisingly warm April Sunday fishing instead of attending church, Wilbur had agreed happily enough. But out in his garage, as he puttered around getting together his fishing gear, he had accidentally gotten a hook caught in his thumb, and that had made him feel clumsy and old and useless. He had thought to himself that Ron was asking him to go fishing only out of pity, to give an old geezer something to do. So he had been taciturn during the drive to the lake, and Ron had been quiet, too. They had parked the car and lugged their gear and a cooler full of sandwiches and beer out to a promising spot on the edge of the lake and settled in for the morning.

It had turned into a good morning. The grass around the lake was pale and new and damp from morning dew, and the trees all around the shore of the lake were just starting to bud. Wilbur had put a fresh worm on his hook and cast his line into the blue depths of the lake, then sat down on the little canvas stool he carried for such occasions, and waited. He drank a beer even though it was only nine o'clock, and felt the heat of the sun on his chest. His bitter thoughts began to evaporate. He thought it wasn't that bad, after all, to be an old man being humored by a younger one. Still, though his mood improved and he made comments about the weather and the possibilities of getting a bite, his mind was on himself.

So he had been surprised when Ron suddenly spoke. "I don't know if I can continue going to church," he had said. "I'd like to talk with you about it, Wilbur. I've got a real problem."

What a revelation that morning had supplied. Wilbur had been stunned, saddened, and envious as Ron spilled out his confession of lust and fornication. So many women, and such good women, had come into Ron's bed, or rather into the bed at the Cozy Times Motel, located fifteen miles away from Londonton. Many of them, according to Ron, had instigated the relationship, but just as many, he was quick to admit, had become his lovers only after a real siege on his part.

"I don't know what I'm going to do," Ron had said. "At first I thought it was just a passing stage I was in, a sort of delayed seven-year itch, that sort of thing. Judy talks now and then about having another baby even though we've been married nineteen years and our children are in their teens. It's a sort of craving she gets from time to time, and it will come on her real strong, and then after a while disappear. I'd been faithful to Judy for a long time, all through the hard years when John and Cindy were babies, and all through the years when we didn't have much sex because we were afraid of getting Judy pregnant. I love Judy more than anything in the world, and I'd rather die than make her unhappy. She's the best person I've ever met. In a way, I worship her. But, well, oh, hell, Wilbur, I feel funny telling you all this, but I'm at my wits' end. I don't know what to do. Is it okay, your hearing all this? Do you feel all right about it? What it is, is—Judy. . . . Sex just isn't very important to Judy. We've even talked with her psychiatrist about this. She can't help herself. I know she loves me. She loves me, and she cares for me, and if she wants to have sex with anyone, she wants to have it with me. But frankly it doesn't cross her mind very often. Weeks and *weeks* can go by without her wanting anything more than a good-night kiss. I don't know. I can't imagine being married to anyone else. I love our home, our family, our life together; hell, I love Judy. With all my heart. But sometimes I feel like some kind of —werewolf or something. I'll be sitting in my office and a woman will come in, and I'll be completely transformed by lust. These women don't any of them mean anything to me, and I let them know it. I don't mean I'm insulting or cruel, but on the other hand I don't lead them into believing that I care for them, or that I mean to have a lasting relationship with them. And you'd be surprised at how many women are happy to have just that. Sex is such a damned problem. Even during those times when Judy makes a point to be romantic and loving, even when I have sex with Judy several times a month, I still get such insatiable desires. God, I should just have my nuts cut off."

The fish hadn't been biting that day in spite of the good weather. Wilbur and Ron had stared out at their steady bobbers and drunk beer and talked about sex, and in the end the only advice Wilbur could offer was the suggestion that Ron go talk to his minister about it. Wilbur never had had an affair outside of his marriage, although he did not admit that, because he was afraid he'd embarrass himself and perhaps alarm Ron. He assured Ron that many men did have extramarital affairs, but in his secret mind he wondered if many men indulged with such frequency. He didn't blame Ron. He could understand what he was doing. And Ron's love for his wife, his concern for her, was so strong that Wilbur could only admire Ron for it.

"Do you think I'm *bad?*" Ron had asked. "Truthfully."

Wilbur had laughed. "Hardly *bad.* But I guess you could get yourself into a difficult situation this way. I mean that somebody could get hurt. Yet I don't know what to say. If it were any other man, I'd suggest that he get busy with other activities—but there's no way you could be busier. There isn't a man in this town who helps the community more than you do. Still—"

There was an awkward moment before Ron picked up Wilbur's thought and bluntly articulated it. "Still it's a shame I'm an adulterer."

"Well," Wilbur sighed. "Lord, I don't know. I'm sorry, Ron, I don't know what to tell you."

The men went quiet for a while and Wilbur had stared out at the middle of the lake where the sun shone so brightly that the water seemed to be all sheen, no color. He thought of what it must be like to be Ron, who had held so many different women in his arms and knew what it felt like to stroke long and short waists, bony and fleshy women, blondes and brunettes. Monogamy was as good a rule as any other, Wilbur thought, because, like other rules, it imposed arbitrary constraints on daily life which made that life less exhausting to live. Breaking one important rule once was like letting just one pregnant rabbit into your house; you'd never be free of the consequences. Obeying certain social laws was often a painful task, but in the long run it made life simpler. Yet it was too late now for Ron to think of all of that. He'd made his decision long ago. Wilbur didn't like Ron any the less for it; he could understand Ron and even envy him, and he felt that every other married man would have, too.

In the four years that had passed since Ron's first confidence, he and Wilbur had gone fishing again four times, once each spring. That was the only time they had really talked intimately, although they saw each other often at parties and church and town meetings. The second spring Ron had said, "Well, I'm not stopping, but I am cutting back," and they had laughed about that and it became a sort of password between them. "The thing is," Ron had said, "it's not dangerous to my health. It won't give me cancer or heart problems or make me gain weight—hell, it helps me keep my weight down! I have gotten more select about the women. I take a lot of care to be sure I don't go with a woman who wants love or a long relationship. But you'd be surprised, Wilbur, at how many women want just a good, easy, free fuck."

"And what about Judy?" Wilbur had asked.

"Judy is a saint," Ron answered. "I love her. She has no idea about all this, I'm sure—"

"But what about the women?"

"What do you mean? I thought I explained that. The women I sleep with don't mean a thing to me—"

"No, no," Wilbur interrupted. "I mean what about those women saying things to Judy or to other women who might talk so that eventually it would get back to Judy?"

Ron's face went as harsh and unattractive at those words as Wilbur was ever to see it. "Huh-uh," he said, shaking his head. "There's no chance. Wilbur, I'm telling you, I'm very careful about this. If I think a woman might talk, I don't mess with her. Most of them don't exactly run in the same social set, if you know what I mean. Wilbur, I know this sounds strange to you, but Judy means more to me than anything in the world. She's a treasure. And I work damned hard, making enough money to keep her happy—it takes a hell of a lot of money to live the way we do. I keep her happy, and I always will. It doesn't hurt her if I have these dumb affairs. Hell, it probably helps. It relieves her of a burden. She's got enough to do without servicing a randy old bull like me."

Wilbur kept his eye on Judy and paid attention whenever Norma talked about her, and it seemed to him that Judy was just about as happy as any woman could be. The Bennetts continued to be a thoroughly admirable couple. Once when Wilbur came upon them suddenly in their kitchen at a cocktail party, he caught them off guard and was given, in the blink of an eye, a perfect tableau by which to divine their private life.

"Oh, dahling, won't you take this tray for me, you great big handsome man, you," Judy was saying. She was obviously mimicking Liza Howard as she sauntered over, hips thrust forward, to Ron. "*My*," she went on, giving Ron the canapé-laden silver tray, "you do have such strong hands."

Both Ron and Judy were laughing, and Wilbur knew in a flash

that Judy could not have imitated that ultimately sexual woman so openly had she not trusted Ron completely. The look they shared with each other was that of conspirators. Ron was safe, in spite of his little affairs, and so was Judy. It was all right.

That night, Wilbur had gone back into the living room and sunk down onto a sofa and for a long while merely watched the other people. They moved among themselves and the drinks and food with such subtle elegance, such gentle fluidity, that from Wilbur's vantage point the entire party seemed choreographed. Mitchell Howard had been alive then, and Wilbur had studied the man, wondering what he thought of his young wife, who was moving about the group restlessly. In fact, Liza flashed on and off. Her changes of mood fascinated Wilbur. One moment she would be leaning against a wall, drink in hand, bored and so still she looked like a mannequin, and the next moment, when a man approached her, she would absolutely glow. Wilbur at this time was sixty-eight, and he thought he certainly didn't have the energy to sleep with such a woman, but for once the idea of voyeurism was intriguing.

He would have liked to see Liza Howard naked. He would have liked to watch her making love to some man. She was one of those women whose entire demeanor changed when a man came near. She would be quite a sight to see in the bedroom. Everyone suspected the worst of Liza, as well they might, for one had only to look at the way she dressed to see what was on her mind. She had little subtlety; everything was on display. Her fabulous beauty was made apparent for everyone to see—and so were her opinions. Wilbur thought this a strange trait in someone so sophisticated. Whether she liked or disliked someone showed instantly on her face and in the attitude of her body, and Wilbur wondered why she did not use more discretion. Could she really be so ingenuous? He thought not. What it came down to, Wilbur decided as he studied the woman, was that Liza Howard did not care about what this particular group of people thought of her.

Still, Mitchell Howard seemed happy enough and it was clear that Liza loved her husband even though he was so much older than she. Wilbur realized after Mitchell's death that Liza had loved her husband even more than he had suspected, for her face took on such desperate lines, as if she were now slashed with pencil marks, as if grief outlined her expressions. The flashing off and on was gone for a while;

she was still beautiful, but harsh and still. Wilbur pitied her. He understood that sense of loss and hopelessness—he had gone through it all when Ricky died. Now and then when he saw Liza Howard at church, he wanted to speak of his sympathy, but she seemed so unapproachable. And as the months passed, she seemed to be making peace with her grief. Now she no longer looked harsh, and if she did not yet flash, she certainly did glimmer, as if containing some new secret fire.

"What does a woman like that come to church for?" Norma had asked, making a little sniffing motion with her nose, as if Liza Howard actually smelled bad.

"Well, she's sad," Wilbur had replied. "She's lost her husband. She's had a difficult life."

"Hmmph," Norma said. "With all her money and good looks? Don't tell me she has had a difficult life. She just makes life difficult for others."

Was Norma right? Wilbur wasn't sure. He and Norma were not given to the sort of personal-philosophical discussions his sons loved, during which the safeguards of the heart were seared away, exposing one's most intimate secrets. They had been through too much together for that—they already knew as much about each other's intimate secrets as it was decent for any one person to know about any other. Now old age was making them even more vulnerable to one another, and as the weaknesses of their bodies became more and more exposed, it was essential that they be ambiguous in what was left to them—their personal life, their speech. There was always a serious danger in being too explicit.

So Wilbur understood vaguely that part of Norma's grudge against Liza Howard was that Liza was a young and beautiful woman, while Norma was old. Wilbur wished she were able to have more charity in her heart toward Liza Howard, but he did not bother to press this. It would only have angered Norma, and Liza Howard was not an important enough person in their lives to be a cause for disruption. Wilbur assumed that by now Ron Bennett had been in Liza Howard's bed and he envied him the experience, not so much for reasons of lust as from sheer curiosity. What was she like? Why was she staying in a community that so continually excluded her?

Wilbur shifted on the pew. He realized he had been staring at

Liza Howard and at the Bennett family for a long time now, and that he had been concentrating on them rather than on Peter Taylor's sermon. But the flame of indigestion which had irritated him was growing more steady, more piercing. With a jolt of fear, Wilbur realized that he actually *hurt*. He wished he had some Tums or Rolaids to cool that burning space between his lungs. He looked at his watch: it was only five after eleven. It would be a good twenty minutes before the church service was over and he could get to his car and home to find some kind of medicine. What had he eaten this morning? Nothing unusual. Eggs, bacon, and only one cup of coffee, orange juice, milk. A good healthy breakfast with no element in it that hadn't been there on previous mornings. Last night's meal had been bland and unprovocative, too, so why was his chest burning like this? Oh, getting old was awful. Every little pain made you think you were being grasped by the hand of death. It was the fear that was worse than anything. He could easily deal with the pain, but it was what this particular pain *meant* that bothered him.

Perhaps life was, after all, only a lengthy and intense purification ritual for the soul. Wilbur was trying to believe this. Perhaps true believers in Christianity were correct when they said this little boy or that little girl died because God was ready for him or wanted her; perhaps some children and adolescents died because their souls were as good and pure as they could ever be, and so they didn't need to go through the ordeals of life. Wilbur could not imagine his son Ricky being any more beautiful in body or spirit than he was at the age of seventeen, when his car crashed into a tree and his strong neck was broken. But Wilbur had always had a messy soul swarming with need and greed: all of his life, it seemed, had been merely a complicated exercise in exchanging one desire for another.

In the early years, his desires had been selfish: he wanted a car, he wanted a girl, he wanted to get laid, he wanted to get out of the Army, he wanted Norma to marry him. Then for a long stretch of time, his desires grew more general: he wanted a house for himself and Norma, and he wanted his children to be born healthy, to grow up happy and safe. Each desire as it appeared had been so passionate—how many times had he prayed that one child or another would recover from some illness or accident! When Ricky died, Wilbur learned a hard rule: there is no correlation between the intensity of the desire and the attainment of that desire. With that knowledge, for a long while he had stopped desiring anything, which was as close to suicide as a man of his moral standards could get. To desire anything at all is to be optimistic. When desire returned to him, it was again unselfish. He wished that Norma were not so unhappy and that he could help his other children in their grief. After a while the little preferences returned—he wanted fish for dinner rather than a minute steak. And that small desire signaled an unconscious resolution on the side of life. Almost in spite of himself, Wilbur wanted things again. But he had been wondering, recently, if he would ever get himself as pure and simple as a child, if he could ever refine his desiring so that he would want nothing but to see God's face.

Right now all he wanted was one thing: for the pain in his chest to go away. If he were at home, he would have gone to the phone and called the doctor, but sitting here in church, in this public place, he felt inhibited. He didn't want to appear to be a silly old man, a hypochondriacal type who made a fuss at every little bit of gas. If he left the church in the middle of the service, it would also be admitting that what was happening inside him was important, of enough importance to interrupt a church service and disturb the community when there were only minutes of the service to be gotten through. He didn't know what this pain meant; he had never felt anything quite like it before. He put his hand up against his chest and pressed, as if he could push the pain back down into the little ball it had once been. But the pain persisted. It gave him a funny feeling, as if all of who he was was being forced to scuttle up high inside his head, so that just behind his eyes he was Wilbur, while the rest of his body was becoming foreign, even treacherous territory. He began to feel scared. Then he thought how foolish it would be to let indigestion frighten him into a heart attack. Concentrate on something else, he told himself, on *anything* else.

Now. Today. After the church service he would go to the back of the church to drink coffee in Friendship Hall—if this pain stopped. There were quite a few people he'd like to talk to, people he seldom saw except at church. He especially liked the few children who stopped their games for a moment to chat with him—although children by and large took little notice of an old man. Packs of children terrified him, with their bright savage energy, but there were five or six individual children whom he considered friends. These children would break off from a game with other children, see that their parents were still involved in the grownup game of drinking coffee and talking, and would drift over to stand by Wilbur. The younger children sometimes seemed to want only that, to stand there, not talking, holding on to his trouser leg with a chubby hand. The older ones tried to carry on sophisticated conversations. Wilbur would kneel or bend in order to hear what the children had to say—they were so small, so close to the ground! The world was surreal from their vantage point, a blur of moving legs, shoes, and skirt hems mingled with floating-down bits of laughter and words. Wilbur thought that being a little child, having to face the vast grownup world, must be almost as frightening as being an old man about to face the black void of death. He knew that for the children who were familiar with him he was a sort of safety spot, a home base, like an old tree in a yard in a game of tag.

His favorite child in the group was Suzanna Blair's daughter Priscilla. The Blairs lived in the same neighborhood as Norma and Wilbur, but Suzanna was so busy teaching and raising her young family and their ages were so different that the Wilsons seldom saw her except at church. When Suzanna and Tom Blair were divorced, Norma had gone into a fit of fretting: *those poor little children,* she had said daily to Wilbur, *living there without their father.* Wilbur had made it a point to stop by to see the children as often as possible during his walks, to check up on them. Of course, he would never know what sorrows the Blair children suffered in private, but when he saw them in their front yard in the daytime, they seemed continually happy and buoyant. They discussed their parents' separation and divorce, their father's move to another part of the state, their trips to visit him and his new wife, with the same easy tone that they discussed other news of their lives—the birth of babies to the pre-school guinea pig, a movie, a broken toy. Wilbur was relieved, and shared this with Norma.

He was happiest in his conversations with Priscilla, who seemed to notice no barrier of age or sex in their relationship. She just considered Wilbur one of her friends. Priscilla resembled her mother so much that she almost seemed a miniature of Suzanna: both the woman and the girl had fine brown hair that curled softly around a fresh, guileless face, wide blue eyes, and an overall apple-round, apple-clean quality of health and good humor. This apple-like quality made Suzanna, who was in her early thirties, appear younger, so that people were surprised at her efficiency as a teacher. In turn, it made Priscilla at six seem older, unabashed and quite capable of carrying on a genuine friendship with a seventy-year-old man. Priscilla had recently invited Wilbur to her birthday party, which would be held next week. Today after church, in Friendship Hall, he would have to ask Priscilla what she would like for her birthday.

He would also, of course, talk with people his own age, about matters of concern to the town: whether or not a flashing red light should be put at Slate's Corner, when the next town meeting would be held, local gossip, affairs, plans. Wilbur had not cared one way or another about running his dry-cleaning business. It had had no poetry in it, and not a great deal of money, either. But it had been a way of making a living while providing a service to the town. He had been efficient and reliable, and in this town where so many women had fur coats to clean and store and so many summer bedspreads and curtains and slipcovers to clean and refresh and then exchange for winter spreads and curtains and slipcovers, he had had a lot of easy duties for a pleasant and familiar clientele. On the whole, he had been satisfied with his business, not for itself, but because it took up so little of his time and mental energy that he was free to take part in all the community activities that interested him. He had seen a lot of things change in Londonton over his seventy years, and he had helped make a lot of things happen. He still attended meetings and people listened to his opinions. But ever since his operation he realized that the workings of this town were now being passed on to someone else, if for no more malicious reason than the simple fact that being flat on his back in the hospital made it impossible for him to do the work. Someone else had to go out and pitch in. He liked to keep his eye on things, though, even if he was no longer essential. Today he would talk with Ron Bennett and Reynolds Houston and all the other men who were active in the community, and they would ask his advice, and he would gladly give it.

Finally Friendship Hall would empty, and he would take Norma's arm and lead her out to the car. They'd drive slowly home, admiring the fall trees along the way. They'd eat a nice big Sunday dinner early in the day, and Wilbur would watch football games on television. Maybe in the evening, if Norma was in the mood, they'd get in the car again and take another, longer drive around the countryside of Londonton, to enjoy the fall foliage. But unless the day took a sunnier turn, they probably would not do that. They'd stay inside instead, and evening would fall early and cool, night would close in—he'd make a fire. They'd have a little brandy. The important thing, he had found, was to keep busy, to be doing things, because being bored or at loose ends made him uneasy. He would feel so pressured, thinking that here he was at the end of his life, with so little time left, no time at all left to waste, and his boredom would turn to panic. So he always made plans.

Now he felt the need to urinate. It came on sharp and sudden and was as insistent as an itch. He fidgeted around on the wooden pew, hoping to trick his body into settling down. He was so intensely aware of all the discomforts of his body that he felt the wool of his suit prickling his skin. He put his hands on his thighs and scratched.

"Wilbur!" Norma hissed from the corner of her mouth, and turned her head toward him enough to give him one of her I-mean-business glares. Ever since Wilbur's retirement and operation, Norma had taken a maternal attitude toward him. Sometimes Wilbur enjoyed being fussed over and tended to, especially when he was feeling weak. Other times he felt downright annoyed by the superiority this attitude implied, and right now he was annoyed. He was no little child squirming in his seat from boredom. He glared back at her.

"I don't feel good!" he whispered.

Instantly Norma's expression changed from irritation to alarm. Now he felt petty for having worried her, and as if chagrined, the pain in his chest lessened, or seemed to lessen in relation to the intensity of his emotions. He was grateful for her concern, and still, after all these years, surprised that one other person in the world could care for him so much.

"Don't worry," he told her. "It's all right. Just a touch of indigestion."

Norma looked at him suspiciously, and her blue eyes took on a feisty look, but she took one of his hands in both of hers and lightly patted it. She turned back to watch Peter Taylor, but she kept hold of Wilbur's hand.

Wilbur thought that tonight when he went up to the attic, he would try to write a poem for Norma. He hadn't done that yet, and he thought it would please her. But he was not sure what he would say. There had been times in his life when he had thought to himself:

When I am old and on my deathbed, I will remember *this*, and be happy. But sitting in the church this Sunday morning with his wife's hands about his and his friends and neighbors gathered in respectful silence, all of them here together, as if in a miniature of life, Wilbur couldn't remember a thing from his past that would make him happier than he was right now. He could think of events that *should* have evoked happy memories: the day Bobbeen DuPont finally let him make love to her, the day he married Norma, the days their children were born, the day they moved into their own house, birthdays, celebrations, vacations, parties. . . . But it was always *right now* that was the important thing. Nothing from the past could outweigh the present, the here and now. Wilbur had hopes that when he became truly old and senile, and lost his mind along with control of his bladder, he'd be given the gift of getting lost in memory, as he had heard old folks do. The closest he could really come to that these days was when he wrote his poetry. Then he stopped seeing the attic or even his wrinkled hand holding the pen, and saw instead the bodies of women, birds on branches, peaches in white dishes, fish in blue water. More than anything Peter Taylor could ever say, the thought of these things existing and going on brought Wilbur consolation against death. No one but a madman sincerely believed he knew the whole truth about death, yet some kind of attempt at belief was necessary. Wilbur believed in life as much as he believed in God. He believed in the people who sat around him in church: they were real and substantial, and when he was dead and gone they would continue to eat breakfast and put on clothes and weep and make love. There was comfort in knowing that. Maybe he would try to write a poem about that tonight. There were many things he wanted to write poems about. He felt an urgency to go to the attic right now. He pressed his hand to his chest and tried to be patient as Peter Taylor continued to speak. The pain flamed up inside him now so suddenly that it took his breath away for a moment, and Wilbur knew that his one last desire was that Life would have as much justification as a poem.

SUZANNA BLAIR

Peter Taylor had just said: "In Jesus Christ we are forgiven, accepted, and loved. And the abundance of his grace has set us free from sin and free to love."

The words caught Suzanna Blair's attention, pulled her up out of her reverie, and made her long to raise her hand and interrupt the sermon, demanding to know if Peter Taylor really meant that—and if God really meant that.

Free from sin. Free to love. She believed in Jesus Christ, and in God; was that enough? If she rose now and said to the congregation of people gathered about her that she loved God and believed in Jesus Christ, but she also loved a woman, would her neighbors reply that she was free from sin and free to love?

Perhaps. Or perhaps they would drive her from the church, from the town, from their hearts. There was no way to know in advance. For Suzanna, it was as if her life had become a house of many rooms, and at the center of this house was sexual love, a clean, fragrant, pure, and perfect chamber. But danger shadowed the windows of that room, and lurked at the doors.

It was necessary to shutter off her life from the eyes and judgments of her community. For the first time ever she had to hide herself. Always before, she had gone through her life happy in the normal companionship of the world; she had always greatly enjoyed the common cheerful rolling around of life, as if she and other people were brightly colored marbles in a game with easy boundaries. Now she had gone outside those bounds, and she did not feel smug or superior; she felt afraid. But she was so much in love, and so happy in that love, that she felt she could not choose to give it up—so what was she to do? She sat quietly in her pew, staring up at Reverend Taylor with what she intended to be a face showing composure and sincere interest, but she was not listening to what he had to say. In fact, she felt that whatever he could say would be irrelevant to her problem. She had not come to this church to hear his sermon. She had come to present herself before God, to say with her presence: Look at me. See who I am, how I love. Help me, please.

Love had never been a problem for her before. She had been born into a lucky family; her parents had loved each other as well as most parents can, and she and her brother and sister had always been close. Remembering her youth, Suzanna searched the patterns of her life for some portent of the woman she was to become—*a lesbian*—but could find nothing of significance. As a child, she had played with dolls more than trucks, but she had climbed trees, and been good at games, too. As a teen-ager, she and her sister had kept their favorite stuffed animals on top of their pink-gingham-covered beds, and hid their forbidden packs of Kool cigarettes under the mattress. In high school, Suzanna had played on the girls' field hockey team, but she had also been president of the Pep Club, and secretly vain of the way her body curved in the short pleated blue-and-white skirt and tight blue sweater with the big gold *S* that the members of the Pep Club wore to the football and basketball games.

She had been neither rich nor poor, brilliant nor dull, beautiful nor homely. She had been normal, and too content in her normality to spend time examining it. When she was seven, she had vowed to marry her father when she grew up. When she was eleven, she decided instead on Elvis Presley, and when she was thirteen, she thought it didn't matter if she ever saw Elvis Presley if only Ronnie Goodwin, the sixteen-year-old who had moved in at the end of the block, would offer her a ride in his maroon-and-gray Chevrolet.

She had fallen truly in love for the first time when she was seventeen, with a boy named David Kittredge, a tall ambling boy who had brown eyes and red hair and freckles all over his body. He was a year older than Suzanna, and captain of the basketball team. They had passed each other in the halls at school but had never spoken to one another. The summer before Suzanna's senior year at high school, just three weeks before school was to start, Suzanna met Dave at Stowerby

Lake, where he worked as a lifeguard. She was baby-sitting four-year-old Jackie Ellison that day, and was sitting with the little boy at the water's edge, intently building a sand castle with him. She had not been aware of Dave's approach; just suddenly planted before her in the sand were his two bony white naked feet. She had been stunned, and had followed the long skinny line of his sun-burned body up and up until she saw his face grinning down at her. He was wearing only blue swim trunks, a white lifeguard hat, and a whistle around his neck on a chain. His skin smelled of Coppertone oil.

"Hi," he said simply, and in the middle of that hot humid day, Suzanna had shivered into goose bumps. The connection had been as quick and definite as that.

"Hi," she said. Dave squatted down on the sand beside her to chat, and that night he took her out for a Coke. In a week they were going steady, and in three weeks, just before he went off to college, she slept with him because she loved him so.

He loved her, too. He came home whenever he could, which meant a three-hour drive from Boston, and wrote letters to her two or three times a week, in spite of the fact that he hated writing. But he was far away, and at college, where there were all sorts of parties, dances, beer fests—eventually he broke off with her, telling her he still loved her, but that he needed to be able to date other girls. Suzanna had been nearly inconsolable, and had finished out her senior year in high school wishing only that Dave would ask her to marry him. Her parents had to force her to enter college, she had so little energy or imagination for anything but Dave. But Dave did not ask her to marry him. He told her again and again he still did love her but wanted to have some fun. So she had listlessly gone off to college—and once there, had been weak with relief that she hadn't married Dave.

For her college days turned out to be full of a sort of gambling joy —there were so many men! Every day she awoke exhilarated with the possibilities ahead of her, and each time she walked down the long corridor of Jardine Hall, she smiled to herself to think that each classroom she passed held a different set of men to flirt with, date, and kiss. She didn't sleep with as many men as she would have liked to, because the birth-control pill was not yet readily available and she had to worry about getting pregnant. Then, too, she did not want to be cheap and easy, so she slept with only the few boys she felt really in love with.

But she delighted as much in the preliminary challenges and temptations, in all the shimmering, unpredictable stages of romance. She liked the way that, during the course of an evening, a boy she was interested in would hold her closer and closer against him as they danced, until their hips touched and his hand moved down from the middle of her back to the small of her back to the rise of her buttocks. He would carefully press her more firmly against him, and she would nestle her face against his shoulder and press her hand against the back of his neck with a corresponding gentleness that let him know it was okay.

When she was a sophomore, Dave finally asked her to transfer colleges and marry him, but she was at the stage he had been at two years before: she was too busy having fun. She couldn't, in fact, imagine being married. She wanted to finish college, teach elementary school, and live a life flitting from one man to another. Her young love for Dave had been so painfully intense and overwhelming that she wanted years of antidote: she wanted freedom and frivolity. She moved through her college years as though at a casino of romance, and enjoyed it all. If a man stopped dating her, she took it in stride, because her relationship with Dave had taught her, if nothing else, how to deal with that sort of grief—she immediately began dating other people, which always proved a quick and certain remedy. And she broke a few hearts herself, unwittingly, and one of them, in the end, was Dave's. When she graduated from college, Dave came to the commencement ceremonies, and afterward, he asked her once more to marry him. She stood before him, still in her black robe, holding on to her flat mortarboard against a spring breeze, and said no. As they looked at each other, she realized that she had come to care for Dave in an almost fraternal manner. The passion, on her side, was really gone. She was sorry she did not love him, because she liked him so. But she could not conjure or force up the emotions that had once so suddenly exploded within her, and for the last time she and Dave kissed, and parted. He went to Oregon to work as an engineer.

Suzanna went to Londonton, to take a job teaching first grade. Londonton was only a two-hour drive from her hometown, only a one-hour drive from her college, so she always had visitors and seldom was lonely. But teaching made her feel grownup, responsible. She began to admire the reliable lives of the teachers and parents of her first-graders; she wanted to live accordingly. When one of her old boyfriends, who had become a stockbroker in Boston, came to see her one weekend to ask her to marry him, she almost accepted, in spite of the fact that she didn't love him.

But she was glad she hadn't, because three days later she met Thomas Blair. He was a newly tenured professor at the local college, and single. They first saw each other in the Grand Union grocery store, where they were each pushing a huge metal shopping cart filled with pathetic little quarts of milk and cottage cheese, tiny cans of vegetables, and plastic sacks with two lonely apples. Tom came around a corner too fast and accidentally slammed Suzanna's cart with his.

"Oh, I'm sorry," he said, and took a good look at her, and smiled.

"That's all right," she said, taking a good look at him, and smiling back.

There was something in Tom that reminded her of Dave—he was tall and skinny like Dave, and moved with the same jock grace. But Tom had dark hair and brown eyes, and where Dave had been cute and appealing, Tom was downright handsome. In those days Suzanna was still slim, and her thick brown hair was cut in a flattering pageboy. She and Tom liked each other's looks. They moved off from each other, each in different directions of the grocery store, and they attempted to direct their attention to boxes of macaroni and paper napkins. But they were very much aware of whether or not the other was in the same aisle. Suzanna was furious at herself for breathing so loudly and because her boot squeaked. Then she didn't see him for a few moments and assumed he had bought his groceries and left. She was disappointed, but plodded along down the dairy aisle, pushing her cart listlessly, and there he was. He came hurtling around the corner again, and almost rammed into her a second time.

"Look," he said, "excuse me, I don't mean to be rude, but can I speak to you? My name is Thomas Blair, and I teach English at the college, and I've just moved to town. I'm single and healthy and have no police record or illegitimate children, and I'd like to know if you would join me for dinner tonight. That is, if you're free. That is, if you're not married, or engaged to someone bigger than I am."

How charming he was! She had to laugh at the thought of someone bigger than he, and she was flattered by the way he rushed his words as he spoke to her, as if he were really nervous at confronting her. He had hunched up his shoulders while he talked, like some awkward boy, as if he had no idea how handsome he really was. Of course she went out to dinner with him that night. They talked, they laughed. Suzanna was entranced. And Tom did not hide the fact that he wanted to make her like him. He kept saying things like: "Would you like me to open the car door for you or not? I don't want to offend you, if you're a feminist, but I don't want to seem rude." And he smiled as he spoke, such a smile that Suzanna wanted to say, "Oh, let me open the door for *you!*" He was thirty years old, a professor with tenure at the college, a man who had just published a book of essays on Charles Lamb and William Hazlitt; yet when he walked Suzanna to the door that first night he was as ingenuous as a child.

"There's a party tomorrow night at a friend's house," he said. "Would you go with me?" He stood before her, shoulders hunched up again, both hands shoved into his jeans pockets.

"Yes, I'd like that," Suzanna replied.

"Great! I'll pick you up at eight!" Without taking his hands out of his pockets, he leaned forward quickly and kissed her—on the cheek—grinned like a little boy, and raced back to his car.

Suzanna let herself into her apartment and leaned against the door with her hand against her cheek. Nothing could have seduced her more than that shy breathy kiss.

The party the next evening was at the home of a junior member of the History department. Suzanna knew she should be glad for the opportunity to meet so many people her own age here in Londonton, but as she followed Tom through the crowd of people to the kitchen to get a drink, she resented all the others. She wanted to be alone with Tom. Everything was very casual: the sink was full of bottles of beer stashed in ice; the kitchen table held paper cups, several gallons of cheap wine, and cheese and Triscuits on paper plates. People were leaning against the refrigerator and stove and walls, talking and laughing, and they all seemed so glad to see Tom. He introduced her and everyone responded pleasantly, but it was obvious that it was Tom's attention they wanted. She could understand why. Tom seemed to know just what tone to take with each person, just how to joke or flatter each individual, and it was perfectly natural for him to stand close to people, to wrap a friendly arm around a woman's waist or a man's shoulder. He was a toucher. People touched him back.

Suzanna made her own way around the house, meeting people,

chatting, and she felt at ease, but she was always aware of just where Tom was, and whom he was with. He was so *popular!* He was so handsome, so endearing—so sexually appealing. She stood in the living room listening to a perfectly nice woman give her tips on the best shops in Londonton, but out of the corner of her eye she saw Tom settle back on the sofa next to a pretty red-haired woman. The two leaned into each other, nestling conspiratorially. Suzanna felt all the emotions of her high school days revive: jealousy, possessive lust, a sense of urgency. It was more a need for protection than a desire to manipulate that made her welcome with unusual warmth the attentions of an unmarried history professor who presented himself before her. She was as charming to him as she could be, and soon they were leaning up against the living-room wall, shoulders touching, their own conspiracy established. Then Suzanna began to feel a steady beam of attention focused on her as definitely as a light. She turned to glance at Tom and saw that he was staring at her with steady intensity. Surprised, she flashed him a proper party smile, but he did not smile back. He continued to stare at her, until she felt caught in that stare, surrounded by it, a fly in honey. The smile slipped from her face; she felt stunned. She felt that she and Tom were caught in a moment of truth: their mutual consuming desire. Next to her the history professor stopped talking in the middle of a sentence, while the redhead leaning against Tom gave him a playful pinch on the arm to remind him of her presence, then turned to see what in the world had so captured his attention. Still Tom stared at Suzanna, and Suzanna at Tom, spellbound. She felt her face go warm and rosy—with wine, with desire, with embarrassment at being so obvious in a public place—but before she could turn away, Tom rose from the sofa and came across the room to her. By then half the party had fallen silent and watchful.

"Let's go," Tom said, and put his arm around Suzanna's shoulders and led her to the door.

Suzanna could not speak. They did not even think to tell the hosts goodbye.

They went down the three long wooden steps of the porch and two feet more before Tom pulled Suzanna to him in a kiss so passionate that all reality gave a little shudder: this was real, this was a point of crisis. She was relieved—she had not misinterpreted his look. She pressed her body against him, and he wrapped his arms around her and kissed her forehead, cheeks, lips, neck, shoulders. He ran his hands down her sides and up the front of her jean-covered thighs; he slid his hands up inside her loose pullover sweater.

"We can't do this—here!" Suzanna gasped. "Tom, people can see us!"

Indeed people could see them. As they turned to hurry toward Tom's car, Suzanna caught a glimpse of several of the party guests openly staring from the windows of the house. She didn't care. She didn't care what anybody saw. She only wanted to be in bed with Tom. They went to her apartment because it was closer, and fell into bed with an urgency that made them clumsy, and they laughed at their own clumsiness, and Suzanna's heart filled with joy at this: their friendly easy laughter in the midst of powerful lust. When they had finished making love, they laughed again, to see each other so disheveled, Suzanna still wearing her necklace and earrings, Tom still in his socks and shirt and tie.

"My goodness, what a performance we gave your friends tonight!" she said, smiling as she unbuttoned his shirt. She did not know then how her words would come to haunt her in the years to come.

For Tom turned out to be, in spite of his Ph.D., a bit of a fool. It took Suzanna a long time to realize this, and in the meantime she married him and they had two children and established a life together. Tom was as addicted to popularity as an alcoholic to alcohol. The need for it ruled his life. For him life was always a drama, and he was not happy unless he was the star. This made him a hard worker, an excellent classroom instructor, and a great help to the college trustees, who could watch him charm the alumni into generous donations. But Tom was not as brilliant as many of his other colleagues, and since charm was not a quality essential to good research, he found time and again that his colleagues' papers were accepted by academic journals and his own were not. Over the ten years of their marriage, Tom's hair thinned, exposing a rather knobby forehead, and he accumulated unwanted weight—he was aging physically, as who does not? But he continued to be encircled by eternally youthful, muscular students and new young faculty members, so he felt his aging even more strongly by contrast. In public he continued with his winning ways, but in the privacy of his home he grew sullen. He did not need to charm Suzanna anymore; she was his already and for good, his wife. He cared for her in his own way, and was grateful to her for all that she provided: love, a home, a pretty life. He liked bringing students home to dinner so they could admire his house with its wood-burning stove and solar greenhouse, his study with its books and stacks of correspondence, his children with their rosy cheeks and sturdy bodies. But of course nothing could compare with the scene he and Suzanna had first set: their desperate passion in the living room and front yard of a faculty member's house for all the world to see. Nothing really compares with sex for drama.

He could have had affairs with some of his students; he was offered opportunities, and some of his colleagues would have envied him. But he did love Suzanna enough to stop short of hurting her in this way. Instead he slowly grew to bedgrudge her because she was growing older also, and heavier, and because she was a mother, tied down to the worries of running a house and keeping people well fed and healthy. He resented her for providing the commonplaces that he could not have lived without. It was not very long into their marriage that he began to turn the full force of his petulance against Suzanna, as if she were responsible for redressing the grievances he suffered.

She continued to love him, but her affections of necessity took on a maternal tone. In what came to be the last year of their marriage, she dreaded all social occasions because of the risk involved. If Tom felt he had been sufficiently admired and appreciated, he came home happy, and made love to Suzanna with something close to élan. But if he felt slighted in any way, his mood turned black the moment they got in the car to drive home, and nothing could cheer him up. Then he would rail against Suzanna, against the boredom of their marriage, the weight on her hips, the pressures of providing for a family which kept him from doing significant research.

One fall almost exactly ten years after they first met, Suzanna and Tom were at a dinner party, and everyone was rather silly with wine. Yet Suzanna was alert and worried, for at the end of the dinner table, next to Tom, sat the newest member of the English department, a young woman who was a guest lecturer in creative writing. She had just published a book of short stories which had received literary acclaim, and she was young and slim and actually very beautiful, with long blond hair. And Suzanna could see from her end of the table that this new young woman was not adoring Tom at all; she was polite to him, but just not interested. Suzanna watched Tom's motions grow wider, larger, in his desperation. She heard his voice grow more hearty.

"Will you go away for Thanksgiving vacation or stay in Londonton?" the man across the table from the blond woman asked.

"I'll probably stay in Londonton," she replied, smiling. "My family's all in Arizona, too far away to travel for just four days."

"Ha, Thanksgiving!" Tom bellowed. He leaned his arms on the table, as oblivious of the spoon he knocked to the floor as if he were drunk, and leered. "Imagine the plight of the poor Thanksgiving turkey—he only gets eaten once a year."

Tom laughed at his own lewd joke, but the blonde only stared at him with complete deadpan disdain, then looked away. After a brief awkward silence, everyone else at the table broke into the sort of nervous babble that follows a social gaffe, and the moment was over. But Suzanna was chilled with apprehension. It was the first time that Tom had stepped over the line and tried to get attention in such a stupid way. And of course he knew he had been stupid; that made it worse.

They fought that night—or Tom fought, while Suzanna cried. She knew she had no power to help get the spotlight back to Tom; she was not beautiful, and she was getting older, she was just a nice elementary school teacher, not destined ever to be famous or distinguished. She liked her life, but feared that her marriage was doomed: she could do nothing more for Tom. And she was tired of nurturing him. In a way he had become a full-time emotional invalid. This life they were leading did not bring out the best in either of them.

But they had been married for ten years, and their daughter Priscilla was five, their son Seth only three; they *were* a family. So it was with mixed hopes that Suzanna at last brought out the crucial word. Divorce. Perhaps, she suggested, they should get a divorce. She hoped that Tom would agree, because she wanted to be free of him and his everlasting needs; but she also hoped for the impossible—that Tom would be so devastated by the very thought of divorce that he would promise to change, that he *would* change.

She had only to watch his face as she spoke to see just which hope would be fulfilled. Tom looked away from her; his eyes went sly. And she could see how he calculated the different possibilities in his mind. On the one hand, he would lose his wife, his children, his pretty home. But on the other—divorce! At last, at least, a drama! He would be invited to dinner by sympathetic women. He could sleep with young slim blondes without any censure. And if he made an ass of himself, he did not have to bear Suzanna's tolerant insights; he could be miserable alone, in privacy.

"Well," he said, raising his eyes to Suzanna, "yes. I think you're right. I think it's best if we get a divorce." He tried to speak with the necessary solemnity, but he could not suppress his joy at the thought of a new life, a new adventure, and as he stared at Suzanna, a huge, uncontrollable smile spread across his face. Suzanna turned away. She sank down onto the sofa and began to cry. It hurt to see him so happy at the thought of living without her. But later, as the weeks passed, it was the memory of that smile which set her free.

Tom moved through the divorce with the ease of a duck through water. This was his element—drama, phones ringing, long sincere discussions over drinks with sympathetic colleagues, hearty greetings of good cheer from people in the community who had only nodded at him before. In fact, this private crisis seemed to perk up the town. Happily married couples felt their bonds reinforced by the contrast of their tightly knit lives with the Blairs' rapidly unraveling one. Divorced and single women, even college students, suddenly recognized Tom as an intriguing and sexual object now that he had come out from under the proprietary mantle of his marriage. The world was just a little more exciting. More parties were given. Tom, seeming younger by virtue of his new bachelorhood, bestowed on those around him a temporary sheen of youthfulness, like a child's chin shining yellow when a dandelion is held near. For a few months people gave, instead of the usual staid cocktail parties, rock-and-roll parties, masquerade parties, disco parties. Couples turned off the television and lay in bed at night analyzing the Blairs' marriage and their newfound duties as friends: Could they invite Suzanna and Tom to the same party? Or should they plan two separate parties? What exactly were their responsibilities? Their new self-importance made them unconsciously fond of Tom, and slightly cautious and resentful of Suzanna—they were afraid she might act sad and depress everyone. But they felt expansive around Tom, and in turn buoyed Tom up, so he was able to see himself as a ship tossed on a turbulent sea, and all the while he was quite safe in his own small pond of life.

For Suzanna it was not so simple. She had first of all to worry about the children, to explain the divorce to them, to wrap her energies around them protectively, to remain alert to any signs of trauma. Tom saw Seth and Priscilla only on Tuesday nights, when he took them out to dinner at Howard Johnson's, where he was almost certainly joined by some other family who found the trio brave and sweet. He gave Suzanna the house when they divorced, and enough child support to make them moderately comfortable, but he was, as he was the first to admit with charming honesty, just not very good at dealing with little kids, and Suzanna was left with the burden of emotional care. When she drove them, each morning at seven-thirty, to the local day-care center so that she could go on to her job at the elementary school, she would often pass Tom as he flashed by in his new peacock-blue warm-up suit. He had taken up jogging, and did calisthenics and laps at the college gym and pool each day, getting back in shape. Suzanna would watch him go by, a handsome, newly lean man, and then she would look at herself in the rearview mirror of the car. She was beginning to have gray streaks in her hair, and she did not foresee the time when she would ever have the energy to teach, take care of her children as she wanted, and exercise her body back into a youthful shape.

For a few months she was depressed—despairing. She had to leave a large spring-break party because Tom had appeared with a marvelous-looking very young girl at his side; she could not bear it. But her children remained healthy, and Suzanna's friends rallied around, and then men began to ask her out, and her life began to take on that tingling feeling of a limb that has been long asleep now coming back awake. There were not many men to date—it wasn't like college had been—because there simply were not many single men in Londonton. Still she felt those old gambling joys returning. Once more when she went to a concert or party or restaurant or even to the post office, she felt the possibilities of the event—she might meet someone.

She decided to work on her master's degree in order to raise herself up on the school pay scale. The college in Londonton did not offer graduate courses, so she had to go to the state university thirty miles away in Southmark. But she decided that was fine. She would like the quiet lonely drive which gave her time to think, and the sense of going off to someplace new, where there would be ideas—and people—she had not encountered before. The class met on Saturday afternoons. Suzanna wrote this schedule on her kitchen wall calendar, and it seemed that the calendar and her life took on a new weight of importance.

The first day of class, however, she was as much frightened as excited. She walked from the parking lot to the large stone building that housed her class, oblivious to the natural beauty of the rolling countryside around the college and to the brisk fall air. She was aware only of the young lithe students who passed her on the walk, and she realized how much of her recent life had been spent in the company of little children or their parents. The people at the college were exotic to her by virtue of their age, and she shrank a bit to see them, feeling by contrast old, plump, and pale. And when she entered the building, the old first-day fears returned full-force: she was afraid she would be late, or early, or that someone would see her studying the classroom numbers so seriously, and snicker at her.

When she thought she had found the right room, she plunged in and took a seat in the first row. To her relief, she spotted a woman much like herself seated next to her.

"Is this Introduction to Interpersonal Psychology?" Suzanna asked.

"God, I hope so," the woman said. "I feel as insecure as one of my second-graders."

They laughed and struck up a conversation, and Suzanna began to relax. Looking about her, she saw there was a mix of students—young and old, male and female, bored and nervous. It was going to be okay. Suzanna took a deep breath and prepared herself to concentrate now on the subject matter.

Dr. Madeline Meade taught the psychology course. When she entered the room, the class stopped talking and came to a casual but focused attention.

How beautiful she is, Suzanna thought.

She was tall, long-legged, slim. She was wearing loose cotton khaki trousers, a white cotton shirt, a navy blazer, small gold earrings, several gold bracelets and rings. Her light brown hair was held back from her face with two tortoiseshell combs. She wore no makeup. Her eyes were blue and striking, her cheekbones high and prominent, her smile dazzling. She moved about the front of the room, introducing herself and the course, writing on the blackboard, leaning on the desk, and Suzanna, watching, felt a physical thump in her lower abdomen, as if she had been hit. Her body went still, and alert.

It happened very fast. Suzanna Blair, who until that moment had never entertained the idea of loving a woman, fell in love with Madeline Meade that day. Of course she did not realize it at first. She only noticed what exquisitely long and slender hands the professor had, and how lean and graceful her body was; but then Suzanna had grown up in the practice of noticing other women's bodies and comparing them to her own, continually surveying the competition. She did not think to herself that she had fallen in love—she did not think at all. She was just so completely alive in the present moment, and completely happy to be able to look at this woman, to hear her voice, to see her gestures. The two hours ended so suddenly; Suzanna felt dismayed. She wanted to approach the instructor as some of the other students were doing, ask a question—any question—but she could think of nothing to say, and so she gathered up her books and notebooks and left.

After that, an amazing thing happened: her life took on the floating, inconsequential quality of a dream. Nothing could affect her. She was not furious when her children fought or angry when a neighbor's dog ruined the last of her garden. She was not tired or hungry or anything at all except an automaton who moved through the necessities of each day until she saw Madeline Meade again. Then the world became clear and real. Everything in her daily life was equal in value except the need to be in class: that was primary. So she seemed serene, because she was always waiting.

She studied furiously and worked on her course paper as if it were a document with the powers of saving or costing her life. Still she did not articulate to herself just what it was she felt. She moved through a life now that was marked by the time of the next class.

She could not sleep, but she didn't jump out of bed to bustle around accomplishing tasks; she just lay there. More remarkably, she could not eat. It was not a matter of choice, of dieting; she could not swallow. Her throat closed as tight as a fist against food. She did not stop to wonder what was going on. She just kept moving forward. She was always thinking: three more days, six more hours, two more hours, until I will be in class. For that was the way she thought of it: in class. The class seemed to be the important thing, as if the room and all the people in it were magnetic and charmed.

But one evening toward the end of the course, Dr. Meade entered the classroom, leaned on the desk, smiled at her students, and told them that the following week she had to be gone for several days to deliver a paper in San Francisco. Dr. Hower would be substituting for her. When Suzanna heard this, something plunged inside her; she felt bleak, bereft. She did not know how she would summon up the energy to get out of her chair and out of the room and to her car. Madeline Meade's announcement forced a discovery that brought despair: the time would come when this course would end and Suzanna would no longer be able to schedule her happiness according to the days of attending class.

So it was not, in fact, the class or knowledge that she loved. Nor was it the novelty of being a student once again, nor being in the company of interesting adults. She could have all those things with her next class, the one she was scheduled to take on new techniques in elementary education.

That day broke her dream-life open. Suzanna walked out to her car holding herself tightly as if she had been wounded. More than anything, she needed and craved privacy so that she could admit to herself just what it was she felt. She was a normal woman, used to discovering the secrets of her soul through conversations with friends. This was different: she had to do it on her own. There was no precedent for a secret as threatening as this. She drove home, paid the baby-sitter, talked to her children, moved through the house normally, but as she stood in her kitchen cutting up bananas and apples for her children's snack, she was in a fury of fear and delight as the seditious knowledge began to spread through her. She gave her children their snacks, sent them to their rooms to rest, and told them she was going to take a bath.

She went into the bathroom, shut and locked the door, and began running the bath water. Then she turned and looked into the mirror.

For a long time she studied her face, not in the superficial way she checked her face before going out in public or in the critical way she searched the superficialties of her face for stray eyebrows or dry skin. She looked into her own eyes and let herself acknowledge the truth: she had fallen in love with a woman.

But after all, what could be done about it? It was silly, once she admitted it. Love a woman? What a humorous idea.

Suzanna mocked herself in the mirror. She pulled her mouth to one side in derision. She turned away from the mirror and stepped into

the tub and forced her body down into water that was so hot it seemed
to purify. She lay back, stretched out full, with mounds of white bubbles covering her like an iridescent blanket. She stared at the blue
bathroom tiles, at the sedative white ceiling, and thought.

She had heard the words: lesbian, homosexual, gay. They had
meant nothing to her, they were just words used to describe people so
far beyond the pale of her life that they had no relevance to her whatsoever, no real existence at all.

Yet now she could remember a scene from her childhood. She had
been about fourteen, and her father had taken her with him on a day
trip into Boston. It was one of those almost miraculously rare times
when both her brother and sister were invited somewhere else and she
had her father to herself. They rode together in the family car comfortably, talking. Suzanna read a book in the reception room while her father conducted his business in an inner office, and then they drove
back home. It was a two-hour drive, and a hot day. On the way home,
they stopped at a roadside café. Her father ordered coffee and Suzanna
a hot fudge sundae.

Sitting at the counter was a strange creature: a woman with hair
chopped short as a man's, wearing gray trousers and a shirt, with a
pack of cigarettes rolled up in the left sleeve of the shirt, exposing a
very muscular arm. The woman was fat and homely and sinister in appearance. "Yaaaah," she was saying to the man sitting next to her,
"they're all turds, every one of them." Suzanna had stared at the
woman—she looked so freakish, and most horrible of all, she wore a
pair of men's wing-tipped shoes.

Finally Suzanna's father noticed the direction of her gaze. "Don't
look at her," he said. He was embarrassed, so embarrassed that
Suzanna sensed that something sexual was involved here. "That
woman's sick. She thinks she's a man. She's—a homosexual. She loves
women."

So that was it. Women who loved women were sick; they were
unattractive to men, disgusting, and one should look away.

But then another image surfaced. Suzanna remembered it from a
text on the modern novel which she had studied in an undergraduate
course. Virginia Woolf. She had been in love with a woman named
Vita Sackville-West; they had been lovers. Virginia Woolf had not
been ugly or dumb or unable to attract the love of men. In fact, she

was beautiful and brilliant and married to a man who adored her. On
the other hand, she had not been exactly a model of sanity and the
normal life.

What *kind* of woman loved a woman? Suzanna wondered, and as
the bubbles from her bath began to dissolve, she saw her body pink
and real beneath the water and her thoughts raced. What kind of
woman loved a woman, what did it mean to love a woman—*how* did
one love a woman? Did she want to *touch* Madeline Meade?

Oh, yes, she did. She did. Very much.

Suzanna rose from her bath shaking and frightened. She wanted
to touch Madeline Meade, and she wanted Madeline Meade to touch
her with her long, elegant hands.

That night, Suzanna could not sleep, but fell in and out of
dreams of Madeline's hands. When she rose on Sunday morning, she
was dizzy from lack of sleep, but strangely refreshed and eager; it was
as if some reservoir of energy had suddenly cracked open inside her.
She went to church, but did not hear the sermon. Instead she sat staring up at the minister as if entranced: she was trying to decide
whether or not God played tricks in love.

She made it through the day by doing laundry, housecleaning,
baking, all her weekend chores, but once again she found she could
not sleep at night. She was exhausted, but alert, she could not rest, her
mind was vivid with dreams of Madeline Meade's hands and face and
voice. When she awoke on Monday morning, she did not know how
she would make it through the day, she was so tired, yet so tense, but
as she stirred her coffee in the kitchen, she considered her calendar and
saw that that afternoon, after school, both Priscilla and Seth were invited to a birthday party. They would be gone for two and a half
hours. She smiled a mad smile at the kitchen door where the calendar
hung, and a lovely desperate daring drove her into the day. She taught.
She dressed her children in party clothes and dropped them at her
friend's house. Then she drove to Southmark very carefully, but very
fast.

The college, as she approached it, looked larger and brighter to
her than usual; it seemed to beckon and shine. Desire had now possessed her completely, and it also made her dull. She had no thoughts
except that she must speak to Madeline Meade. She did not worry
about her children, her parents, her friends, her God; she was intent

on one thing only. She did not even stop to wonder whether or not she, Suzanna, was lovable. She only knew she had to see this woman, to present her with the knowledge of her love, and to see where life would take her then.

Madeline was in her office, seated at her desk, talking on the phone. She was laughing. Suzanna stood with mute appeal in the doorway until Madeline looked up, noticed her, smiled, and mouthed, "Come in." Madeline pointed to a chair, and Suzanna sank down into it. The actual presence of this woman she loved did not frighten or calm her; it only made her feel more strongly the need to get this thing done and said before the hidden knowledge broke her apart.

When Madeline hung up the phone, Suzanna said, "I need to talk with you. May I close the door?"

"Of course," Madeline said.

Suzanna shut the door, sank back into the chair, then faced her professor and said, "I think I am in love with you."

Madeline's expression did not change. Finally she sighed. Then: "That's very flattering. I'm not sure how to respond. This sort of thing happens, you know, between students and professors, or patients and therapists. I think what you mean is that you admire me, because I am a professor, because I teach—"

"No," Suzanna said. "Please give me more credit than that. This is not a schoolgirl's crush. I do admire you. But I *love* you. I want to touch you."

Madeline hesitated. "Well, then," she said. And she stretched out her hand across the desk, her long slim hand with fingers wearing two thin silver rings, her wrist dangling gold and silver bracelets, her arm elegant and easy in its gesture.

Suzanna gently placed the palm of her hand against the palm of Madeline's hand, and with that most delicate pressure, her entire body went warm and wet; her mouth filled with saliva.

Suzanna held Madeline's hand—their flesh touched. "I love you," Suzanna said. She did not feel courageous or frightened; she felt completely alive.

"You know," Madeline said, smiling, "this could get complicated. I think we should go get some coffee, and walk together, and talk." She withdrew her hand.

"I've horrified you, haven't I?" Suzanna said. "But I can't apologize."

"No, you haven't horrified me," Madeline said. She rose from the desk and crossed the room and opened the door. She looked sad. "Please. Let's go get some coffee."

They said nothing as they walked over to the student union; they did not speak until they were seated in a booth with their coffee cups in front of them.

"Now," Madeline said, "listen to me. I do not take what you're saying lightly. But it's all a little bit crazy, you know. I don't know you very well, even though I've enjoyed having you in class. You're a good student. You're smart. You've got good instincts. Still—Suzanna, you're a mother. You're part of a community. You teach little children. You need to think of all these things."

"I can only think of you."

"What makes you think that I could love a woman?"

Suzanna was stunned. "I—I didn't *think* you could. I guess I didn't consider that at all. I mean"—and she smiled—"that I'm a woman. I mean you know I'm a woman. I'm not making sense. I mean that I only thought that I love you, and that you are a woman, so this is—strange—for me to feel this way. But I don't know, I didn't think —*could* you love a woman? My God, I know so little about you. I've assumed from what little you've said about yourself in class that you're not married, but—oh, God, are you in love with someone? Are you living with a man—someone?"

Madeline smiled. "I want to be so careful," she said. "*You* must be so careful. If I tell you things about me, then we will be making some kind of relationship, and there's real danger there. Please, listen to me. It does not matter whether I'm living with someone or whether I can love a woman. It does matter that you were married to a man, you have little children, you teach in public schools. Please stop and think of those things."

"Oh, I do think of them. I love my children—I love my life. But I *am divorced*. And now I love you, and I can't stop. Couldn't we— couldn't we have an affair?"

"I can't answer that now. I think you should take some time to consider the implications of what you're saying, and to imagine all the possible consequences. You must be aware that homosexual love is not acceptable in this society."

"But—"

"It was once viewed as a disease, an illness. Now it is considered only a sordid aberration."

"Please—"

"Do you want to be called a lesbian, a homosexual, a queer, a dyke? Do you want to be thought of as weird, an outcast? Do you want to have a judge take your children from you? Do you want your children called names by other children because of what you've done? Could you live with yourself? I'll tell you, an affair is one thing, but a homosexual affair is something completely different. It can destroy your life forever."

"But do you think you could love me?"

"Oh, Suzanna. I think you are beautiful. You seem good, intelligent, and full of grace. If I didn't admire you and care for you a little already, I wouldn't be so frightened for you. *You* should be frightened. You must be careful."

"Then you are not saying that you could not love me."

Madeline grinned. "You *are* persistent."

Suzanna smiled back. "I am obsessed."

The two women were quiet a moment, caught up in a strong and mutual steady current of desire, and their smiles both widened slightly as they understood the fierce and subtle acknowledgment of their state.

Then Madeline turned her head aside and said softly, "Obsessions seldom cause people anything but grief."

"I want to kiss you. I feel desperate. I long for you."

"Suzanna, aren't you frightened?"

"No. Yes, of course. But I can't help this. I'm frightened, but I'm also so full of joy to be sitting here, looking at you, to be hearing your voice, to be telling you that I love you."

"Have you loved a woman before?"

"God, no. I've never even thought of loving a woman before. No, this is strange for me, and yet it seems completely right. Have you ever loved a woman?"

"I think you should go home and think about all we've said."

Madeline rose abruptly, tossed her Styrofoam coffee cup into the wastebasket, and walked from the room. Suzanna had no recourse but to follow.

"Go home now," Madeline said.

"Please. I want to kiss you."

Madeline stared at Suzanna a long moment. "All right, then," she said. "Let's go to my office. We'll shut the door, and we'll kiss, and then you can see how you feel about this love of yours. You can see if you do not feel repulsed and disgusted to be a woman kissing a woman."

Suzanna walked beside Madeline back to her office, and all the while she felt as though she were burning; she could not get her breath. Her professor walked rapidly, and the easy elegance with which she usually moved had diminished; her body had gone tense.

Inside the office, Madeline shut the door and turned to Suzanna.

"Well?" she said.

Suzanna had thought that Madeline was much taller than she, but as they stood facing each other, she realized that Madeline's superior height was due in part to her slimness, which gave an illusion of height, and in part to the shoes she wore. When Suzanna went to Madeline, she had to look up, to take her professor's face in both hands and gently bring her face down; and so they kissed.

"Wait a moment," Madeline said, and she stepped back and took off her shoes. Now she was only slightly taller than Suzanna. "This is better," she said. This time when they kissed, their bodies touched, up and down.

"Oh, dear," Madeline said at last. She put both her hands on Suzanna's shoulders and pushed her away, but gently. "This will never do," she began.

"Yes!" Suzanna cried.

"Wait, I don't mean that. I mean it will never do here, now. Not on the college campus. Not while you are my student."

"I'll drop your course."

"Don't be silly. There are only three weeks left. You'll need this credit, and I can assure you you've already earned an A for the work you've done. We have to wait."

"I can't wait."

"Listen to me. We hardly know each other. Let's spend the next three weeks just talking. We can be together this way. We can have coffee and talk. We can become friends."

"I want to be your lover," Suzanna said. "I don't want to wait."

"Why? Are you afraid it won't last?" Madeline asked. "Do you think that what you feel will disappear in three weeks?"

"No—*no*."

"Then we have to wait. And you have to do some serious thinking."

Another student knocked on the door then. Suzanna wanted to scream at him to go away, but he had an appointment with Madeline. It was Suzanna who had to leave, and she hated it. She walked to her car, drove home, thinking all the while of Madeline's soft mouth, of the pressure of Madeline's breasts and curves and hips and legs as they had been pressed against her own. She was so aware of her own body that mere breathing, mere shifting in the car seat as she drove, seemed physical acts full of exotic and sensual possibilities. She felt reincarnated or transformed, and her new body seemed as luminously edged as the William Blake drawing she had seen on the cover of textbooks: everything within her, body and soul, was inspired.

Suddenly, there was her house, a small, yellow Colonial, with autumn flowers, chrysanthemums and daisies, against the outer walls. There was her front door, with the brass knocker her husband had installed, and her daughter's doll forgotten on the front step. There was the entrance hall she had papered and decorated and swept, and there was the large wooden-framed mirror in the entrance hall. This was a lovely, normal house, but there in the mirror was Suzanna, a woman she no longer knew.

She stood in front of the mirror, confronting her image, staring at her own face. Back in her own home, she felt disoriented. She was afraid. She walked to the mirror and touched the glass reflection.

"You are Suzanna Blair," she said. "You are a mother and teacher. You love a woman. You love Madeline Meade. You love a woman."

She was overcome by a terrible shaking, much like the trembling that had possessed her after the birth of her children. It was the shaking that follows severe physical shock. She shook so hard that her teeth chattered. She wrapped her arms around herself but gained no steadiness.

She went into the kitchen and leaned against the sink. Everything around her looked so endearingly normal, and she thought: I have made this room cozy and comfortable—I am capable of many things. She ran cold tap water into a glass, and looking down into the glass as if God were invisibly waiting for her there, she said, "Listen, God. You've got to help me. If what I feel is wrong, you've got to let me know. I'm afraid."

But there was no sound in the kitchen save the tiny ticking of the stove clock and the whispery movements of the cat who came to sit by the cupboard door, looking at Suzanna with inscrutable eyes.

"Well," Suzanna said, and brought the glass of water to her lips. But the slight touch of the glass to her opened lips stunned her and the cold water that entered her mouth seemed to reawaken the desire that now lay sparkling, ready, within her. From now on every sensual pleasure would remind her of Madeline, and of the joy that shot through her when Madeline's mouth met hers. Suzanna touched her lips with her fingertips, and stood trembling, bemused, fascinated, until some inner instinct brought her to look at the kitchen clock, and she realized it was time to pick up the children from the birthday party.

The next three weeks she met Madeline ten times for coffee in the college union. She told Madeline about her life, and drew small bits of information from Madeline about her life. Madeline had gotten her Ph.D. at the University of Wisconsin. She was thirty-two years old. She spent her summers in England. She was working on a book. Madeline told Suzanna many details about the research for her book, an anthology of psychoanalytic literature written by women. She told Suzanna little about her personal life, yet it seemed they had so much in common. For when Suzanna would recount an incident about Seth and Priscilla's squabbling, Madeline would laugh and remember a similar childhood experience, or a case study, which would in turn remind Suzanna of a joke or a book or a memory, and their words and thoughts and ideas would tumble out together so that very quickly their experiences seemed joined. It was as if they rapidly built a mutual edifice with these words, a house familiar and comfortable to both of them, so that when they saw each other, they were immediately at home—safe, yet excited, for there was so much else to create and explore.

There seemed to be no inequality in their relationship, for

Madeline had a Ph.D. and the prestige that gave her, but Suzanna had children and a different kind of knowledge. They were different but equal; there was to be no hierarchy, dominance, or submission. They built their domain about them with instinctive balance, just as within themselves they balanced eagerness and courtesy in their speech. They inundated each other with words: it was, for this period of time, their only way of touching.

The semester finally ended. Madeline left Southmark to spend the Christmas vacation in New York with friends. She promised to call Suzanna when she returned, and she promised that then, after the vacation, if Suzanna still wanted to, they would spend some time alone together in a private place.

Suzanna took Priscilla and Seth to her parents' home for Christmas. Her parents told her that her divorce obviously suited her: she had never looked better. It seemed to Suzanna that her nervous system had somehow speeded up, as if hoping that if it worked faster, time would pass faster, too, and so she found herself always racing at the edge of her emotions. She burst into tears when she saw old friends, when carolers came to the door singing "Silent Night," when the children saw what Santa had brought them Christmas morning. She ate and drank too much. She played in the snow with the children until they begged to go inside and rest. Finally the holidays were over, and she and the children returned to Londonton.

The day before she started teaching again, Tom showed up at the house. He was tan and healthy from two weeks in Bermuda, and he played a bit with the children, and informed Suzanna that he had taken a job at another college at the opposite end of the state, three hours away. Suzanna smiled, wished him well, and thought to herself that this seemed a stroke of luck, for with Tom gone from town she would have a freedom she hadn't felt before.

Madeline came back from New York early in January. She called, and invited Suzanna to her home for a drink. Suzanna was nearly ill with anticipation, but she found that once she was actually there, inside Madeline's house, with Madeline physically present, she did not know how to begin. For once she had trouble talking. She was terrified and shy.

The women discussed their holidays from opposite ends of the sofa. Madeline spoke of the plays and galleries she had been to in New

York, Suzanna of her parents and children. They drank wine, then more wine. Suzanna told Madeline that Tom was moving away. Madeline was curious, more curious about Suzanna's marriage, in fact, than Suzanna was; Suzanna had suddenly come to look upon her past and her husband as if they had no more substance than a dream.

"Oh, please," Suzanna said at last, "won't you ever tell me about yourself? Have you ever been married? Have you ever loved another woman? Have you ever loved a man?"

Madeline smiled. "Yes," she said.

"Yes? Yes, what?"

"Yes, I've been married, I've loved another woman, and I've loved a man. My life has been different from yours, Suzanna. You are in a transitional state now, but I think that most of your life you have enjoyed the company of people and their established patterns. I mean, you like to teach, you like your children, you have your friends. I prefer solitude, travel, books, ideas. No one has ever meant—very much— to me. My marriage was very brief and sad, but"—she smiled—"not too sad. What I'm trying to say to you is that yes, I can go to bed with you. I can be your lover for a while, since 'lover' is the term that's used. But I can't promise you anything more than that. I can almost certainly promise you that I won't be monogamous, faithful, whatever. Oh, I don't mean that I treat these things lightly. But I may not be capable of treating what is between us with the seriousness you would like, and you should decide now if it would be worth it to you, given the way I am."

Suzanna sat watching Madeline, who now slowly paced the room as she talked, and she thought how beautiful the woman was, slim, elegant, reserved. Everything about her was disciplined and somehow bounded, edged. By contrast, Suzanna felt bulging, limp, and eager. She was astounded by her own courage when she simply rose, went toward Madeline, and took her in her arms.

"Please, let's not talk anymore," she said. "It's all right, you know. I'm not a child."

They stood in the middle of Madeline's living room, with the curtains pulled shut and the lights on full; they held each other and kissed and embraced. Suzanna ran her hands over Madeline's hair, over her shoulders and arms and back. Then, trembling, she touched Madeline's breasts. She put both her hands on the cotton shirt that covered Madeline's breasts and simply laid them there gently, as if afraid that this touching might cause their flesh to flame up and harm one or the other. But Madeline only sighed and stood, acceding. Suzanna ran her hands down Madeline's fine slender waist, down her hips, and pressed her palms against Madeline's thighs. Still they kissed. Madeline touched her fingertips to the tips of Suzanna's breasts, and Suzanna's heart knocked so strongly throughout her body that she swayed and nearly fell.

"I think I'm going to have a heart attack," Suzanna whispered into Madeline's hair.

"This is what bodies are made for," Madeline said.

Then she smiled and began to unbutton Suzanna's shirt. Her hands on Suzanna's bare skin were cool and light. Still standing, the women took off each other's clothes: shirts, belts, jeans, underclothes. They stood before each other naked.

"How different we are!" Suzanna cried. She realized how unusual it was to see another woman's body naked. She was short and round and fleshy; Madeline was lean and bony, so that her breasts seemed impertinent. They held each other then, and skin touched skin so sweetly it seemed a coming home. In Madeline's bedroom, they lay on top of the thick violet comforter and explored each other's bodies with their hands and lips.

Suzanna said, "I want to touch you first. I want to show you that in spite of everything you don't need to be a teacher to me." And she lay stretched out against her lover, and kissed her lover's mouth, and moved her hand in a meandering line from the hollow of Madeline's throat to the rise of her breasts, down the smooth flat stomach, to the swell of pubic hair. She placed the whole of her hand between Madeline's legs, and pushed her legs gently apart, then parted the swollen rise of flesh and touched the mauve and hidden clitoris. Madeline was so wet between her legs with thick liquid. Then Suzanna did the forbidden thing: she found the eager rounded rim and slowly slid her two longest fingers into what she could not see— that tiny silk-lined cave, which was now slithery with juices. Suzanna explored, fascinated, she moved her wrist, her fingers, and took care to be gentle, and at last, with a little shove, she touched with the ends of her fingers a minute protrusion which hung stalactite-like and soft inside Madeline's vagina: it was her cervix.

"God," Suzanna said, "how interesting women are!"

Madeline said, "Don't stop."

What could she not find to do? The possibilities seemed infinite, and Suzanna wanted to do everything at once. She slowly spread her two fingers apart, and Madeline's vagina responded; it went wide, then wider. Suzanna raised herself onto one elbow and looked. Madeline lay stretched beneath her, totally given over to the experience, naked, vulnerable, displayed. Her eyes were closed and she had flung one arm over her face as if to hide. A flush had crept across the top of her breasts and up toward her neckline; her nipples were distended; her pelvis arched. There is no more satisfying sight than that of a lover receiving pleasure—and there are no more satisfying sounds. Such subtle changes in touch or angle or movement or rhythm could bring such low and luscious moans—and then, without warning, such gasping for breath. Madeline's eyes opened, she stared at Suzanna, a demand, an entreaty, then clasped her eyes shut and grasped the sheets with both hands as if to keep herself from falling off the edge of the world. Suzanna gently turned and moved her hand until Madeline's vagina clenched itself in helpless spasms around Suzanna's fingers. With her own hand she could feel her lover's ecstasy spread in waves throughout her body, like rings circling out from a stone cast into water. She withdrew her hand, which was fragrant and sticky, and brought her body down against Madeline's body. Both women were shimmering with sweat as they lay together. Suzanna smoothed Madeline's hair. Madeline lay silent, and slowly her breathing returned to normal.

"Well," she said when at last she opened her eyes, "you're right. You don't need me to be your teacher. But still—roll over."

There is, Suzanna found, the most exquisite variety to a body. A tongue, which can lick light and wetly flat across the skin, can become sharp, bone-like, a precise point. When a lover cares, there is almost no end to the eloquent transformations the hands are capable of. When there is love, the pleasures of the body flow through with the urgency of music, and what was once a dull and everyday set of bones and organs and skin becomes buds, froth, blossoms, becomes undulating fabric, becomes a giant bell. Madeline climbed Suzanna's body, she caressed Suzanna until her whole being went tintinnabulous with joy. She was relentless and imaginative with Suzanna, until at last she

collapsed next to her on the bed. Both women lay against the sheets
with their limbs intertwined and their hair damply trailing over the pillows. They were as limp and redolent and delicately drawn out as con-
volvuli—as morning glories.

The bedroom reeked of sex. Madeline sat up and pulled the tumbled covers up about their shoulders, then lay on her side so she could
see Suzanna's face.

"Well," she said. "Well. Now we've begun."

It was hard to be a woman in Londonton. It was easy enough to
be a married woman, a wife and mother, but in spite of the propaganda of liberation, it was still implicitly assumed in Londonton that
the primary qualities of a good woman were chastity and humility.
After their divorce, Tom moved to another town, but he appeared back
in Londonton often for parties or college dances, and each time he
brought with him a different woman. How he was admired for this
ever-expanding collection of lovers! For of course it was always made
apparent that the current woman slept with him. One weekend he
might arrive with a young blonde, and the next weekend with an older
brunette, and a weekend after that with the young blonde again, and
all of this only delighted the people of Londonton. But women in the
town were not allowed the same privilege of implied promiscuity. The
kindest thing that was hoped for them was that they would somehow
manage to get marired again, fast. Liza Howard was considered a
woman to be spurned because she slept with married men, and yet
those very men were the darlings of every social occasion.

Suzanna learned all this because, as the months went by, she
found it necessary to camouflage her relationship with Madeline by appearing to be involved with men. Once at a party at Pam and Gary
Moyer's, she had met Gary's half brother, who had come up for a football weekend. She liked the brother, whose name was Chad, and was
pleased when he asked her to go to dinner with him the next night. In
fact, she slept with him, and enjoyed his presence so much that she let
him stay the night. But he was only twenty-four, thirteen years
younger than Suzanna, and no sooner had Chad left than Suzanna
was deluged with gossip about herself—in her best interests, everyone
said. How could she let a man spend the night—she shouldn't do that

to her children. And what was she doing with a man so much younger than she, it was a little embarrassing, wasn't it? It made her seem cheap to have picked up that boy at the Moyers' party, cheap and . . . lascivious; and those were not qualities admired in first-grade teachers.

"My God!" Suzanna would want to yell (but never would). "I've been dating those men for *you!*" By you, she meant the entire town, which had miraculously transformed itself into one all-seeing eye and one eternally whispering mouth. Nothing escaped the town, and everything was judged. Suzanna fed the town the red herrings of her little escapades with men in order to distract them from what was growing more and more important in her life: her love for Madeline.

The months went by, and Suzanna loved Madeline, and Madeline loved Suzanna. This frightened them both, and they both kept attempting affairs with other people in order to make their love seem frivolous, but this never worked. The months went by and the two women continued to find that they were happy in each other's company, and slightly lamed alone, as if they had so quickly grown part of each other's bodies. They took such sheer pleasure in each other's company. They fit each other.

For a while, Suzanna had feared that perhaps it was only the thrill of the forbidden that was driving her again and again to Madeline's bed. For there was certainly that thrill. Lost in the wet and fragrant landscape that lay between her lover's legs, that even at its most spread and exposed promised with its intricate convolutions that it hid more than it revealed, Suzanna would marvel. She would think: I am making love to a *woman!* I am touching a *woman!* But after two years, the shock value had disappeared, and their lust was no longer fueled by novelty or desperation. In fact, the lust finally burnt itself out. Oh, it flared up from time to time so that Madeline might call Suzanna in the middle of the day to say, "I must come see you, *now.*" But it was not the distinguishing quality of their relationship. All the other lovely properties were there, flourishing and growing—devotion, caring, concern, interest, compassion, conversational delight, goodwill, laughter. Suzanna and Madeline might sit in bed, naked and cross-legged, delicately teasing the nipples of each other's breasts; they might lick the juices from each other until their own faces grew hot and sticky; they might occasionally spend whole nights building the ecstasy between them until their backs shimmered with sweat and their breasts were sore and they fell apart panting. But that was the way of all lovers, and they knew it. What they had found went beyond that, and encompassed friendship as well as lust. More than the nights of love were the days of love, when they took simple pleasure in preparing a meal together, in lying side by side reading books, like any normal married couple who had the luxury to read in bed because sexual needs were satiated, and would be satiated again and again.

Almost two years after they had first slept with each other, they were down in Suzanna's basement at eleven o'clock on a Sunday night. By this time Madeline had come to be a welcome part of the household. The children liked her and thought nothing of it when she sometimes spent the night. They thought of her as a good friend of their own as well as of their mother. This Sunday night she and Suzanna were putting the finishing touches on two small, intricate dollhouses that the women had made from scratch for Seth and Priscilla at Christmas. They had been inspired to this task by the pleas of the children, who had seen a quaint miniature tree house in a toy store. That tree house had been priced at over two hundred dollars. "Hummph!" Madeline had said. "We can do better than that ourselves!"

She had bought the boards and saws and paint, and Suzanna had dug up bits of fabric, old swatches of rug and curtain, and together the two women had constructed the houses—the Rabbit Home for Priscilla and the Raccoon Home for Seth. Now they were sitting on newspapers, wearing old paint-streaked shirts, very carefully trimming out the windows and doors. Suzanna looked up for a moment, and saw Madeline there near her, her tongue pushed to the corner of her mouth in concentration. Madeline was intent on her task, and the thought of what that focused intensity could bring when they were in each other's arms made Suzanna shiver. Suzanna had not realized before that it was possible to have both in love: ecstasy and companionable ease.

"I want to marry you," Suzanna said to Madeline. "I really do. I want to marry you and share my house with you and my life with you and my children's lives with you. I want to invite friends to dinner, and you and I will both be hostesses. I want—"

"Sssh. Don't," Madeline said. "It's childish to wish for the impossible. You'll only hurt yourself."

"But I want it so much!" Suzanna said.

"You have too much to lose," Madeline replied.

That was true. There was no argument, there was no solution. Both women bent their heads and resumed painting in silence.

After two years of living in such happiness that it was like moving about in rarefied mountain air, Suzanna had decided to confide her secret to some of her friends. The first friend she told lived not only in another town but in another country; she responded to Suzanna's letter by writing: *"C'est merveilleux! Je pense que l'amour est si rare qu'on doit le prendre comme un cadeau de Dieu."* And Suzanna thought her friend was right: it was marvelous, and love *was* so rare that one *should* take it as a gift from God. This gave Suzanna the courage to confide in a friend who lived in town. Lana was divorced and had had a series of unfortunate affairs with men. She was a feminist and a bit of a radical. Suzanna had counted on her approval. But Lana had surprised her with vague censure. "I don't know," Lana had said, "there's something about this that frightens me. I think this sort of thing could undermine society, and we already have troubles enough. And then, of course, you must think of the children—"

Of course, the children. Always the children. Why, Suzanna thought, were women thought unfit to raise and nurture children because they touched their hands to a woman's body rather than to a man's? For it had come down to that basic and particular event.

Lust between women was of the same quality as lust between the sexes. There was not one whit of difference. Lesbian love was no more violent or gentle than heterosexual love; it is the individual who makes the difference, not the gender. There were in Londonton two sisters who have never been married, the Misses Toomeys, and they went everywhere together; why could not Madeline and Suzanna do the same? They kept every bit of sexual expression confined to the privacy of a bedroom, behind locked doors, or far away from the children at Madeline's house. Carnality did not steam off their bodies or glow about them as they walked. They cooked dinners together, ate and joked with the children, strolled down tree-lined streets to buy ice-cream cones, and never in those two years did the children wake in their dreams with fears or do any other thing to indicate that they knew that their mother loved Madeline except as a friend. They came to love Madeline, too.

Tom did not know about Suzanna's love for Madeline, and

Suzanna was terrified that he would find out. After two years of collecting what was almost a harem of women around him, Tom had recently announced his engagement to a girl of nineteen who sold airplane tickets in a travel store. Tom had told Suzanna about this one weekend when he brought Priscilla and Seth back from a visit—it was a three-hour drive from Tom's house to Suzanna's and the two parents had fallen into the habit of stopping in for a cup of coffee before facing the grueling drive home. This weekend, Tom had told Suzanna he was to marry, and suggested that it might be wise if the children came to live with him. He missed them so. It might be good for the children to live in a home where a father figure and a mother figure lived together, instead of Suzanna's home where they seldom—according to what the children had told him—saw a man.

Suzanna did not know if a threat had been implied in Tom's speech, but she was frightened. I must start dating men! she thought, all in a frenzy, but Londonton was so small that there were few men for her to date. And she really didn't want to date: she was thirty-seven now, and found the little games necessary to dating embarrassing and tiresome. She was a grown woman, and she found her life quite full. She loved taking care of her children and her house, spending time with Madeline, working on her master's degree, teaching at the elementary school. Her life had reached that rare and satisfying balance of pleasure and gratifying work. But her work was jeopardized, also, by her love, and this seemed such a hopeless tangle to her: that the same parents who came to her time and again to tell her how wonderful she was with children, how much the children loved her, how much they had learned from her, what a wonderful teacher she was, what a wonderful person she was—these very same parents would recoil from her in horror and drive her from the children's sight if they knew she loved a woman.

What was she to do? Suzanna had begun attending church the month she first made love to Madeline. She went simply to present herself before the face of God for punishment or rebuke or whatever He willed. She thought she would make it clear to Him, by coming before Him regularly this way, that she was ready to do His will, if He would make it clear. For example, she had thought, when she was first so furiously given over to the throes of lust, that one of her children would be hurt. It seemed logical, and then there would be a clear and simple message—but it did not happen. Seth and Priscilla thrived. Suzanna's work went well. Tom was happy with the divorce and his new wife; the roof did not fall in, the ground beneath Suzanna's house did not shudder and split, no plague arrived, the children stayed healthy and were not hit by cars or bitten by dogs—so what was Suzanna to think?

Oh, God, is this a trick? Suzanna would ask. She was continually weighing the happiness she felt with Madeline with the ferocious judgments handed down upon lesbians in the local and national news. It began to drain her more and more—the pretense that she was not in love and was therefore not happy, and the secret-keeping from her friends and community. But she was afraid, for her life and for her children's happiness. There were women in the town who would not hesitate to destroy her without even attempting to understand.

Last summer at a church picnic she had been standing behind Judy Bennett, watching Seth and another little boy scrabble with each other over a Frisbee. They tusseled, and Seth, being stronger, won, and instantly the fight was over and the other boy ran back to catch the Frisbee that Seth tossed to him, and he threw it back to Seth. They went on playing. But Suzanna heard Judy Bennett say to Pam Moyer, "Oh, look at the Blair boy. He's over there, trying to take a toy from little Bryan Haskell. Well, what can you expect from a child like Seth —he's the product of a broken home, you know." Tears had shot into Suzanna's eyes. She had wanted to pummel Judy Bennett in the back, to scream in rage and frustration, to shake and shake the woman until her body broke open and compassion entered in. But she had only walked away, trembling so violently she thought she might faint. If Judy judged that little boy so harshly because his parents were divorced, what would she do to him if she knew his mother loved a woman?

People were still skeptical of women who were divorced—but not of men who were divorced. People were still frightened of women who were divorced, as if they held some kind of primitive and tainted power. Women not sanctified by the presence of a husband seemed by no choice of their own to appear to married women with an almost witch-like aura; and women who loved women were considered fallen past witchery and into the black outlands of evil.

But perhaps that was an exaggeration, for Suzanna had friends now who knew her secret and, beyond being happy for her happiness, did not care. These people saved her life.

"Oh, for heaven's sake," Ursula Aranguren would say whenever Suzanna got carried away with her fears. "*Everyone* has a gay relative by now. If Madeline moves in with you, this town will buzz like a hornet's nest for maybe a week or two, and then turn its attention to something else. We're sophisticated people, after all. Life is too short to squander—live your life!" But Ursula Aranguren did not have children. She could afford to be remarkable.

"I have to admit," Leigh Findly said, "when you first told me, my first reaction was fear—I think I thought you might make a pass at me and I wasn't sure how to handle that. Not to insult you, Suzanna, but you're not my type! And then I was—wary—for a while. I suppose I thought you might start showing dirty movies in your home or, well, proselytizing. But after all these months, well, I feel fine with you, perfectly comfortable. I'm beginning to understand: you don't love a woman, you love a person."

For that was it. Suzanna loved a person, and that person loved her, and the gender of that person was not the point. As the months went by and the emotions deepened past lust and wild exhilaration, Suzanna came to feel that perhaps this person—Madeline—was the person she could spend her entire life with, for kindness and generosity and good humor and mutual respect were all there. They could even argue and resolve the arguments without damaging their estimation of each other or crimping their loose and dear companionship.

It was society, this town, that could provide the hurt that would come, to them or to Suzanna's children, and nowhere in this town was a group of potential judges gathered in greater numbers than in the very church where Suzanna sat. Her position seemed impossible. She wanted to rise from her pew, to speak her defense before the community, to beg for their charity and support. But she could not do this one thing: she could not trust her neighbors.

She saw no hope. She sat beneath the shining whiteness of the sanctuary's dome and wondered if she must live in terror all her life.

REYNOLDS HOUSTON

The chairs in the chancel of the church were antique, carved from rosewood and upholstered with striped rose and gold velvet. They conveyed a majesty that seemed suitable to this territory that supposedly belonged to God. But they were not comfortable chairs; Reynolds Houston thought that perhaps these chairs had been designed in accordance with that ancient pedagogic belief that discomfort of the body sharpened the receptivity of the mind. In any case, Reynolds felt like a stork perched on a thumbtack, and thought he must look as awkward as he felt. There was no way to settle all his long bones gracefully on this little chair. Reynolds, over fifty-four years of life, had learned to discipline his extremely tall and narrow body out of most of its gawkiness; he had learned to dress himself fastidiously. He would never be thought of as a particularly handsome man, but he was distinguished, and knew he was considered elegant. In an attempt to compromise comfort with dignity on such a small space, he now leaned forward, rested his elbows on his knees, and touched the tips of his fingers together so that his hands pointed downward in a V. This posture placed the pressure of his entire upper torso on his shoulders and arms and made it a strain to lift his head—or maybe it was simply that he was so very tired that any posture at all would have weighed him down.

Reynolds was an academic man; a professor of Greek and Latin at the local college, and privately an extremely well-read scholar and philosopher. He was a private man. He had devised a life of solitude for himself, a life limited because of complicated philosophical reasons. But in the past week he had been confronted with a personal dilemma of such magnitude that he had had to ask others for help. He had been presented with a crime committed by one of the most outstanding members of his community, and he was being forced by the strength of his own principles into what seemed to him to be an almost violent act. Certainly by calling attention to this crime he was going to violate another person's life. But he did not see what choice he had.

Reynolds had built his solitary life on one dream: the perfectability of man. He tried to be a pefect man himself, and he tried to believe that the people he lived among were striving for the same goal. He had thought it possible that Londonton was a model town, one of the best gatherings of human beings on earth. He had needed to believe that.

Eighteen months ago the people of Londonton had been drawn together in a new and exciting endeavor: they were building a youth recreation center. Quite probably this was Mitchell Howard's idea, at least at first, for he had been a philanthropic man and a concerned citizen, the sort of man who would notice that the young people of Londonton needed such a place, and the sort of man rich enough to think a building within the realms of possibility. However, Mitchell had died of a heart attack shortly after the first plans for the center were drawn up, and while no one person claimed the center as his own idea, everyone closely involved with the project seemed to feel that he or she had been intimately associated with its inception. It was as if the town itself had had the idea and spread it through the minds of its citizens through the drinking water or the air. At any rate, it was an idea that aroused great enthusiasm throughout the town, and after the first early discussions about it over coffee or cocktails, five men got together and made themselves into a committee in charge of the construction.

On the official Londonton Recreation Center Foundation committee was Jake Vanderson, who was almost as wealthy as Mitchell Howard but not nearly as bright or kind. Still, he donated the land to build on and $100,000 of his company's money. Gary Moyer, a lawyer, donated his time in setting up the initial contracts. Daniel Weinberg, a local surgeon, and Reynolds Houston were also on the committee. The other member of the founding committee had of course been Mitchell Howard, and when he died, his wife Liza became a nominal member of the committee; it had seemed the only correct thing to do, especially since Liza had donated $150,000 of the Howard money to the rec center fund. But while the other members automatically sent her letters notifying her of business meetings, she never attended any of them, never showed any interest in the center. They let her name remain on the roster listed on the stationery they had had printed up for their money-raising drive.

Gary Moyer had spent a few days studying the municiṛal and state statutory requirements on public buildings, and he had decided very quickly that in order to save a lot of red tape and hassle, the five members of the committee should join together to form a private charitable organization; this way it would be tax-exempt, and the five members of the committee would be free to make certain decisions without the interference of public officials. One of the main reasons the five decided to form in this private way was to preclude the necessity for putting the job of building the center out to bid. Every man on the committee knew just which contractor he wanted to build the center, and they were unanimous on this, they wanted no discussions, no competition: they wanted Ron Bennett.

Ron had been building houses and small buildings in Londonton for as long as anyone could remember, at least twenty years, and what he built was of fine quality, and lasted, and they were buildings to be proud of. He was a good man, a good worker, he was the best, and he was one of them, a real member of the community. There was no doubt in anyone's mind that if he built the center it would be built with the best quality and the least money that was possible. They appointed Ron contractor; he estimated the cost of the center at around six hundred thousand dollars. Mitchell and Jake gave their vast donations, and the members of the committee set out to raise the rest of the money from the town itself. It was an exciting time for the town, a time when everyone who lived there felt a surge of belonging, a surge of civic pride; and almost everyone, rich and poor, contributed what he could.

On June 3, half the town had turned out to watch the mayor of Londonton shovel the first load of dirt from a plot of ground next to the Blue River. The earth was broken, the building begun. That day and in the long summer days to come, people from Londonton, young and old, would stroll by to lean against a tree or a pile of lumber, watching the foundation being dug, the cinder blocks being placed, the giant grinding machines lifting the earth and replacing vacant space

with man's materials. In its own way, the building of the rec center
stirred within the hearts of the Londonton population a communal
pride and warmth of the same sort that barn-raisings had caused a century before.

Reynolds, too, often stopped by to watch the construction. He
would never use the rec center, which was to be devoted exclusively to
the children of the town, but even so it was a building of great importance to him—he saw it as a monument to human achievement and accomplishment. He had helped raise the money; now Ron Bennett and
his men were raising the walls, and this building would stand for years
as a haven for the community's children and a hallmark of the community's optimistic affiliation.

Now all of that had changed.

Last week Reynolds had attended a formal dinner for the local
alumni of the college. Seated on his left had been Ben Martin, who
owned a large hardware store in Southmark, thirty miles from Londonton. There were two small hardware stores in Londonton, but if one
wanted something more elaborate than a few nails or a garden hose, it
was necessary to make the thirty-mile drive to Martin's Lumber and
Building Supply in Southmark. Much of the lumber and other
materials for the rec center were coming from Martin's. Ben Martin and
Reynolds knew each other only slightly, but they were amiable men,
made more amiable by the excellent meal and abundant wine and
cordial reunion atmosphere. As they finished their desserts, and before
the speaker was introduced, they discussed the new rec center.

"Tell me," Ben said, bending closer to Reynolds and dropping his
voice, "is Ron Bennett having some personal trouble? Perhaps I
shouldn't pry."

"Personal trouble? I don't think so. Why do you ask?" Reynolds
replied.

"Oh, it's nothing. I shouldn't talk shop here. But on a lot of Ron's
orders, he's been returning about half of the materials. It's not like him
to make such big mistakes on estimating what he'll need. Last month
he ordered sixty thousand feet of copper pipe and returned more than
half of it. Well, it's of no consequence."

It *was* of consequence to Reynolds, who appreciated that he was a
bit of an old maid busybody but could not help being curious and
worried. He had never liked to let minor problems go unsolved, be-

cause they could blossom into major problems if left untended. He knew that Ben Martin's words would buzz at him unless he settled the matter to his own satisfaction. So the next day, last Sunday, he walked to the town hall, let himself in with his own key, and went into the office where Ron kept the blueprints and financial records for the rec center.

Reynolds did not turn on a light. It was sunny enough outside and bright enough inside to see without artificial help, and he did not especially want any passersby to know someone was there. He had a perfect right, every right, to be doing what he was doing; still, he felt clandestine. This was, he suspected, an unsavory task, and he was not even sure what he was looking for. But he thought he had found it when he came upon the bill submitted in Ron Bennett's handwriting for sixty thousand feet of copper pipe—and, after a thorough search, found no corresponding credit slip.

The committee paid Ron in portions as the work progressed and different stages of the building were complete, so that the few checks that had been written out to him already were large: forty thousand dollars, eighty thousand dollars, sixty-five thousand dollars. Ron in turn paid his workers and the various establishments from which he bought his materials: Zabski Steel, Martin's Lumber and Building Supply, Mazani Window and Glass. Reynolds was in fact the man who glanced at Ron's itemized bills and made the check out to him. Now he studied the figures more carefully and realized, with a slight chill, that of the six hundred thousand dollars allocated for the building, over three hundred and fifty thousand had already been spent. How could that be possible? The swimming pool had not been started yet, the heating system was not in, nor were any of the interior walls. Ron had been complaining of inflation—everyone had been complaining of inflation—but surely this was unusual. He wondered how it fit in with Ron's recurrent mistakes in ordering supplies at Martin's.

Reynolds was bewildered, which was a state of mind he had never enjoyed. And he was uncomfortable, and wished he had not sat next to Ben Martin at the alumni reunion. But Thursday, he drove over to a small town between Londonton and Southmark to visit the owners of Zabski Steel. He entered a rather grime-covered metal building and, feeling conspicuous in his three-piece tweed suit, asked for Mr. Zabski. After much shouting, a man in a greasy navy blue cover-all appeared.

"Mr. Zabski?" Reynolds said. "I'm Reynolds Houston, from London. I'm on the committee that's in charge of the rec center building."

Mr. Zabski was not impressed. "What can I do for you?"

Reynolds realized that no insidious subtlety would work with this man: he had to make the plunge.

"We paid you for forty-five thousand dollars' worth of hot tar and gravel and other roofing material, and then we returned almost half of it."

"So what?" Mr. Zabski said. "I reimbursed you guys. I gave the check to Mr. Bennett a month ago."

Reynolds stared at Mr. Zabski.

"So?" Mr. Zabski said, taking the conversation into his own charge after several moments of silence. "So what do you want?"

"Nothing," Reynolds said. "Thank you."

Back home in Londonton, he sat in his study, doodling figures on a pad. He was torn. He wanted his suspicions disproved; but he did not want to prove himself a man who dealt in suspiciousness. He decided to sleep on it. Friday evening he dialed Gary Moyer's number. Gary was a lawyer, a member of the committee, and one of Ron's closest friends.

"Reynolds," Reynolds said to himself as Gary's phone rang, "you're probably going to make an ass of yourself."

But that was not what had happened. Gary was as appalled at Reynolds' suspicions as Reynolds himself had been. He canceled a Saturday afternoon tennis match in order to join Reynolds in the town office. They went over the books together, and Gary called Mazani Window and Glass. When he had finished talking, he put the receiver down and bent his head to rest in his hands.

There seemed to be only one conclusion: Ron Bennett had been siphoning money from the committee by ordering twice as much material as he needed, returning half of it, and pocketing the refund himself.

They had no way of knowing exactly how much money Ron had appropriated for himself, because the merchants were bound by common courtesy to keep secret the exact amount they charged the contractor for each item. Usually they gave a discount ranging from two to twenty percent. Some of this was passed on to the buyer, and some of it went straight to the contractor; it was one customary way the contractors made money. But the merchants were able to give out information about the amount of materials bought and returned, and everywhere, Ron Bennett had returned almost half of everything that he had bought and the rec center committee had paid for. If Reynolds and Gary were anywhere close in their figures, Ron Bennett so far in the past six months had kept for himself refunds amounting to a little over a hundred thousand dollars.

"Well, you know," Gary said quietly, raising his head to look sadly at Reynolds, "John just graduated from college, and Cynthia is only in her junior year at Smith. It takes a lot of money to put kids through college."

"Still," Reynolds began.

"Still," Gary said, then sighed. "Listen, Reynolds. We have to discuss this with him first before we tell the rest of the committee. This is going to destroy him."

"I don't like the sound of that," Reynolds said. "This is going to destroy him. He's been stealing money from every family in Londonton as surely as if he were a thief entering their homes at night, taking money from their pockets. He's a crook."

"I know, I know. But maybe we're wrong."

"Do you think so?"

"No. I don't see how we can be. In fact, I'm not all that surprised; I've almost been expecting something like this. Pam had mentioned to me that she thought the Bennetts were overextending themselves financially. But Reynolds, he's a friend of mine. Do me a favor. Make an appointment to go see him tomorrow night, to tell him what we suspect. I'll go with you. I want to go with you. But I just don't know if I can face him—" Gary's eyes filled with tears. "If this is true, it's just an awful damned shame. It just breaks my heart. Why should he ruin himself like this?"

"I'll make the phone call," Reynolds said. "I'll call now." But when he dialed, the number was busy, and although he tried off and on the rest of the evening, he wasn't able to get through to the Bennetts until Sunday morning, just before church. Judy Bennett had answered cordially; when he said he wanted to drop in that evening to visit with Ron, she had sounded pleased.

Now Reynolds sat in church, looking out at Judy Bennett, who sat so serenely at her husband's side. Poor woman, he thought; she would soon feel that when she let Reynolds in the door she was letting a viper into the house. Reynolds was glad he had thought to ask Peter Taylor to join them this evening; the minister's presence would surely provide a sense of comfort to them all.

Reynolds could only guess at the outcome of the meeting. Perhaps Ron would return the money, perhaps he could prove they were wrong, or he would admit they were right. What would they do then? They would probably have to prosecute. They would certainly have to call in another contractor, and let the town know what Ron had done. They would have to raise even more money somehow, much more money, before the rec center could be completed.

Reynolds had over the years learned to control his emotions, and he was not a passionate man to begin with. But now in this consecrated building, he felt a holy anger rise within him. He felt like some kind of human volcano about to erupt. He hated Ron Bennett, and this was as intimate and powerful an emotion as he had ever felt for any living man or woman. He hated him not so much for the individual act of greed and corruption as for the repercussions this would have on the broader community. The money was almost beside the point— but not, of course, entirely. One hundred thousand dollars was a lot of money, especially when it had been raised from the personal donations of almost every single family, rich and poor, in the town. Ron had done worse than merely steal money; he had violated the trust of the town, and he had done it in a despicable manner, casually, taking the town's trust in him for granted. He must have thought the committee was made of fools. He must have held—he must hold—his community in contempt. And he was not an outsider—he was one of them. People in such a close community judged themselves by each other, and if an adult or child performed a noble act, each individual felt himself capable of just that much more nobility. In this democratic little society, the members of Londonton looked at each other to reflect the best in themselves. Ron Bennett would reveal to them all the selfishness which bred in every man's heart. The center itself would lose its aura of communal dignity and unity; the atmosphere of the town would turn angry, vengeful, and grievous.

Reynolds had been wrong all along, a fool, to hope that humankind differed from the rest of the physical universe and could somehow shoot away from the deteriorating course that nature followed and aim at uniquely human heights. Now Reynolds knew that in spite of his hopes, mankind, represented in this instance by that fellow citizen Ron Bennett, was doomed to fail, one way or the other.

This sad knowledge Reynolds took personally, and it was the final blow in a summer of disappointments. Like a man hanging from the edge of a cliff, Reynolds felt he would now stop grappling and clawing for a fingerhold in the infirm ground of optimism and slide down into the metaphorical arms of the only faith that was trustworthy: despair.

It would be such a relief to despair at last.

All of his life, Reynolds had clambered up the treacherous and unassisting ground of hope, trying to believe that men were not bad and that life was not senseless. He had come at an early age to believe in the perfectability of man: this seemed to him to be the *point* of all life. He also learned very quickly that as an individual, and one not given to theatrics or incendiarism, he had little chance of changing the course of humankind in general. He was an optimist, not a madman. So he set about to control what he could control: himself. He decided that he would try to be a perfect man.

It was easy to be perfect while he was young. His parents taught languages in a prep school just outside of Boston. They had little money, but lots of hauteur. Reynolds was their only child, born late in their lives, and he was delighted to find how effortlessly he could earn their approval. He had only to sit quietly with them in the damasked living room of their apartment with his head bent over a book. He learned to read at the age of four (he didn't intend that, he was too young then to think about perfection, his precocity was pure accident). His parents made much ado about this, so he felt doubly blessed: what seemed to them to be compliance was to him a natural pleasure. He simply loved to read. This was fortunate for him, because his parents read so constantly that it seemed to him as a watching infant that reading was actually another vital bodily function, like breathing or walking or eating. He learned to fit into his family almost immediately. His father would sit in a huge armchair, his mother would recline gracefully on the couch, with her stockinged feet on a pillow. Reynolds would lie on the floor between them, and they would all turn pages in silence together. In the winter there would be the accompanying crackle and warmth from the fireplace; in the summer breezes and birdsong would drift through the open window and over their bent heads and engrossed consciousnesses. In the winter, his mother would at some point in the evening serve sherry to her husband and herself and hot chocolate to her son. In the summer she served sherry and lemonade.

When Reynolds turned six, and his mother realized that he had grown too mature for Little Golden Books and the picture books she bought for him, she took him one Saturday afternoon in the fall to the great public library. Reynolds would always remember that day as the happiest day of his life.

Until then, the world had been divided for him into two categories: the Safe, which was man-made, familiar, limited, and comprehensible; and the Dangerous, which was natural, strange, and too huge to be understood or organized (because of this, the Dangerous was also often boring). Their own home represented the first, as did the little grocery store where his mother shopped, and the homes of friends and other human dwellings. Reynolds had been confronted with the Dangerous only twice before, once when his parents took him to the ocean, and once when they took him to the mountains. Those wild vistas shrank in his mind in comparison to what vaulted above him when he entered the library: a whole new category, the Amazing, this vast and beautiful space which had been shaped by human minds and hands. The ceiling rose open for floors above him, and he could see, behind iron balconies, rows of books with people moving quietly through those rows. The floor beneath his feet alternated as far as he could see in large black and white squares. Their pattern was broken by tall oak counters where people stood checking out or returning books. In one direction stood an enormous alcove with wooden boxes of drawers lined up and golden; Reynolds would soon learn that this was the card catalogue. In another alcove rows of tables were occupied by people of all ages and sizes, bent over books. Everywhere he looked, he saw grownups walking slowly, reverently, speaking in whispers.

His mother led him through the aisles, softly explaining the library to him, and as Reynolds saw row after row of books unfold before him, he was filled with utter joy. This was the most beautiful place in the world. This was what Man was meant for. He understood in his own childish way that in this building Man had come close to enclosing the infinite.

Before he was ten, Reynolds was so addicted to the written word that words had more meaning to him than the objects or people they represented. Of course he excelled in school, except in recess and gym, but he was such a large boy that he could avoid being bullied. He was not the sort of child who wears glasses and blows up the basement doing scientific experiments—he did not want to do experiments, but only to read about them. The fact that all of human history, experience, actions, and emotions could be listed, explained, catalogued, organized, and analyzed satisfied him immensely.

So it was that from his earliest childhood he developed a preference for life bound up in books to life as it was lived. He was tantalized by the idea of perfection, and irritated by real life, because it was so sloppy. Something, in real life, was always going wrong. He attempted a few personal relationships, but was always disappointed: people were so messy, so easily hurt. And life never did provide that tidy resolution that made the ending of even the wildest novel so gratifying. Reynolds isolated himself; he withdrew more and more each year into the world of the mind.

As he grew older, he developed the intelligence and insight to realize just how narrow his life was. He did not become a friendly person, but his philosophy of life became friendly. He felt more charitable to people in general, and was able to remain that way by staying aloof from most people. This made it possible for him to believe in the perfectability of man, and to believe that the people he lived among were valuable and good.

While other men and women loved each other physically and emotionally, he loved the world and its inhabitants abstractly. He was pleased when he saw signs of heroism, kindness, or even intelligence in other people; he was depressed when he heard or read of people caught in demeaning acts. He disciplined himself, worked hard, and decided to devote himself to his fondest hope: the ultimate perfectability of man. He became a professor; it was the only life he wanted to live, and he was very good at it.

Now and then someone drunk or foolish would ask Reynolds whether or not he was ever lonely; his honest answer was always no. Over the years he learned to treat himself to all sorts of pleasures that more than made up for whatever he might have missed for lack of human interaction. He attended concerts, ballet, theater. He learned to cook with fastidious skill, and to know about wines. And finally he came to live his life in what was for him the almost perfect relationship with human beings: he taught at the private college in Londonton and became the dean of students there.

This was, of necessity, disciplined and careful work, and Reynolds excelled at it. In fact he helped the students much more than any sentimental gusher would have; although the students from time to time thought him a cold fish, they were later to write him letters telling him that he was the man who had done the crucial and perfect thing in their lives.

His college and his town became everything to him. He found here a source of solace and encouragement in the midst of an imperfect world.

He liked the gatherings of man at formal ceremonies such as convocations, graduations, trustees' dinners, baptisms, weddings. It was the shape that pleased him, the form. He liked to look out over a hall full of long, rectangular tables spread with white linen; the tables radiated out from the central dais with the regular pattern of chemicals in a trusted formula. He liked the elongated slender shapes of silverware framing the round plates in a design that was repeated routinely and symmetrically down the length of the tables. Man needed definition and order; it said something about the achievements of man. When the hall filled with men and women of all ages, sizes, shapes, and cultures, Reynolds could look out at them from his raised table with approval: those professors and administrators were for this limited time putting aside their petty grievances in order to sit together in harmony at an academic banquet. Rivals passed each other the salt; regional enemies discussed national politics; competitors bent their heads toward each other in order better to hear tales or jokes. All these contestants in the academic strife dropped their metaphorical swords for the space of one evening, and applauded as one the guest speaker. No matter that they would all go muttering out to their cars afterward, disgruntled with the speaker's words or even more incensed at an adversary's subtle insults. Still, for the period of three hours, two hundred men and women could be seated together in harmony, and that was an achievement not to be derided.

Town meetings also filled Reynolds with pride, for although those people opposing tax cuts nearly always came to blows with those advocating tax cuts, still in this forum human beings could present differing views in a mature and dignified way. Reynolds attended town meetings partly because he cared about the community—and he was listened to because he always spoke so intelligently, with clarity and good intent. He also went partly to watch what he considered the evolution of sophisticated man in progress.

For similar reasons he had attended church. The structure of the church service was even more appealing than the form of college dinners, for here the sensual appeasements of food and drink were not provided, and people had to sit together for almost two hours actually concentrating on words. It had given Reynolds great pleasure in all seasons to welcome members of his community into church, to escort them to their pews when he ushered, to look out over them when he served as lay reader, to stand with them as a member of their community when they rose to sing their hymns.

He was something of a philosophical pack-rat, he knew. He scurried from town hall to college assembly, sniffing out, trying to detect and collect signs for remaining optimistic about the future of his fellow man. He had relied on his town for inspiration.

Sometimes he simply walked around the town, slowing his stride when he came near a home which enclosed what seemed to him a particularly admirable family. He liked looking at the windows of houses where the curtains hung in such a fashion that they seemed to him, as an outsider, to be framing a little diamond of bright, mysterious, inner life. He liked the design of Londonton; the way it was neatly bisected by Main Street, ornamented by the winding Blue River, divided into explicit areas: college, residential, commercial. Reynolds approved of the way man had laid his shapes upon the land so that the town itself seemed to have sprung up from the ground as naturally as the trees.

Sometimes during his walks, Reynolds would pause to chat with an acquaintance. He would lean up against the brick building which sheltered the dry-cleaning business that had once belonged to Wilbur Wilson. And he would reflect that the permanence of this brick building was satisfying; the gritty, wicker-like pattern of layered bricks had been there for decades and would endure for decades. It was a shame that an individual good man could not have the same powers of longevity.

Reynolds admired Wilbur Wilson, for even though the older man

was not educated, he had become wise, and it settled Reynolds' soul to
know that such a man existed. Sometimes in the past Reynolds had
taken his raincoat or sportscoat into Wilson's Cleaners, and had rested
against the high counter while Wilbur leaned across from the other
side; they would stand there for a long time, talking in a quiet, comfortable way, about local news and events. Reynolds would look down
at their hands as they talked. His own were usually folded neatly, but
Wilbur's were always gently stroking and smoothing out the fabric of
whatever item it was that had been placed on the counter for his care.
Wilbur obviously respected substance; he treated all garments as if
they had dignity, because he had his own dignity, and believed
implicitly in the worth of the world and its materials. Reynolds' hands
were long, smooth, and fluent, and when he looked at his hands and
then at Wilbur's, he hoped that when his own hands had grown
gnarled and wrinkled like Wilbur's, his spirit would be as refined and
smooth and fluent as Wilbur's spirit. It was the flesh, the voices of people like Wilbur that helped Reynolds keep his intellectual faith in the
perfectability of man.

But now Wilbur was not enough, and the superficial prettiness of
the town did not suffice. It had been a difficult year for Reynolds, and
he was growing old.

In May of this year, a senior at the college who was the son of
friends of Reynolds' had been discovered cheating: he had plagiarized
not one but several papers for various courses. Reynolds and the ethics
committee had had no recourse but to expel the boy from college; he
could not graduate. What a waste, what a shame that had been, for
the boy was not stupid or even incorrigible, but merely lazy. The
news of his misdeed had nearly destroyed his family, especially the
mother, who had struggled so hard to impart the proper values to her
son. All of graduation had been clouded for Reynolds by this one
senseless episode.

Then a disaster of greater dimension had unraveled around
Reynolds' life, and the worst of it was that he had not realized until
the very last what was happening. He, who prided himself on his dis-
cernment, had been duped.

Reynolds served on many of the college's committees; the other
professors trusted his judgment, and he found this responsibility
satisfied his desire for human interaction. He had taught at the college

for over twenty years, and was known for his charity and equity; people confided in him. At the beginning of the summer, he was visited in his office at the college by a tall, strikingly attractive young woman named Lana Maccoby. Lana was a junior professor in the English department; she had a Ph.D. and a wonderfully warm way about her. She hadn't published much, but was working on a book of criticism of contemporary American women poets; and she was an excellent teacher. The students flocked to her courses. Reynolds was not in Lana's department, so he had never had cause to spend much time with her, but he supposed he liked her as well as he liked any human being, and thought she liked him.

When she entered his office on that muggy June morning, she was wearing jeans, rubber thongs, and a T-shirt with a picture of Miss Piggy on the front. She looked more like a student than a professor, and she was so pretty and pleasant to look at that it was a real shock when Reynolds realized that she had come to him for a serious reason.

"I need your help, Reynolds," she said. "I've just heard that the administration is going to make Sandra Tyroff chairman of the English department."

"Well," Reynolds said, leaning back in his typing chair, "someone has to be chairman." Only six weeks before, Maxwell Ellison, who had been chairman of the English department for years, had died of a heart attack. Reynolds was on the college committee on appointments and promotion; he was aware that a search committee had been formed to study possible candidates for the vacant chairmanship and to advise the president and Reynolds' committee of their recommendations.

"Yes, of course," Lana said, "but it shouldn't be Sandra Tyroff. You can't imagine. No one likes her; everyone is horrified that she has been suggested as a possible candidate."

"Well, you know we need a woman in a chair at this college," Reynolds said.

"No one believes that more than I do, Reynolds, but Sandra Tyroff is the wrong woman. She is unimaginative, tyrannical, dictatorial, to the point of insanity. No one in the department can deal with her. Reynolds, it will be a disaster if she runs the department."

"Why?" Reynolds said. "Give me some definite examples."

For the next three hours, Lana Maccoby gave Reynolds definite examples. She also gave him a list of names of other members of the department who had asked her to represent them in discussing this situation with him. Obviously, because of the nature of the problem, it was necessary to keep their discontent secret, because the wrongs that Sandra Tyroff had committed were of the subtle sort that slid snakelike through the department, leaving distrust and injury, but no telltale sign. There was no one deed of misbehavior that could disqualify her for the job. But there were so many devious, petty, arrogant acts that after hearing about her, Reynolds thought Sandra Tyroff sounded like one of the nastiest people he'd ever heard of.

Still he could not judge her on the word of one person; he spent the next month phoning and visiting other professors in the English department. The evidence built fraction by fraction. Sandra Tyroff had snubbed this person, slighted that person, listened to another professor's advice then done the opposite thing, taken credit for others' actions, accused unfairly, refused to listen. Hour after hour Reynolds sat in the homes of the junior professors, listening as they or their spouses spoke of indignities and injustices done to them by Sandra Tyroff. Because it was summer, various members of the department were off at different times on vacation, so Reynolds could not deal officially with the problem until early in September when the new semester began. He then sent out a memo, calling together a special session of the search committee and the committee on appointments and promotion. He spent a great deal of time and care on his agenda, but because he had never had any dealings with Sandra Tyroff himself, he had to rely on the professors in the English department to put forth their own case. He sent memos to everyone he had spoken with over the summer.

The meeting was held on a Thursday afternoon when the September sun was so warm and the day so clear that it mocked any kind of intellectual activity. How could all not be right with the world? But Reynolds worked himself up to a full stand of righteous indignation, and left the heat of the sun for the cool of the college building, because he meant to represent the people who had entrusted him with their fears and who relied on him to see justice done. He strode into the conflict, his shoulders stiff with rectitude.

Seated around the oval table were Sandra Tyroff, the chairman of the search committee, and various members of the committee on appointments and promotions. Not one member of the English department was present.

Reynolds sat down and looked at his watch. Too much was at stake for him to indulge in any comfortable small talk with anyone else in the room; that would mitigate the seriousness of this case. He looked at his watch again. After fifteen minutes, it became apparent that no members of the English department were going to arrive. Reynolds took his memo out of his briefcase and studied it: no, he had not printed the wrong date or time.

"I'm sorry, gentlemen, Miss Tyroff," he said at last. "It seems I've called you together for a meeting that for some reason is not taking place. Let me only ask you—any one of you—to do me the favor of going to Ms. Maccoby's room and asking her to come here. She was the one who began all this, and I'm amazed that she isn't here now. Either everyone in the English department has been killed in a bizarre series of accidents, or I've been abandoned."

Because he was smiling, speaking lightly, the others were relieved; a professor from the Philosophy department went off and returned with Lana Maccoby. She greeted everyone with friendly smiles, sank into a chair, and looked at Reynolds.

"Ms. Maccoby," Reynolds said, "would you please tell the committee why you object to Sandra Tyroff being named chairman of the English department?"

"Object? But I don't object," Lana said. She even looked surprised.

Reynolds was speechless for only a moment. "You mean you did not come to my office earlier this summer to ask me to help you prevent Ms. Tyroff from gaining the chairmanship of the department?"

"Why ever would I want to do a thing like that?" Lana asked.

"You are denying that you came to me on June 7, at ten o'clock in the morning, and spent three hours describing to me the various reasons that Sandra Tyroff should not be made chairman of the English department?"

Lana did not pause. "Of course I don't deny that I visited you one day in June in your office, although I must admit I can't pinpoint the time and date with the precision you've given it. But you must have completely misunderstood me. I didn't mean for anything I said to be misinterpreted as a vote of no-confidence in Ms. Tyroff."

Reynolds stared at Lana, then smiled. He felt like a fool in front of everyone there, but he knew he was not as much a fool in their eyes as he was in his own. He shut his briefcase.

"Ms. Tyroff, Mr. Carpenter, my colleagues," he said, "it seems there has been a mistake. I ask your forgiveness, and hope that you'll let this matter drop. Please forget that I ever called this group together."

"Well!" "Oh!" "Humm, yes!" people said, rising from their chairs with as much ado as if the chairs were physically hindering them. People left the room awkwardly, except for Lana Maccoby, who smiled graciously at everyone before she slid away. Reynolds approached Sandra Tyroff.

"I'm sorry about all of this," he said. "I don't know quite how to explain it to your satisfaction—"

"It's perfectly clear," Sandra Tyroff said. "Don't apologize for what you can't change. You're simply an old-guard, conservative, male chauvinist. You can't bear it that a woman will be made head of a department at this college that didn't even admit women when you started teaching here. Oh, I understand desperate measures like yours."

"My dear lady!" Reynolds began.

"I am not your dear lady," Sandra Tyroff said. "I am your equal."

With those words, she swept from the room, her sharp, pretty face held so high that Reynolds feared she might smash into the wall from lack of level vision.

He sat back down in his chair and folded his hands in front of him. His heart was thumping indecorously in his chest. Another professor sat down next to him; otherwise the room was empty. The door to the hall had not been closed by Ms. Tyroff when she left so that Reynolds sensed a vacant, looming quality in the air around him.

"I don't know what happened," Reynolds said to his friend.

"One of the facts that might have bearing on this case is that Ms. Tyroff was made vice-president of the American College English Association at their August convention," his friend said. "She'll be president automatically next year. She's powerful now—too powerful for anyone in her field to risk her enmity. I don't imagine anyone in this college will challenge her now."

"But why didn't anyone tell me?" Reynolds said. "I feel such an ass."

"Well," the other professor said, "I don't know. I don't think it was a malicious act, though, Reynolds. I suppose that some of the department members assumed that someone else—Lana, anyone else— would be passing the word on to you. Then, too, this has been a blow, I'm sure, to many of them. To be blunt, they need to save their skins. They must feel defeated, and cowardly, and confused."

"I don't feel cowardly," Reynolds said, rising. "But I certainly feel defeated."

In the days that followed, he asked various English department members, when he came across them casually, why they had not appeared at the meeting or at least let him know they were not intending to appear. They all said that they felt that their individual cases were not important enough to be aired publicly, that they had not realized how seriously Reynolds was taking it all, that they had assumed other members of the department would be there, that they had not realized. . . . He never did talk with Lana Maccoby again, because she proved efficient at avoiding him, and he could not bear to exacerbate the situation by calling her at her home. He could understand why she had backed out at the last minute, although he did not admire her for it; he thought people should stand by their principles, or what were principles for?

Sandra Tyroff was made chairman of the English department. Now Reynolds, who before the summer had been on friendly terms with everyone in the college, found himself avoided, even disliked, by an entire department. They were the cowards, the pretenders, but he had no proof. He felt like a man who had lost his home through a freakish act of nature.

And now, the knowledge of Ron Bennett's crime.

Now Reynolds stared out at the congregation that sat so raptly listening to Peter Taylor's sermon. There sat the Bennett family, their heads and shoulders forming a little scalloped set against the white wooden pew—how perfect they seemed. Reynolds had almost believed they were perfect, a whole family of perfect people, perfectly interacting; and he hated them for duping him. Yet it gave him no pleasure to know that before this day was over, their complacent lives would be shattered. The Bennetts would never know it, but they already had their revenge on Reynolds: they had ruined his life as much as he would ruin theirs.

He was in such despair now that he could no longer believe in God, or in man, or in his work. He could believe in nothing.

Now it was only October, and he was only fifty-four years old, yet when he looked out at his students as he talked to them in class, he did not see their youth and beauty, but instead the skulls beneath their shining hair, the greedy fangs behind the smiling lips, the perfidious hearts beating beneath the alligators on their socially accepted shirts.

He was impatient with students now. Just this week a timid young junior came to him to complain in a voice tight with fear that the head of the English department, Dr. Tyroff, was constantly treating her in an insulting and intimidating way. Was it possible, the girl wanted to know, for her to drop Dr. Tyroff's Shakespeare seminar and take something else?

"No," Reynolds said. "I won't let you drop the course. Go back and fight your way through it. This is not a nursery school. Whatever Dr. Tyroff is handing out to you is marshmallow fluff compared to what you're going to face in the rest of your life. Grow up. And don't come back to my office. You've got to handle this on your own."

The girl left, nearly in tears, and Reynolds could tell that she was not one of life's fighters. But he was past caring. Let Sandra Tyroff destroy the girl—he didn't care. And once he had articulated those words to himself, he knew he had lost the meaning of his life. He would have to stop teaching for a while; he could not teach if he did not care.

Reynolds had applied for a sabbatical. At the middle of December, as soon as the first semester ended, he would be leaving Londonton. He was going to rent an apartment in Seattle, because he knew no one who lived there, and it was a big enough city so that he wouldn't have to become friendly with anyone. Also, it was on the other side of the continent. If he liked Seattle, he thought he might just move there, and leave his tenured post at the college.

He would also stop attending church. He could no longer be satisfied with the teachings of the church. There were still times in the days of his life when the sight of people walking under trees or when a fresh breeze swiftly skimming through an opened window, rippling the papers on his desk, would make him aware of some sublimity in the world. It had to be explained somehow. Life had to be explained somehow. But he did not any longer think it could be explained through Christianity.

The idea of Christian perfection was wrong, impossible. Reynolds knew that now. Man could never be perfect, the world was not perfect, and so God could not be perfect. The workings of the human eye were signs of everyday miracles and such miracles could not be denied. But neither could the Holocaust, the Inquisition, or the Peloponnesian War; neither could cancer, famine, or greed. The world was flawed. It was a beautiful, ornate, revolving bowl that had been cracked from its conception in the hands of a flawed maker, and everything within it reflected inescapably that basic, deep, ineradicable imperfection.

So this was the last time Reynolds would attend a Christian church. It occurred to him that if he gave up teaching and churchgoing both he would isolate himself from his fellow man. But he was too tired, just now, to think of any other way to live. He had no reserves left. He knew that most people lived their lives by performing a delicate psychological operation: they lifted themselves daintily from the sordid world and set themselves apart, so that whether they smiled or cried depended entirely upon the singular events of their individual day. Reynolds had never learned that trick. And so he was defeated . . . by the young boy who cheated, by Lana Maccoby, by Ron Bennett.

The ushers were passing out the collection plates; the service was almost over. Reynolds rose with the others to sing the Doxology: "Praise God from whom all blessings flow. Praise him all creatures here below. Praise him above Ye heavenly hosts. Praise Father, Son, and Holy Ghost."

He no longer believed the words he was singing, but this did not bother him now. It did not matter. Nothing much mattered.

AMANDA FINDLY

Why did Mother have to sit *here*?

It's lovely being home for the weekend, lovely coming to church with Mother just as always. But why did she choose to sit up here on the fifth row from the front? Michael always sits in back!

Well, it's not Mother's fault; she doesn't know about Michael. I didn't see him when we came in, and I can't very well turn around now, crane around looking past everyone else to search him out. There are so many people here today that he might not even see me in the crowd, especially since he doesn't know I'm home. I should have called. But I promised myself I wouldn't—wouldn't call him, wouldn't write him, would wait until *he* contacted me. Damn. Oh, damn.

And it's hard sitting here so close to Reverend Taylor, practically right up under his nose. I'm trying to look respectable, but all I can think of is his son. His first son, who is my first lover. It makes me smile to see Mr. Taylor, looking so pure and pious behind the pulpit in his black robe, as if sex wouldn't dare enter the atmosphere he inhabits. And all the while his own son is to sex what champagne is to wine.

At least, he is to me.

I've been away at college for just six weeks, but it might as well have been six years. I feel so much older. Ages older. You couldn't tell it from looking at me, but I've got an old mind hiding in this eighteen-year-old body. What does it mean that Michael is a year younger than I am, that I'm eighteen and he's only seventeen? I *thought* it meant

that we were too young really to be in love. Too young really to be in
love—that sounds like a bad song. I think it *was* a bad song.

There's no way I can sit in this church, looking at Mr. Taylor, and
not think of Michael. Of course it seems there's no way I can be anywhere and not think of Michael, but it's especially difficult when Mr.
Taylor looks so much like Michael. Or, I suppose it's that Michael
looks like Mr. Taylor, since Mr. Taylor came first. They are amazingly
good-looking: tall, slender, dark-haired, blue-eyed. Michael is so handsome that I don't think I could have made love with him if he weren't
a year younger than I am; I needed to feel that slight edge of superiority that age gives, to balance out the advantage his good looks give
him. I'm pretty enough, with blond hair and a slim enough figure, I'm
not worried about myself, I'm *fine*. But Michael is extraordinary. Although now that I've been away from him for six weeks, it's not his
looks that I remember and miss, but Michael himself: the *feeling* of
him. He is like a vein of marble hiding in a mountain: quiet, glisten-
ing, vivid, inviolate. I could never capture him with my sculptures. I
could never capture Michael with *one* sculpture. But I can envision
sculpting him again and again and again, each time never quite captur-
ing his essence, but each time creating a work I love.

I did not ever think so much would come of it.

Because Michael is younger than I am, I never had paid much attention to him until this summer at a church picnic. I spent all summer waitressing at a local restaurant, making money for college, all my
thoughts aimed into the future. That Sunday I had gone along to the
church picnic partly out of boredom, partly to please Mother. I messed
around with the little kids, tending them so their parents could social-
ize in peace. I like children, and I had baby-sat for most of these children at one time or another over the past few years. It was a hot day
for June, clear and bright, and I was wearing short shorts and not
thinking at all about myself and how I looked. No one that mattered to
me was around. I bent over to pick up a little boy who'd just tripped,
and when I stood back up, I saw Michael Taylor staring at me.

He was several yards away, alone, separate from everyone else,
leaning against a tree, looking a little bored and disdainful. Our eyes
met, and something about the way he looked at me made me quickly
glance down at my blouse—for an instant I was afraid that the buttons
had come undone and my bra was showing. His look was a look that

made me feel that way. I fiddled around with the toddlers some more, and when I casually looked back at him, he was still staring at me.

I grew up here in Londonton, and the Taylors moved here a long time ago, so I've sort of known Michael for about ten years, I guess. He's been as insignificantly indigenous as the Blue River or the college buildings. This summer I had caught glimpses of him around town from time to time; I had thought, "There's Michael Taylor, working for the landscape company." He was always working shirtless, sweating, trimming hedges, shoveling, mowing the grass on gracious lawns. I knew he was around, but on the eleventh day of this June, it was as if I were seeing him for the first time.

I stood there, patting a baby against my shoulder, and I met Michael Taylor's stare without embarrassment—although it was a comfort having that baby there as a shield; I'll bet she's never been patted so hard in her life.

I think I fell in love with him right then. I certainly desired him, and that desire was as strong and clear and certain as a light coming on in a dark room. I really don't understand why they don't talk more about sex in the Bible; we are raised to want to be *good*, and to believe we can control our lives and our actions, but I'll tell you, when I stood there looking into Michael's eyes, I had as much control over my future as if I'd been tied down to a railroad track in front of an onrushing train. Why don't we admit it? Sex has nothing to do with the wills of human beings. It's a sort of universal law of physical energy exchange, and human beings are just the helpless transformers or converters. I have a theory—which will never be tested—that if everyone in the world refrained from sex simultaneously for five minutes, in those five minutes the earth would fly apart, or fall out of orbit, or stop spinning. The energy of the earth is sexual, there's no doubt about it. Of course I wasn't thinking these things when I looked at Michael Taylor; I was just thinking: *well*. And then, why not? After all, he's a year younger than I am, and I'm going off to college in two months, so if it turns out to be awful, I won't have to see him every day. I was wondering how in the world I was going to make a date with him tactfully—we hadn't said over ten consecutive words to each other in years—when he strolled over and said to me, "Let's go for a walk by the river later. Okay? I'll meet you at seven by the bridge."

"Okay," I said, and before I could say anything else, he walked away.

I didn't tell Mother or anyone else where I was going. Michael Taylor, the *minister's* son, and a year younger than I—what could I want with him?

Yet when I saw him walking toward me through the high grass near the bridge I was overwhelmed by the magnitude of my blindness in the past. How had I lived in the same town with this boy and not *seen* him? For he was beautiful, beautiful, tall, and sexy.

We walked along the river, talking in a kind of daze about our summer plans, where I was going to college, little things. Before long we were out past the Mt. Grace Dairy, sitting by the river under an overarching stretch of willows. By then the sky was growing violet, and the willows formed a cave of shadowy light around us.

We sat on the soft grassy bank, tossing rocks into the water, almost not talking, but comfortable together. After a while Michael leaned over and kissed me. He took my shoulders in his hands and held me firmly while he kissed first my neck, then my chest, my breasts, my arms. Then we eased down onto the ground and he lay on top of me, kissing me while his hands moved and lingered. Russian hands and Roman fingers, I thought of the old joke at first, and then I thought: How can a minister's son be so sexy? I wondered if I should tell him that I had never made love with anyone before, but I was afraid that if I did tell him that, he would stop. So I said nothing. I just kissed him back.

I kissed him and kissed him. I wrapped my arms around him, I ran my hands down his long back. Almost without being conscious of it, we took off our clothes, bit by bit, they had become impediments. What a surprising luxury it was—a multitude of delirious sensations shot through me. I could feel the swirl of grass under my back and legs, and the more delicate, intricate prickle and press of Michael's thighs and arms and chest against my smooth skin. No sooner would his sweet mouth leave my breasts or neck or face wet with kissing than that spot would be dried by his warm breath as he exhaled, whispering, "Oh. Amanda."

What stuff the skin is—seeming to be smooth, all of a piece, and yet it is shimmering, electric, and multiplex. My body felt like the control panel on a spaceship, with lights flashing in every imaginable rhythm and hue. When Michael came into me, I gasped and for a moment I was afraid: this was all new. "Oh," I said, and Michael answered, "Oh," smiling down at me. So I held on to him and let him lead, lift, carry me on our lilting voyage out of this earth, yet centered in my body and Michael's and our bodies joined. Yes, Einstein, there is another dimension, and I know what it is.

We went on and on together until Michael suddenly hunched up, dug his face into my shoulder, and moaned. I understood what had happened, yet was disappointed. I almost cried—I didn't want it to end!

And it didn't. We lay side by side for a while, whispering, then we started all over again.

It was almost midnight when we walked back toward town, following the gleam of starlight reflected in the river. We walked with our arms around each other, leaning against each other, tired, not talking. When we got to the bridge, he kissed me softly and said, "Same time tomorrow night?" I said yes, and walked home, smiling. That we would be able to do the next night what we had just done—that we might have an entire summer of such nights!—made me want to spin cartwheels in the street. I wanted to shout, "Thank God I'm alive!"

When I got home, I called out to Mother that I was there, and she called back, "Good. Now I can go to sleep." I saw the light in her bedroom flick off. I thought about taking a bath, but I didn't want to wash off any of the lingering sensations from my skin. So I just took off my clothes, and crawled into bed and lay there hugging myself. I could hardly sleep, I was so excited. I had learned from experience that masturbation can provide a quick, vivid, tense explosion of pleasure, like a shot from a gun, but I had not been prepared at all for what I had experienced with Michael. And it seemed to me as I thought about it that what we mean by sex is simply happiness, the kind that meanders and blossoms and unrolls over us and in us all at once, leaving us flushed and calm and grateful.

I could not sleep all night, I was so happy—about what had happened, about what would happen. I'm still dazzled by the knowledge that no matter what unkindnesses life doles out, it also has provided us all, in advance, with this miraculous source of pleasure. It seems a decent gesture on life's behalf, magnanimous and democratic, the best and most exquisite gift.

We spent almost every night together for two months. We walked along the river or went off in his car, or occasionally, when Mother was out, knew the luxury of my big soft bed. Michael had a job with a local landscape contractor and spent his days working in the sun. I spent my days inside, waitressing. I worked from seven in the morning till three in the afternoon, when I would rush home, put on my bathing suit, and sit out in the sun with a book and a glass of iced tea. But some days it rained, or there were errands to do, and I never did manage to get a good tan. It only mattered because I felt like such a pale, cool creature next to Michael; but when Michael lowered his brown body over mine, it was like the sun coming out all over me. His skin was browner, more glowing with the day's heat with each passing day; oh, how I welcomed that warmth! When I slid my arms around his body, it seemed I could feel precisely how the muscles of his back and arms grew firmer, more substantial, as the days passed. At times I felt almost maternal, as if I could sense that here was a boy changing, even as I held him, into a man.

I loved his body. I loved it. I loved the feel of his body against mine. I ran my hands over him, over his back, arms, chest, legs. I cradled his sex. I longed for clay and stone, to sculpt a permanent reproduction of this masculine perfection. And I dreamed of new, uncaptured shapes. Could I ever express in tangible materials this pure, easy, complete, sensual happiness that seemed to bloom out from us into the air? What form would it take? Would it be rounded, burgeoning, and complicated, like a braid? I would sand and polish the surface to a silky fluidity. For we did glow, Michael and I, with the pleasure of ourselves. It seemed that sometimes we coalesced with our heat, like two different metals, into a new and shining mass.

Afterward, Michael would roll onto the ground next to me, and we would lie there, holding hands, panting. Sweat shimmered on our skin, and as it disappeared into the cooling air, we watched the leaves above our heads grow dappled with the failing light, then gray, then seem to vanish completely, as if night had dropped a curtain: so the world arched above us deep and soft.

When we were together by the river, or in bed, we seldom talked, except in that funny, intimate language that lovers use about parts of the body and what we're doing with them. Yet there was no awkwardness between us. Michael taught me how to enjoy silence, and I was glad for this, because like a blind person whose other senses expand and heighten, I found myself luxuriating in a clearer, more complete physicality once I stopped searching for and using words. At times, as I walked along the river, my arm wrapped around Michael, his arm enclosing me, I pictured myself as some kind of fruit: blunt, plump, dumb, juicy. I wanted nothing more.

Yet I often wish now that I had spent more time talking with Michael. In many ways I don't know him. He hides himself. He is aware that there is a black streak bred into him, like a vein of black running through a block of marble, and it frightens him. It worries me. He is smart, so smart that he has achieved cynicism young. He is handsome, much loved by his parents, lucky in the world, and yet he is angry at himself and those who love him. He feels they are forcing him into a mold he cannot fit. In this we differ: his parents are ultra-traditional, mine are divorced, and ultra-flaky. I think I prefer my parents, perhaps because they aren't quite so certain of what is True and Good and Right. Michael feels so pressured by his family, by their very love. Talking about them sets off a gloomy stain that darkens his face and our life. When we were alone together along the river, that black streak always receded, and all that rich intensity became sexual. That was what I wanted.

But now I wish I had talked to him more, drawn him out more, because I keep thinking of him while I'm at college. I keep thinking of not just his body and the pleasures it brought, but of him, Michael, the person. He is more important to me than I thought—it may be that I love him.

We parted so casually. That last night together, he walked me back to my house around midnight—I had to leave early the next morning—and stood there with his hand on my arm, just below my shoulder. It was not childish, not a simple holding of hands. It was a grownup gesture, an unconscious gesture of detainment. But why couldn't we speak of it? We said so little. We were such fools.

"Well, write me."

"Okay. And you write me. I gave you my address."

"Okay. Well, have fun."

"You too. Goodbye."

Then he was gone. I went inside, leaned against the front door and thought: *Stop it!* Stop feeling this way! He is *seventeen* years old!

He's a *kid! You're* a kid. Call him your first love, call him your summer love, but don't fool yourself by thinking he's anything more. Go to college. Sleep around.

Well, I have—and here I am, back home, certain that Michael is what I want.

But does he want me—and in the same serious way?

I suppose I should talk with Mother about this. We've always been so close. I could always talk with her about anything. About sex, for instance. We've discussed sex. When I was a little kid, Mother was determined that I would not grow up thinking that sex was something dirty or terrifying. Once in the third grade a friend of mine started teaching me "dirty words." Mother fought fire with fire. She made up a little song, with my help, that we used to sing occasionally on road trips or on housecleaning binges. It went:

> *Does your vagina come from Virginia,*
> *Does your penis come from France,*
> *Do your ewes have uteruses,*
> *Is there a scrotum in your pants?*
> *BOOBIES BREASTS NIPPLES BALLS!*
> *SPERM OVARIES DECK THE HALLS!*

By the time I was nine, Mother had told me all about menstrual periods, masturbation, the function and appearance of every bit of male and female reproductive apparatus, childbirth, contraception, abortion, social disease, and slang sexual words. I was a veritable storehouse of information, and consequently I was very popular and self-confident. I could make myself the focal point of a group of kids at any moment I chose, simply by quietly revealing the secret of whatever word or fact seemed mysterious at that point. When I was fourteen, however, I was quickly relegated to second place by Katie Potter, who was *doing* it instead of just talking about it. Katie was admired and envied by many, including me. It's one thing to talk about sex and giggle about it, and quite another to be alone in a dark basement rec room with a warm living human boy. In spite of all my knowledge, I was terrified. I knew that if I had sex, I would get pregnant, or get syphilis, or herpes, or I'd ruin my reputation, or worst of all, I'd take off my pants, and the boy would look at me, burst out laughing, and tell me that some part of me was absurdly misplaced. So it wasn't until this summer with Michael that I actually knew what all the talk was about.

When I turned sixteen, Mother said to me, "Mandy, I've told Dr. Laughlin that he has my permission to prescribe birth-control pills for you whenever you ask. And he is not to inform me that you've asked for them. I want to give you your privacy in this particular matter. Of course you know I hope you won't take the pill—it can have bad side effects; we've been through all this. On the other hand, I hope you will take the pill if you start"—and here my own mother, who had sung that crazy sex song when I was little, began to fidget around for the proper word, as if we had never discussed sex before in our lives—"sleeping with someone. In any case, it's up to you; Lord knows I've told you everything I know."

The first few nights when I came home at midnight from being with Michael, I felt that the scent of sexual satisfaction must have preceded me by a good hundred feet, broadcasting the news of my activities to any adult or animal in the area. Each night I would call up to Mother that I was home, and each night she would say, "Good. I'm glad you're safe. I'm going to sleep." Once, after about two weeks of this, she said, "You're staying out awfully late awfully often. I hope you're not falling asleep at your job." I reassured her that, on the contrary, I was a powerhouse of energy; she looked at me sharply for a minute, then left the room, muttering that she had to make a note about something.

One rainy afternoon when the restaurant was closed and I had the day off, I scrounged around in Mother's record collection and found an old Kingston Trio album. One song seemed to have been written for me. It was about two lovers who walk along the Seine at night, and after I found the record, whenever I did the dishes or cleaned house, I found myself humming, "When will I again, meet him there, greet him there, on the moonlit banks of the Seine."

But Mother never did say, as I expected her to, "Why on earth are you mooning about this way? Where do you go every night?" She just continued to wait up, call out good night, say she was glad I was safely home. Because she didn't question me, I grew shy about the subject. And what happened, what continued to happen, between me and Michael seemed so extravagant, so *extreme*. It was so much more than

I expected. I didn't know how to explain it to Mother properly. I was afraid to say, even to myself: I think Michael and I are in love.

I should talk to Mother now. Maybe she can help. She's always helped before, in her own way. At the beginning of the summer, before I started seeing Michael, a weird thing happened, and if I hadn't been able to talk to Mother, I'm not sure how I would have sorted it out.

I was asked to baby-sit the first Saturday night in May for the Halsteads. The Halsteads really are crazy people. When Dr. Halstead moved to town and bought the huge stone house on Cherry Street, he had a beautiful sign painted and hung on the end of his driveway, announcing that he had named his house Bedside Manor. Mrs. Halstead and Mrs. Moyer are good friends, and for Mrs. Moyer's birthday, Mrs. Halstead made Dr. Halstead sleep at the Moyers' house so she could have a huge party for Mrs. Moyer. I had to take Nina and Nicholas Halstead, who are old kids, eleven and twelve, to a movie, because I can drive, and I was supposed to keep them out as long as possible, then bring them up the back stairs of the house and stay with them until I was sure they were sound asleep. Because Mrs. Halstead gave Mrs. Moyer a surprise she didn't want her kids to know about. What a surprise—a male stripper!

Mrs. Moyer isn't the kind of woman who would ordinarily appreciate a male stripper, or at least I didn't think she was, but then I know most of the women who were at that party, I've baby-sat for them over the years, and I never saw any of them act the way they did that night. Mrs. Vanderson was there, which wasn't surprising, because she loves parties so much, and Mrs. Aranguren was there, and Mrs. Bennett (she was the only one who didn't act like a fool), and of course Mrs. Moyer and Mrs. Halstead, and about five other women I've never baby-sat for. They started the evening with a buffet supper and champagne—when I arrived to pick up the kids for the movie, I saw two cases of champagne in the kitchen, and by eleven o'clock, when I returned to put the kids to bed, most of the bottles were empty. As I went up the stairs to put the kids to bed, I heard the women laughing, and I shook my head thinking how awful they were all going to feel the next morning.

I wasn't sure what to do after I got Nina and Nicholas to bed. They fell asleep right away, in spite of the laughter coming from downstairs. I sat in Nina's room for a long time, wondering how to slip out without bothering anyone.

Finally I came out of Nina's room and walked down the hall to the stairs, and bumped right into the stripper. He was gorgeous, and he was wearing a skintight black tux with no shirt and a gold lamé bow tie. He couldn't have been much older than I was, perhaps he was twenty-two, and he looked shocked and embarrassed to see me in the hall.

"I'm the baby-sitter," I said, trying to be polite.

"Well, I'm the stripper," he replied, and grinned. "It's an easy way to make a buck," he added.

"I suppose," I replied, although what did I know about it all?

We stood there for a moment longer, insulated by the thick carpeting and the elegantly papered walls, while the women's laughter rose up the stairs and curled around us.

"Well," he said, grinning again, "I guess I'd better go do my act."

He walked away from me and flicked the light switch at the top of the stairs, giving Mrs. Halstead a signal, and she started the music. It was that old da-da-*dah* stripper music from *Gypsy,* and that boy did such a sexy entrance down the stairs that I'm surprised the banister didn't melt.

I knelt in the corner of the upstairs hall, where I could peek around and watch the show. No one saw me, and they were all too drunk and wound up to care if they had. So I got to watch the guy do his act.

He was good. But I also saw the faces of the women watching him, and I wish I hadn't. It made me sad. All those women, in their *forties.* I thought it was pathetic that they were so interested in a boy's body. Surely, I thought, they were past all that.

As soon as the stripper music ended, some disco records came on, and that guy could really move; he was *fabulous.* In the first place he was actually a fine graceful dancer. But of course there was more than that. He was sexy. When he started doing bumps and grinds and taking off his clothes, I stopped looking at the women's faces. And he flirted with the women, as if he thought they were all unbearably attractive. I don't know how he stood it. I thought they all looked stupid; I was embarrassed for them. They laughed and clapped and whistled and yelled, "Take it off! Take it all off!" And he did.

In the most tantalizing way possible, he took off his jacket, cummerbund, trousers, shoes, and socks, until he was out there dancing in front of them in nothing but a gold lamé bow tie and a gold lamé jockstrap. In spite of myself, I was fascinated.

Then Mrs. Moyer said, "Honey, I'll give you fifty dollars to take that off," pointing at the jockstrap. I nearly fell down the stairs in shock. Mrs. Moyer, who's always campaigning for politicians and being serious about local issues! The stripper told her, teasing, slowly moving his hips as he talked, that he couldn't take off that last piece of clothing; it wasn't part of the act. However, he could be raffled off at the end of the act. The money would be split—half would go to him, half to Mrs. Moyer for her birthday present. Whoever won him could go into the guest bedroom and have him at her service for three hours.

The women laughed nervously at that—but something different was in their laughter then, and although Mrs. Halstead was doing a great job acting like an auctioneer and making the raffle one big comedy act, some of those women got deadly serious during the bidding. Well, I wasn't even drunk, and I hadn't made love with anyone yet, and I still couldn't help but wish I could enter the bidding, too. He was so sexy. But of course I didn't have any money, not *that* kind of money. I was relieved to see Mrs. Bennett, who up till then had been laughing too but generally seemed embarrassed, lean back in her chair with a look of disapproval on her face. She didn't bid even once, which made me glad, because I've always admired Mrs. Bennett. The highest bidder was Mrs. Aranguren, who is so exotic-looking that I couldn't imagine her ever *bidding* for sex, but she paid three hundred dollars. She didn't look the slightest bit ashamed when she went up the stairs with the boy's arm around her waist. In fact, she gave everyone in the living room a big grin and wave, and yelled, "Eat your hearts out!"

I had to scurry off to the back stairs which led down to the kitchen so that Mrs. Aranguren and the stripper didn't see me when they reached the second floor. They went into the guest bedroom and shut the door and I never did hear another thing about it.

I went down into the kitchen, where Mrs. Halstead was starting to make coffee, and she asked me, since I was still there anyway, to help clean up the mess. And it *was* a mess. But I got to hear the women discussing the stripper. Some of them were pretending it was all an intellectual or political coup: women's lib. Mrs. Moyer said it was great that they had got to yell "Take it all off" and "Let's see your buns and boobies" to a man. But some of the other women were sad. One woman, whom I was glad I didn't know, cried, "I'll never see such a handsome male naked again in my life. I hate getting old!" She sat down, or rather fell down, into a chair and bawled until another woman sort of carried her out to a car and drove her home.

I never dreamed that sort of thing could happen here in Londonton, and in fact Mrs. Halstead told me she had had to import the stripper from a bar in Southmark. She didn't say how much he cost, but she indicated that he was pretty expensive. I helped her clean up the kitchen, and then I drove home, feeling stunned and depressed.

Mother was waiting up for me as she always does, sitting in bed reading. When I came in, she called out for me to come in and say good night. She patted the bed next to her, and I plopped down with my head on a pillow and talked to her the way I have so often done after a night out. I told her about the party, every detail, and we both got to laughing so hard that Mother nearly fell out of bed.

"How wonderful!" she whooped. "I told you that under the beautiful surface of this town there lies a hotbed of depravity and vice!"

"But you know," I said, "Mother . . . it makes me feel a little *sad*, and I'm not sure why. The thought of those old women leching after that young man. Mrs. Moyer, Mrs. Halstead—they have children. Mrs. Moyer and Mrs. Bennett have children almost as old as that stripper. Seeing them look at that guy that way makes me feel sick. And sad."

Mother stopped laughing then, and just looked at me for a minute. She smiled, but her eyes went serious. "Loss of innocence," she said. Then she did something she hadn't done for a long time. She reach out and pulled me up against her, and as she talked she held me as if I were still a child, and stroked my arm.

"You're so young," she began, and I said my usual "Oh, *Mother*." But she went on. "I mean you're young enough to still believe the best of people, and seeing below the surface makes you sad. Innocence is bliss, and all that. But, Mandy, those women aren't bad or even pathetic because they liked watching that male stripper. Women in their forties are just as much sexual creatures as young women, maybe even more so. And thank heavens for it. We older women have the same desires—just not the same opportunities. Desire, my darling, goes on and on, even when youth fades. You'll learn all this in your own good time, but for now, don't judge older women, those women, too harshly. You're young and lovely, everything is on your side—so be kind. Let us old women have a turn at enjoying the sight of young men's bodies."

As Mother spoke, she kept her arm wrapped about me, and held my arm in hers, and in her absentminded, almost oblivious way, she traced circles on my inner wrist with her thumb. It was a sweet caress, and now as I sit here in this church, I am aware of Mother, sitting only inches from me, her hands folded quietly in her lap. It is unusual, that quietness, for her hands are seldom still, always working on her pottery.

Over the years I have watched her hands shape a multitude of vases, bowls, cups, and figures on her pottery wheel, so that when I think of Mother, I first envision her articulate hands. When I was little, and sat with her through concerts or speeches or church services on days when there was no Sunday school, I used to play little games with her hands. I would slide her rings off and try them on all her fingers; I would open and close her fingers in contrived patterns. Little nonsense games, just keeping in touch with my mother. Now I am too old to do such things. I'm nineteen, and I wouldn't dare sit playing with my mother's hands in church. Still, I sometimes think I would like to hold her hand again.

It seems to me that there is nothing like the flesh for telling. The skin's silent eloquence is more powerful than a million spoken words. I think of the few boys with whom I have in various ways made love—and especially I think of Michael. We are often so clumsy. I'm eager to grow older, for surely as I do I will learn more grace and control in touching. Now Mother reaches in her purse for the envelope which contains the church offering; her arm grazes mine, and I feel the familiar comfort of it. I sit firm, I don't tighten up. She is my mother and her flesh is familiar. I remember in an instant the back rubs she gave me when I was sick, the times she knelt to draw me to her to console me when I was sad, the brisk competent gestures with which she fixed my dress or brushed my hair when I was small. We seldom touch that way anymore; we seldom touch at all now. I'd be embarrassed to take her arm in public. But I'm eager for new and different embraces from others, to take the place of those I'm leaving. I'm yearning for Michael's touch above all. And I'm longing to continue my work with clay, to see if I can, with my own hands, mold that clay into some kind of celebration of all the touching I have known.

I want to be a sculptor. I'm going to be a sculptor.

I'm afraid to tell my parents of my decision. They'll be alarmed. Since their divorce, my parents have not trusted each other. Daddy will think Mother has exerted some kind of influence over me, making me want to become a sculptor because she's a potter. Mother will just be furious—because the influence she's wanted to exert over me hasn't worked. She has never wanted me to live an "artistic" life, because her own life has been so hard. She will think I'm dooming myself to a lifetime of poverty, solitude, and eccentricity as a potter, and she's always yearned for me to be normal. She wants me to have a career as a teacher or a file clerk, something easily set aside while I have children so that I can hold a marriage together. She doesn't want me to be overwhelmed and driven by my work. But I have to be a sculptor; I can't help it. I look about this church and feel drawn by the beauty of all these human bodies. There is such adroitness in the ways arms and legs angle, bend, and flex. There is such a fine reciprocity between muscles and skin. When I talk to people, I am usually tongue-tied, or bored, or embarrassed by the banalities we exchange, but if I could learn to shape clay skillfully enough, I could show them how beautiful they are, and how I love them in my own way.

I know I have a talent for sculpting, too. My art teacher at college has told me so, and I can't think why he would lie. It's going to be rough at the end of the semester when Mother sees my grades and realizes that I dropped anthropology and took sculpting instead, in addition to my other art courses. But I don't even care if I get a degree, I just want the art courses. If only I can make Mother understand.

Earlier in this service, I watched Priscilla and Seth Blair leaning up against their mother, and I envied them their innocence and dependence. Mrs. Blair and her children incline toward each other in all their movements, with the natural interdependence of a family. They seem to have nothing to hide from one another. But that will change as they grow older; it always does. Still, I envied them this morning, and wished for that childhood relationship with my mother, that comfortable trust. I wish I could tell my mother I'm going to be a sculptor—if I had when I was little, she would have laughed and bought me a set of modeling clay. But in the past few years she has often said to me when I brought home good grades from art class that she'd rather I got pregnant at sixteen by a sailor than become an artist. Why does she say such things to me? Why does she think she knows what's best for me? She might have had a tough life, but we are two different people. She's willing to tutor and encourage other kids who want to learn how to pot or sculpt—why can't she encourage me? It's the damned words, I think. Mrs. Blair protects her children's bodies with her own, but as they grow, the tactile safeguards will disappear, and she'll protect and direct them with words. And it will all get screwed up. I love my mother and I know she loves me, but touching is so simple and true, and words are so complicated and often misunderstood. When Mother and I talk for any length of time about my future, about my art, we invariably end up disagreeing.

I want her to give me her blessing; I want her to let me be a sculptor. I need her. She was so wonderful this weekend when I came home all in tears.

At college I was determined to forget Michael, to date older, more sophisticated boys, to have lots of fun. And in six weeks I had three relationships—none of them glorious.

The first boy I dated and slept with was a smooth-talking senior. I was impressed that he paid attention to me, a freshman, but it was stupid of me to be so thrilled, because his only interest in me was as a fresh body. Screwing was, for him, like putting another notch on a gun. I found out too late that he was trying to set some kind of record before he graduated. I was more relieved than hurt when I discovered all this, because it explained why having sex with him was so much like taking my driver's test had been: a quick run-through with an impatient partner.

The second boy I met in my freshman comp. class. He was cute and clever and witty, and I thought we might become a couple for a while, because we enjoyed each other so much. We dated for a month, and got along well, laughed together, had fun. But he seemed alarmed instead of pleased when I said I would sleep with him—*he* asked, so why did he seem amazed and upset when I said yes? We went to his room just one time, for he lost his sense of humor and wit. He fumbled and bumbled and practically came in his pants and neither one of us had much fun. After that one night he avoided me. Now he even sits on the other side of class. I can't get him to talk to me. I'm beginning to see that sex is a complicated matter, and I'm even more grateful for the ease I had with Michael.

The third boy I slept with at college is the reason I came home. At least he's one of the reasons I drove home this weekend. Or perhaps it's Paula Barry's fault as much as Chad Bawden's. Well, of course, part of the fault is mine.

Paula is going to be an art major; we have a lot in common, live in the same dorm. We have—had—an instant friendship, learned to confide in each other, to turn to each other when we wanted to celebrate or talk. So she knew about all the boys I dated, and she knew about the crush I had on Chad Bawden.

Chad's a junior, a history major, and a basketball star. And he's *nice.* He's one of those rare men who can handle being handsome, popular, and a good jock without getting snobbish. He's easy to be quiet with, and that quality reminded me of Michael. I smiled at him until he asked me if I wanted to join him for a Coke, and I flirted with him over the Coke until he asked me to go to the movies. Part of the delight of it all was talking with Paula about it later. "Can you imagine!" I would say to Paula, smug with accomplishment. "I *saw* Chad, and I wanted to get him to date me, and I *did* it!" It was such fun listing each of Chad's enviable qualities to Paula: his wealthy parents, admirable background, good grades, athletic honors, his easy kindness, his easy laughter. Chad was right for me. He was the person I should have fallen in love with, and I wanted very much to fall in love with him. On our fourth date, we slept together in his apartment off-campus. We actually *slept* there, after making love, and woke up with each other in the morning. He brought me coffee in a cracked mug and told me I looked beautiful there in his messy bed, and I burst into tears which I could not explain to him or to myself. Why did I feel so bad when I had gotten what I wanted? Why did I wish that instead of being with this nice, acceptable man, I wanted to be with taciturn, difficult Michael—Michael, a *kid!* I drank my coffee and reached my arms out to Chad, determined to love this lovable man.

I'll never know if it would have worked. For two weeks, we spent most of our time together. But Thursday my art teacher told me after class he wanted me to come back at four to discuss my project with him, and of course I agreed; I was excited by his special attention. I had told Chad I'd meet him at the deli at four, and I had no way to call him, so I asked Paula to go to the deli to tell him I'd be late. I had a great meeting with my art professor, who thinks I might be able to do something really fine, and I practically flew to the deli afterward. What a brilliant fall day it was—crisp, clear, sunny—one of those days when I feel the world has been created just to make a place for me to be alive in.

When I got to the deli, no one I knew was there. I went back to the dorm, and Chad wasn't there. Neither was Paula. I waited around, feeling more and more whiny, and dinnertime came and I didn't hear from Chad, and night came and Paula didn't return to the dorm. I could hardly sleep that night, I was so suspicious—and my suspicions were correct. The next day Paula came into my room, glowing and pathetic with guilt. She told me she was in love with Chad and he was in love with her.

"I don't know how it happened," she said. "I told him you'd be late, so we sat down to drink a Coke while he waited—and things just happened."

I suppose if I'd really been in love with him I would have been too hurt to confront him, but as it was, I was more angry than anything else. So when I passed him in the hall that afternoon, I stopped him.

"Hey," I said, "what happened?"

"What do you mean?" he asked, looking embarrassed.

"I *mean*, why didn't you wait for me?"

Chad looked truly puzzled. "Paula said you weren't coming," he said. "She said you had a date with someone else, someone important. She said—I thought—she said that now that you were seeing this other guy, I shouldn't count on seeing you anymore. You sent her to—let me down easy."

What could I have done? Yelled, "Paula is a liar"? I was so hurt and angry that I could only turn and walk away.

Later, as I was walking to my dorm, I saw Paula come out, and she couldn't stop smiling. Chad was on the steps waiting for her; he bent to give her a quick kiss, then they walked off, holding hands.

I skipped my last class, threw my stuff in the car, and drove the hour's drive home as fast as I could. Everything else faded in importance before this event, this double betrayal, and I couldn't decide which was worse: Chad's dropping me so easily for Paula, or Paula's betraying me by lying to get him.

And at the very back of my mind, tempting as a fragrance, was the knowledge of Michael. Home was where Mother was, but home was also where Michael was.

Thank God Mother was home when I arrived. It was five o'clock when I burst unexpected into the house. Mother was sitting in her jeans and sweater in the living room, reading the newspaper. She took one look at me and rose up from the sofa, letting the paper scatter.

"Why, darling," she said, "what's wrong?"

That little overture of sympathy was all it took for me to burst into tears, and I raced to the sofa and collapsed in her arms. I told her all about Chad and me and Paula.

"I don't want to go back to college," I said. "I can't stand the thought of living in that place. Every day I'd have to see Paula and Chad mooning around with each other. Every day I'd be reminded of— of everything. She *lied*. How could she *do* that when she knew how I felt about him? How could *he* do that when we'd been so close? Oh, I hate them both. Mom, I really don't want to go back there. I want to stay here or switch colleges."

"Mmm," Mother said. "I see. Do you think you'll find a college where this sort of thing won't happen, where everyone is perfect?"

By then I was lying on the sofa with my head in Mother's lap, and she was smoothing my hair with her hand. I was calming down, feeling safe, there on our old comfortable sofa, staring at the wooden pine coffee table whose grain and knicks were as familiar to me as the creases of my hand.

"You've been betrayed before, you know," Mother said.

"Nothing like this," I replied.

"At the time it seemed even more important." Mother said. "Remember when you were in the first grade? Cindy Patten was your best friend. You girls were inseparable. You and Cindy went to the drugstore. Cindy stole some lipsticks, then told her mother that *you* had taken them and put them in her coat pocket without her knowledge. She swore you took them. You swore you didn't. It was hard knowing whom to believe—"

"Well, *Mother!*" I said, halfway sitting up with indignation. "I *didn't* take them. *She* did. I saw her!"

"I know. I know. I believe you, for heaven's sake. But think about it—you were so mad at Cindy you didn't speak to her for a whole week. Then little by little the two of you drifted together again. And that's just one incident I can remember. That sort of thing happens all the time, everywhere."

"Then it's a rotten world."

"Sometimes. Sometimes it's pretty good. Be careful in your judgments—he who is without sin casts the first stone—"

"Mother! I've never done anything like this!"

"Oh, nonsense. Of course you have. We all have. Remember the time you and Diane Maloney went to the library? You were in the sixth grade then, and you were best friends. The library had just gotten in a huge new book on fashion, hairdos, finding your own style, beauty hints, all that stuff, geared to young teen-agers. Diane found it first. She called you over, all excited. 'Look what I found! This is the only thing I'm going to check out today. I'm going to take it home and read every page.' And you looked *so* superior; you said, 'I can't believe you're really interested in that. How embarrassing. Well, if you're going to carry it around, you can walk home by yourself. I don't want to be seen with you.' You psyched her into putting it back on the shelf, and when she did, you grabbed it, said, 'Ha-ha, now *I* get to read it *first!*' "

Mother and I both began to laugh. "That was a terrible thing to do, wasn't it?" I said. "I'd forgotten about that. But I was so scared about going into seventh grade; I wanted so desperately to look gorgeous and sophisticated—"

"And Diane didn't?"

"Well, Mother, we ended up sharing the book, after all. She came over and we looked at it together, after all!"

"That's true, but don't miss the point. You *did* do a sleazy thing to get what you wanted. Maybe Paula wanted Chad more desperately than you did. Maybe they really fell in love. Anyway, you can't stop going to that college because of that. If everyone ran away because of one or two betrayals—well, civilization wouldn't function at all." Mother was quiet for a time, stroking my hair. Then she said, "I think you should go to church on Sunday."

So here I am. Sitting here, I feel safe, at home, yet I can't help seeing things from a new perspective. I guess I'm growing up, getting jaded. Everyone in this church must at one time or another have betrayed someone. Everyone must have lied or cheated.

Several of the married men in this church have tried to have affairs with Mother. I can remember her refusing gracefully on the telephone, at the swimming pool, embarrassed because I was listening. I remember, when I was about fourteen, how Mother cried for weeks because Jake Vanderson had been calling her. His wife was off in Bermuda at a women's golf meet. Mr. Vanderson took Mother out to dinner at a restaurant way down in Southmark so that no one would see them. Mother came home that evening and started crying so hard she could scarcely make it up the stairs. I was terrified. She had never been this way before. I kept asking her what was wrong, and she finally told me.

"I want to have an affair with Jake," she said. "He's handsome, intelligent, witty, sexy. Oh, God, I'm *so* attracted to him. And Lillian is such a drip. All she cares about is spending money. She has no compassion, no charity. I don't owe her a thing. But I made a promise to myself when your father and I were divorced that I would *never* have an affair with a married man. And I won't, I swear I won't. But oh, Mandy, how I would like to spend just one night in his arms. He's so tall—"

It was weird to see the Vandersons in church after that. They always looked so proper, so perfect. He wore such elegant clothes— tweed suits with vests, silk ties, and everyone, even the minister, treated him with such respect. For a while I lived in fear that some Sunday I'd jump up in the middle of a sermon and yell, "Mr. Vanderson, how dare you look so perfect when you're really such a creep, trying to have an affair with my mother, making her cry!" But I don't know, after a while Mother got involved with someone else, and it all just faded in importance. Now when I see the Vandersons, I think nothing much except "Well, there are the Vandersons." Of course, now I also think of Mrs. Vanderson laughing and trying to look seductive at Mrs. Halstead's party with the male stripper. People are so strange.

Liza Howard is another one. It's like having a cheetah lounging over there in the pew, some sleek cat who doesn't belong in church. When I was little, I used to wish I were the most beautiful woman in the world. But after seeing Liza Howard, I wonder if amazing beauty isn't a kind of curse. At least it must be a responsibility; she must feel she has to make use of her beauty in some way. She doesn't seem to be interested in politics or feminism or art or a career or the town or anything except the way she looks. And the few times I've seen her in town she's always been doing something like vamping the UPS man. I think she's trapped by her beauty. There's no way she could ever live like a normal person, because she gets treated the way celebrities must —when people are confronted with her, they get tongue-tied and act silly. She is so absolutely beautiful that she makes everyone else feel inferior, and embarrassed, as if we chose the looks we were born with. So we are dazzled and inept in her presence, and furious at her when released from that presence.

Most beautiful people—fashion models, movie stars—give us hope, because they are human, and we think, well, maybe if I had my hair cut that way, or wore that shade of lipstick, I could be beautiful, too. I think that trying to be beautiful is not just vanity, it's a celebration of existence. We are fluffing up our feathers against the cold of life, we are shining as brightly as we can while we can. I love seeing people at Mother's cocktail parties, or the people I baby-sit for when they are dressed up to go out for an evening. They are not dressing to show off or attract; they are dressing up in order to make their existence gleam, as a sculptor will polish stone to make the surface shine. They must be thinking: Here I am. I'm alive, a unique reality in this world. And in this way we encourage others, because being human is usually such a difficult task, and we are so fragile and transient. Every human being who shines warms us, and makes us feel the glitter of being alive.

But Liza Howard's beauty is not generous in that way. It is demanding, obsessive, extreme. I think that absolute beauty is as terrible as absolute ugliness, just as great wealth is as destructive to a person's soul as great poverty. Liza Howard is a person who has been gifted or cursed with an extravagance, and like any person who stands outside the bounds of normal society, she is an outcast, and deserves to be.

And yet—and yet. I sometimes feel that with my sculpting I am also standing at the brink of a life that would be demanding, obsessive, and extreme. If I turn to art with the devotion I know it needs, will I be making myself an outcast? Is this why Mother worries that I might be an artist?

Mother and I watched Liza Howard enter church this morning, and I leaned to Mother and said, "Why does she keep coming to church? She doesn't belong here."

Mother said, "Oh, leave the poor woman alone. We're all orphans in this world, all struggling to pretend we've found a home."

I'll have to ask her sometime if she thinks that statement is true of the Bennetts. There they sit, the perfect Bennetts, except that dumpy Cynthia's off at college, winning honors so she can be written up in the local paper. A great deal of my childhood was spent wishing that I had Mrs. Bennett for a mother instead of my own. Now I'm beginning to appreciate Mother and be grateful to her for the way she raised me, but for years I've longed for Mrs. Bennett. Mrs. Bennett is *perfect*; she's just like someone from a magazine ad. She always looks serene, organized, gentle, and quiet. Mother, even when she's sitting perfectly still, *looks* noisy. When you look at Mrs. Bennett, you can tell just by watching her sit that she doesn't even *own* a pair of ripped underpants. I'll bet her underwear is folded up neatly in her dresser drawer with a bag of fresh sachet tucked alongside. I'll bet her shoes are lined up in her closet instead of tossed in, and the good ones are carefully tucked into a quilted shoe bag. I can imagine her bedside table: it is surely not cluttered, but neither is it dull. I'll bet she has a clock, a lamp, a Wedgwood dish, and a leather-bound book on her bedside table. I can't imagine her sitting the way my mother does, surrounded by books, magazines, letters, pillboxes, photographs, memo pads, pens, telephone books, tissue boxes, ashtrays and cigarettes and matches . . . Mother always has two or three liqueur glasses sitting on her nightstand with a residue of sticky liquid coating the bottom of the glass and filling the air with the smell of crème de cacao or Baileys Irish Cream. Mrs. Bennett undoubtedly takes her nightcap in the living room with her husband and rinses out the glass and puts it in the dishwasher before going to bed.

Now I'm learning to appreciate Mother, but still the sight of Mrs. Bennett and her family brings out a yearning in my soul, like the sight of autumn leaves or spring flowers. Mrs. Bennett just seems like such a normal mother, and she and Mr. Bennett seem to be really a couple.

I'm glad Mother and Dad are divorced. It happened a long time ago, and I think it was the right thing for both of them. When I sit very still, trying to summon up in my mind a picture of Mother and Daddy together, when they were still married, I find myself becoming nervous, because all I can remember are the times when they fought. Perhaps they always fought, were always fighting. In my memories, that's how it was. It was like living in the middle of a penny arcade: potshots were flying everywhere, tilt lights were flashing, sirens were ringing, it was all noise and speed and cheap danger, but never any prize. Now Dad's remarried, and he's nice to Irene, and they get along fine. Dad and Irene seem like a real couple. I can't imagine why Dad and Mother ever married in the first place.

Well, yes, I can, of course. They must have fallen in love. There's no controlling love, and it's almost a miracle when the proper people fall in love with each other.

Just look at John Bennett and Sarah Stafford. He's as handsome as a movie star, as charming as a prince, and she's got the personality and beauty of a brick. What can he possibly see in her? And forget the looks, John Bennett is a good-time boy, and I don't think Sarah Stafford knows how to *spell* the word "fun." What he sees in her I'll never know. They must have fallen madly in love, I can't imagine what else could have happened.

At least he is officially engaged at last. He's twenty-three, five years older than I am, but I've had a crush on him all my life. Every time I saw him at church or just walking down the street, I used to get hot all over. My knees went weak, I'd grin like a lunatic, and invariably do something gawky, simply because he was *there*. Well, I suppose half the girls in this town have been lurking around secretly hoping that the miracle would happen and gorgeous John Bennett would suddenly see one of us and fall in love. It's funny, now, though, because John Bennett doesn't seem very attractive to me anymore. He seems kind of slight. I think this must be because I know Michael now, and anyone compared with Michael seems pale, vague, and boring.

Still I envy the Bennetts; I envy them, and the Wilsons, and the Moyers—all those people who live here, who have found or made a home. They're *settled*. They have ended up in this town; I was only begun here. I feel a part of Londonton, yet I know I must leave. It is as if Londonton were a spinning rock, more faceted than a prism, and each facet an individual; together we make a whole. I must hew my shape, my particular self, from the massive refuge of this town—but how? How will I transplant myself? I'll probably have to teach art in a public school to support myself. It is almost certain that I won't be able to return to Londonton for good. Do all the young people of a town leave it with the speedy free-falling ease of pebbles in a rockslide? It is an amazing thing to think of, how we are all spinning helplessly through the space of life.

Spinning. This morning I cannot keep the idea of motion from my mind. My head is full of spinning globes, and I wish I were at the studio at school because I can almost see what kind of sculpture I would produce if I could get my hands on clay. Several smooth globes protruding at various spaces from a rough rock—I can see it in my mind. What a trick it would be to capture such self-assured motion in a static form!

In some ways I wish I hadn't come home. If I were at college, I could go to the studio right now . . . But if I hadn't come home, I would not have this idea in my mind.

It was last night that brought me this idea.

It was after midnight, and Mother was asleep. I had put on my old fuzzy pajamas which I've worn since I was fourteen. They're too short in the arms and legs now and would never do for college, but it was nice finding them here at home. Wearing them made me feel childlike. I opened the window to let the cool night air in, and lay snuggled under my comforter, waiting to go to sleep. Instead, I hallucinated.

When I was a little girl, I used to be both terrified and exhilarated by summer nights. My parents would leave the windows open, and kiss my forehead, and go far away downstairs, leaving me at the mercy of the summer creatures who urgently whispered their secrets to me through the open window. I would clutch my bed for fear that otherwise I would float right up and out the window into the blinking night —*they* wanted me to come, the crickets, birds, bats, and ghosts. For I was just as much a part of them as I was a part of the daylight human world, and *they* were no more frightening and mysterious than my parents and the human world they moved in. *They* wanted me, *they* needed me, *they* called to me, "Come, come come come," or "See, see see see."

Sometimes, if I got up the courage, I'd jump out of bed, race over to the window and slam it down, shutting out the night noises. Then I'd fall asleep, although Mother would always make a fuss the next morning: why had I shut the window, did I want to suffocate? I could never explain. Other times I would burrow under my pillow and cling tightly to my bed until at last the sounds ebbed away and I slept.

All those feelings returned to me last night, perhaps because I was back home after an absence, perhaps because I was in my childhood pajamas, perhaps because the window was open—I don't know. I lay there, prepared to fall asleep, and instead I was in a flash wide awake, keenly aware of myself, my bed, the open window, the black October night air, which was more chilling and silent than the air of summer. Then began that sinking feeling in my stomach, a lightness in all my limbs, as if I were being lifted up in a current of air. And all at once, without warning, while I was still gripping the sheets of the bed, I was also slipping with marvelous ease out the opened window.

Once outside, the night brightened and I could see everything clearly, although the mums which leaned against the house beneath my window were drained of color. Everything was a shade of radiant gray. I had no control at all over the speed or direction in which I floated, so I lay passively, breathing quietly, while beneath me the house and its familiar boundaries slid away. I was flying, or floating, effortlessly around the curve of the world. The yards and rooftops of the neighbors passed beneath me, and I lost all fear. I was over-whelmed with love and something close to pity to see the way we humans have tried to subdue the wild world with lines. As I looked down at Londonton, I could see so many right angles in our structures, poised against the sweeping curves of the natural world: houses, churches, intersecting roads, all in such careful order, guarded, gilded with right angles and bright trim, as if our points and apexes could de-fend us by puncturing the spherical truths of nature that persist in de-scending on our lives with the regularity of rain.

At the edge of town, I saw beckoning the silver and blue flash of light advertising the Blue Moon Dance Hall. I longed to reach down and touch it, bright bauble that it is, but the moment I moved my arm I found myself propelled with even greater speed up and off into the night.

The world spun one way, I spun the other. Wind rushed by me, murmuring, gushing, until I felt like a scarf rippling out. The earth spun steadily past me. I could see grass flowing into mountains, moun-tains melting into oceans, oceans rising to sand beaches, marshland climbing into pastures, and all that land dappled with angular shapes built by humans—their towns and cities.

At last I rose, or fell, up even higher, so that I saw only green and blue, glittering light and black, jungle and glacier alternating as the world whirled relentlessly by, a majestic merry-go-round.

This was far enough. I did not want to go any farther, to see any more, to know any more profoundly. I grabbed my pillow and put it over my head and bit into it as I had when I was a child trying to stop nightmares. I did not want the Dreadful Thing to happen; I did not want to run into God.

After a while, when I was sure I had settled back down safely in my own bed, I took the pillow off my head, turned on the light, looked around the room. Then I got out of bed and shut the window. I didn't want God coming into my room, and I didn't want to hallucinate myself out the window again.

I think people go to church for many reasons, but one of the main ones surely must be that we don't want God to come too close—who *really* wants that? Not me. It's frightening to think of. It's a much more bearable arrangement for us to meet Him regularly in one accordant spot, the church, and at one time, Sunday mornings. Mother says she enjoys church because it's the one place she feels she can really feel His presence. I can't wait till I'm older and calmer and can feel the way she does. I get tired of shutting Him out of rooms. I'm aware of His presence everywhere. If I even *think* of doing something wrong, or if I've done something bad or bitchy, well of course He's always there, like a looming shadow. But I don't mind that as much as I mind His appearance during the good times—when I'm driving my car down the highway, singing along to the car radio, or racing around in the bathroom getting ready for a date. Suddenly there will be a brightness in my chest and in the room or car, as if someone flashed on a light, and the common stuff of life seems suddenly precious, miraculous. I want to stop the car and kiss the yellow dividing lines on the highway, I want to touch the square tiles on the bathroom walls as if they were precious gold. Then I can scarcely move for gratitude, and amazement that out of the black empty void these things were created: my warm flesh, cold white tiles, delineated roadways you can trust to go where they've gone before. Sometimes I'm glad for this appearance, and I say, Thanks God, I love it all. But sometimes it's frightening. Once or twice when I've been driving, I've gotten so high just thinking about it all that before I know it, I'm going seventy-five miles an hour. That's

great; what will I say when I wreck the car someday: sorry, God
got in the car?

I can't talk to most people about this. It embarrasses most people
to talk about God. I can talk to Michael about God. I can talk with
Michael about God, about my work, about my hallucinations, about
my art. If I told him about last night and my vision, he would not
laugh at me. He would put his arms around me and pull me close to
him while I talked. He takes me seriously, and takes care with his answers. He would understand that it is this sort of crazy vision that I
need to have now and then in my life if I'm ever going to be a good
artist. It's the sort of thing that I can't help happening to me, that I
want to happen to me, because it opens up new worlds for me to work
from. But I also need what Michael gives me: that special sense of
being grounded in the earthly present. I could do so much, roam so far
artistically, if I knew he was physically there for me to come home to,
to bind me to the real.

I am in love with him. I need him. I want to be with him.

But how does Michael feel? He hasn't called or written me these
past six weeks. Maybe he's forgotten me. Surely not, surely not *forgotten*— But maybe he doesn't feel the same way. Even if I do manage to
find him today, shall I tell him how I feel—that I *love* him? Will that
embarrass him, frighten him away? Oh, God, if only I had the courage
to shape my life as willfully as I shape clay.

Oh, God, where are You in all this? Are You watching? Do You
care? Are You responsible for the way it is between Michael and me?
Have You got a message for me here, anywhere? What shall I do?

PETER TAYLOR

The service was almost over, and Peter Taylor was not satisfied. He did not feel it had been a successful morning. Something was in the air.

There were Sundays when, during a sermon, he could feel the individual attention of each and every person focused so intently on his words that their combined concentration became almost a tangible thing. He often felt this—that he could stretch out his hand with a swift sure move and capture it, then hold it out as a gift to God: the fluttering and wary intelligence of these believers.

Once, when he had been speaking on the Trinity, he had announced that for him Jesus Christ was as real and actively present in his everyday life as his car or house or family. The congregation as one had been shocked at these words, and their usual colorful quietness had gone white, tense, and electric. He had had one awesome moment of feeling at the center of their fierce and hopeful regard before someone sneezed, someone else shuffled, and the tone of the room dropped back to normal. And of course almost immediately some of the more conservative members of the group began to shift uncomfortably on their pews, obviously anxious lest Peter lapse into some sort of unseemly evangelical spiel.

Those moments of unified consciousness were rare. Still, most Sundays were better than this one. Today everyone seemed to be so twittery. They sat with their heads cocked dutifully in his direction, but their eyes were glazed. Clearly they were occupied with their own thoughts. Some people stared out the windows or up at the carved moldings. Even Wilbur Wilson, who could always be counted on for

almost fierce attentiveness, kept fidgeting about in his pew like a bored
child. During the end of the sermon, which was supposed to have been
uplifting and even cheering, Suzanna Blair's face had slowly grown
more and more woebegone, as if she had been hearing him preach
about some sort of hell—and in the back of the church his own son
Michael stared at him with a stony and unremittingly black stare.

The congregation rose to the opening chords of the organ music
and raised their hymnals before them; they seemed to sigh and rustle
with relief as they stood. They began to sing "Love Divine, All Loves
Excelling," and as they did, Peter let his eyes and his thoughts rest for
a moment on Michael. His greatest fear was that there really was a
God who would chastise him for not ministering well enough to his
congregation, or for interpreting Him and His words incorrectly. But
in this fear was a kind of hope—that if he prayed, thought, read,
worked hard enough, he could perhaps do some part of it right. So in a
strange way his fear made him optimistic, energetic, eager. So much
yet remained to be done and seen.

But his greatest sorrow was of a different quality, for his greatest
sorrow was that he had somehow failed his elder son. This seemed a
permanent and enduring emotion, for he felt that even God was more
forgiving and less judgmental than Michael. And with God there
would be—God willing—more chances, days and months and years of
new chances, to redeem and distinguish himself as a minister. But
Michael was seventeen now, planning to leave home at the first opportunity. Peter's time of really influencing Michael was almost over. He
had only a few more chances, and this knowledge carried with it not
relief, but despair.

This was not what he had intended; it was never what he had intended. He had planned to provide for his children a love so broad and
vast and sturdy that it would stretch under and around them all their
lives, as naturally and endlessly as the earth beneath their feet and the
air they breathed and moved through. This had been one of the major
efforts of his life. Peter felt he worked every day to build and
strengthen this benevolent domain. He wanted his children to be
happy and secure. But for some reason his elder son had always refused to make himself at home within the province of Peter's love.
This was most obvious now, when Michael had attained some sort of
physical manhood. He was taller, weighed more than, Peter. In the

past year Michael had hulked through life like some science-fiction hero of adolescent fantasy, with eyes like laser beams that could cut in one searing instant through the parental bonds of love. But this hauteur had not begun in adolescence—it had begun years and years ago, and Peter could remember the exact moment of that first chilling knowledge.

Peter and Patricia had had happy childhoods and intended the same for their own children. They worked hard, read the best child-rearing books, hugged, kissed, cuddled, held their tempers but disciplined firmly. They forgave readily, and spent countless hours biking with or reading to or rocking or making cookies with or somehow *being* with Michael and his younger brother and sister. Michael had had colic as an infant, temper tantrums as a baby, and nightmares as a child, but by the time he reached school age, he was a handsome and winsome little boy who was respectful to teachers, good at sports, academically bright. His younger brother and sister, Will and Lucy, had adored him in spite of their normal childish spats, and Michael had, in his own rather undemonstrative way, always equally adored them. He had loved and needed his mother with a ceaseless, fierce, shy passion. But his father he had judged from the start.

Michael was six when Peter first began to notice what he later came to call in his own private thoughts Michael's Stuffed Animal Stare. It was a look Michael favored only his father with. Peter might suggest that Michael eat with his fork instead of his fingers, or insist that he brush his teeth, or hang up his coat, some trivial task, and Michael would turn to look at him with eyes that had gone blank as buttons, remote, aloof, removed, dispassionate. The first time this had happened, Peter had knelt down and taken his unwilling son into his arms.

"Why, Michael, what's the matter?" he had asked, alarmed.

"Nothing," Michael said, his beautiful eyes still cold, his tiny body rigid in refusal, and Peter was as deeply hurt at that moment as he ever was in his life.

Later that night, as they lay holding each other in bed, Peter told Patricia about this, but she had only smiled.

"Well, darling," she said, "he's a boy. He's starting to rebel. I guess he'll be rebelling from you now for the rest of his life." She had

actually seemed to find this somehow rather sweet, and in turn Peter
was reassured.

But when Michael was seven, a more dramatic and somehow pro-
phetic event had occurred for what seemed very little reason. Michael
and Will and Lucy had been in their basement playroom playing
house one night after dinner. Peter had gone down to inform all three
children that it was time for bed. Will and Lucy had immediately set
up their normal whine. "Oh, no, Daddy, just let us play a few more
minutes, we've got a good game going, please, Daddy—"

But Michael had instantly gone red with rage, burst into tears,
and yelled, "I hate you! I hate you! You think you can boss everything!
I wish you were dead! I wish you were killed in a car accident!"

Peter had stared at his son, stunned, for one long moment, then
he had crossed the room and yanked Michael around and swatted him
good and hard on his jeans-covered bottom.

"Don't you ever say that to me again!" Peter had screamed. He
had turned Michael around then, placed a hand on each small shoulder, and gripped him tight. "Do you hear me? Don't you ever say such
a thing again. That's a *terrible* thing to say to anybody. That's the
worst thing to say. You should be ashamed of yourself."

Will and Lucy, then five and three, had burst into tears at the
sight of their father in such a rage, but Michael only went very still.
He did not cry out when he was spanked, nor did his father's words
bring the sign of a tear into his dark and secretive eyes. This had sent
Peter into an even wilder fury, a truly desperate state, for he wanted
some acknowledgment from this child of his that he had not meant
what he said, that he did love his father—that he did *not* wish him
dead.

"Well, I'll move away if that's what you want!" Peter had shouted,
knowing even as he spoke that this should be too irrational and incredible a threat for even the young ones to take seriously. He flung himself
from Michael and stomped across the room to the bottom of the basement steps. "I'll pack my suitcase and move far away and you'll never
see me again!" he cried.

"No, Daddy, *no*," both younger children had wailed, and run to
him, faces strained with real panic. Peter felt a surge of shame as his
younger children grasped his legs, attempting to keep him from going,
but his eyes were riveted on his elder son, who had started this insane

scene, and who stood now so stony-eyed, unmoving, and adamantly mute that Peter knew in one chill moment that this son would never beg him to stay, and that there really was some substance to his seven-year-old hate.

But Peter did not deserve this hate, he felt, and he did not hate his son, although at that moment he was so furious that his hand clenched at his sides and he longed to cross the room once more, to slap that sullen, blank-eyed look from Michael's face. Lucy and Will continued to scream. Patricia came rushing down from the second floor, where she'd been taking a bath. She had not even taken time to wrap her wet hair up in a towel, and water dripped in rivulets down her blue bathrobe, making dark streaks from her shoulder to her breast. She stopped at the top of the basement steps, hand grasping the banister, eyes wide with fright, searching the room for some awful sight.

"What happened? Is someone hurt?" she asked.

"Daddy's running away from home!" Lucy wailed.

"Michael wishes I were dead," Peter said.

He realized immediately how immature he sounded, standing at the base of the steps, tossing his complaint of wounded pride up at Patricia like that. But he could think of nothing he could say that would make it better. He felt temporarily helpless, Michael's words had hurt so much.

"Everyone's tired," Patricia said. "Come on, Michael, Lucy, Will, it's time for bed. No more messing around."

Her normal, patient, irritated voice calmed them all, and the children, relieved that the scene was over, went with unusual silence up the stairs to get ready for bed. Still Peter stood at the foot of the basement steps, caught in his confusion and misery.

"You must come say good night to them, you know," Patricia said softly before she shut the basement door.

Peter sat down on the steps for a few moments and tried to think the scene through. What had happened? Why? How could his son say such a violent thing to him with so little provocation? Good God; he was thirty-eight years old, and a minister, and in an instant he had let his own seven-year-old son reduce him to a rage of insecurity and doubts. What should he do now? What would a perfect father do? What would God want him to do?

He waited until the children had brushed their teeth, put on their pajamas, and been tucked in bed by Patricia. Then he went up to the bedrooms. He spoke first with the younger ones, telling them he was sorry he had frightened them, that he loved them and would never leave them, never run away, that he wouldn't say such foolish things again. Both Will and Lucy, in the privacy of their own rooms, went teary-eyed, and wrapped their arms around him, and snuggled up against him, and Peter felt the blessed bliss of mutual love.

So when he went into Michael's room, he was calm. He had decided that Michael could not have meant what he said, and he was ashamed that he had reacted so angrily. He did not want Michael to be frightened of his own anger, his own words. He wanted to hold his son, to reassure him.

"Well, son, let's make up," he said, approaching the side of Michael's bed, smiling down at him. At that moment Peter had nothing but goodwill and love for his son in his heart.

But Michael lay rigid in the bed, eyes cold. "Not yet."

Not yet? What in hell did that mean, and how in the world had Michael come to possess such arrogance?

"All right, then," Peter said, suddenly berserk with despair, "let's fight. Are you ready? Come on, tough guy, get out of bed and let's fight." He rolled up his shirt sleeves and yanked the covers off his son, exposing the slight severe body in the blue-and-white-striped pajamas. "Come on, come on, you little creep, you don't want to make up? You want to fight? You want to hold a grudge because I sent you to bed? Get up and put your money where your mouth is!"

Michael sat up in bed, his skin bloodless, white as chalk, his face set.

"Peter?" Patricia said, coming to stand in the doorway.

"Please," Peter said, nearly choking in desperation, "let me handle this." He turned back to Michael. "Well, kid, ready to fight?" He made a fist and advanced on his little boy.

Michael's face flushed then, and he burst into tears. "No, Daddy," he said. "Please." He hid his face behind his arm.

"Oh, God," Peter said, tears coming into his own eyes. He collapsed on the bed next to his son and just sat there a moment, stunned. Then he pulled Michael toward him, and Michael did not resist, but lay there in his arms, a heavy, awkward, ungenerous bundle.

"Michael, I'm sorry. I wouldn't have hit you. I love you. I love you. I don't understand why you're acting this way. I love you." He talked on and on, rocking Michael, rubbing his back, until the little boy's sobs abated. Finally he said, "Are you all right now? Can you go to sleep?"

"Yes," Michael said.

"Do you want a drink of water? Do you need to go to the bathroom?"

"No," Michael said. "I'm all right. I'm just tired."

"All right, then, son. Go to sleep. Good night. I love you."

"I love you, Daddy," Michael said.

Peter tucked the covers around his son, kissed his cheek, and left the room. He felt like a monster. He felt he had wrung the words "I love you" out of his son. He had needed terribly to hear those words, but he wondered what it had cost Michael to say them—and why, dear God, it had cost him anything at all.

From then on it was never clear and easy. Michael remained a good, smart, likable child, popular with friends and teachers, quick to learn, good at sports, a fine son. There were even times when Peter could *see* Michael working to break through whatever barrier it was that kept him from giving to his father the spontaneous love he gave to everyone else. At those times Peter felt deep pity for his son. He went along, doing the best he could, showing his love for Michael in every possible way, refusing to give up, hoping that someday it would change.

Peter took the duties of his ministry very seriously, and he believed that one of his major responsibilities was a symbolic one: he should present before the community an exemplary life. He should try to be wise, serene, and benevolently judicious—whether he was or not. And he was very good at helping others with their personal problems, he had a gift for it. It was only his own family, and more precisely just his elder son, whom he could not handle. So because he felt it would be a failure on his part to ask for advice from anyone, he tried to learn the secrets of fathers surreptitiously.

He volunteered to help with Cub Scouts, Boy Scouts, soccer and baseball Little Leagues. He covertly watched and listened to the other men as they dealt with their sons. He was surprised at the range and varieties of fathering. Some men were brusque and even officious. Some were warmly affectionate, given to gentle cuffing of their sons now and then because it was the only way they had to touch their sons' bodies. Some were so absentminded about it all that the sons in response danced attendance on their fathers. Well, Peter thought, *there's* an idea, and for the next few months he tried to be distant and aloof—in a kindhearted way.

But Michael didn't even seem to notice. His attitude certainly did not change. Finally Peter went back to his old ways, because it was too much of a strain otherwise. He hugged Michael when he could and tried not to mind that he was not hugged back. He visited Michael's room at night, just as he visited Lucy's and Will's, to tuck them in, kiss them on the forehead, ask casually, "Everything okay?" in case there was a problem that could be discussed best in the quiet of the night. Will and Lucy would sometimes confide in him their secret fears and worries, and sometimes they would simply blither on about the happenings of the day or ask how space shuttles worked—anything to keep from having the light turned out and sleep imposed. But Michael always, always answered, "Yes, everything's okay." There were nights when Peter had wanted to grab his son, shake him furiously, and cry, "No, everything is *not* okay! You're a secretive, ungenerous, unloving child, and that is NOT okay!"

Peter read books on child rearing. He memorized entire passages from Dr. Spock: "The child after six goes on loving his parents deeply underneath, but he usually doesn't show it much on the surface. . . . From his need to be less dependent on his parents, he turns more to trusted adults outside the family for ideas and knowledge. If he mistakenly gets the idea from his admired science teacher that red blood cells are larger than white blood cells, there's nothing his father can say that will change his mind."

Peter recited this passage to himself like a mantra the year that Michael began to hero-worship Chet Elliott, the man who coached the soccer league Michael played in. Chet was a handsome young man and a great coach, and that was all that Michael could see. Only Peter and the other adults in Londonton knew about Chet's adult life—he was a garage mechanic who at thirty showed no signs of marrying. He spent every evening in local bars, drinking to a loud-mouthed, happy-hearted excess and eventually taking to his apartment whatever local girl wanted to go—and there were plenty who wanted to go, because Chet was handsome. He was easygoing, sauntering, quick to laugh, unambitious, unconcerned. He was also a wonderful, hard-working coach, because he loved games, and without even meaning to, without really thinking about it, he instilled all the best values into the boys he coached. He taught them how to play hard and fair, how to balance competition with sportsmanship, how to demand the most from their growing bodies. Then he went off at night to get drunk and slaphappy, and once about every six months he ended up in the doctor's office with a venereal disease. But the boys he coached didn't know what Chet did with his nights, and the fathers could see no sign that Chet's nights ever affected his coaching, and so they kept him on—it was, after all, a voluntary, non-salaried job. They were grateful to have him. The boys adored him, and Peter liked him very much; everybody did, it was impossible not to. But it was a hard year when Michael had Chet for a soccer coach, because no one had ever before aroused in Michael such openhearted exuberant adoration.

He sang Chet Elliott's praise morning, noon, and night. When he had free time, he went to the Gulf station and hung around watching Chet fill cars with gas or tinker under the hoods. One night at dinner, Michael stated that when *he* grew up, he was going to be just like Chet Elliott.

"Good, dear," Patricia had replied, smiling. "I hope you'll still live in Londonton. Then I won't have to worry about my car ever again. I'll just let you take care of it."

Peter just stared at Michael, then asked Lucy a question about her school field trip. He was trying to put Michael's claim into perspective. Michael was a child, and his crush was a child's crush, and it was all part of growing up. But Peter was wounded, for Michael had never once said that he wanted to grow up to be like his father. And Chet Elliott—he wasn't the sort of man Peter would ever want his son to be. He didn't even have children of his own. He had no education, no sense of personal destiny and responsibility. Other than his sex, Chet Elliott had *nothing* in common with Peter.

"You expect too much from Michael," Patricia said one night.

"I expect him to love me," Peter replied.

"He does love you, in his own way," Patricia said.

"When I was his age, I followed my father around like a shadow. I thought my father was God."

"Michael is different from you. You are different from your father.

Peter, you know that Michael has a stubborn streak in him. The more you ask, the less he'll give."

"But why? Why?"

Patricia wrapped her arms around Peter as if he were the child. "I don't know, honey," she said. "I wish I did know. I know how he hurts your feelings. Oh, children are just the hardest things. I think all we can do is love Michael, and let him be."

Peter had done his best to do just that: to love Michael, and to let him be. Still he was always on the alert, hoping for a change, even a slight one, and as the years passed, the burden of his relationship with his son settled on him like a weight on his back. He could not turn easily to any other thing or person: that burden was there, weighing him down, hindering him always just that little bit.

The year Michael turned sixteen was a horror. Michael got his driver's license and proceeded to smash up his mother's car, then his father's, and then a neighbor's. It was only through the kindness of the neighbor, who refused to press charges against Michael for "borrowing" his car, that Michael avoided being arrested.

Then the Defresnes caught him naked with their naked daughter in their TV room at midnight one night. The Moyers found him with their son and three other boys drinking and smoking pot in the basement underneath their son's electric-train table. Bartenders called to say they'd done him the favor of kicking him out of their bar because he was obviously underage. Peter had to love his son and *not* let him be; he had to discipline him, punish him, and set down some stringent rules to protect him from himself.

He found Michael a job as a dishwasher in a local restaurant. He drove Michael there at seven o'clock on Friday and Saturday nights and picked him up and drove him home at one in the morning. He let Michael play sports, and he let him attend any school function that others attended, and he let Michael drive to these, but only with Peter seated in the front seat next to him. He did not let Michael date or even go to movies with friends for several months after the car accidents. Gradually Michael seemed to settle down, although Peter feared the boy was merely hiding his rebelliousness until a future time. And if Michael had been cool toward his father before, he was no longer so. Now he hated his father with a fury, and let him know it. His contempt for his father seemed so deep and strong that it was finally an integral part of his personality and showed in the very stance of his handsome body, in every stare from his cold, judgmental eyes.

God, what a mystery this son was! Peter felt helpless, doomed. Lucy and Will remained loving, tolerant, affectionate children, and their relationship with Peter was full of easy love. He could not understand, he could not think it out—why it should be so different, so difficult between himself and Michael.

At least this summer Michael had calmed down a bit and stopped acting like a hood. He had gotten a job with a local landscape contractor, and the strenuous outdoor work seemed to have a healthy effect. Michael seemed to, in his own jargon, mellow out. He became punctual, reliable, and almost miraculously talkative. At the breakfast or dinner table, he talked voluntarily about the work he did, the people he worked for, or he told jokes he had heard from the contractor and his crew. As Peter watched this son of his, who seemed to grow larger and certainly more tanned every day, it appeared to him that, perhaps for the first time, Michael was happy. And Peter was glad for this happiness, and sorry that it had taken so long in his son's life to arrive. Because he was afraid that this happiness might be a temporary thing, a delicate china teacup accidentally set down on the hood of an idling car, he was very careful to do nothing that might provoke any changes. It bothered him that almost every night after dinner Michael took off for solitary walks by himself. He told no one where he was going, or rather, they knew, but only vaguely. He always said that he was just going for a walk, around the town, or along the river. They could hardly follow him to see if this was true. And he always returned home at the time they demanded, and he never asked to use the car, and he seemed to spend almost no money. He was never seen with the troublesome bunch Peter was so wary of—so Peter thought that it could be possible that Michael was only walking around the town, enjoying the summer nights, perhaps thinking about his future. . . . Peter let Michael be. It was the gentlest summer the family had ever had together.

But when Michael started back to school, things changed. Peter and Patricia were not aware of it right away, because on the surface things remained fine. They let Michael drive the car on weekend nights, and he always returned home at an early hour, with the car undamaged. Some weekend nights he didn't go out at all, but stayed home watching television with the family, or reading by the fire. His happiness, though, had disappeared; he seemed to have lost it. But he was as calm and cooperative as he had been that summer. They had had no reason to worry about him until, just this week, the principal of the high school had called and asked them to come in.

Michael had been in school only six weeks, but the principal said that it was already apparent that if he continued as he was, he would fail every class. He was innately intelligent enough, there was no doubt about that. He had scored very high on the IQ tests, and there was probably no limit to what he could do if he put his mind to it. And he was no longer the discipline problem he had been in his junior year in high school. He didn't instigate minor classroom rebellions or smoke pot in the rest rooms or act in an insubordinate manner. He was always polite, even courteous. But he did not do his work. He did not pay attention. He would not care.

The principal of the school, Dan Ford, was a friend of the Taylors'—he attended the Episcopal church, but he had lived in Londonton as long as the Taylors, and they knew each other from parties and community functions. They had goodwill toward each other, and because of this, Dan was taking special pains to present the information carefully to the Taylors.

"I have to tell you, Peter," Dan said, "this kind of behavior often indicates that the child is not getting enough attention from his parents. That the parents are not spending enough time with the child."

"If we spend any more time with him," Peter said drily, "we'd have to sleep in bed with him at night."

"I know," Dan said, laughing. "I know. You and Patricia couldn't be better parents. That's why I feel at a loss as to what to suggest to do. Perhaps Michael should see a psychiatrist. But you certainly do need to do something."

Peter and Patricia drove home from the meeting in stunned silence. During the past six weeks, while Michael had been so politely failing his courses at school, he had shown almost exemplary behavior at home. He had, it was obvious, learned the necessary behaviors that kept the surface of the family life smooth: he was courteous, civil, obedient; he helped with the dishes and housework when asked, carried in the groceries, carried out the trash. Now they would have to probe beneath this accommodating surface, and they were afraid of what lurked below. They were afraid of the process of investigation, as if cutting through to the truth would wound their son, or set off some delicate mechanism that would cause him to explode.

But it was not Michael who exploded.

As soon as they got home, they called Michael into the living room and told him what the principal had told them. They told him that if he continued this way, he would not only lose all chances of getting into a decent college, he would also not even graduate from high school.

"That's okay," Michael had said calmly. "I don't want to go to college. The only reason I've been going to school is to keep you guys from freaking out."

"But, Michael," Patricia said, "you *have* to go to college."

"No, I don't," Michael said, with that cool, controlled tone that always made Peter want to shake his teeth out. "I don't *have* to go to college. I don't even have to graduate from high school. In Massachusetts, as soon as you're seventeen, you can quit school without your parents' permission."

Peter rose and walked out of the room.

Now he stood at the pulpit of the church, staring out at the congregation, and at his elder son, who had his hymnal raised dutifully before him, but who did not sing. Five days had passed since Michael had made his announcement, and Peter had still not decided what to do about it. His instinct was to do nothing, for he feared that anything he did or said at this point would be wrong. Peter felt explosive with righteous indignation, and he knew in his mind that he was right to feel this way. But he also knew that he could not face his son with his emotions, not when Michael was so cool and Peter was so hot. They might break and lose each other, like hot liquid poured into a cold glass.

Each night for the past five nights, Peter had waited until everyone else in the house was asleep, then he had pulled on his old corduroy robe and padded barefoot down the carpeted stairs, through the hall, and into the privacy of his study. He could not sleep, and he could not think while lying down, but he did not want to inflict his insomnia on anyone else, so he did not turn the light on in his study, but merely paced about the room in the dark. There was enough light coming in the windows from the moon and the streetlight to illuminate the room sufficiently so that as he walked he did not bump into any furniture—but he had nothing to illuminate the problem which drove him to this pacing. He came to the conclusion that his failure toward his son was not one of commitment or devotion or love, but simply of imagination. He could not imagine his son.

If Peter believed anything, it was that a person as privileged by life as he was, and in turn as Michael was, should use his God-given capabilities to help the world along. It didn't matter how—Peter honestly didn't care if Michael became a doctor, philosopher, naturalist, actor, scientist, or poet. But he should become *something*. Peter thought that any child who had been raised in such a loving home, with such an affluent life with so many advantages, owed the world— owed *Fate*—a debt. What made life worth living if not helping the world? Man must look past himself to live. If he serves only himself, his soul shrivels and dies. Peter believed this as firmly as he believed in God, and if there was any one value he had tried to pass on to his children, this was it. In fact, for Peter this belief was not an intellectual one that could be instilled, but an integral way of life, as natural and necessary as breathing air. Yet his elder son did not in any way seem to live or believe this. He did not want an education; he did not want to discipline and train himself in order to go out in aid of the world. Peter truly could not imagine what kind of person this boy was, who had flourished so perversely in his house, as odd and inexplicable as a solitary penguin thriving in a hot jungle.

When all was said and done, it appeared to Peter that he and Patricia had accomplished nothing more, with all their best efforts, than to keep Michael's body alive. There were no signs that they had in any way touched his mind and soul.

Peter had managed one more conversation with his son since the discussion with the principal of the high school, and that conversation had been pretty much of a deadlock. No, Michael was not planning to go to college. Yes, his decision was absolute, final; he had given it much thought. Yes, he intended to finish high school, he supposed, if only to keep his mother from being upset. No, he didn't know what kind of work he'd do after high school. Did it matter? He just wanted something that would give him enough money to move out of his parents' home and live in his own apartment. No, he wasn't taking drugs. No, he wasn't depressed. Yes, he was sorry to cause such pain, especially to his mother, but the honest truth was that he just didn't want to go to college. He didn't like studying. There were other things he'd rather do. Oh—work with the landscape contractor. Or with Chet Elliott down at the garage. He was pretty good with his hands and liked that kind of work.

During this conversation Peter sat still, vowing to remain calm in spite of his amazement. He couldn't have been more dismayed if Michael had suddenly begun speaking a foreign language.

"Well, son," he said finally, "I guess you know I'm deeply disappointed by all this."

"I know," Michael said, and his voice was flat. As he spoke he did not in any way expose his feelings, neither distress nor triumph at hurting his parents in this way.

"I hope at least you'll finish high school," Peter said after a pause. "Your mother and I really want you to bring your grades up so that you can graduate."

"I know you do," Michael said, and proceeded, in silence, to stare his father down.

Peter did not know what to do. He spent his nights pacing his study and his days attempting to appear normal, as if that would make things fall into their normal places. But life was suddenly weighted. Everything resonated.

Just last night the family had been gathered around the dining-room table for dinner, and it was a comfortable enough dinner. Lucy and Will filled the air with gossip and laughter and minor complaints about homework and ice skates. Patricia had served a thick fish stew with homemade bread and a green salad, and after the meal all five Taylors leaned back in their chairs a moment, enjoying a full and agreeable silence. Then the children rose to clear the table while Patricia brought in homemade apple pie and ice cream for dessert. Peter watched Patricia cutting and serving the pie, handing the plates around to her family, and the three children talked, and the moment seemed calm.

"Hey, I heard a joke," Michael said. "Jesus is crucified and goes to heaven, see, and he walks through the Pearly Gates and goes up to God. He says, 'Hi, God!' But God is looking real sad, so Jesus says, 'Hey, God, what's the matter? You sure do look sad.' God says, 'I am sad. I've made a son. I created him with my own hands. And now he's dead.' Jesus says, 'Hey, God, you're wrong. *I'm* your son, and I'm not dead!' God looks at him. Jesus holds out his arms and says, '*Father!*' And God holds out his arms and says, '*Pinocchio!*' "

Everybody laughed. Will, who was thirteen, even went into one of the laughing fits which had come on him at adolescence; he laughed so hard that tears streamed down his face and he had to be pounded on the back. Peter laughed, too, amused at the joke and wondering immediately if he could somehow work it into a sermon, when he was struck by a fresh doubt: had Michael been trying to tell him something? Was Michael saying that fathers, even God, were incapable of recognizing their sons? Did Michael mean that Peter would prefer a wooden marionette to him? It was exhausting. Everything was fraught with significance.

Last night, for the fifth night in a row, Peter had waited until his house was dark and silent, then he rose from his bed, took up his robe, and went downstairs to his study. He could see by the moonlight that his study held peace. The afghan was folded neatly over the back of the leather sofa, his papers lay in neat piles at right angles to each other on his desk, and in the center of his desk, on the leather-rimmed blotter, lay his sermon, typed and corrected and waiting for Sunday morning. Peter stood a moment, surveying this domain, his domain, his ordered sanctuary of a room which sat in the middle of his house like a staunch desert isle set down in a turbulent sea. He crossed to the window, and looked out at the world, and wondered if he was growing old. Why else should it calm him to be awake at night, when the house was silent and everything inside and out all muted into shades of gray? He had begun to appreciate the world at night, and in the winter, when snow made the world white, and in the summer, when everything was green. He liked seeing the world all of a piece, unified by color, unfurling away from him in a banner of visible unity. This flashy season, fall, disturbed him. In the daylight he could see the fields around Londonton stretching away from the town like a rumpled patchwork quilt: here a block of green, there a block of bronze, over there a forest of deciduous trees brandishing branches of crimson, scarlet, orange—colors of warning, colors of alarm. This fall did not make Peter feel nostalgic, nor did it make him feel chilled at the thought of the coming winter, the symbolic season of death. It made him think instead of how variegated the world was, how myriad and uncontrollable were the possibilities of life. How dangerous life was. He wanted to tuck away his family, all of them, into his house, and surround the house with snow so that they were all shut in, warm and safe. He wanted nothing golden glinting in the distance, beckoning his son away so soon. But surely these were an old man's thoughts?

"Peter."

Peter turned to see Patricia standing in the doorway in her blue cotton summer nightgown.

"Come in," he said. "Join me. I can't sleep."

Patricia shut the door behind her. She crossed the shadowy room and stood at the other end of the long casement window. "What are you looking at?" she asked.

"The world," Peter said. "I keep thinking how vast and dangerous it is. I'm afraid to let Michael wander out into it."

Patricia laughed softly. "Peter," she said, "Michael wants to get an apartment in town and work at a garage. I would hardly call that wandering out into the vast and dangerous world."

"Why is he doing this to us?" Peter asked, and he softly hit the windowsill with his fist.

"He's *not* doing this *to us*. He's just doing it."

"I want him to go to college."

"I know you do. He knows you do. But it's his life."

"What does that mean—it's *his life*? Who gave it to him? When did he gain control of it? Legally, I suppose it will be his life when he's eighteen. Then he can get married, own land, be drafted. But I suppose if you want to get realistic about it, it was his life when he turned sixteen and got a driver's license. Well, I guess if he has the right to go out and kill himself in a car at sixteen, he should have the right to ruin his life at seventeen."

"If you're going to look at it that way, Peter," Patricia said, "then it was his life the day he learned to walk."

She left the windowsill and crossed the room. "I think we both deserve a drink," she said, and picked up the brandy decanter.

Peter was quiet a moment, occupied with his thoughts, but he watched Patricia as she poured the brandy into glasses, and he could not help but notice how in the darkened room the light from the window caught and glinted off the cut glass, off the golden liquid, off Patricia's pale and shining hair. Patricia brought him his glass, then went to the leather sofa and sank down in one corner of it, drawing her bare feet up under her, pulling the afghan down about her in a nest.

"It's getting cold," she said. "I'll have to get out all our winter nightclothes. I need my good warm nightgowns." She fussed about, wrapping the afghan over her shoulders, and it seemed to Peter as he watched that there was something ageless and endearing about his wife curled up like that with the afghan draped around her like a shawl. As she rearranged herself and the cover, her bare arms, neck, and feet shone smoothly, a wealthy substance, glossy against the muted leather and wool. She sat there smiling up at him, vivid, gleaming, real.

"It seems harder for me than for you," Peter said. He sat down at the other end of the sofa, and sipped his brandy. What he wanted to do was believe that she was magic, eternal, that if he threw himself before his wife now and implored her, she could make things change.

"You expect more of him than I do," Patricia said. "You want so desperately for us all to get things *right*."

"What's wrong with that? Of course I expect a lot. And I do all I can to provide every kind of assistance I know."

"Yes, that's true. You are wonderful that way. But do you think you might be a little limited in your views of what is right?"

Patricia smiled as she spoke, and she raised her glass to her lips. The afghan fell from one shoulder, exposing the bare flesh of her arm and neck and the soft blue cotton of her nightgown curving down around her breast.

"There are many different ways to live a life," she said.

She twisted on the sofa so that she faced him, her back against the sofa arm, her legs extended. She pushed her two bare feet up so that they were braced companionably against his thigh, and she bent her knees, and the skirt of her nightgown rode up a little, so that the smooth stretch of her leg gleamed.

Peter realized that he had not looked at his wife for a while. Their bodies were as familiar to each other as all the other daily things which dwelt where they belonged within their lives. And as he looked at Patricia, he saw how she had changed. She was forty-five, and still slim in her clothes, but her body had taken on a roundness and a soft solidity. He touched her knees carefully, then ran his hand up and down her leg for the warmth and the comfort.

"It's possible, you know," Patricia said, smiling at him from the other end of the sofa, "that your father wanted certain things of you. Perhaps he wanted you to stay on the farm, to follow in his work. Perhaps he was puzzled when you went off so readily into the dangerous world. Perhaps he was hurt because you left the farm so easily. That beautiful, safe home."

Peter listened to his wife, but now the words were less important than her hushed, beguiling tone. It was almost as if she were singing him a song. Absentmindedly, he ran his hand from slender ankle up the swell of calf, over a silken knee and down her thigh. Here, at the apex of her legs, was a concentration point of body heat, and as naturally as any animal moving toward warm comfort, he extended his arm just a little further until his hand came to rest in the heated hollow between her legs. She was naked. The sweet surprise of this made his heart thump. He pushed his hand against the furry swell of her crotch, and pushed again.

"Hey," Patricia said, so softly that it was more an exhalation of breath than a word.

"Hey," Peter replied, with equal softness.

They smiled at each other in silence, and suddenly there they were: just Peter and Patricia, who loved each other. In one sleek and generous second, everything else in life fell away, leaving them alone in all time and space. Peter put his brandy snifter on the floor, turned to Patricia, and carefully pulled her hips down toward him, moving at the same time so that he could kneel on the sofa between her legs. Patricia held her arms up to him and he unsnapped the waistband of his pajamas and slid them down his hips, then gently lowered himself down over her. They moved together, moist and murmuring, smiling at each other, looking in each other's eyes, pleased, happy.

Finally Peter just lay there, curled between Patricia's legs, his head on her breast, her arms wrapped around his back. She stroked his arms and shoulders and smoothed his hair.

"I love you," he said.

"And I love you," she answered.

They fell asleep like that in the shadowy room. At some point in the night they shifted positions so that Patricia could cover them with the afghan, but they didn't really wake up until the strong morning light brightened the room. Then they sat up, feeling cramped from the strange positions. Patricia's shoulders were chilled, and so were Peter's feet. But they were happy.

"Well," Peter said, adjusting his pajamas and robe.

"Well, yourself," Patricia said.

"I'll make coffee."

"I'll go shower and dress, then come down and make breakfast. It's only seven-thirty. There's no rush." Patricia rose and stretched. "Oh, my aching back," she said. "I'm getting too old for this."

"Oh no you're not," Peter replied, and wanted to embrace her again, but did not, because he felt suddenly and strangely shy, and strangely smug.

He had moved through the kitchen this morning like a traveler who has come home after a long and arduous journey. Each pedestrian household thing shone cleanly, and he felt great gratitude toward his wife for putting their house and their lives together with such grace. He dug a measuring cup into the ground coffee beans like a man digging into a treasure, and when the coffee was brewed and the rich aroma filled the air, he just stood in the kitchen, smiling at the toaster and the butter dish, a man happy with his life.

Patricia came into the kitchen, wearing a quilted robe, her hair freshly shampooed. She smelled of herbs and perfume.

"Ummm, coffee," she said.

Peter took down two mugs, poured the coffee, handed a mug to his wife. "I think you seduced me last night," he said.

Patricia smiled. "Why, Peter, what a thought!"

"Did you have any ulterior motive?"

Patricia measured a spoon of shimmering white sugar into her mug. "Well," she said, smiling at him, "perhaps when I first came down to the study I did think of distracting you from your worries about Michael. There are three other people in this family who want your attention, you know. But believe me, my love, after a while I wasn't thinking anything at all."

Patricia set her mug down on the table and came over to wrap her arms around Peter. They stood there a while, just nestling against each other.

Then Peter went upstairs to shower, and as he stood under the steaming water, he felt brisk and hearty and confident: he felt he had regained perspective on his life. He knew there could be no mother more fierce in her love and protection of her children than Patricia. He knew that the health and happiness of her family was her main concern. During the eighteen years of their marriage there had been times when they had argued and disagreed, and even weeks at a time when they had been too angry at each other to make it through with more than a pretense of civility. But they had always trusted each other. They had an honorable marriage.

In the past few months, as Peter realized he was approaching his fiftieth birthday, he had come to view his marriage, when he stopped to think of it at all, as a finished thing, a fine accomplishment, almost a tangible object that he and Patricia had built together. Something, say, as useful and well matched and necessary to their lives and their children's lives as their walnut dining-room table and chairs. Now he saw that they were not finished, not set in any limits. No. He had seen Patricia through fresh eyes last night, or she had been a new person, or both: she had been a subtle, glowing temptress, and he had been an ardent lover, with a passion both renewed and new. How grateful he was for the variety and complexity of people's lives. And he hoped he could manage to extend to his elder son, and to his other children, this new generosity of understanding. He wanted to be brave enough to give them freedom, to let them be whatever they wished to be.

But now he sang the last stanza of the hymn, and although he saw Patricia standing there, he also saw Michael, whose face was set, whose handsome eyes were fixed with their Stuffed Animal Stare. Immovable, sullen son! Peter had to look away. Michael might be one of the most important people in his charge, but he was not the only one, and if he were to allow Michael the freedom he desired, then he, Peter, would have to allow himself an equal freedom of thought. After all, his furious concern was doing little good.

So Peter let his eyes rest on Patricia until the anger subsided and the joy returned.

Then he turned his gaze to the other people in the church, his congregation.

Something was wrong with Wilbur Wilson. All the other members of the church were standing, singing this final hymn, but Wilbur had stayed seated in the pew, his head bowed—in prayer? illness?—his body curved. Beside him Norma Wilson stood turned sideways, holding her hymnal dutifully in her hands, but her eyes were cast downward, as if she did not dare stop her vigilance for a moment. Then Wilbur looked up at Norma, and nodded, and Peter breathed a sigh of relief. Perhaps he was only sick, perhaps he had a touch of flu.

In another pew, Suzanna Blair stood with her hymnal in one hand, and with her other hand, she was buttoning her jacket around her. She had put the first button in the wrong buttonhole, so the jacket hung crookedly. She seemed to be awkward now, ill at ease. Peter renewed his resolve to ask Judy Bennett to speak with Suzanna, to offer help.

Judy Bennett stood in the front pew, her head held high as she sang the closing lines of the hymn. On either side of her stood her husband and son, like a pair of tall male bookends, but Peter suspected it was she who supported them rather than the other way around. Peter admired the symmetry of the trio as they stood there, such healthy, clear-eyed people, and he felt a twinge of envy that the Bennetts' son had fit himself into their lives so well. He wondered what it was they had done *right* where he as a father had gone wrong. How had they managed to raise a son who stood at their side with such content?

Liza Howard had already put her hymnal in its wooden rack in front of her, and now she stood with her hands raised, holding the collar of her mink coat up against her neck and face. She was staring, dreamy-eyed, at Johnny Bennett, and a sleek fat-cat smile played on her lips. Slowly she rubbed her chin into the silky collar of her fur coat. Steadily she gazed at Johnny Bennett, with slightly lowered eyelids: a sinister, compelling look. My God, she is bewitching, Peter thought, and just then Johnny Bennett, pretending to bend to put his hymnal in the rack, turned slightly and looked back at Liza. Peter could not see Johnny's expression, but he could see Liza's: her eyes flashed in recognition and she slowly opened her mouth and touched the tip of her pink tongue to her soft pink upper lip. Her smile widened. Johnny turned back to face the front. He had been turned toward Liza for only a few seconds. But Peter could see from his vantage point how Liza stood now, eyes glittering. She and Johnny were conspirators; there could be no doubt. But what could Peter do about it? What *should* he do? For now, he tried to focus on the rest of the congregation while his thoughts cleared.

Leigh Findly was sharing a hymnal with her daughter Mandy,

but neither woman was singing. Mandy was half turned to look toward the back of the church, her body tense, and Peter could see enough of her face to tell that she was biting her lip. She was searching out someone—who? Beside her, Leigh looked down at her daughter with smiling curiosity, then, as the last word of the hymn was sung, nudged her. Mandy started, looked up at her mother, and the two women shared a quick affectionate glance before turning to the front and staring up at Peter with expectation. He could sense from their attitude of forced composure that the moment the service was over they would lean into each other and laugh.

Behind him, Reynolds' voice swelled powerfully and held the last note of the hymn. That man had the breath and stamina to outlast the organ, Peter thought. He was grateful for Reynolds' presence in the church, and in fact he always kept Reynolds and his knowledge and critical intelligence in mind when he wrote his sermons. It kept him from getting sloppy. Peter couldn't imagine why Reynolds needed to talk to him today, but it pleased him to think that he might be able to be of some help to this solitary man. "A matter of grave concern," Reynolds had said when he asked Peter if they could talk after church. Well, Peter was not worried. Reynolds was a grave man, his problem was probably intellectual.

The hymn ended. The organ music swelled, faded, died. The members of Peter's congregation looked up at him for one brief moment, then bowed their heads as he raised his arm to give the benediction. Peter saw them all then, old and young, rich and poor, glad and worried, and he loved them. Suddenly a longing flared up inside him, and he wanted to tell them that they were beautiful, that as they stood before him, they seemed ensconced within the church like precious vessels, and that all the objects man holds dear—velvets, jewels, perfumes, silks, silver, gold, houses, and even land—were thin and meager substances compared to their own persons. It was a miracle that the vast electric energy of their minds and hearts could be contained within a fabric so smooth and complete as skin. They really were true miracles, each one of them, and in his mind, he bowed down before them all. He loved them, these members of his congregation, he loved them, body and soul. He wished he could keep them just as they were at this moment. He wished he could keep them safe and happy forever.

Instead, he lifted his hand high in blessing and spoke the usual
ceremonial words: "May the grace of our Lord Jesus Christ and the
love of God and the fellowship of the Holy Ghost be with us now and
forevermore. Amen."

In their loft, gathered around the organist, the choir very softly
sang the choral amen. Mrs. Pritchard's plump fingers began to press
out a gentle postlude, Handel's *Allegro*. Peter Taylor walked down the
five steps from the chancel and passed down the red-carpeted center
aisle of the church, to be at the door to greet the congregation when
they filed out. The members of the First Congregational Church of
Londonton raised their bowed heads slowly, as if awakening from a
dream, and moved politely from their pews out into the day.

PART TWO

Sunday afternoon and evening
October 18, 1981

The last notes of the *Allegro* resonated through the sanctuary. Peter Taylor reached the central doors which opened onto the narthex, and waited there to greet the members of his congregation. Gary Moyer, who had been ushering, pushed the high brass-trimmed main doors open to the outside world. The chilly October air entered, making the hem of Peter's black robe tremble.

While his father was occupied greeting his parishioners, Michael Taylor managed to slip out the door, past the knot of handshakers.

Pam Moyer also slipped out onto the narthex without greeting Peter; she wanted to be sure that the bulletin board in Friendship Hall was ready.

Liza Howard passed through the line, then stood slightly to the left of the main doors, ostensibly easing her brown kid gloves over her hands. It was a difficult task; she had so many large rings. Her expression and posture were those of a person relaxed to the point of boredom, but she was alert. She was watching for Johnny Bennett to come, shake hands with the minister, greet other members of the congregation, and then to set eyes on Liza. They would look at each other briefly, and smile. Just those few seconds of recognition and conspiracy, just that one electric pinpoint of contact, that rush of lust—that was what Liza wanted for a little snack right now before leaving church and going out into her day.

The sanctuary emptied; the entrance hall filled. People moved in and out of the various doors leading from the narthex to the basement, which held Friendship Hall, or to the nursery, or to the Sunday school rooms and bathrooms. Friends searched out friends, parents looked for children, children raced up the choir-loft stairs to hide from parents and giggle with friends; people shook Peter's hand and went out the front doors, then came back in again, having remembered a message they wanted to give someone, and went through the door leading to Friendship Hall.

Wilbur Wilson said to Norma after they had greeted Peter, "I don't feel very good. I think we'd better forget the coffee hour and go on home."

"Oh," Norma said. "All right. Just wait one moment, though. I have to ask Flora about the auxiliary meeting. Okay?"

"Okay," Wilbur said. "I'll wait here." He leaned up against a wall and watched people come out of the sanctuary.

The Bennett family approached Peter Taylor. They had been sitting at the front of the church, and were among the last to leave. The sanctuary was nearly empty now, and the entrance hall was crowded. Voices echoed; people said, "Excuse me, please," and squeezed past each other.

Reynolds Houston shook hands with Peter, said, "I'll talk with you after coffee hour," and walked toward the door leading to Friendship Hall. It was then that he felt someone rudely nudge him in the back—in fact, it was actually quite a hard shove. He moved aside, turning to see just who it was that had affronted him. In the very act of turning, something in the air alerted him: something more significant than rudeness had just happened. He turned quickly enough to see Wilbur Wilson buckle and crumple to the floor.

"Norma," Wilbur said, and his knees came up to his chest with pain. The tiles were cold and he was surrounded by legs and shoes.

"Oh, *my!*" someone said, and the room around Wilbur went still for a moment with shock, while people at opposite ends of the entrance hall began to call, "What's happened? What's going on?"

Reynolds squatted down so that Wilbur could see his face. "What's wrong?" he asked.

"My chest hurts," Wilbur said. "Oh, God, I think I'm having a heart attack."

"You'll be all right," Reynolds said. "We'll get help." But Wilbur's eyes closed—he had passed out. Reynolds rocked back on his heels, frightened at the sight of someone so startlingly out of control, then he put his hands on the floor and pushed himself up. "I think Wilbur Wilson's had a heart attack," he announced.

"Wilbur!" Norma cried. "Please let me through!" She began to claw her way from the end of the room to the center where Wilbur lay.

"Is there a doctor here?" Peter called, knowing as he spoke that there wasn't. Many doctors were official members of the church but few of them came regularly. "Call an ambulance," Peter said. He looked to see who was standing closest to the door leading to the upstairs offices. "Pam," he called. "Hurry. Call an ambulance."

The hallway surged with action. Pam Moyer raced up the stairs and everyone else turned toward the spot where Wilbur lay. Many of them tried to push forward to see him, as if it could not be true until they had actually set eyes on the man.

Judy Bennett moved through the crowd, looked down at Wilbur's inert body, and said with authority, "Stand back. Someone give me a coat; he needs to be covered up. Everybody stand back. He needs air."

"Coats! Air! *Christ!*" Liza Howard said. "He needs CPR. Doesn't anyone here know CPR?" She glanced around quickly, her expression indicating clearly that it was only too obvious that the fools gathered around her had no knowledge of CPR. Then she sank to her knees, so swiftly that the sides of her coat flew upward like the wings of a bird. She tore her gloves from her hands and dropped them, then quickly loosened Wilbur's tie and collar and shirt. She placed her ear against his chest, and at the same time grasped his wrist, but quickly and unceremoniously dropped it. She took Wilbur's head in her hands and gently flexed it backward, then she pinched his nostrils together and put her mouth to his. She took her mouth away, and in what seemed to the onlookers an obscene gesture, she brought her right leg over Wilbur's body so that she straddled his hips with her knees, careful not to let the weight of her body touch his. She pushed both hands down hard at the center of his lower chest, and pushed again, and again, and again, and again, then brought her mouth down over Wilbur's once more.

The room buzzed with whispers.

"What's she doing?"

"CPR."

"What's that?"

"Cardio-pulmonary respiration."

"Resuscitation."

"Look how gray he is!"

"How old is he?"

"I called the ambulance," Pam Moyer called from a doorway. "They're on their way."

"Let Norma through," someone said.

Norma dropped on her knees next to her husband and took his hand, but carefully kept out of Liza's way.

"Is he breathing?"

"Is he okay?"

"Is he dead?"

Liza worked on, oblivious to the questions, intent on the rhythm of counting as she pushed Wilbur's chest and breathed into his mouth.

Several children came clattering down the choir-loft stairs or up from the basement. "What's happening?" they asked in shrill voices, and were shunted off down the stairs to Friendship Hall by adults who had suddenly gone stern, as if solemnity were necessary to save Wilbur's life. Everyone else stood still, helpless witnesses to the scene, and if there was ever a time in the history of this congregation when the members thought as one, it was now. "Oh, God, help him, let him live," they prayed, in that silent, individual way that people pray at points of crisis. Occasionally Norma Wilson's voice broke the silence: "Oh, God, oh, God," she cried.

Liza worked on, like an expensive machine, pushing on Wilbur's chest, breathing into his mouth. From above, her pumping body in the thick mink coat looked like that of an animal; people could see nothing but the brown fur and her shining blond hair. When she leaned forward to breathe into his mouth, her bottom rose high in the air, so that she seemed involved in some weird sexual parody. Peter Taylor had moved through the crowd and knelt down next to Norma, touching her shoulder gently in support. For a terrifying moment this tableau seemed frozen, eternal; Wilbur would always lie there, dying; Liza would always kneel above him, forcing him to live; the members of the church would stand around him, captured there, helpless, forever.

But an ambulance siren screamed in the distance and then screamed closer and abruptly stopped. Two men and a woman came in through the high wooden church doors and went immediately to Wilbur. The crowd automatically pushed back to make room for them. Liza did not stop or look up, did not break her rhythm until one of the attendants placed an oxygen mask over Wilbur's face.

"He's alive. He's breathing. He's responding," one of the men said. He looked at Liza, who had brought her body off of Wilbur's and was just kneeling there by his side. "You did a good job," he said to her.

Then the attendants got Wilbur's inert body onto a stretcher and people cleared a path so they could get him out the door.

"Can I ride with you?" Norma asked, clutching the sleeve of one of the men. "I'm his wife."

"I'm sorry, but we've got work to do. You'd get in the way. You'll have to have someone else drive you," the man said, and then they were out the door.

Almost everyone clamored at once, offering to drive Norma to the hospital, but Ron Bennett, seeing that the woman was too stunned to decide, pushed through the crowd, took Norma's arm, and led her out the door.

"I've got my car keys right here," he said. "My car is just over there."

So it did not strike anyone as especially strange when John Bennett pushed his way through to where Liza Howard was, still kneeling on the black and white tiles. Like father, like son, people thought, if they thought anything about it: two kind and helpful men.

John knelt down next to Liza. "Are you okay?" he asked softly.

She had just been sitting back on her heels, her head down, as if trying to catch her breath. Now she raised her head and met his eyes, and her own blue eyes shimmered at him. Johnny wanted to lift her up in his arms, this unparalleled creature, he wanted to carry her over the threshold of the church and out into the world as if she were his bride.

"Let me take you home," he said. "I'll drive your car for you."

He rose, and Liza gave him her hand, that hand which moments before had seemed such an efficient, competent, inhuman thing, pushing life back into Wilbur's chest. He helped her to her feet.

People began to crowd toward her now.

"Liza, that was wonderful!"

"Liza, you were marvelous. You saved his life!"

"Liza—"

But she would not look at them. Johnny, as if protecting her, led her out the doors.

Mandy Findly, who had been too much behind other people to see anything, now was shoved forward by the crowd, and she tripped on something. Looking down, she saw that she was standing on Liza Howard's brown kid gloves. She bent down and picked them up and smoothed them out; how supple, how deliciously soft the skin was! What kind of creature was Liza Howard, Mandy thought, to be capable of saving a man's life, and yet to own such glamorous gloves?

Judy Bennett watched her husband lead Norma Wilson through the tall main doors and then her son lead Liza Howard out the same way. She was slightly surprised at Johnny's actions, but she thought: How like him, to be like his father, like *all Bennetts,* thoughtful, helpful, taking charge. Her husband and son had risen chivalrously to the occasion before any other males, and Judy felt proud of them, and a little smug. She turned to search out Pam and Gary Moyer, who would be only too glad to drive her home.

So Judy Bennett did not see how her son kept his arm around Liza Howard as they went down the sidewalk toward Liza's black Cadillac.

"You were wonderful," Johnny was saying to Liza. "You were *magnificent*. Shit, you saved his life!"

"Yes," Liza said, "I probably *did* save his life. At least that part of life that's important. When there's a heart attack, it's the brain that goes fastest. It dies in the first five minutes."

They came to the black Cadillac and stopped. Johnny opened the door for Liza and she slid in. When he had crossed around and settled himself behind the steering wheel, he looked over at Liza. She was sitting very still, staring straight ahead, as if she were looking at some scene from some other time.

"Well, damn, honey," Johnny said. "I just can't get over it. That whole church full of people, and you're the one who knew what to do. Were you a nurse once? How'd you come to know stuff like that?"

Liza turned toward him, but did not look at him. "I know *stuff like that*," she said, "because I married a man who had already had two heart attacks. When I knew I was going to marry Mitchell, I took a course in CPR, hoping that if—if the occasion ever arose—" Liza broke off.

"But Mitchell died of a heart attack, didn't he?" Johnny asked.

"Mitchell died of a heart attack," Liza said. She glared at Johnny. "He died in bed right next to me as we slept. He didn't do me the favor of giving me the chance to help him. I woke up that morning, and he was lying there in bed next to me, and he was dead. The doctor came and said that Mitchell had had a heart attack. My God, the *irony* of it. There I was, completely prepared to save his life, and he lay right next to me and *died*. The fool. Why couldn't he have just reached over and tugged my arm?"

Johnny stared at Liza, entranced. He had never known any woman who was quite so calm and also so passionate. She had turned her face sharply away from him in a firm motion, and as she sat next to him now, fierce and arrogant, she was contemptuous of tears. To Johnny she seemed a magical woman. If he had not been totally enslaved by his love for her before, he was so now.

"I'll drive home, Liza," he said, for he could think of nothing else to say.

They drove in silence, too occupied with private thoughts to speak. Liza was thinking that in China, Japan, one of those places, they believed that if you saved a person's life you were then responsible for that life, like a parent. Or was it that the person then owed his life to you? Whichever way, she wanted no part of it. She was glad to have been able to save Wilbur Wilson's life, for she liked him, but she could foresee the consequences of her action, and it almost made her ill. Mrs. Wilson would have to call her to thank her, and all the do-gooders who had stood around gawking would be in a frenzy now, wanting to be the first to call her to praise her so that they could in turn call each other and discuss it. People did that sort of thing, milked every ounce of drama they could out of a situation; and then they liked praising people for a virtuous or valorous act, because it made them in turn seem virtuous or valorous for having recognized it. This was just the sort of self-important, picayune community that grasped at such occasions as opportunities to puff itself up and give *awards*. Oh, God, she would really die if they tried to give her an award, but she could just see how they would all fuss and flurry around, trying to make her one instinctive act into something larger, so that there would be room enough for them all to own a part of it. She could not bear it. Simpering hypocrites. She would not answer the phone today, to speak to people who had shunned her before. No. She would pack and leave town today. Let Johnny come with her today, or not at all.

Johnny was thinking that Liza was a true heroine. He was thinking that it had to *mean something* that she had saved a person's life, and *in church*. He always had been just a little afraid of Liza, because of her sexual power, and now he admitted to himself that he was still in awe of her, but that it had somehow been proven to him that it was okay, this awe, this love, it was good. How could a woman who saved lives not be good? In fact, he was immensely aroused. He wanted to possess this magic woman, sexually and in every other way. He wanted her to be his.

He parked the Cadillac in front of the Howard mansion, and they went in. The house rose cool, vast, and shadowy around them. Liza turned to Johnny but did not really see him. She had that out-of-focus, preoccupied look that made her large eyes seem even more enormous.

"Thanks for driving me home," she said. She laughed shortly then, as a thought occurred to her. "Now how are *you* going to get home?"

"I'm not going home," Johnny said. He wanted the drama of the morning to last. "I'm not leaving your side ever again," he said. He drew her to him, and held her tightly against his body.

"Oh, Johnny." She was exhausted.

But her reluctance only made him more ardent. He could not have explained the subtleties of this moment—they stood there together in the entrance hall, still in their coats, in each other's arms. He could not have compared this moment, when Liza just leaned against him, her arms hanging at her sides, her long body almost limp, her whole being still, with all the other times they had held each other. Those other times Liza had been the seductress, supple and elegant, but busy, busy—busy doing things to him. She had been the one in charge. But now she was soft with a languorous indifference, cat-like; she was a different woman, and Johnny did not know why, but he was as excited as if he were holding a new lover in his arms. He bent to put one arm under her knees, and with a graceful swoop he did what he had always dreamed of doing with a woman: he picked her up, thick fur coat and all, up, up into his arms, and turned to carry her up the stairs to the bedroom. Liza drew her arms around his neck and let her head droop against his chest, thinking, oh, well, she had played the heroine; now he could play the hero.

But just then the phone rang, startling them both so much that he almost dropped her. The phone seldom rang in this house.

"I cannot bear it," Liza said, and meant it.

Johnny turned away from the stairs and carried Liza into the library. A white-and-gold telephone sat on the long mahogany library table, ringing imperiously. Johnny knocked the phone onto the floor with an elbow, and the ringing stopped, but only to be replaced by a woman's voice saying, "Hello? Hellow? Is this Liza Howard's residence? Hel-low?"

"Oh, rip the damned thing out of the wall," Liza said.

Johnny looked at the phone, looked at Liza, then set her as delicately as possible right down on the library table. He bent down and yanked the phone cord. It did not come out easily. He pulled again, and then harder, faster, again, and finally the woman's voice was done away with, and he turned back to Liza, a dead phone cord hanging in his hand.

Liza smiled, and then, with one long movement, she slid her arms behind her, as if slowly stretching, and leaned back, back until she was lying on the table. Her head nestled against a pair of brass bookends holding a leather-bound set of dictionaries; her outstretched arm softly struck a crystal ashtray, and it fell to the carpet with a thud. She lay there, a sleek strange sight, with her knees bent exactly at the end of the table so that her legs hung down as if broken. She was motionless, waiting, and as Johnny looked at her, at all that richness, smooth skin against silk fabric sinking into silk-lined fur against polished mahogany, he longed to sink into her. He dropped the phone cord and eased himself between Liza's legs. The table was a perfect height: he slid his hands up her thighs under the silk of her dress, and the fabric of the dress made a slithery sound as it drew away from her legs. She was wearing a garter belt and hose and underpants—of course underpants, she had been at church. She just lay there watching as Johnny unsnapped the garters, then reached up with both hands and slipped her lacy beige panties down. He unzipped his trousers, and pulled Liza to him, and, bending his knees slightly, thrust into her. She was moist; she closed her eyes; she scarcely moved. She didn't have to: Johnny was moving to her, pulling her hips toward him with both hands, moving his own hips to hers as rhythmically as a machine.

"Johnny," Liza said suddenly, and when her eyes flew open, it was as if a door had been flung wide, exposing secrets. Needing to grasp on to something, she reached for the back of the leather sofa which stretched along the length of the library table, but Johnny pulled her toward him just then, and instead of gripping the sofa, she only managed to drag her nails down it, leaving five long rippling marks irrevocably in the dark leather.

In the weeks they had known each other they had done many things with each other's bodies to give pleasure, but this was an act of a different sort. It had about it the binding intimacy of seeing the other in illness or fear or extreme joy or pain. *Now*, Liza thought, as Johnny finally cried out and gripped her thighs so tightly she knew her skin would show bruises, now either he will run or he will be bound to me forever. His head was bent back, his eyes closed, and he stayed that way as his body relaxed against her, and when he finally lowered his head to look down at her, she saw that he was afraid.

"Johnny Bennett, in the library, on the library table," she said, smiling, to ease the situation.

"Liza," Johnny said, "did I hurt you?"

"No," she lied, and reached her arms forward so that he could take her hands and pull her up into a sitting position. She wrapped her arms around his back and pressed her head against his chest and they stayed that way awhile, catching their breath. Liza could feel how Johnny was shaking, ever so slightly, and she held him tighter.

"I didn't mean to hurt you," Johnny said. "I can't help how I am when I'm with you."

"I know," she answered. "Sssh. I know." She brought her hand up and placed it gently over his mouth. The expression in his eyes alarmed her: he looked so *sincere,* and Liza knew just how terrified a boy like Johnny Bennett would be if he suspected he actually *loved* a woman like her. It was okay to indulge himself in one last pleasure binge, to spend himself sexually in one prolonged and carefree spree; but he would not be able to approve of himself if he felt true affection for a woman he had just fucked as if she were a whore. He was, in his own way, as Victorian as Charles Dickens in his morality, and Liza knew she had to act fast if she were to keep the situation light—if she were to keep him.

"I'm starving," she said. "Aren't you? I could eat a horse." She nuzzled into his shirt and bit his tummy, then worked her mouth down.

"Hey," he said, and bent down and bit her back. He pulled her face to his and kissed her cheeks, her eyes, her neck, but Liza tossed her head away from him, laughing, and cried, "Food! I need food!"

So he pulled her to her feet and they hurried, arms wrapped around each other, down the long carpeted hall to the kitchen. Johnny turned on the radio and found a station that played rock music. He opened two bottles of British ale, put dill and garlic pickles on a plate. Liza buttered thin rye bread, then piled slivers of rare roast beef on top, and covered it with chunks of Boursin cheese, then melted it all under the broiler. Finally they sat across from each other at the kitchen table, eating the sandwiches, licking the dripping butter and cheese from their fingers.

"I think we should leave today," Liza said when she had almost finished her sandwich. "I think we should go *now*—just throw our things in a suitcase and go."

"I don't have any clothes with me," Johnny said. "And I can't just go home and pack up my stuff—"

"Never mind about clothes," Liza said. "We'll fly to New York. We'll buy you a whole new wardrobe. We'll go someplace where it's hot and you won't need anything but shorts—"

"Let's go to Mexico," Johnny said, for her enthusiasm was contagious and his second ale combined with his memories of the morning made him feel fervently young and alive, and eager to express this youth, this life, in some dramatic way. "Let's go to Acapulco. We'll just swim in the ocean, we won't need any clothes at all."

"Yes, Mexico," Liza said. "We'll swim in the ocean, we'll get lost in the crowds, no one will ever find us!"

"If I can't take any clothes, you can't, either," Johnny said.

"All right," Liza said. "Fine. But I will have to pack some necessities—jewelry, money, traveler's checks, checkbooks, and, my darling, birth-control pills—it won't take long."

They were childish, triumphant, like adolescents hurrying to pull off a trick and escape. They left the dishes on the table and went rapidly through the house. Liza swooped up what she needed and threw it into a canvas-and-leather traveling bag. This was the sort of thing she loved to do, this was the sort of thing she was born to do—wild, brash, extravagant acts of escape—and she glowed as she moved. Johnny followed her about, nearly ill with excitement, caught up in the momentum, needing to be caught up in the momentum so he wouldn't stop to think. It seemed to him that if he could just move fast enough and not lose courage, he could escape the fate of Wilbur Wilson and every other human being in this town. He could run away from death. He could make certain that he would never keel over in the entry of a church or nearly die in front of an entire town.

"Ready!" Liza called at last, and Johnny called, "Wait!" He ran back to the kitchen and grabbed up a six-pack of ale and a bottle opener, thinking himself immensely clever and responsible for remembering the bottle opener. They went out the door, slamming it with gusto, and threw the canvas bag in the back of the Cadillac, and jumped in.

"I'll drive," Liza said. "I know the road from here to the Hartford airport like the back of my hand—like the front of your hand!"

Johnny laughed and opened an ale and the golden foam shot up and out of the bottle, cascading down over his slacks and her silk dress. They laughed at this, and it did seem *right,* as if the beer had caught their mood and was spontaneous, explosive, mischievous, like them. Johnny turned the car radio to a rock station, and sang loudly to the songs he knew. From time to time he reached across the seat of the Cadillac to press kisses onto Liza's face, neck, arms, and breasts.

"My hair's a mess!" Liza yelled at one point, when they had stopped at a toll booth on the turnpike and she caught a glimpse of herself in the rearview mirror. "I look insane, Johnny! Why didn't you tell me! Here, trade places with me. You drive while I fix my hair."

"Oh, no," Johnny said. "Huh-uh. You drive. Leave your hair like that. It looks great. You look like you just finished making love. You look all disheveled and—*handled.*"

She smiled at him. "Keep it up," she said, "you've got the potential to develop into a truly decadent person."

"Good," Johnny said. "That's exactly what I want to be." As he spoke, he realized that what he said was absolutely true. He felt he had discovered a genius within himself for a vocation his parents had

never told him existed. He had never been trained for this new life—
and yet, he was sure, it would suit him very well.

Liza had turned the heater on against the October chill, and the
car filled with warm air that circulated the aroma of their two bodies
and the perfume of those bodies and the smell of spilled ale through
the car. They abandoned the Cadillac in the airport's long-term parking lot, and within two hours of making love in the library, within two
and a half hours of Wilbur Wilson's heart attack, they were seated on
a plane to New York.

At that moment, Peter Taylor was standing outside his own
house, and his eyes were lifted upward. He was studying the gutters.
He had just returned from the hospital, and had changed into his favorite old khaki pants, a plaid flannel shirt, and a pair of blue-and-
white and slightly decomposing sneakers. This side of the house was
sheltered by an enormous old catalpa tree which Peter threatened repeatedly to have cut down. It had beautiful fragrant flowers in the
spring, white petals streaked with pink and fluted lacily around the
edges. When the children were little, they put a flower on each finger
and paraded around pretending they were little old ladies wearing
gloves. Once a year, for about two weeks, the tree was spectacular with
these flowers, but at almost every other moment of the year, it was a
trial. After the trumpet-shaped blossoms bloomed, they shriveled and
fell, clogging the gutters along this side of the house. Then the tree
sprouted long skinny pods, like wooden string beans, which also fell,
with a dry clattery sound, into the gutters. Now it was fall and the
giant heart-shaped leaves were falling—catalpas seemed to be the last
trees to bloom and the first to lose their leaves. They were clogging the
gutter again. If Peter didn't get the gutter cleaned out soon, the first
strong rain that came would cause the gutters to overflow, making
brown streaks down the house, and worse, causing all the water to
back up and flood down just where the back door opened, so the
Taylor family would have to forge through a giant puddle just to get
out of the house.

Probably the gutters weren't crucially full yet, but it was better to
be safe than sorry.

Besides, Peter was anxious and worried and full of a sense of dread. He had that all-wired-up feeling. He needed right now to be outside in the fresh air, working physically, on a concrete, manageable problem. Not for the first time he wished he had a woodlot so that he could go cut fireplace wood with a bow saw until he panted and sweated with exhaustion and his mind was worked clean of all images but those of the splintering wood.

He had been dissatisfied this morning in church. Then there had been the crisis with Wilbur. Now, just a few short hours later, he wished he'd had the sensitivity to interpret the atmosphere of his church more accurately. He felt very much now as he had often felt as a parent who considered his child spoiled and bad-tempered only to discover that the child was in fact exhibiting the early signs of an illness. He felt guilty, as if he'd been dense. But then, he told himself, what good would it have done if he had been anxious? It would have changed nothing.

Will came out of the house and toward his father.

"Michael's not in his room," he said. "I don't know where he is. He split right after church. Want me to help with the ladder?"

Peter looked at his younger son. Will at thirteen was short and actually a little puny for his age, but for just that reason it wouldn't do to refuse his offer of help with the ladder. He would have preferred it, though, if his older son, who was so large and strong and graceful with this sort of thing, had had the thoughtfulness to stick around. Peter had told the family at breakfast this morning what he hoped to accomplish in the afternoon. The only ladder they had was an old-fashioned wooden one, cumbersome and heavy. He and Will would manage to carry it from the garage and get it propped up against the house, but Peter wasn't thrilled about climbing up to the top of the second floor— where the roof rose in a peak it was a good forty feet from the ground —with only his ninety-five-pound son bracing the ladder. Where was Michael? Well, Peter would climb the ladder with a superstitious sense of security: so much else had gone wrong today that he couldn't believe the ladder would slip and he would fall, too.

"Yeah, Will, let's get the ladder," he said. He followed his son into the garage and for a few moments was totally occupied, trying to disengage the old relic of a ladder from the garden hoses and bikes and ski poles and garden tools in the garage. Why was their garage so untidy? Just why on earth had anyone seen fit to keep *three* broken hockey sticks? "How did this place get to be such a mess?" he said.

Will shrugged. "I don't know, Dad. It's always been like this."

"Well, it's terrible!"

"Oh, I don't know," Will said, hefting his end of the ladder and giving it a tug. "I think it's pretty normal—for a garage. All the other garages I've seen look pretty much like ours."

"What makes you such an authority on garages?" Peter asked, amused and touched by his son's good nature. And the boy was surprisingly strong; he was certainly carrying his end of the ladder well.

"You'd be surprised," Will said. "I must spend as much time in garages as in living rooms. More. You know, Sam's building a go-cart, his brother's helping him. It's neat. Chet Elliott gave them a used lawn mower engine. And we found three great old wheels out at the dump and—"

"You go out to the dump much?" Peter asked.

"Yeah, it's really neat there. You'd be surprised at the things you can find. People throw out the best stuff!"

They carried the ladder to the side of the house, Will talking all the way. Lord, Peter thought, if he could somehow just siphon off an ounce of this son's enthusiasm for life and inject it into Michael, what a help that would be! They managed to get the ladder propped up against the house.

"Now you stand there like this," Peter said, "and brace the ladder."

"Sure, Dad," Will said.

Peter climbed up the ladder, and Will kept on talking about Sam's go-cart, yelling so his father could hear. Thank God, Peter thought, as he reached the top and peered into his leaf-packed gutters. Thank God for the reality of these hard white clapboards and his son's chattering optimism. Peter reached into the gutter and grabbed up a handful of crackly brown leaves. They crumbled in his fist and he tossed them to the ground.

"Want me to get a trash bag, Dad?" Will called up.

"Not yet," Peter said. "You stay down there and hold the ladder."

Actually the ladder would probably do fine without Will; it was Peter who needed the bracing presence of his son. He scooped up leaves, tossed them into the air, scooped again. The world looked fine

from up here, clear, clean, organized. From this vantage point, as he
half stood, half lay against the ladder, he could look down into his
daughter's bedroom. She had placed her white desk under the window
and arranged in perfect symmetry her pens and pencils, school notebooks and pink-and-gold diary, cat statues and a little shellacked
wooden box holding—what?—paper clips, rubber bands? Lucy was
such a tidy child. The window frame enclosed the scene so that it
looked like a picture: "Child's Desk," by Lucy Taylor.

Seen this way, from the outside, through glass, framed by wood,
her desk took on the features of an oil painting, a real still life, captured as if for eternity. What elegance the objects of ordinary life had
when isolated and bordered in this way, Peter thought, and he hoped
that as Wilbur Wilson lay in the hospital, drifting helplessly through
unknown countries of pain and strangeness, scenes like this from his
own life would pass by him, Alice-in-Wonderland-like, for him to see,
remember, take comfort from.

By the time Peter had taken off his vestments and arranged plans
with Patricia and gotten to the hospital, Wilbur was already in the
Coronary Care Ward, being cared for by Southmark's best cardiac spe-
cialist. Peter joined Norma and Ron Bennett and the six or seven
others who had come to help Norma in her vigil in the waiting room
on the fourth floor. The doctors were working on him, people told
Peter. It would be five or six hours before they would know for sure
what his condition would be. But one thing was certain: he was alive,
and in much better shape than he would have been if Liza Howard
had not come to his aid so quickly. "Imagine that woman knowing a
thing like CPR," everyone kept repeating, "just imagine." Peter sat
with Norma, talking with her, holding her hand. Then he led them all
in a prayer for Wilbur's quick return to health.

Norma seemed fine, even self-possessed, although of course almost
an hour had gone by since the attack, and what Norma was feeling
was probably tempered by exhaustion and relief.

"I've asked Bertha to bring me my knitting," she told Peter. "I'll
be okay if I can just get my hands on my knitting. I never was very
good at just sitting still and waiting."

"Yes," Peter said, "I think this kind of waiting is the hardest kind
of work we can do." But then he thought of Wilbur, lying near death
on his hospital bed, and knew that Wilbur's work was even harder: he

had to fight to live. "Norma," he said, "I'll stay here with you as long as you want me."

Norma patted his hand, as if she were comforting him, and smiled. "Peter, that's very kind of you. But go on home. They told me he was conscious for a few moments. He's doing fine. And I've got plenty of other people here to keep me company. I just feel certain I won't be needing you in any official capacity today. But I am grateful you came. Thank you."

It was true that Norma didn't need Peter for company. As he rose to go, several other friends crowded into the little room. There weren't enough chairs to go around.

"Oh, Norma," one woman said, and bent to embrace her. "I'm so sorry."

But Norma pulled back. "Don't cry yet," she said. "Don't be so sorry just yet. He's alive. Is Bertha here yet? Did she bring my knitting?"

Peter drove home, thinking of Wilbur and what a loss it would be to everyone if he died. Wilbur provided a strong, solid streak of color in the pattern of Londonton's people, and if he died, that particular part of the daily design of their lives would fade, would cause a rough and obvious absence. But maybe he would not die. Norma was a tough old soul, and he admired her for her staunch refusal to grieve a moment too soon. Peter had spent many hours in similar situations, trying to comfort a person whose loved one lay ill. He had thought, as a young minister, that it would get easier as he grew older and more experienced, that he would learn the right things to say and do. Well, he hoped he had improved, was less clumsy, more sensitive, more articulate. He was by now fairly good at comforting. But it never got any easier for him in the privacy of his own heart and soul. Remembrances of former griefs did not lessen the pain of new ones. Fear and pain were always the same: intolerable. And beside the hulking shadow of death, everything else paled.

So the cold metal of the gutter and the obdurate wood of his house were as satisfying to Peter's touch as light and a cold hard floor to a man who has awakened from a nightmare. Peter climbed down the ladder and moved it along the house, then ascended once more, tossed down more crackling catalpa leaves.

"Dad," Will called up after a while, finally bored with his passive job, "you know I've got a soccer game at three-thirty."

"It's not even three yet," Peter called down. "You've got plenty of time." Then, relenting: "Actually, Will, if you've got other things you want to do, go ahead. I'm just about done with this gutter, and I think the ladder's okay by itself. I'll get your mother to help me carry it back if you're not around."

"Great!" Will whooped, and raced off to the garage. He came out a second later, pedaling his ten-speed bike. "I'll be at Sam's for a while!" he yelled, and sped off around the corner.

"Be careful! Slow down! Watch where you're going!" Peter called; it was an old habit, hard to break. If Will didn't know how to handle himself on a bike by now, he never would. Still Peter felt that old anxiety begin to throb in his breast, a pulse by now as natural and familiar as that which carried his blood, a pulse which began the minute the children left the house on their own and didn't stop until they were all safe in bed, tucked in, asleep. Why couldn't children stay home? Why had anyone been crazy enough to invent cars? Why couldn't everyone just *walk*?

"Peter? Reynolds Houston wants you on the phone," Patricia said, walking around the corner of the house just in time to be showered with a fall of crumbled leaves.

"Sorry," Peter called. "I didn't see you coming. Tell him I'll call him back. I just want to finish this gutter."

Patricia shook her head, trying to shake the leaves from her hair. She was wearing jeans and a bright red sweater. He loved her for that red sweater, that bright announcement of life.

"Well, he sounded worried. He said it was important."

"Oh, great," Peter grumbled, and began to climb down the ladder.

"I'll finish for you," Patricia offered. "I don't mind."

Peter jumped off the ladder and landed right in front of Patricia as she touched the wooden sides.

"Look, *don't*," he said. "Okay? Don't climb this damned ladder today, okay? I'll finish it after I talk to Reynolds. Just go on in the house and cook or something. I've got my hands full without your falling off a ladder."

Patricia gave Peter her old squinty-eyed summing-up look. "You grouch," she said. "You haven't had lunch. You got out on this ladder right after going to the hospital. I'll fix you a sandwich. Come in the kitchen and eat before you come back out. Do it for me; I hate it when you're grumpy."

"I don't feel very hungry right now," Peter said, and it was true. Every time someone in his congregation died, Peter lost his appetite, but although he fought a weight problem every day of his life, he never did appreciate this way of shedding pounds.

"Peter," Patricia said.

"All right." Peter smiled. He put his arm around her and pulled her to him. "I like your red sweater," he told her. "You cheer me up." They walked into the house together and Peter went to the phone, to talk with Reynolds Houston, whom he had missed talking with after church because of the confusion during Wilbur's heart attack.

Mandy and Michael were down by the river.

They had been there for almost two hours. After Wilbur Wilson's heart attack and the ensuing commotion, Mandy had pushed her way through the crowd and out the high front doors of the church, meaning to chase after Liza Howard to return to her the leather gloves she had dropped and forgotten. But there was something about the sight of Liza's statuesque figure, wrapped and protected by her thick mink coat and John Bennett's embracing arm, which made Mandy walk less quickly after her, then stop altogether. How beautiful they were together, those two tall blondes, and when they stopped by the long black Cadillac, they looked too good to be true, like an advertisement for champagne—or Cadillacs. Mandy bit her lip, pondering. She could envision herself, gawkily running down the walk, waving the gloves, intruding on the gorgeous intimacy of those two shining people—she couldn't do it. She'd give the gloves to the church secretary. Mrs. Howard could stop by the church and pick them up herself when she remembered them. John Bennett got into the Cadillac and the car pulled off; Mandy went back into the church.

She stood for a few minutes just inside, taking in the scene, searching the crowd to see if Michael was there. She couldn't find him; had he somehow already left? She panicked to think she might have missed him, and panicked again to realize how much it meant to her to see him. She moved then, heading for the door to the basement and Friendship Hall.

"Oh, hi, darling, here you are," Leigh Findly said, coming out of the door just as Mandy was about to enter. "I've been looking for you. Are you all right? You look pale."

"Oh, listen, Mom, I found these gloves Mrs. Howard dropped. I ran after her to give them to her, but she'd already left. I've got to give them to the church secretary."

"I think she's downstairs. Reverend Taylor's going right on over to the hospital now, and so are a few others. There's not going to be a regular coffee hour today, now, of course. Why don't you go on down and give the gloves to Mrs. Allen, and I'll wait for you here. It's terrible to admit, after poor Mr. Wilson and all, but I'm starving for lunch. It's such a treat to have you home, I thought I'd take you to the Long House for lunch."

"Oh, Mom. That's so sweet of you—but, well—Mom, there's someone I've got to see. I mean there's someone I've got to find and talk to. I mean, well, could we have *dinner* at the Long House? I was thinking maybe you could just go on home and I'll walk home—pretty soon."

Mandy looked at her mother, loving her for her love, and at the same time wishing she would disappear right now into thin air so that she could get on with her search for Michael.

Leigh looked at her daughter. "The color's returning to your face," she said, and smiled. "All right, dear," she said. "I'll go on home. Of course we can go to the Long House later. And we've got food at home if we want to be lazy. Call me if you want a ride. It's colder out than you'd think." She kissed her daughter's cheek and left.

Mandy scouted through the basement, but found no sign of Michael. She did manage to get the gloves to Mrs. Allen, who was *so* glad to see Mandy again, and who wanted to know *all about* how she was liking college, and how did she like her courses, and did she feel homesick. Mandy wanted to scream, "I've got to go!" Instead she answered the older woman's questions politely, and when she finally escaped, she was nearly in tears. The church was almost empty of people upstairs and down. There was no sign of Michael.

"Goddamnit," Mandy said under her breath. She wondered if she would have the courage to call Michael at his home. She went out the front doors, nearly ill with disappointment.

And there was Michael leaning against one of the high white columns, waiting for her.

"Hi," he said. "I was looking for you."

"I was looking for *you*," she said, and she just stopped dead in her tracks, smiling, weak with relief at the sight of him. One last departing couple came out of the church just then and accidentally hit her in the back as they opened the door on her dumbfounded figure.

"Oh, excuse me," Mandy said, and came alive again, moving a few steps toward Michael, gingerly, as if there were something between them that might break.

"Want to go for a walk?" he asked—and then something did break: the tension between them, the invisible wall of their mutual apprehension.

"Oh, yes," Mandy said.

"Let's go down by the river, then," Michael said.

They walked side by side, not holding hands or touching.

"I didn't know you were going to be home this weekend," Michael said. "You should have let me know."

"Well, I didn't know myself that I was coming home until Friday afternoon," Mandy said. "I just had to get away for a while."

"So what did you do all day yesterday?"

"Just hung around with Mom. Talked and stuff."

"Why didn't you call?"

"Well, I—I didn't know if I *should* call. I mean, when I left for school, we didn't agree to keep in touch or anything. I didn't know if you'd want me to call."

"I want you to call," Michael said. "That's about all I do want."

Mandy went light-headed, breathless with pleasure.

They walked in silence then until they came to the bridge where they had met that first time, and all the other times in the summer. The grass around it was now brown and brittle, but still high, and it made a rustling noise as they half walked, half slid down the embankment. Mandy's coat caught on a high, prickly brown weed, and she stopped to tug her coat away, then turned back and, slipping on a muddy spot, she skated down the final few feet to the bottom of the hill, where Michael caught her in his arms.

She grinned up at him. "These are not the best shoes for this kind of walking."

"It's fine with me," he said, and smiled back down at her, and they stood there, holding each other, looking at each other, inhaling the other's presence like a long-desired, exotic drug.

And here they were again, next to the river, which ran bright and rapid over the pebbled bed. They were away from the town now. They were in *their* place. Michael kissed Mandy, and kept kissing her until a car passed over the bridge above them and a kid yelled out the window: "Whoowhee!"

"Come on," Michael said. He hugged Mandy to his side, and she hugged him back as they walked along the rocks and sand of the river's edge toward the countryside.

"I found out something," Michael said. "I found out that I'm not happy when you're not around. I've been miserable since you left."

"Oh," Mandy said. "Oh, Michael. That's wonderful."

"Thanks a lot."

They smiled. "I haven't been exactly happy myself," Mandy said, and her heart raced.

It was difficult walking along the river's edge. The sand was mucky and wet and Mandy's shoes kept getting sucked down. The sky was still overcast, and a chilly wind swept by, but did not sweep any of the thick puffy clouds away. The world around them was cold and muted, as if all the heat, light, and grace in the world had been concentrated somehow into their bodies. Finally they came to a bend in the river where an arrangement of sloping bank and boulders made a kind of shelter, and they slipped inside the little roofless cave and settled themselves on the sand.

"Will you ruin your coat?" Michael asked.

"Oh, Michael, I don't care about my coat," Mandy said, and reached her arms up to him, and pulled him to her.

They kissed again, with the confident delight of children on Easter morning: searching, finding, searching, finding, here and here and here, treasures, surprises, sweet candy, joy, more and more and more of it. Mandy nudged her head into the navy wool blazer covering Michael's chest and hugged Michael and felt her body hum with pleasure as he ran his hands over her, rediscovering all its swells and hollows.

They could not touch each other enough. They could not hold each other close enough. The wind blew above them, making the limbs of trees click and sway, sending occasional flame-colored leaves swirling down onto Michael's hair, Mandy's legs. The river poured by, silver, hurried, and now and then the wind caught in the rocks and buffeted and called out softly. There was no way they could make love, not in this cramped space on the cold sand, but there was an erotic novelty even in the impediments of sand, coats, sweaters, hose, wind, and cold.

"Oh, *God*," Mandy cried out all of a sudden, without thinking, "Michael, I love you!"

Michael raised his head and looked at Mandy. They were both shocked by her words.

"Mandy," Michael said, "I love you, too."

Then they were embarrassed, and sat up, straightening their clothes. For a few moments they were very busy not looking at each other, as if they were both guilty of some inexcusable blunder. Mandy recovered first, and looking at Michael's face, which was turned away from her so that she could see it only in profile, she saw, or thought she saw if her perceptions were right, signs of real conflict. He looked so troubled.

"Michael," she said, gently putting her hand on his arm, "it's all right. We can love each other. That doesn't mean we have to *do* anything about it."

"But I want to do something about it," Michael said, and he turned and looked at Mandy with such love that that moment, that expression, was one she would remember all of her life.

They leaned back together against the rocks then, and looked out at the rushing river, and talked about the things that they could do about their love. There were so many possibilities. They could do nothing, or they could start writing to each other, and seeing each other on weekends, or they could get married.

All this talking made them shiver, or perhaps it was simply the October chill. But finally Mandy said, "Oh, let's go home and get warm and have something to eat. Aren't you hungry?"

So they walked back along the river and scrambled up the bank to the bridge and made their way to Mandy's house along the familiar streets and sidewalks. This time they held hands all the way, past the houses, shops, the church, for anyone to see, and they were very aware that they were doing this, as if they were committing some loud, attention-getting deed, like blowing bugles or beating drums.

"Mandy?" Leigh called, hearing her daughter come in the door. "Where have you— Oh, *hello!*"

Leigh stopped and smiled at the sight of Mandy and the boy she had at her side, both of whom were wearing about the same amount of Mandy's lipstick and mascara on not entirely appropriate spots of their faces. So this is what Mandy was doing all summer, Leigh thought. "Come in and have lunch," she said.

She heated up homemade vegetable soup and brought out some rye bread, and chatted casually with Michael and Mandy, or rather at them. Mandy dropped the napkins, forgot where they kept the butter, and set four places. Michael just sat, such a huge man in this kitchen that was so accustomed to only one or two women. He cleared his throat often and answered Leigh's friendly chatter with monosyllables that seemed to have been tortured out from his depths. *Oh, God*, Leigh thought, they really are in love. Eating with them was almost painful; each slurp and clink of soup or silverware seemed to reverberate. Leigh had been in love like this, more than once, so when lunch was finally over, she said cheerfully, lying, "Mandy, Michael, I hope you don't mind, but I was planning to drive down to the Southmark hospital to see how Wilbur is doing. I'll be gone about three hours. I've got some errands to do, too."

"Oh, that's *fine,* Mom," Mandy said, not stopping to wonder what possible errands her mother could have on a Sunday afternoon.

"Well, I don't want you to feel hurt, I mean since you're only home for the weekend," Leigh offered.

"Oh, nonsense, Mom, go on," Mandy said. "It's fine. Michael can keep me company." She was trying to be pert, but at her last sentence she couldn't help the smile that lit up her face, the silly grin.

Leigh turned away, pretending to look in her purse for her keys, in order to hide the tears that had ambushed her. That child is lost, she thought; and she was sad that Mandy was so grownup, and glad that she was so happy, and envious all at the same time.

"Well," Michael said, the moment Leigh had gone out the front door. "Now what shall we do?"

They didn't even stop to kiss first; they just raced, like children, to Mandy's bed.

My God, I'm in a spaceship, Wilbur thought when he opened his eyes. They've gone and made me an astronaut; here I am all wired up to beeping machines, uniformed and strapped in and monitored and prone in my own little solitary capsule. I only wish I knew where they were sending me.

There were four wires attached to what looked like little suction cups stuck to his abdomen, and an IV stuck into his right hand, which was tied, as was his left hand, to the bars of the bed. There were tubes up his nose, and he knew without seeing that there was a catheter in his penis. There was a curtain pulled around his bed and various machines hung and stood and clicked and dripped all around him.

I'm not very happy about all this, Wilbur thought. But thank God, I'm not dead yet.

"Oh, good for you, Mr. Wilson," someone said, coming into his view. "You're awake." It was a tall, skinny, gray-haired nurse. She touched his arm gently, an introductory gesture. "I'm Selma. You're in the hospital, you know, and I'm going to be your nurse for a while. How do you feel?"

"Ready to go home," Wilbur said.

"Ha-ha," Selma replied. "Listen, hang on, I'll get your wife for you. I know she'd like to come see you. Just for a minute or two."

"All right," Wilbur said. "You go get her. I'll just wait right here."

He wished someone would cover his chest; it looked so scrawny from his vantage point, so bony, so goddamned pitifully *frail*. But he supposed that any covering would disturb all those wires. What few chest hairs he had curled around his nipples, gray and lank. He wished now that at least he'd been a hairier man, had a chest with hair so thick and matted that it would cover his vulnerability. He just looked *too bare*.

"Wilbur," Norma said, and bent down to kiss his forehead. She had such a strange expression on her face—as if she were proud.

"Can you tell me what time it is?" Wilbur asked.

"Honey, it's just about three o'clock."

"And still Sunday?"

"Still Sunday."

"Well, that's all right, then," Wilbur said.

"Yes, you're going to be fine. Probably the worst you can expect for the next few days is a good long spell of boredom. But you should see the people in the waiting room. Everyone's out there, and they all want me to give you their love. They're all pulling for you."

Wilbur could see them there, a crowd of people, really pulling for him, tugging on the lifeline that would bring him back down from this eerie outer space where he floated, back to the solid earth. "Well," he said, confused for a moment.

"Wilbur, do you remember anything that happened? Do you know that it was Liza Howard who gave you CPR?"

Those words yanked Wilbur right back to reality. "Liza Howard?"

"She got right down on top of you in her fur coat and silk dress and gave you mouth-to-mouth and pushed on your chest."

"Well, hell," Wilbur said. "Mouth to mouth with Liza Howard and I didn't even know it. I wouldn't call that fair." But he grinned, just to think of it. "Would you thank her for me?"

"Yes, I'll call her when I can. Stop grinning like that, you old reprobate. Stop thinking that way, you'll get your heart all to racing."

"It was my heart, then."

"Yes, it was. I thought the doctors had told you—"

"Maybe they have. I'm not too clear about the past few hours."

"Sorry, Mrs. Wilson, but your time's up," Selma said.

"Selma," Wilbur said, when he was sure Norma was gone. The nurse was busy checking something at the foot of his bed. There was something about the way she wore her gray hair that reminded him of his grandmother, and so he didn't feel too humiliated to ask his question. "Can you tell me how I am? I'm not going to die right away, am I?"

Selma looked startled, as if his question had no relevance to his situation. "Why, no, Mr. Wilson, you're not going to die right away," she said, coming up closer to his face and smiling. "You're going to be fine. You just need to rest."

"I'm afraid to close my eyes," he admitted. "It's like when I was a little boy. Sometimes at night I couldn't go to sleep. I was afraid that once I closed my eyes and—let go—I wouldn't ever wake up again."

"I promise you you'll wake up again," Selma said. "It's been a very minor attack, Mr. Wilson. The more rest you get, the faster you'll recover."

Oh, I do love women who take care, Wilbur thought. I do love women who know answers and make things safe. It's possible that he said aloud, "Selma, I love you," or he might have just thought he said those words as he closed his eyes and fell away from his poor puny body into a generous sleep.

Priscilla and Seth had been invited by another family to go to Southmark Plaza to see Walt Disney's *Cinderella* and then to eat at the new Pizza Palace, so Suzanna had dressed them up, tucked money in their pockets, and waved them off to their afternoon's delights, smiling all the while at the thought of what delights *her* afternoon would hold. She could not remember when she and Madeline had been able to make love in the daylight—either they were always teaching or the children were around. At night, by the time the children were in bed and really asleep, Suzanna was so tired. But now it was Sunday afternoon, and a good four hours of freedom and light stretched out in front of her.

Up in her bedroom, she closed the curtains at the windows that opened onto the street and pulled back the curtains on the windows that gave onto the back yard. There was no house immediately behind her, no way that anyone could see in unless they happened to be parachuting by. The sky was overcast and the wind was blowing, tossing the amber leaves of the ash trees behind the house in a steady dance. It was a chilly day for October, and it looked chilly: a good time to be inside.

Suzanna stripped her bed and carefully spread on the new sheets she had bought, silvery-colored satiny Christian Diors. She had stood for at least fifteen minutes in the department store in Southmark worrying over these sheets: should she buy them? They were sinfully expensive. But they were also on sale. And they were so tempting, so luxurious. Now she smiled at her purchase as she smoothed the shimmering fabric across her bed, transforming it just as Madeline had transformed her life, from an ordinary thing into a thing that could shine with magic and beauty.

She looked around her room, pleased. It was *her* room now,

painted the colors she had chosen, colors Tom would not have liked: oyster-pale walls with silver-blue woodwork and doors and mauve curtains and chair and spread. The sheets went perfectly with the room: they glimmered as the room did, opalescent.

She went downstairs and found the silver ice bucket—a gift to her and Tom when they married—and filled it with ice, and found the one bottle of champagne she had in the house. She carried it up and put it on the bedside table, then made another trip downstairs and up, bringing a silver platter with grapes, sliced pears, cheddar cheese, and bars of Swiss chocolate. She had been saving the champagne and the chocolate for a special occasion, and she had decided that today that occasion had arrived. She put the platter in the middle of the bed, and two long-stemmed crystal champagne glasses on the other bedside table. There, now. She stood for a moment, savoring the sight of all this silver, all these pleasures, until Glutton, the cat, appeared from nowhere, attracted by her incredible radar, to leap in one swift movement onto the bed. She was a beautiful cat and would have fit in nicely with the scene, but her eyes were clearly on the cheese, and weird cat that she was, she probably would have nibbled on the chocolate, too. Suzanna grabbed her up, tossed her out in the hall, and shut the bedroom door.

I'm ordinary, Suzanna thought, just a schoolteacher in a tiny New England town. I'll never shape the world, I'll never have glamour or drama or fortune or fame. I'm verging on chubbiness and middle age, and someday Fate will crush me just like it's crushing poor Wilbur Wilson. But I can make this day special. If only for today, I can be the happiest person in the world.

She stripped off her church clothes and hung them up, instead of tossing them over her chair as she often did, then took out her white terry-cloth robe and went to the bathroom. She showered, powdered, and perfumed herself, looked at herself in the mirror. But the habit of being critical, even demeaning, about her own body was too strong within her, so she wrapped her robe around her body and thanked heaven that Madeline saw her with different eyes.

The doorbell rang then: Madeline. She came in, wearing jeans, a beige knit shirt that looked very much like a waffled undershirt, and a blue down vest.

"Well," she said, eyeing Suzanna in her robe. "Look at you!"

"I told you," Suzanna said. "The children will be gone for four hours. Let's go upstairs." Out of force of habit, she locked the front door, and after they had climbed the stairs and entered the bedroom, she locked that door, too.

"Well," Madeline said again, when she saw the silvery bed, the champagne, the tray of fruit and chocolate. "Look at all this. What a treat, Suzanna!" She turned to embrace her.

"Let's get in bed," Suzanna said. "I want to talk to you seriously."

"Shall we take our clothes off?"

"Of course."

But when they were finally settled, naked, sitting cross-legged, sipping their champagne in the middle of the bed, Suzanna realized she wasn't going to be able to concentrate. She could never look at Madeline's naked body without wanting to touch her.

"Oh, dear," she said to Madeline. "I was wrong. We'd better put on some robes at least. I really do want to *talk* to you."

Madeline rose from the bed then, and Suzanna thought that she was going to get a robe, but instead she turned, took the silver platter from the bed with one hand, and Suzanna's champagne glass from her with the other, and set them on the table. Then she came back to the bed and knelt down just behind Suzanna, and lifted Suzanna's hair, and spoke whispering against her neck.

"We can *talk* later," Madeline said. "We can *talk* over the telephone. We can *talk* when your children get home." As she spoke, she ran her hands lightly down Suzanna's shoulders, back, neck, arms, and finally, so lightly, around and over her breasts.

"Yes," Suzanna said. "Yes. All right." She sat perfectly still, all her senses alert, receptive, as Madeline dallied her long slender fingers slowly over Suzanna's skin. They had done this before, they had teased each other's bodies awake, but rarely with such elegant restraint. Madeline would not let Suzanna turn to embrace her. She stayed behind her, sliding her tongue down Suzanna's spine, nibbling at her shoulder blades, her hips, her back, all the while moving her fingers gently over Suzanna's breasts and waist, until finally Suzanna was too weak to sit, and sighing, "Madeline," she slid downward on the bed. Madeline very slowly kissed and touched Suzanna, as if she were designing her body, each limb and finger, each rise and fall of flesh. Pleasure swirled in Suzanna's body, just beneath her skin; pleasure beat in Suzanna's blood and throbbed at the pulse in her neck, the pulse in her groin. Still Madeline kissed, licked, touched, all in a sliding motion, up and down Suzanna's body, until Suzanna felt pleasure flowing in her like a liquid, curving through her limbs as if she were a riverbed and pleasure were the river, eddying and building and rushing through the channels of her body, until it stopped in desperation to pound and billow, caught, blocked, between her legs. She was hot, moist, frantic. "Madeline, *please*," she said, and before her eyes closed, she saw Madeline's smile. At last Madeline put her hand between Suzanna's legs, and her mouth on Suzanna's breast, and slid her long cool body against Suzanna's, and with the elegant expertise of a locksmith, she fiddled, turned, slid, and thrust her fingers until the lock of Suzanna's body opened and the floodgates of her pleasure surged full and burst. Suzanna was carried away in pleasure.

She lay a long time just holding on to Madeline before she opened her eyes.

"That was lovely," Madeline said softly, looking at Suzanna with fond love, kissing her forehead and cheeks, smoothing her damp hair.

"Yes, oh, yes, thank you," Suzanna said.

"My pleasure," Madeline replied, and meant it. It was true. For when they made love to each other the pleasure was doubled; it echoed, as now, when Suzanna rose above Madeline's body, and felt her own body fill again with pleasure at the sight and thought of her hands and mouth on Madeline's breasts and stomach. She loved Madeline, loved giving her pleasure—and she knew just how sweet a particular dabbing at this moist spot felt; the sensation flickered in her own skin. The joy was twinned.

They let it build. Madeline's body was already eager, wet, and rosy, from loving Suzanna, and as Suzanna loved Madeline, her own body reawakened and in its greed attained a new level of awareness. They were caught up in a private cove of sexual sensation, and now Madeline rippled sleekly in the shallows of pleasure, smiling, eyes open, as she trailed her fingers in Suzanna's hair. And now she was sucked down into a violent whirlpool, tugged relentlessly under. Her fingernails dug into Suzanna's back as she grasped for something to hold on to, and the slight stinging of Madeline's nails sank into Suzanna's skin and, sinking, became pleasure, became a greed, so that Suzanna was soon caught up in her own wet search, plunging over Madeline's hands down toward a finer, deeper, more intense level of ecstasy. Finally they were so soaked and slippery with sweat and saliva and other juices, so shaken from their explorations, that as Suzanna lay spread-eagled against the silver sheets, gasping for breath, Madeline had only to ease her body down over Suzanna's, so that breast touched breast, mouth touched mouth, thigh slid against thigh, and the damp matted pubic mounds touched, pressed, pushed, and they arched against each other shuddering. Pleasure ran through and over them in an exquisite tense line; they were caught on each other.

They drew the covers up over them and lay together. Suzanna scooted on her stomach over to the edge of the bed to get a good look at the clock: three hours had gone by.

"Umm," she sighed. "We should get up. Get dressed. Want to talk now?"

"I don't think I'm capable of anything else," Madeline said, smiling. She stretched out a bare arm and pulled Suzanna to her. "Dear thing," she said, nuzzling her hair. "I do love you."

"I do love you," Suzanna said. They lay there a few minutes more, then rose, showered, dressed, and carried the champagne and food downstairs to the living room. Finally they were seated, just like two friends having a chat, in case the children walked in, across the coffee table from each other.

"Now," Madeline said, "what do you want to talk about?"

"I want to live with you," Suzanna said. "I want you to move in with me. I don't want to wait any longer."

"Suzanna—"

"No, Madeline, listen. Today at church, I was praying, oh, God, please give me some kind of sign. Well, and of course nothing seemed to happen. But as I was leaving church, when the service was over, an older man, Wilbur Wilson, had a heart attack. One moment he was walking along, smiling, and the next minute he fell to the floor, clutched his chest, and nearly died. Maybe he will die. I suppose he would have died right there if Liza Howard hadn't give him artificial resuscitation. It caused quite a commotion. Poor old man—he's awfully nice. I called the hospital a little while ago—he's alive, he's resting comfortably, his condition is good. But, Madeline, as I stood there watching him, I realized how short life is. How fragile life is. Madeline, I don't want to wait any longer to live with you. Who knows how much longer we have to live, and why should we wait till the children are gone and we are old and cranky to share our lives? Madeline, I don't want to wait any longer. I want you to move in now, this week."

"My sweetest Lesbia, let us live and love," Madeline said. She rose, crossed the room to get a cigarette, lit it while still standing.

"What?" Suzanna said.

"It's a poem by Thomas Campion. I came across it the other day; you made me think of it. Or it made me think of us.

"*My sweetest Lesbia, let us live and love,*
And though the sager sort our deeds reprove,
Let us not weigh them. Heaven's great lamps do dive
Into their west and straight again revive,
But soon as once set is our little light,
Then must we sleep one ever-during night."

"Oh," Suzanna said. "That's lovely. That's just what I was saying. Madeline—"

"All right," Madeline said, and came back to the sofa, sank down onto it, flicked her cigarette at the ashtray. "Let's take all this step by step. We agree on the fact that we love each other, that we want to live together. Forget for a moment your children, the community, our jobs, your ex-husband—which is a lot to forget. Think about us living together: where would I sleep?"

Suzanna laughed, surprised. "Why, in my bedroom, of course."

"Where would I put my clothes?"

"In my closet, silly. Oh, I know it's crowded, but I can easily weed things out. Hang some of my things in the guest bedroom—"

"My records? My furniture? My *books*?"

Suzanna stared at Madeline. Her face fell. "Oh," she said, "I see."

Madeline came up from the sofa, moved to Suzanna, knelt by her legs, and looked up, hugging her. "Suzanna, don't look that way. *I want to live with you.* But if we do such a major thing, we can't do it halfway. We've been doing it halfway for two years now. If you really want me to live with you, then we have to talk about it seriously. We have to talk about anything that could be a potential problem. You can't just squeeze me into this house, a bit here, a piece there. I'd go crazy. I'm a grown woman. I'm used to living alone, to arranging my things, the things I've collected and loved for years, all around me, the way I want them. I have to have a study to work in, to keep my books in, to grade papers and make lessons, and I have to have more room for my clothes than a corner of your closet. I don't even know if we could work it out in this house."

Suzanna looked at Madeline, stunned. "But—" she said, and waved her arm slowly outward, looking about her. Madeline knew exactly what Suzanna meant by this; she meant: But *my house*. This house that I've made so beautiful. The hours I've spent choosing the right wallpaper, the perfect shade of paint, decorating the children's rooms, painting the woodwork—how could I give up my beautiful house?

"I see," Suzanna said at last. "I'm asking you to give up your beautiful apartment, and it's just as difficult for you as if I were to give up my house."

"Well, perhaps not quite so difficult," Madeline said, and leaned forward to kiss Suzanna on the cheeks, the forehead, the mouth. She smiled, then rose and settled back again on the sofa facing Suzanna. "I'm used to moving around, after all. I've lived in six towns in the past ten years. But now I've got tenure at the college, and though I'll admit I never thought I'd end up staying at Southmark, I'm beginning to see the charms of the area. Mainly—you. I'd like to settle here. I like the college and my colleagues and the students. And I love you. I want to live with you. I don't mind moving from my apartment. But if we are going to live together, Suzanna, I can't live in *your* house. *We* will have to live in *our* house. Don't look so dismayed. I don't envision us fussing over whether to put chintz or Haitian cotton in the living room. I'll be delighted to leave all that to you. I love the way you've made this house look. I'd sell my furniture gladly. But I have to have my own study, a place for my books, my desk, my papers. I have to feel free to light a fire or move a chair or buy a lamp . . ."

"We'd have fun in the kitchen." Suzanna grinned. "I mean, if we combined my Cuisinart with your escargot set and my wine with your wine rack—"

"We'd have a lot of fun in the kitchen," Madeline agreed. "And in the bedroom. But there's something else. If you're really serious about living together."

"God, let me pour some more champagne," Suzanna said. "Okay, go ahead. What else?"

"The children," Madeline said. "We'd have to have some rules or agreement about my relationship to the children. If I move in with you, Suzanna, that means I move in with your children, and if I do move in, I want it to be for good—"

"Oh," Suzanna interrupted, "so do I!"

"For keeps. So we'd have to talk seriously about the children. The decision about just what and how much to tell them is entirely yours, of course. I'll abide by whatever you decide. I like Priscilla and Seth and I think they like me. I can imagine all of us living together quite happily. But if we do live together, I can't just play sweet auntie to them. Let's say, for example, that I want to take a bath and they've just bathed and dropped their towels all over and left their toys in the tub. They do that, I know. I've seen you go in and straighten up after them. My instinct is to march the little munchkins into the bathroom and say, 'You made the mess, you clean it up. Hang up the towels. Put the soap in the bowl—'"

Suzanna laughed. "Their soap is disgusting, isn't it? They're supposed to be able to color on their skin with it, and on the tub and the walls, then wash it right off. Instead, it dissolves and settles in the tub in little black or brown or red hunks—"

"Well, you see, Suzanna, what I'm saying. I'd want to make them clean it up."

"I know, and you're probably right. It's just that usually, at the end of the day, it's easier to do it myself than to make them do it."

"I'm not criticizing your way of raising the children. I'm just saying I'd do it differently sometimes. So we'd have to make it clear to each other and to the children just what kind of jurisdiction I'd have."

"My God," Suzanna said. "It's complicated."

"I'll tell you something," Madeline said. "About six years ago I—went with—a man who had a little boy. The boy's mother was dead, and the man, who was completely reasonable and intelligent in every other way, was crazy where this kid was concerned. He was so determined never to let his son suffer again that he refused to spank the boy, or punish him, or yell at him, or threaten him—God, that child was a holy monster. Lincoln was handsome, charming, wealthy. He asked me to marry him. If it hadn't been for little Lincoln, Jr., I might have. But I couldn't *stand* the thought of living with that kid."

"I didn't know you had almost married—"

"Suzanna! I'm not trying to make you jealous. Stop it. My God, *you* have been married. You have two children. And I want to live with you. I'm telling you, I love you, and I love your children. But I want to do it right."

"Money," Suzanna said.

"What?"

"Well, if we're talking about everything, we'll have to talk about money. I mean, about sharing the mortgage and the groceries—there's three of us and just one of you, of course. We'll have to sort all that out."

"Yes. These are all touchy issues."

"Are you sure you want to get into all of this?"

"Yes. I'm completely sure. Are you?"

"Yes, I'm completely sure, too."

"Well," Madeline said, and raised her champagne glass. "I think we should drink to that."

They toasted each other, and kissed.

"I think we're quite wonderful," Madeline said. "We've drunk almost an entire bottle of champagne and yet look how intelligent we're being."

"We *are* wonderful," Suzanna said. She rose, left the room, came back with a pad of paper and a pencil. "It will be like a maze," she said, settling down, curling up against the arm of the sofa. "We'll have to wend our way through the perils of Money, Children, Society, House & Furniture—"

"To get to the prize—Living Together," Madeline said.

"Well," Suzanna said, licking the pencil tip. "Let's start at the beginning."

"We're already way past the beginning," Madeline said. She rose and kissed the top of Suzanna's head. "And the nicest thing about this game is that we can get little rewards every step of the way."

Behind the brass andirons a bright fire was flaming in the Bennetts' family room. The cats, Rags and Flapper, lay stretched on the hearth, warming their tummies, and Bruce, the black Lab, lay in the middle of the braided rug, gnawing on a rawhide bone. Ron had changed into the clothes Judy had laid out for him: gray wool slacks and a white cotton shirt for Sunday-afternoon comfort and a wine-colored Ralph Lauren sweater for the company that would be arriving any moment now. He sat at one end of the kitchen reading the Sunday *Times.* Judy was at the other end of the room, wearing red-and-yellow plaid slacks and a yellow turtleneck sweater. She was slicing radishes rose-style and arranging them attractively on the canapé platter. From time to time Ron would read her something he found particularly interesting in the *Times,* and she would comment or laugh. When the phone rang, she said, "Don't get up, darling, I'll get it," and wiped her hands on a dishcloth. Ron vaguely overheard her conversation. Judy sounded friendly, normal, so he didn't pay much attention to what was said. He was surprised when she hung up the phone and came over to him, sitting down across from him on the edge of the rocker.

"Ron," she said, "I'm worried. I'm really worried."

Ron put the paper down. "What's the matter?"

"That was Sarah. She was calling for John. I had to tell her that he'd gone off on an errand for us and wasn't back yet. Now if he isn't with Sarah—"

"Judy, I've said it before: John is twenty-three years old now. He's a grown man. He's only living here until he and Sarah get married. You can't expect him to check in with you every hour like a little boy. This is still his home, but we can't keep tabs on him all the time."

"But this isn't like him. You know it isn't. It's almost four o'clock. He knows the Talbotts are coming for dinner. They'll be here any minute."

"*He'll* probably be here any minute, too. Or maybe he won't. Maybe he's not interested in meeting the Talbotts. They seem young to us, but they probably seem old to him."

"But I've set a place for him in the dining room. He knows I was expecting him for dinner. He's never inconsiderate. I'm not saying that he should ask us for permission to go places, but I do expect him to be courteous enough to let us know if he'll be here for dinner or not."

"Well, I promise to speak to him about it when he comes home. But don't get so upset."

"I can't help it. I—oh, I just feel so nervous. He's been acting strange for weeks now. Not showing up for meals, disappearing at odd hours, staying out all night—"

"Come on, Judy. He's a grown man. He has to have his private life. Look, he's getting married soon. He probably just wants to have a little time to—to sit around and drink beer with friends. Be irresponsible. Take long walks and think about life. That sort of thing."

"What if he's still with that Howard creature? That's the last time we saw him today, going out the church door with her. I suppose he meant to drive her home, but then how was *he* to get home? And why should he be so nice to her anyway?"

"Johnny's nice to everybody. Why don't you call the Howards' house and see if he's there."

"I called. No one answers."

"Maybe they went down to the hospital."

"No. I called there, too. No one has seen him—or her."

"Well," Ron said. "I don't know, then. I've run out of guesses."

"I think we should call the police."

"Oh, for heaven's sake, Judy!" Ron said, and in his exasperation he began to fold up into neat rectangles the various sections of the *Times* he had been reading and scattering around. "He's only been gone from your sight for *four hours*. The police wouldn't even take you seriously. Judy, honey, this isn't like you."

She rose and went to stand close to the fire, warming her hands, her back toward Ron. "I know it isn't. I'm sorry. I just feel so— Maybe they were in a car accident."

"Maybe they went out to a restaurant and are having a long lunch."

"Oh, *Ron*." Judy turned from the fire and glared at her husband. "Why on earth would John go to a restaurant and have a long lunch with Liza Howard? He doesn't even *know* her. To say nothing of what it would *look* like."

"Well, it's just as likely that they're having lunch somewhere as it is that they're in a car accident somewhere."

"I'm not sure which would be worse."

Ron laughed, stood up, and took his wife in his arms. "Judy," he said, "what a terrible thing to say."

"I know. I don't mean it. Of course I don't want him to be in a car accident. But I don't want him . . . getting involved . . . with that Howard woman, either. You know what she's like."

"I don't think anyone knows what Liza Howard's like," Ron said. "But let me remind you for the fiftieth time: John is a grown man. He can take care of himself. He's not about to 'fall into her clutches' or whatever dreadful thing it is you're imagining."

Judy pulled away, unconvinced. "I *hate* this!" she said. "I'm going to call the police. Just to find out if there have been any accidents."

"All right," Ron said. "Fine. I'll go take a place off the table. The Talbotts will be here any moment."

But the Talbotts were there right then, lifting and dropping the brass lion's-head knocker. Judy stared at the phone, looked at Ron, then smiled and sighed.

"Oh, all right," she said. "He'll probably turn up just as we've sat down to eat and are putting the first bites into our mouths." She walked out of the kitchen and through the long hall to the front door, rearranging the expression on her face as she walked so that by the time she opened the door she looked serene again.

"Hello!" she said to her guests. "How lovely to see you! Come in!"

What's that word, Wilbur thought. That word that means that man can adapt to almost any condition. *Atrophy?* No, no, that's not the word at all. What's the matter with my mind? I'm getting so old and *muddled*. What *is* that word? There was that show on television the other night, about the pioneers who settled the midwestern United States. What a lot they had to contend with: savages, wolves, droughts, floods, insect plagues, crop failure, tornadoes, and always the constant repetitive hard work. Norma had said that she could have stood all that, but she couldn't have taken the isolation. She said it's a good thing she hadn't been a pioneer woman, because the loneliness would have killed her. No television, radio, telephone, not even any neighbors close by—she would have died of it. But I don't know, Wilbur thought, it occurs to me now that if she had *had* to, she would have survived. I have to believe that, I have to believe that she would have survived that isolation—that man can survive almost anything. But how do people survive the worst? How am *I* going to survive this?

I hate lying here, helpless. I'm scared to death. No. Not *that* scared. But I *am* scared, and I don't think I can stand it. I don't want to be here. It seems I've been here years already. The room's dark and I'm weak, helpless. Goddamn, I never was much good at this sort of thing. I used to have to have a stiff drink before going to the dentist. The pain never bothered me; it was that feeling of being trapped in the chair. Well, I'm sure trapped now.

Where are the doctors, where are the nurses? Where is Norma?

Oh, God, where's my sense of humor? I always said to myself that when my time came, I wouldn't lie around on my deathbed sniveling and crying, losing dignity, letting self-pity drip down my old face. Where did I hear that story about the man who died—he was a priest or a cardinal or a statesman, something. A great man. He was lying on his bed, his family all gathered around him, waiting for him to die so they could mourn him and get on with life. He'd been dying for hours. The young ones must have been bored; I don't blame them. Death-watches can't be fun. One of them whispered, "Is he dead yet?" Another said, "I don't know. I can't tell." "Well," another said, "feel his feet. If they're cold, he's dead. Everybody's feet are cold when they die." "Except for Joan of Arc's," the old man said, and then he died. Imagine that. Imagine having the self-possession to make a joke like that when you're dying. Well, I think I could pull it off right now. I think I could be pretty funny—if only I had an audience. If someone were here right now. It's hard to be funny all by yourself. I wonder if God has a sense of humor. I wonder if there will be laughter in heaven. I don't see how, because I don't see how there can be laughter without imperfection. Banana peels. If we're all perfect in heaven, what will we have to laugh at? Maybe we'll get to watch what happens on earth; that would be nice. I'd like that. Still, if I had my way, I'd rather *be* here on earth some more, rather than just watch. Even if I have to be confined to a bed or an old people's home, I'd like to stay alive awhile longer. I can't imagine how anyone who's healthy can commit suicide. I can't imagine anyone I know committing suicide. Life's too tempting. I'm not afraid of dying, but I don't want to give up my life on this earth just yet. Not without a fight. I *will* fight. I'm not that old. There's so much left I want to see and say and do—"

"Wilbur."

A skinny, gray-haired figure in a nurse's uniform slid into Wilbur's view.

"I'm glad to see you," Wilbur said.

"I've been here all the time," she said.

"I hate having my hands tied. It scares me."

"Ah," the nurse said. "I wondered why you were getting so agitated. You do realize you're in a hospital, don't you? You've had a heart attack."

"Yes. Of course I realize that. But I don't see why I have to have my hands tied."

"Well, I'll make a bargain with you. You promise not to pull out the equipment—don't even touch it—and I'll untie your hands."

"Okay. Thank you."

"You're welcome." The nurse released Wilbur's hands, then began to pump up the blood pressure cuff on his upper arm. "A hundred twenty over eighty," she told him.

"That's good, isn't it?"

"That's good. Let's take your temperature."

Wilbur marveled, as he had when he was in the hospital for his bladder operation, at hospital technology. The thermometer was a prong stuck in his mouth and attached by a cord to a little white metal box which he knew from experience printed out his temperature digitally. I might as well be in a spaceship, he thought.

"Ninety-eight flat," the nurse said. "That's fine. How do you feel?"

"Tired," he admitted. "What's your name?"

"I'm sorry, I thought I had told you. I'm Selma."

"Selma. A good old-fashioned name. Well, Selma, I'm tired, but I—I keep getting scared."

"Wilbur, you're doing fine. You'll probably be sitting up in the morning eating scrambled eggs and complaining about them. You just need to rest."

"I know. But it scares me to drift off . . . to let go . . ."

"I'm here with you all the time."

"You are? All the time?"

"That's what intensive care is all about," Selma laughed. "Why do you think it's so expensive? Now you go back to sleep and the next time you wake up we'll get your wife in here to see you again."

Wilbur dutifully shut his eyes. Selma's words floated through him like the fluids from the IV: *I'm here with you all the time.* That was better, then, that was all right. That was really all that was necessary, one friendly human being to stand watch. Now I lay me down to sleep, I pray the Lord my soul to keep. Let Selma watch me through the night and keep me safe till morning light.

"Thank God that's over," Judy Bennett said as she watched the Talbotts' car lights disappear down the drive and out of sight. She waved again, although no one could see, then shut the front door and leaned against it, sagged against it. "I thought they'd never leave."

"It's only seven-thirty," Ron said. "They weren't here very long. And I thought they were nice. You're just upset because Johnny hasn't come home. Come on, I'll help you clear the table, then we can sit down by the fire." He put his arm around Judy's shoulders as they walked toward the dining room.

Judy began to stack plates. "You've forgotten. Reynolds Houston's coming at eight."

"He is? Oh, God, that's right. I'd forgotten. What did he say he wanted?"

"I don't know. He just called and asked if he could stop by."

"He probably wants to talk about the rec center. He's one of the Big Five on the board."

"Why can't he talk to you about it during the week, during working hours? Why does he have to spoil a Sunday evening?"

"He probably doesn't think of it as spoiling a Sunday evening," Ron said. "Maybe he gets lonely on Sundays. He lives alone."

"That's his choice," Judy said. "He shouldn't inflict himself on others just because—"

"Hey," Ron said, and took Judy into his arms in an awkward hug; she held a pile of plates in one hand and a gravy boat in the other. "You really are out of sorts. Come on, now. Reynolds is a bit of a bore, but he's not that bad. Besides, you won't need to talk to him at all. Why don't you just go on up and get into bed and watch TV or something?"

"I'm too nervous, too worried about Johnny."

"I know. I know. But, honey, I'm sure he's all right. You've got to let him go."

"You don't think we should call the police? It's been seven hours now."

"I don't think you should call the police."

Judy pulled away from him, her mouth set in a little moue of disagreement. "Well," she said, "let's get the dishes done."

She felt so tired. The pills, and then the alcohol at dinner, the energy she had expended being charming, had drained her. Yet she was so anxious about Johnny. And anxious about Reynolds Houston. It was the worst combination of feelings. When she got like this, the best thing to do was go to sleep, for she couldn't be sure now just what effect another drink or pill would have. But she couldn't sleep, not yet. She carried the dishes into the kitchen and scraped them under hot running water, then stacked them in the dishwasher.

Ron came in with more dishes, then crossed to the other end of the room to stoke up the fire. "Good dinner," he said.

"Mmm," Judy answered. She was thinking that she would have to take *something* if she was going to get through the rest of the evening. Or she could slip off to bed as soon as the dishes were done; Ron wouldn't mind being left alone with Reynolds, and Reynolds hadn't said he wanted to see her. That was what she would do, then—go to bed. If it weren't for the mess in the kitchen, she'd go upstairs now, but she couldn't leave the kitchen like this. It was the main disadvantage of the house, this huge kitchen–family room. Whatever mess was in the kitchen could be seen from the fireplace area, and for Judy, if even a bowl was out of place, the beauty of the room was thrown off.

Ron continued to stack the dishes. Judy rinsed, scrubbed pots and counter tops with practiced, efficient movements. Then she sponged down the top of the stove, the oven door, the refrigerator door, and each of the cupboards. She did not ordinarily do this after every meal, but she had been playing a little game with herself all evening, betting that Johnny would walk in the door before dinner was over—and as long as there was some cleaning to do, dinner was not officially over. Besides, if she stopped moving, she'd fall over. She was stuporous, exhausted, and each movement derived from the force of great will power. But she kept moving.

She set out Armagnac and two brandy snifters on a brass tray on the long pine table and placed the raspberry pie, two plates, two forks, two cloth napkins next to it.

"The whipped cream is in the refrigerator," Judy said, at last. "If you want to offer Reynolds some dessert. I think I'll go on up. I don't feel very well."

"Fine, sweetie," Ron said. He looked at her carefully. She has had too much to drink again, he thought—he knew the signs. She never got silly when she'd been drinking, nor loud nor boisterous, but rather very sleepy and melancholy. He leaned against the refrigerator, and pulled Judy against him, and kissed the top of her head. He ran his hands up under her yellow sweater, stroking her back in soothing circles. He could feel the tension in her, and he felt a deep pity dive within him, and a deeper love. She was a sweet woman, and she had spent so many years of her life protecting her family that she could not break the habit. He could not say to her what he suspected: that Liza Howard, who, he assumed, was as close to being a nymphomaniac as anyone in Londonton could ever be, had managed to lure Johnny into bed today. He couldn't blame Johnny for going—he'd gone himself. Any man would want to go to bed with that woman, at least once—especially a man about to end his single life in a proper marriage at the age of twenty-three. No, he even half hoped Johnny was with Liza now, enjoying the thrill of illicit love. Illicit sex, rather, which was something completely different and just as enjoyable in its way. Johnny would look back on it in years to come, when his life revolved around making enough money to keep his family happy, and he'd be glad for the experience. But Ron could not express all this to Judy; she would not approve. Ron could imagine just how she would disapprove, how she'd worry—about what Sarah Stafford would do if she found out, about venereal disease, about morality. We are a good pair, Ron thought, stroking his wife's back: she is the heart of the house, the warming furnace, the illuminating light, and I am the protecting frame, the wooden supports, the barricade against the outer world.

From where he stood, he could see the long stretch of family room. He had added the room onto the original old frame of house; he had put down the wide-board floors himself and raised the walls. But Judy had created the room, she had worked the magic that made it cozy and attractive. It gleamed with comfort. She was always busy around this room and the other rooms of the house, dusting, sweeping, puffing up pillows, rearranging, and the rooms glowed with her care. Just so did she busy herself around her family, fussing over their appearances, infusing them with the right spirit, keeping them healthy in body and soul. He could not be angry with her for her fretting over Johnny. He rubbed her back, around and around, and kissed her hair.

Judy realized that she had nearly passed out, leaning against her husband, feeling his comforting touch. She had had too much to drink, too much, because she had started taking the Valium so early, and had taken so much today. Well, it was just as well, for otherwise she'd be frantic now, worrying about Johnny. Sarah had called again during dinner to ask if he'd gotten home, and Judy had lied: he went down to Southmark to check on Wilbur Wilson, she had said. The Staffords didn't know the Wilsons; it wasn't likely that anyone they knew would be at the hospital. Judy hadn't been able to think of any other excuse, and she hadn't wanted to tell Sarah the truth, that she didn't *know* where Johnny was, that the last she'd seen of him, he was going out the church door with Liza Howard. What would Sarah think? She didn't want to worry Johnny's fiancée—or anger her. But what if Sarah called again, later tonight? What would she say then? Ron's soothing strokes lulled her, made her want to slide right down into sweet oblivion. She pulled away.

"I think I'll go upstairs," she said. She felt warm, weak, lazy. "I'll take a little nap. But I'll set the alarm for nine-thirty. If Johnny isn't home by then—"

"Then we'll start calling around," Ron said. "But, Judy, he might spend the whole night out. He has before. If he's—really involved in—something, he might not think about calling home. I don't think you should worry. You go on to bed. I'm sure Reynolds won't be here long."

"Well," Judy said. "Be sure to offer him some pie." She went down the hall and up the stairs, and stopped halfway to call back, "Thanks for the back rub." But she was so sleepy that she didn't call loudly enough; Ron didn't answer.

She went on up the stairs and into her bedroom. The rich brown shell-patterned afghan she had crocheted was folded neatly at the foot of their king-sized bed. She set the alarm clock for nine-thirty, then collapsed on the bed, pulling the afghan up over her. Before she even thought to take her shoes off, her head hit the pillow and she fell into a blank sleep.

Downstairs, Ron checked his watch. Reynolds would be here in ten minutes; he was always punctual. Ron wandered back through the dining room to reassure himself that the table had been completely cleared and the silver candlesticks and bowl put back in their established place in the center of the table. Judy would be upset if she woke up in the morning to find even a silver bowl out of place, it would make her feel she had been lax, sloppy. She worked so hard, set such high standards, and over the years Ron had come to rely on this sense of pride she lived by. Their house seemed an oasis of stability in a troubled world; no matter how messy the town politics or other people's lives or the world news, here was their house, set down firmly on the earth, clean, solid, well tended, uncluttered, unscarred. A refuge.

Ron went back into the family room and looked it over to see if anything needed doing. The cats had nestled together in one of the rockers, and Bruce had sneaked up onto the corduroy love seat. Judy didn't like the animals on the furniture, because of their claws and fur and smell, but they looked so utterly peaceful there that Ron hadn't the heart to make them get down. Pretending not to see them, he checked the rest of the room. The wood rack next to the fireplace was getting low. He might as well fill it up now.

He went out the door to the woodpile stacked against the house and, once outside, stopped to look up at the sky.

It had not been a pretty day. It had been cloudy, cool, and gray, and now the wind which had been threatening all day was rising in earnest, and a hint of rain was in the air. Tree limbs tossed, dry leaves clattered. The night had a brooding, ominous feeling about it, and Ron shivered and was glad to have on his sweater. He began to stack logs against his chest. He always thought it such a shame when the brilliant display of fall foliage was ruined by early wind and rains. Too bad that man, with all his technology, couldn't control the weather just a little. Well, it certainly made him appreciate his house and all those things in his control that much more.

The heel of Ron's shoe caught on a rotting board, and he kicked it back in place, shaking his head. The whole porch floor was going to have to be replaced soon. It had weathered through a good many years, but now it was past whatever salvation paint and repair could give.

Judy had been asking Ron for months now if they couldn't turn this open porch—it was really just a floor sticking out in the L of the back of the house, with the roof covering only a third of it—into a proper glassed-in porch. She had always wanted a "wicker room." Straw rugs, white wicker chairs and chaises with puffy cushions covered in bright flowered fabric, plants and hanging flowers all around. She had a collection of pictures cut from various home-decorating magazines.

"Just because our children are growing up and leaving home, we don't have to move our lives into a little box," she said. "I don't want to be that way. My life doesn't end when the children move out. *We'll* still be here, Ron, and after all our hard work, we deserve the best house we can have. Oh, it would be such fun to have a wicker room. I could give the loveliest dinner parties in the summer, with candles on every table." She had spread her hands out in front of her as she spoke, as if the tables were there before her then, instead of the slanting, decaying wooden floor. "And think how cheery it would be in the winter," she said. "It would be like having a bit of summer in the house in the winter."

"It would be expensive to heat," Ron had said, feeling like an old fussbudget, a spoilsport. "It's on the wrong side of the house to get any solar-heating effect." Then, seeing her face: "I'll think about it, though."

"Johnny's through college," she said. "I mean, since we don't have to pay his tuition—"

"Yes, you're probably right," Ron said. Not to agree would have alarmed her, and he did not want her to know that he had any worries about their financial state.

How do men please their wives? Ron thought now, pushing an armload of wood into the black iron circular wood rack, then going back outside. Women were such mysteries. Always wanting more. More and better. Maybe God made them that way to keep men from getting lazy. Maybe it was women's wanting that was the vital force behind the gradual perfection of the species and the world. It was too bad that it was Reynolds who was coming over now. He didn't know a thing about women; he'd be no good at this kind of discussion. This was the kind of thing Ron always mulled over with Wilbur Wilson, and Ron felt a sharp thrust of pain, missing him now. If Ron had a best friend in town, it was Wilbur, and the thought that Wilbur might die—well, it was terrifying. All the times that Ron had gone fishing with Wilbur, or just over to sit with him when he was recovering from his operation, all the times they just sat around together, shooting the breeze—Ron didn't suppose he had ever in his life had any human contact that was closer, or meant more, than those times with Wilbur.

For the truth of it was that if there was any one human being who knew the *real* Ron Bennett, it was Wilbur Wilson. Wilbur had enough knowledge and the skill to know just how good a carpenter and contractor Ron was; he could actually look at what Ron had constructed and appreciate it. So he had a better understanding of Ron as a professional man than any of the members of Ron's immediate family. And he knew Ron's secrets—and loved him still, with a love which was different from any other Ron had known, because there was no hint of forgiveness about it, and thus no hint of judgment. It was simply acceptance, the rarest thing. Ron did not feel sad to think that Wilbur knew him more truly than Judy; Judy was his wife, a sensitive and proud woman. She needed his protection. She could not have borne to know all the awful truths about Ron's complex life and needs. There was no reason she should know all the truths—they were not even relevant to her.

Back outside, Ron stuck his hands in his pockets against the bitter wind, and walked around the side of the house to look down the driveway at the road. No sign of Reynolds Houston's car; no sign of Johnny. Now Ron had no doubt in his mind that Johnny was in bed with Liza, yet another bit of information that would have distressed Judy, but which made Ron smile. Liza Howard. What a fabulous fuck she was. Ron would never be sorry he had slept with her, of all women, because of all people Ron had met in his entire life, only she had brought with her, as rich and tantalizing as her perfume, a sense of glamour, and it was this experience above all others which Ron had with each passing year thought he would never have, and longed for. He had experienced love, sex, passion, friendship. He had worked hard enough to surround himself with security. He had made friends who were wealthy. He had traveled to small islands with white sands, pink drinks, and shimmering hotels. But none of that was glamour; not even Jake and Lillian Vanderson were glamorous. They were simply rich. All of Ron's adult life he had spent in a scurry of activity, trying to get enough money in the bank so that he and Judy would never feel threatened, trying at the same time to build up in the community an equal account of respectability and belonging. Ron did not think one could be both respectable and glamorous. He did not even really want to be glamorous, because glamour carried with it, he thought, an ever-present tinge of danger, a promise of impermanence. But he wanted to *touch* glamour, to grasp and hold it to him, to bury his head in it, to breathe it in, and for a few hours on two different occasions, he had. With Liza Howard.

In spite of the fact that he had seen her naked, and in intimate and revealing positions, he could not think that he knew anything about her. She was so foreign to his way of life as to seem completely unreal. Oh, she had a beautiful body, and she was fabulously capable at sex. Too capable. She was too experienced, sleek, a mannequin come to life; she seemed almost inhuman. A man could be absolutely care-free with her, and sometimes Ron thought that was the essence of glamour and of all the experiences in life which he would never have. Freedom from care, responsibility, accountability. Freedom to touch just one person in this world without worrying about the consequences of that act. A carefree moment seemed to Ron the rarest thing a man could have in life. So what better person for Johnny to spend some of his remaining bachelor hours with? Johnny would come home tonight or tomorrow, exhausted and amazed, with a self-conscious grin on his face; Ron was sure of it. He turned away from the road and went back around the house, took up more logs, and went inside. It was so cold out for October, so raw.

He had dumped the pile of logs into the wood rack and put a new log on the fire and was considering helping himself to some of the Armagnac when he heard the car pull into the driveway. Then, to his surprise, he heard another car pull in, and the slamming of several doors, and voices.

He walked through the unlit front hall and looked out the long strip of glass that bordered the front door. It must be Johnny, he thought, but it wasn't. Holding their coats closed and their hats on against the rush of autumn wind, Reynolds Houston, Gary Moyer, and Peter Taylor came up the flagstone walk toward the house. They were not smiling and talking easily with each other—Ron could see as the front-porch light fell on them how grim and set their faces were, and he knew in that instant why they had come.

It was one of those times in life when eternity rolled by like a great ball of ice, touching his skin, freezing and paralyzing him. He would stand there forever, cold with fear, trapped in the knowledge of what he had done and terrified of the consequences of that act. He wanted to die.

But the doorbell rang, and the icy ball rolled past him and away, leaving him real and alive, caught in the present moment. He moved normally, because he had to. He flicked on the hall light and stood exposed in its glare.

"Reynolds," he said, opening the front door. "Hello. And Gary. Peter. What a surprise. Come in. Come on back to the family room. We've got a fire going. It's such a nasty night."

"I know," Gary said. "Terrible weather for so early in the fall. Still, I remember two years ago, all of October was like winter, with temperatures in the thirties, and then November came on like Indian summer, warm and bright. But by then, of course, the leaves had fallen. You know, the trappers tell me the muskrats are building high this year. A sure sign we're in for a lot of snow."

Gary's blithering had taken them down the stretch of hall and into the family room. Ron took their coats and put them casually across the pine table, then handed out snifters of Armagnac—no one refused—and shooed the dog and cats off the chairs. Finally they were all settled in a charade of companionship around the fire.

"Well, gentlemen?" Ron asked. It wouldn't do to pretend he thought this was just a social occasion. "What can I do for you?"

Peter looked at Gary, Gary looked at Reynolds, Reynolds looked at Peter.

"Ron," Gary finally said, "there seems to be a problem with the rec center fund. It seems that more money is gone from the account than there should be at this point. For the amount of work done, I mean."

Reynolds drew a slim notebook out of the breast pocket of his tweed jacket. "We have some figures," he began.

"—that we'd just like to check with you," Gary intervened, leaning forward. "Ron, some of this might be my fault, you see. When we formed this committee, well, since we all knew one another, I just didn't bother with a lot of the legal details that perhaps I should have bothered with. I mean, if we had done this another way, for example, we'd be having regular accounting meetings once a month."

"Of course, Gary. I understand," Ron said. "It's perfectly reasonable that you and the rest of the committee would want to go over the records. It's fine with me. And it's fine to do it on a Sunday night in front of a fire with brandy, instead of down at my office, which does not have these comforts."

"Our figures indicate—" Reynolds began.

"Well," Gary interrupted again, "this is sort of a special meeting, Ron, I just want you to understand that. It's really a—just a secret meeting, just the four of us here. We haven't mentioned any of this to the other members of the board, to Jake Vanderson or Dan Weinberg. We thought we might be able to settle it with just the four of us."

"I'm just here for moral support," Peter Taylor added, smiling.

"Moral support?" Ron asked.

"Our figures indicate," Reynolds said again, his beautiful voice rising only slightly in volume and clarity, "that in the past six months you have bought materials for the rec center, paid for those materials with checks from the fund, then returned half of what you bought for cash refunds. And not passed those cash refunds back to the rec center fund. There is at least one hundred thousand dollars unaccounted for."

So soon, Ron thought. How have they discovered this so soon?

"I see your problem, gentlemen," Ron said, still smiling. "Yes, Gary, you're right. We probably should have bothered more with the legal details, in order to prevent just this sort of misunderstanding. I assume you believe that I've personally pocketed the money."

"Well, not exactly," Gary began.

"More or less exactly," Reynolds said, gazing with an almost scientific interest at Ron.

"I don't have the figures with me," Ron said. "This paperwork is in my office. We could go there tonight, if you want. It's true that I haven't handed back the cash refunds to the fund. What I've done is something I think much more sensible. I've been putting the cash into money market funds. Now, they're not as safe as the bank savings account, I know, but over the short term they pay a lot more interest. It just seemed silly to me to be getting five and a half percent on our money when we could be getting anywhere from fifteen to eighteen percent."

"You've invested the money in your name," Reynolds said.

"Of course," Ron answered. "But I have it in a special account, not connected with any of my personal money, and I intend to draw out the money when I need it further along toward the end of the job."

"And what will you do with the interest earned?" Reynolds persisted.

"It will all go into the building fund," Ron replied. "Every bit of it."

"Then the one hundred thousand plus dollars which have been given to you in cash refunds will be plowed back into the building fund," Reynolds said.

"Yes, of course," Ron replied. "I really wish you had called me about this on the phone. I could have answered your questions immediately and you wouldn't have had to expend such energy worrying."

"Well"—Gary almost stuttered in his relief—"I wish you had let us know that's what you're doing, Ron."

"I know. I'm sorry, Gary. But you remember what a fuss Jake Vanderson made when we discussed different banks. He would have been most upset if we hadn't used Londonton National. I suppose I just didn't want to get into it with him."

"What you are telling us," Reynolds said, "is that if we asked for it, you could reimburse us, the fund, in the amount of around one hundred thousand dollars."

Ron smiled at Reynolds without a trace of displeasure. "Yes, that is exactly what I'm saying. Would you like to go down to my office now?"

"Oh, well," Gary said, "I don't think that's necessary. Now that we understand—we were afraid the center wouldn't get built, Ron, because of shortage of funds. A hundred thousand dollars is a lot of money for a town this size. I don't think we could raise it again if we had to. We just want to be sure the job's going to be done as promised, for the amount you bid."

"It will be," Ron said.

"Are you bonded?" Reynolds asked.

"No," Ron said. "I'm not. A payment and performance bond is legally required only if the contractor is doing public work, for the federal or state government or the township. It's expensive, and in this case, unnecessary."

"That's one of the reasons we decided to form a private charitable organization," Gary reminded Reynolds, now totally on Ron's side. "In order to cut through all the bureaucratic red tape and hassle. If we'd gone public, we would have had to put the job out to bidders and accepted the lowest bid. As it is, we all wanted Ron for the job, and from what I've heard, the quality of construction and materials is excellent."

"And it will continue to be," Ron said. "I'm sorry you were concerned with this money issue. I've never dealt with such a large sum of money before, you know, though I have built some rather expensive houses—houses approaching the cost of the building. But it seemed a waste to me not to have the money accruing more interest in the money markets. Believe me, we'll use every penny of the interest in finishing the center off right." He smiled at the men and leaned back in his chair.

"I'm still not quite clear on this," Reynolds said. "It seems to me that either you have *accidentally* made repeated mistakes in ordering materials, in which case you have been incompetent, or you've *purposely* made those mistakes in order to put the refunded money into money market funds. In which case you've been devious."

There was a long and uncomfortable silence in the room then, and the four men stared at the fire rather than at each other. The only sound was the expletive gasp of a giant log which finally buckled under the heat of the flames; it rolled against the andirons, sighed, and burst into flames.

"Well," Ron said at last, still keeping his voice light, "those are harsh words. I haven't meant to be either incompetent or devious. I think if you look at the *building* itself—"

"The point is," Reynolds persisted, "this is supposed to be a group effort, based on mutual trust. I'm finding it difficult to understand how you could take it upon yourself to handle this much money in this way without discussing it with the other members of the rec center committee. It seems to me that you might have mentioned it to Gary, since he is a lawyer, and one of the five members of the committee, and your close friend. Since so much of this is being handled so casually, I'm surprised you didn't casually clear it with him."

"Look," Ron said, cornered into anger, "I don't have time to *casu-*

ally do anything these days. I've been working eighteen hours a day, six days a week for months now, trying to get the rec center built, trying to get it built *right*. I've got three crews of seven men each working under me to supervise, and that building is going up beautifully; it looks good, it is solid, it's the best piece of work you'll find in the state of Massachusetts. I don't have time to fiddle around with all the little nitpicking details of paperwork, and to be quite honest, chatting with the Big Five members of the board is the last thing on my mind. But you might not be able to understand what I'm saying, Reynolds, since you're a college professor. How many hours a week do you actually have to be physically at work? Nine? Twelve? You've got more leisure time to worry about the niceties, the proprieties, than I do—"

"Well, now," Peter intervened, leaning forward, "you've got a valid point there, Ron. A lot of this misunderstanding is probably due to the fact that we've somehow let you shoulder too much of the burden. You shouldn't have to be worried about the financial aspect of it; your function is with the actual building itself, and we are all in agreement, I'm sure, that you are doing a fine, first-class job of that. What we need to work out is some way to provide you with more assistance as far as the paperwork goes."

"Yes," Gary said eagerly. "Of course. Peter's absolutely right. You know, much of this is my fault. I should have set it up more carefully."

"I think we all should get together tomorrow morning," Reynolds said. "We can meet at Ron's office. He can give us a check for the amount he had put into the money market funds, and we can call a meeting of the five members of the board to decide what to do with the money from that point on. It might be that we'll want to do exactly what Ron has chosen to do, to put it into money market funds. But I think handling that money should clearly be the prerogative of the board."

"You're right," Gary said. "Absolutely right, of course, Reynolds."

"It will make things a lot easier for you, Ron," Peter said.

"And in the morning we can also discuss possible ways to make all the paperwork side of the building easier for you too, Ron," Gary said.

"All right," Ron said. "That's fine. Fine. What time shall we meet?"

They agreed to meet at ten o'clock, and then, disguising sighs of relief, they all rose and made ready to depart. They carried brandy snifters to the pine table, gathered up their coats and hats, cleared their throats.

"Does anyone know how Wilbur Wilson is?" Gary asked, more to change the subject and the atmosphere than out of a need for information.

"I called just before I came," Peter replied. "They said his condition is good, and he's resting comfortably."

"Well, thank God for that," Reynolds said. "What a day this has been." He turned to Ron and held out his hand. "Ron, I'll say good night. I'm sorry to interrupt your Sunday evening this way."

Ron's hesitation was only a heartbeat long; then he held out his hand and smiled. "Not at all. I'm sorry to cause you all such concern. I'll see you in the morning."

He ushered the three men to the door and saw them out into the night. It had begun to rain, a fine, steady, fat rain that made plopping sounds on the leaves and walks. The men hurried to their cars. Peter had come alone in his car, and Gary had ridden with Reynolds. The headlights flared as the rain distorted the circles of light into stars. It had grown even colder, so cold that Ron stopped to wonder if it might snow. Certainly it was almost sleeting now.

He shut the door. His heart was pounding so that the blood drummed in his ears. He had to lean against the wall. Then he walked back to the family room and poured himself another brandy. He pulled his chair close to the fire and sat there, staring at it, sipping the brandy, thinking; and he could not get warm.

Leigh spent most of the afternoon and early evening at the Southmark hospital. She had gone in order to give Mandy and Michael some time alone, and also to help Norma Wilson in some way, perhaps only by showing up, by letting her know she cared. But the pale green waiting room off the Intensive Care Ward had been so packed with people that in the end it was almost like going to a party. The social atmosphere was heightened by the good news that Wilbur had regained consciousness several times and had been quite lucid. He was said to be in good condition and resting well. The people crowded into the little room had a feeling of reprieve—maybe this was not to be a tragic day after all—and it made them overcome with a sense of gaiety and good fortune. They were pleased with themselves for being there. Leigh talked with Norma awhile, but spent most of her time chatting with others, catching up on old news and the latest developments in people's lives. She sipped lukewarm coffee from a paper cup as happily as if it were scotch, and when she finally left the hospital, she had a bit of a buzz on from all the caffeine.

Just before she left, she called home to alert Mandy to the fact that she would be arriving soon, and to say she'd pick up a pizza on the way: What kind of pizza would they like? When she arrived back at the house at seven o'clock, she carried an extra-large extra-cheese deluxe pizza in a limp cardboard box.

As if trying to prove that she had had nothing much else to do, Mandy had cleaned up the kitchen after lunch and laid out clean place settings for dinner. The children—for that was how Leigh thought of them, in spite of the fact that they were both taller than she and had probably been spending the afternoon in bed—ate with such gusto that Leigh wished she had thought to buy two pizzas. She didn't have much food in the house—with Mandy off at college, she kept a sparsely stocked kitchen—but after they had finished the pizza and a salad, Leigh went into the living room and got the big brass bowl that was piled high with fresh pecans, walnuts, filberts, almonds, Brazil nuts, all still in the shell, brought it back into the kitchen, and put it in the center of the table. They sat passing the nutcracker around, munching nuts, sipping wine.

"Mom," Mandy said, "uh—we've got something we want to tell you. Talk with you about, I mean."

We, Leigh thought. Well, well. "All right," she said.

Michael worked away at cracking a Brazil nut as if his life depended on it.

"Michael and I are in love," Mandy said. "We want to get married."

Leigh flinched, as if she had been hit in the stomach. The news hit her there, she could physically feel the blow. "Isn't this awfully sudden?" she finally said.

"Mom, I've known Michael for years, and I've been—seeing—him all summer," Mandy said. "I thought when I went off to college that we'd forget about each other. But we can't."

Leigh studied her daughter, a pretty girl, full of promise, lithe and quick, with her nerves running eagerly just under the surface of her skin. She was easily moved, easily awed; Mandy always had been swept off her feet by even the most ordinary things in life. Still, she was no fool. She was learning to channel her private ecstasies into art, and she had never yet made a stupid decision because of emotional blindness. Leigh had high hopes for her daughter. Mandy could be somebody. And be happy, too—Mandy seemed to be one of those rare individuals who was capable of having both prizes. So she had to take what her daughter was saying seriously.

In the past few years she and Mandy had gotten into the habit of trusting each other. Perhaps it was because there were only the two of them alone in the house. Mandy's father came to visit, or sent for Mandy, now and then, but his interest was slight. He was a busy man, and his love was really only a form of cordiality. It had been difficult for Mandy to come to terms with this, and for a while she had blamed her mother, and for a while she had hated both parents, but that was long ago, when she was just entering her teens. She had worked it all through, and for three or four years now, Leigh and Mandy had had an ease in their relationship that stemmed from mutual respect. Leigh didn't want to lose that. She didn't want to frighten Mandy away with arbitrary grownup rules. She knew how skittish young people were—she could remember her own youth. And it was more than a pose, a ruse: Leigh *did* have faith in her daughter's judgment and intuition. If Mandy thought it would be good for her to marry this boy Michael, then very probably it would be. But still—they were so young! She could not help but think that they needed some kind of protection at this age, even from themselves.

Leigh turned her gaze to Michael, who had gotten the Brazil nut open and was now digging the meat out. He was a handsome boy. Leigh would have to give Mandy an A for taste. If he was nothing else at all, he was certainly handsome, even beautiful, with vivid coloring and good bones. Thick black hair. But was he at all intelligent? Did he have a sense of humor? Integrity? Common sense?

"Michael, how old are you?" she asked.

Michael raised his eyes to hers, and in that instant, though he did not know it and Leigh would never have admitted it, he won the battle. His gaze was so clear and direct. It signaled: Here is a good person. There is enough animal in us still, Leigh knew, to sniff that much out in each other.

"I'm seventeen," he said. "I'll be eighteen in December. I'm still in high school. I'm a senior. I'm not making good grades, because I honestly find high school boring. But I'm not stupid—if you want to check my IQ test—"

Leigh burst out laughing at this, and in turn, they relaxed and smiled. "Look, you two," Leigh said. "You're both intelligent, I believe that. And you're in love, I can see that. But why do you have to get married? Why don't you just see each other on weekends and, well, write letters during the week. If you've really only been—seeing—each other just this summer, such a short time, you can't know everything about each other that there is to know. You might be surprised at how much you could get to know about each other through letters—" But she could see by the glaze that began to pass over their eyes that she had lost them. She was silent for a moment.

"Mom," Mandy said, "we want to be together. We don't want to be separated. We don't want to see each other just on weekends."

"I was thinking," Michael said. "I could come to Northampton. I could get a job there. There are lots of things I could do. I'm a good worker and I'm good with my hands. I could work in a garage, or with a builder, or with a landscape contractor like I did this summer. I could support us. Mandy and I could live in an apartment, and she could continue school. I know you don't want her to drop out. I don't, either."

"But I want to sculpt, Mother!" Mandy burst out, and Leigh turned to see by her daughter's expression that she was more terrified about this admission than she was about her love for Michael. "And Michael would help me. Carrying the heavy stuff, the materials and things."

"Just a moment," Leigh said, and rubbed her forehead with her hand. Was any parent ever prepared for this sort of thing? Did any human being ever feel confident about this kind of decision? So much hung in the balance. "Michael," Leigh said, "what will your parents think about all this?"

"My father will be furious," Michael said. "Not because of Mandy. I mean, he'd be furious no matter who I'd want to marry. And my mother—my mother will be worried. I guess she'll be like you—

convinced that we're too young to make a serious decision like this. But, Mrs. Findly, I believe that there's no one age when everyone gets smart. I'm sure experience improves everyone's thinking, but I feel that some people get smart young, and some people never get smart at all, no matter how old they are."

Leigh smiled. "Yes," she said, musing. "I sort of believe that myself. But, Michael, don't you want to go to college? Surely your parents want you to. I don't see how you could both go to college and support yourself—"

"I don't want to go to college. At least not now. I'm not interested in any of it. I—I'm tired of words. I don't trust them. I want to work with things that are real. Of course my parents want me to go to college, but I've talked with them about it and told them I don't want to."

"Oh, God, your poor parents," Leigh said. "They have their hands full with you."

"They do," Michael agreed. "You see, they think that life should be lived in a line. You're supposed to touch certain checkpoints along the way. They want me to be on the way to someplace, and it's always an uphill climb. Well, I can't do that. I don't want to go where they want me to. I—it's like I see a whole different area of life to live in that they can't even see. It's hard to explain," he conceded.

Leigh was quiet for a while, remembering. She thought she knew what Michael meant, and his words drew her sympathies. When she had been their age, she had desperately wanted to go to Paris, to "be an artist," to live among artists—to sleep with artists. She had dreamed of living in a garret on the Left Bank, posing nude for artists who would fall in love with her and make her famous, immortalizing her in their art. And she would turn the tables, sculpt her lovers, and become famous herself, for her art, immortalizing them. She would sit at the Deux Magots, sipping Pernod and saying witty things, and she would never marry or have children, and she would never grow old. But her parents were merely amused by her dreams, and said that of course she was not going to Paris, she was going to college. And she did go to college. Then she married, and she had a child, following that rigid line that society delineated through ambitious love of parents for their children, until the time came when she could pretend no longer, and she got divorced.

Since then, she had lived more or less as she pleased, potting, having lovers; but it was a tamer life than she had wanted for herself, and a more limited one, bounded always by the needs of her daughter. Mandy had to come first. Leigh did not regret this—Mandy was reason enough to make any life worthwhile. And Leigh knew that her early dreams had been greedy and unrealistic; it would have been most unlikely if everything she dreamed had happened. More than likely she would have been hungry, cold, and lonely in Paris; she would have gotten a venereal disease from a lover and gone home admitting her talent was a small one.

Still, why should she join with other grownups in this ritualistic coercion of young people onto the straight and narrow path?

Mandy was rolling a filbert back and forth on the table. Michael was just sitting, waiting.

"Look," Leigh said, "this is a lot of news to hit me with all at once. You two have had a while to think about it. I should surely have some time. Whatever your—career choices—are, Michael, it's something you have to work out between you and your parents. And it certainly wouldn't be fair for me to give you my blessing and force your parents into the position of being the heavies. Look . . . look. If you two think you'll be happier if you're together, well, why do you have to get married? Marriage is so complicated. There's so much legal stuff, so much hassle. Why don't you two try living together for a while?"

"Mother," Mandy said. "Michael's father is a minister!"

"I know that. But he might agree with me. Marriage is so *final*." Then Leigh smiled at herself, and stopped, considering her own divorced state. "Or it should be. At any rate, once you're into it, it's hell getting out—and I know, I *know*, you two think you'll never want to be apart. But, Mandy, I felt the same way about your father once. Look, kids, it's true that some people never do get smart, but over the centuries human beings have learned a few things. You have to admit that. And one of the things we've learned is that marriage is a hard job. The library is full of books about adolescent love—don't bridle like that, you are still both adolescents! Now listen to me. Everyone falls passionately in love and wants to be absolutely *attached* to the other person, but this fades. I promise you, it fades. Every other person in the world will tell you that, even if they're happily married—you can't sustain passion. And it's foolish to make a crucial decision when you're in the throes of passion. Don't badger me, Mandy. If you want me to consider all this seriously, you've got to lay off a bit. If you love each other so much, it will keep."

"Mother," Mandy said, "I know this is a lot to hit you with all at once. But I bet if you went back to those books in the library, those reference books you're talking about, you'd find out that there is no one perfect age when people start doing things right. I don't want to wait till I'm twenty-five to start working seriously as an artist. I want to start now—I *have* to start now if I'm going to get anywhere. And I can do it. My school work is easy, I can do it with my left hand, and still have time and energy to do the sculpting I want to do. And if Michael were with me—"

"You'd be cooking dinner for Michael and doing his laundry!" Leigh snapped.

"He'd be cooking my dinner and doing my laundry!" Mandy said.

"Really?"

"Really," Michael said, and smiled.

"Well," Leigh said. "Well." She stood up, restless with emotion. "I need a drink," she said. She took her time, opening a new ice-cube tray, refilling the empty one, finding the jigger to measure the scotch, stirring the drink slowly. "Look," she said finally, "this is so complicated. Let's go into the living room. Maybe a change of scene will help."

Once in the living room, with the lights turned on against the evening's dark, they settled into sofas and chairs and looked at each other expectantly.

"Well, Mom?" Mandy said, and spontaneously grinned at her mother, as if to say, you can't fool me, I know you're on our side.

"All right," Leigh said. "Let's start over. Mandy and Michael, you say you want to get married. Mandy, you say you want to go to college and learn to sculpt. Michael, you say you want to drop out of school, do some manual labor, and keep house so Mandy can work. Am I right so far? Okay, now, let's say that your parents, Michael, and Mandy's father and I all want the same things: for you two to be happy, but also to—make something of your lives. Not to make any mistakes now that would ruin your lives."

"I'm better since Mandy," Michael said suddenly, eagerly. "I really am. I could tell my parents that, they'd have to admit it's true. I mean they don't know about Mandy, but—"

"You're failing high school and you're *better* since Mandy?"

Michael shrugged, grinned sheepishly. "Last year I did a lot of dumb things. Wrecked some cars. Took some drugs. I was feeling— trapped, I guess. Since Mandy, life looks different."

Leigh was silent.

"Mother," Mandy began.

"Sssh!" Leigh said, waving her hand. "I'm having an idea." She sipped her drink, then said, "Here's a thought. Michael, what do your parents want for you right now, this year? What simple thing?"

"They want me to finish high school, I guess," Michael said. "They want me to get good grades."

"All right," Leigh said, "then promise them you'll do it. Wait a minute, I'm not finished. Promise them you'll make decent grades and finish high school. But do it in Northampton. You could move to Northampton, take an apartment with Mandy, live together for the rest of the school year and the summer. Then, if you still feel like it, get married. Michael, I think this is an excellent solution. It will give your parents what they want most, and enable you to do what you want most."

"If Michael goes to school, how will we pay rent?" Mandy asked.

Leigh shrugged. "You'd both have to take part-time jobs, I suppose. If you're serious about this, you'll clean houses or wait tables in the evenings, on weekends—"

"That wouldn't give us much time to be with each other," Mandy said.

"Yes, well, welcome to real life," Leigh replied. "Besides," she added, "you can apply the dorm money to your rent, and—I'll help out a little. Just a little. I don't want you two setting up a playhouse and thinking it's married life."

"I think it might work," Michael said, leaning forward. "Look, Mandy," he said, because now Mandy looked worried, unconvinced. "We'd get to live together, sleep together all night, start our lives to- gether. You were planning to sculpt on weekends anyway, you won't want me hanging around then, I'll be able to work while you're at the studio." He was silent a moment, then turned to Leigh. "I don't espe- cially want to finish high school. I don't see the value in it. But I know it's something my parents really want. And I think I could do it easily, if I could be with Mandy. It would be like just another job. I think if

I promised my parents I'd finish high school, they'd agree to let me live with Mandy. Not that they're going to be crazy about the idea. Oh, God, it's going to be a real war. It's going to be awful."

"Okay," Leigh said, "I think we've gone as far as we should go. I think we should get your parents involved in this now—even if it is a war, Michael. Look, let's call your parents. Let's go over to your house and talk to them. It's not fair otherwise, and, Michael, your parents are nice people. They're intelligent, they're kind. They might have some good ideas. Shall I call, or you?" Leigh noticed as she talked how white Michael had gone, and she wondered if it were possible that any person could be frightened of someone as compassionate and intelligent as Peter Taylor. Well, she supposed, parents and children never do see each other as outsiders do, because something—some intimate knowing love—always gets in the way, distorting things.

"It would be better if I called, I guess," Michael said. He rose, went into the kitchen to use the phone, came back. "Okay," he said. "Dad's gone but should be back soon. Mom says to come on over. I guess we should go."

"Look, you two," Leigh said as she rose, "don't be so—so *serious* about all of this. It will all work out somehow. The important thing is that you've found each other, and really love each other, which is a rare thing. Don't get depressed if you can't have everything you want immediately. You've got your whole lives ahead of you." But again as she spoke, their clear young eyes took on that glazy barricade, and Leigh thought how no one ever believes that he's got his whole life ahead of him, or if he does believe it, it doesn't really matter. Today is what always matters, this day, this week, this month. When you're young, you want it all now. Growing old is perhaps just a matter of learning how to arrange your life so that you can wait for what you want in reasonable comfort. Leigh sighed. She had thought she would have a quiet weekend with the Sunday *Times,* and instead she had a daughter who wanted to get married to a boy who didn't even want to finish high school. Leigh put on her coat, gathered up her car keys.

"Hey, Mom," Mandy said as they all walked out to the car, "you didn't ask the one question all mothers are supposed to ask if their daughters say they want to get married right away."

Leigh stopped in her tracks. "Mandy," she said.

Mandy laughed delightedly, as if she had just made a wonderful joke. "No, Mom, I'm not," she said. "But I thought I'd give you a thrill."

"Listen," Leigh said, sliding behind the wheel of the car, "you've given me all the thrills I can take for one day."

"Well," Michael said, sliding into the back seat next to Mandy, slamming the door heartily, "forward into the fray!"

Goodness, Leigh thought, pleased, he knows the word "fray." She smiled, and headed the car toward Peter Taylor's house.

"Wilbur, are you all right?"

Wilbur opened his eyes, stared up at the nurse who was leaning over his bed. What was her name? "Selma," he said aloud.

Selma held his hand and looked at her watch, checking his pulse. "I thought you were choking," she told him. "You gave me a scare."

"I think I was laughing," Wilbur said, and began to make the low chuckling sound that had frightened Selma. "I was thinking about a friend who died. His widow, actually. Want to hear the story, even if it's a little racy?"

Selma gently replaced his arm on the bed and leaned companionably against the bars. "Sure," she said.

"Well, Norma and I have been friends with the Watsons for oh, I'd say thirty years now. Horace and Flora Watson. He's a plumber—was a plumber, he's passed on—and we got to know them through church. You couldn't meet a nicer couple, but you never would think that either one of them was much to write home about as far as looks go. Just nice plain New England folk. Well, Horace is about my age. Was. He died about six months ago. For the past two or three years he'd been ill, and he'd sort of shrunk, you know how you do when you get older. But he was always too stubborn to admit it, or I guess he didn't want to face the truth about how old and sick he was. But he used to go around looking so damned awful. All his clothes were too big for him. The sleeves of his jackets hung to the middle of his hands and his pants bagged and trailed on the ground; he looked like an old tramp. He'd lost all his hair and most of his teeth; he was sixty-eight, and not what you'd call a pretty sight. Well, he died, and we were sorry to see him go.

"About two weeks after his funeral, Norma and I had Flora, his widow, over for dinner. She was still grieving, of course. So after dinner, while we were having coffee, she said, in her sweet little old sad voice, 'Well, I went through some of Horace's things before we buried him. I came across a picture of me that Horace always did love. An eight-by-eleven photo, just of my face. It was his favorite picture of me, I think. I took the picture down to the funeral home and went in to where Horace lay in his coffin and placed it face down on his fly. He was buried that way; that's why we had a closed coffin. You don't think that was sacrilegious, do you?'"

Selma burst out laughing. "My, my," she said, "what a sweet story. They must have been happy together right till the end."

"Yes," Wilbur said, "it makes you feel good to think about it, doesn't it? Though I'll tell you, Norma and I had a tough time keeping a straight face when Flora told us that. Norma finally composed herself and said, 'No, I don't think so, Flora, and I'm sure Horace would have liked it.' What else could she have said?"

"Would you like me to get Norma for you now?" Selma asked, fussing with Wilbur's covers.

"No," Wilbur said, for his eyes were closing in spite of himself. "I'm feeling a little sleepy. I think I'll just rest a little first, a few minutes. Then I'd like to see Norma."

"Whatever you want," Selma said.

Whatever I want, Wilbur thought, closing his eyes, letting go of his grip on the world so that he seemed to float. If only that were true, whatever I want. What would that be, if I could have just one thing right now? One thing. I won't ask for my youth back, for my liver spots and wrinkles to disappear, for Norma and me to be young again. I won't ask for Ricky never to have died. What would I ask for if I could ask for whatever I want—but something reasonable? To see God's face? No, I'm not that brave. To see Ricky when I die? Well, if everything I've believed all my life is true, I'll see him anyway, somehow. Not to die? Everyone has to die.

I know what I want.

There was a game I played when I was seventeen, just finishing high school. We all thought we were so worldly-wise then, so smooth. I hadn't met Norma yet. I mostly hung around with the guys—Virgil and Henry and Luther. I wonder what happened to them. We had a club, what did we call ourselves? The Yankee Clippers. We were the smoothest guys in high school. That was 1928. Hmm.

One Saturday night in early May when we were all feeling full of piss and vinegar because school was almost over and we all knew we were going to graduate, we had a party over at Virge's house. What did we drink—beer? We thought we were pretty wild. And those girls were there, hanging around in their cotton frocks, looking shy and brash all at the same time. The moon was shining; we were all out-doors. I can still remember how the world had that green smell of new grass and spring.

We all sat on Virge's big front porch drinking beer and smoking cigarettes and showing off to the girls. There must have been about twenty of us there. Then George Wilson's older brother who had been off to college for two years till he flunked out got us going on this game. I suppose teen-agers nowadays would think it pretty silly, but back then it was exciting.

All the boys went behind the house. In the back yard the house blocked off the moonlight, so it was darker there, and the grass was taller. It felt wild. One by one we'd get a girl, tie a blindfold on her, and gently lead her around to the back. Then we'd tell her she could join the Yankee Clipper Club if she played the game right.

"Take off one item you're wearing that you won't wear to bed to-night," we said.

Well, they'd giggle and titter and wrap their arms around them-selves and look silly, but they all wanted to join the Yankee Clippers—no girls had ever joined it before. So finally they'd take off a shoe. We'd say, "Now take off another item you're wearing that you won't wear to bed tonight." Off would come another shoe. "Now take off an-other item you won't be wearing to bed tonight," we'd say, and then they'd start to get worried. If they wore jewelry, they'd take that off, and if they had sweaters on over their blouses, they'd take the sweater off. But right about then was when they'd panic and say, "Well, I don't think this is a very nice game, and I don't want to be in your stu-pid club!"

Bobbeen DuPont was one of the girls who wanted to be in the club, and when my turn came to go around to the front yard and bring a girl to the back, I knew I just couldn't stand to put her through it. It seemed mean to tease them like that, and even though it seemed to us they could easily guess the secret, no one ever did. I suppose those girls were too frightened to think straight. But I didn't want to put Bobbeen through all that worry, so after I tied the blindfold around her eyes and was leading her around the house, I put my arm around her and pulled her to me and whispered, "It's the blindfold. Take off the blindfold."

What I want is for someone to do just that for me: to come put his arm around me, to whisper just a few words that give me a hint, a clue. I don't just want it. I expect it. I don't know if the guide will come in the shape of a man, a woman, or an angel, but I do expect a human shape, for we are created in the Lord's image. I would hope that it would be Ricky. It would be so nice if I could hear Ricky's voice saying, "Come on, Dad, it's all right." But there's got to be someone. "Yea, though I walk through the valley of the shadow of death, I will fear no evil: for thou art with me." That's what He promised, and I'll be damned if I'll die without some kind of guide at least touching my arm, at least giving me some kind of sign.

But all I can hear is the beeping of those medical machines and Selma's whispery noises as she fiddles around the bed. I guess my time hasn't come yet, after all.

It was as if he had become a ghost and was floating in air slightly above his body, looking down, watching. The fire and the brandy had no power to warm him. His own skin seemed made of the same clear glass as the snifter he held in his hands, as if he had stopped being human. He was so still, so cold. He looked down upon himself, sitting there by the fire, and felt pity for himself, and regret, and a great fondness. *You damned fool.*

All of his life he had worked hard, so hard that it seemed to him he had achieved as much command over his fate as any man could. Looking back at his life, it seemed to him that only once had he lost control so swiftly. It had been so long ago, and now Ron knew that it had not been significant—but then, *then* it had seemed overwhelming, not merely the most important thing in life, but the only important thing. Had he ever really been so young?

He had been in high school, playing center on the varsity basketball team. His senior year they'd had a great team, one of the best, and they went to the state semifinals. With the score tied and just six seconds left in the game, Ron had taken control of the ball, dribbled down court to *his* spot, and with the cool perfection attained through a thousand and one practice shots, sent the ball spinning straight up and over to the basket. Unbelievably, this one time, the ball did not go in. It wavered on the rim and fell back, down into the hands of the opposing team's star player, and the next few moments seemed to move in slow motion to Ron. He was too dismayed to move, except to turn and watch as nine other men raced back up court and, while the crowd in the bleachers roared in ecstasy, Tommy Henderson made the final score of the game, winning the semifinals for his school and his team with that one shot as surely as Ron had lost it for his.

This isn't real, this can't be true, Ron had thought, standing dumbfounded as the rest of the gym went into a frenzy of noise and action. *This isn't fair, this isn't right, this isn't how it is supposed to end.* He had not been able to think that life could continue past this point. For all he knew or cared, the whole world could come to a halt right then. There was nothing else to live for. It had not seemed to him that *he* had done anything wrong: he had stood where he always stood, and tossed the ball with the exact gentle force he always used— no, *he* had not made a mistake. It was only possible that the world itself had moved minutely, the basket, the court, the fieldhouse, shifting imperceptibly just a half inch to the left. He had stood rooted to the boards, struck dumb with amazement at the arbitrary movements of the world, until finally another team member had come over and wrapped his arm around his shoulder and led him off to the locker room.

Now the same sort of thing had happened. This was truly important; it was grownup real life, it was life-and-death; but it was the same kind of thing: it was an error made not so much by Ron as by the mysterious shiftings of the world, and this time he had really lost the game. It was not fair. But he did not see how his life could continue past this point.

It really was as definite as that—as that long-ago ball wavering on the rim of the basket, then falling back. The action was complete and irreversible. It had not occurred to Ron then that he could miss; it had not occurred to him now that he could get caught. It had never been arrogance on his part, though, but more an acknowledgment of the way the world was run. It was as if, all those years ago in high school,

he had made a tacit agreement involving the rules of the game of basketball, the Newtonian laws of mechanics, and the precise discipline of
his own body—yet something had gone awry. Now, after all these
years of playing at the game of grownup life among the complicated
and often contradictory rules of men, he had once more missed his
mark by just that hairbreadth—that invisible and fatal dividing line.
He did not know if it was a whim of Fate that had brought him to this
point; or the result of years of choice which had ever narrowed as he
chose: but it seemed to him that with each choice of his life, he had
chosen on the side of good. Yet ultimately he had failed.

When Ron was a little boy, he often saw pictures of his father in
the Boston newspapers. In the photographs, his father was dressed in a
tux or a three-piece suit, with his thick black hair perfectly brushed; he
would be presenting an award or a check for some charity or opening
some theatrical night. Because he was so young, Ron had trouble connecting this grand gentleman with the sly, unshaven drunk who cried
at the dinner table and slept in the living-room chairs.

By the time he was a teen-ager, he was not troubled by the contrast, for his father's alcoholism by then had ruined him; he was no
longer photographed on evenings out because he no longer went out.
He lived in the downstairs study, drinking, holding long nonsensical
conversations with himself, coming out occasionally to look at Ron and
say genially, "Well, you're turning into quite a handsome boy, aren't
you? I was handsome once myself!" Sometimes he was gone for months
to clinics or hospitals that promised to dry him out, but it didn't make
much difference to Ron's life whether his father was around or not.
Ron was an only child; his mother's main concern was for her husband. So Ron learned to take care of himself. The house he grew up in
had belonged to his mother's family. His mother had been born there,
as had her mother and grandmother before her. It was a tall Victorian
mansion full of splendors, but as the years passed, the house deterio-
rated and finally became a drafty shell. There was no money for
repairs and Ron's mother began to sell off the furnishings to pay the
bills. So Ron got used to things vanishing from the house: oil paintings
off the walls, rugs from the floors, antique furniture from the rooms
and halls. Finally, his parents also vanished from his life: his father
died of cirrhosis of the liver, and his mother of cancer a few months
later. His mother's house, such as it was by then, was put on the

market and sold, and that money, combined with the trust fund his grandmother had left him, saw him through college. He mourned his mother, because he loved her, and because he had been so powerless in his childhood to change her life for the better, but on the whole he felt relief to be free—set free of the spell of his parents' foolish sad lives, and just as surely free of the ever-pervasive drifting-out smell of alcohol he had lived with in his tall, beautiful, deteriorating home.

At nineteen he had known exactly what he wanted: to live a life as good, dependable, and conservative as his father's had been wasted and bad. He wanted to marry, to provide a safe and happy life for his children, to work well at some job. He began working for a building contractor in the summer, and immediately loved it. When he graduated from college, his professors advised him to go on to a school in architectural design, but Ron was not interested in cities or corporate buildings; he wanted to build homes. Safe, strong, lasting homes. When the day finally came when he was settled in Londonton, with two houses contracted for and his wife, Judy, pregnant with their first child, he felt triumphant, even rescued—it was so easy, living a good normal life! He was not doomed to repeat his father's mistakes. Then, when his two children were born, healthy and perfect, and Ron was becoming successful in his business, he decided that there was only one prayer he need repeat for the rest of his life: "Dear God, just let my wife and children lead long and happy lives—*I'll* take care of myself." For he was sure of his competence by then; he could muddle through on his own, because he had learned the rules of men and buildings and knew how to stick to them.

He doubted that many men got as much satisfaction from their work as he did. He had built houses with his own hands, and he could drive through Londonton and see these houses still standing, as solid and everlasting as the hills, and know his work was good. He had enjoyed the physicality of the work: the heft and perfume of lumber, the sleek force of nails, the evidence of measuring tapes and levels. He would drive out to the houses he was constructing on Sunday afternoons when no one else was around, and walk around on the subflooring, running his hands on the structural beams, thinking how he was building worlds within the world, and his the safer, the more sheltering. His houses were expensive compared to those of other builders, but Ron did not cheat his customers or lie or cut corners. His materials and workmanship were the very finest. He was proud of each house he built. He was proud of himself.

It seemed to him that with his own hands he had worked his way out of a nightmare and into a sort of paradise: he did work that he loved, and his wife and children were safe and happy. Surely this was the definition of a good man: to do honest work, to provide security and happiness for those under his responsibility. What a pleasure it was to him to buy a scarf for Judy and a toy for the babies, to buy sirloin steaks for dinner and good wine, to buy a swing set for the children and a car for Judy, to buy ponies for the children and a fur coat for Judy—providing pleasures for his family became addictive for him, the passion of his life. There is no greater luxury in the world, Ron discovered, than that of giving pleasure and happiness to the people one loves. This joy was redoubled by his knowledge of his wife's childhood: she had suffered the embarrassments of her parents' bankruptcy, she had gone without the clothes and other things she wanted, and as he gave his wife more and more, he felt he was in some way redressing the wrongs and sorrows of at least one person's childhood. And Judy *cared* about her possessions so much. She took care of her home and her family and the material objects of their life with the devotion of a nun toward holy things. She was tireless, uncomplaining, graceful in her organization; she made the materials of their lives clean and shining. Nothing in their lives was dirty or frayed: what he provided, she preserved.

It was not Judy's fault, nor the children's, nor Ron's—it was no one's fault that their desires slowly began to burgeon and surpass his income. At first it was almost imperceptible, and it all seemed completely reasonable: a swing set for little children and tennis camp and cars and colleges and clothes with the right labels for big children. A scarf for the bride of one year; a fur coat for the bride of fifteen. There is so much in the world to enjoy. When the Moyers rented a house in Nantucket for the summer, it seemed a good idea for the Bennetts to do the same. And the winters in New England are cold and long—it was nice to be able to fly to Bermuda or the Bahamas for a few days in February. If one is going to buy a piano, one might as well buy a Steinway baby grand. The children would be off on their own soon and that giant expense would be done with; why not provide as much pleasure as possible for them all now? Ron's savings dwindled, then disappeared. He took a second mortgage on his house. He took out loans. He did not tell Judy any of this, because it would have worried her too much. And he was not doing anything that he couldn't handle. The United States was built on credit. Looked at in the right light, we can say that we are only borrowing our lives from God—and if we can borrow from Him, then surely we can borrow from man and his institutions.

Ron did not believe, even as he sat drinking brandy in front of the dying fire, that his choice had been wrong. He was a man who lived by a strict set of values. And which is, after all, *bad*: to cause your family to suffer or to borrow money from an inhuman entity that doesn't even know it's gone?

When he had agreed to build the Londonton Recreation Center, the last thing on his mind had been the money. He had wanted this job—even though up until then he had built only houses—because of the honor involved; in this way he would be able to leave his mark firmly on the town. He would die knowing that generations of children would play happily and safely in the building he had built. It was a kind of immortality. But it had turned out to be a more difficult operation than he had thought. He had had to contract out much of the work to roofers and plumbers and electricians, but still the basic design and structure of the building were his, and his standards were the ones to be measured up to. This building would last forever. The work consumed his life; he had no time to do other houses or even the odd garage or family room or cosmetic work that he usually did at nights, on weekends, to augment his income. State licensing fees and insurance rose; health insurance rose, inflation hit hard. One Monday afternoon he found in the mail the tuition for his daughter's first semester at college, the college she had longed to go to all her life, and that afternoon he didn't have the money to pay it and couldn't see where it would come from. He did not think he could get another loan from the banks when he had so many outstanding. Later that day, with this personal problem on his mind, he returned some materials to Martin's Lumber; he had by a sheer mistake in adding ordered twice what he needed. The refund he was given was so close to the amount of Cynthia's tuition that it seemed fated, a message: here you are. He had gone to his bank, put the check into his account, and paid Cynthia's tuition that day.

How it had spiraled, how he had come to lose control so completely, he did not know. In the past year it seemed that his life had splintered off into fragments, so that no matter how fast he spun or how quick he was, some things flew past his reach. When as a young man he had built houses, he had actually built those houses with his own hands, and it was this that had given him the greatest pleasure. As he grew older and more experienced, he learned to savor the intricacies of manipulating blueprints and designs, but still it was the actual work that he loved. He found his job as the contractor for the Londonton rec center more complicated than he had planned; he had to spend so much time on paperwork and ordering and signing and supervising that he had to have his crew do the actual work. It was as if someone else were raising a child while he gave directions from a distance. It was an unsatisfactory time for him, but he was committed, and he worked harder than he ever had in his life. When two personal loans came due, he did not have the time to consider the morality of it; he simply ordered more material than he needed, returned the material, and used the refund to pay off the loans. He planned to deal with it all later, when he had the time, when he was not under such pressure.

There were times, more and more of them as the work on the rec center progressed, when Ron was overcome with an emotion he had not felt before, at least not since childhood. He was lonely. He was lonely because now he carried a burden which he could share with no one—not his wife, not his friends, not even Wilbur Wilson—and that burden was the fear that he was after all not capable of carrying out the building of the rec center. Now, while he was caught in the middle of it, he realized that there was a possibility that he did not know enough, had not had enough experience, to do it well. Oh, *he* could have built it himself, with his own hands, given enough time; he could have done that. But he had to supervise the construction, oversee and hire and fire men, mediate between workers, satisfy the building inspectors, and spend hours on forms and regulations and paperwork and codes from intricate legal texts—it was the paperwork which really got him down. It bored him, and it irritated him. At the end of every day he went home exhausted, not with the sensual exhaustion of well-used muscles and a physically tired body, but with the draining, depressing, grim, and petty exhaustion of mental strain. When he awoke each morning, he had to shoulder a fresh burden of doubt before he even

went out the door, so he was tired from the start. But everyone around
him seemed pleased with his work; they all leaned on him, the
members of the recreation committee, his workers and subcontractors,
his family, they all leaned on him with confidence.

In the midst of all this, the money he took, not steadily, but occasionally, as the need arose, seemed incidental, really. He could not
focus on it. He could not see it as anything but a minor irritation in a
maze of multiplying problems. It was around the middle of August
when he realized that the money he had taken, bit by bit, refund by
refund, had mounted up to almost seventy-five thousand dollars. This
had not frightened him; it had annoyed him. Yet another problem to
be dealt with. He had taken another refund, amounting to around
twenty-five thousand dollars, and invested it in money market
certificates. He had not been completely clear on this matter—finance
was not his field and he did not have time to make a study of the various investment possibilities—but he planned, in a blurred but determined way, to keep investing the refunds in money market certificates
until the interest earned equaled the amount he had borrowed from
the rec center fund. But it was a vicious circle he had entered, for in
order to earn as much money as he had taken, he had to take more.
Time was against him. He would have to give the committee an accounting when the center was complete.

At the end of August, he and Judy celebrated their twenty-fifth
wedding anniversary, surely an occasion not to be slighted. Judy had
openly yearned for a diamond and emerald ring, but Ron had to disap-
point her. He had no money. He could not tell her this, not in so
many words, for he suspected that Judy, for all her show of capability
and strength, was in a way the frailest of them all. He knew that she
exercised secretly in order to keep trim, and he suspected that she had
other secret habits that kept her going. At this point in his life, he
didn't have the energy to imagine just exactly what these secret habits
were . . he was afraid to know too much. He was certain only that
he must protect Judy from as much stress as possible. He had the memory of his father to warn him of the consequences of too much pressure
on too weak a personality. But it made him lonely to know he could
not share his problems with Judy. And he felt stingy for not giving her
the ring.

That weekend, Cynthia and Johnny had surprised their parents with a celebration dinner party at Londonton's finest restaurant. Dinner for fifty, and lots of champagne. It was a glorious evening, one they could never duplicate, one Judy deserved. Of course Cynthia and Johnny couldn't pay for it; Cynthia was in college and Johnny had just graduated, so they did the natural thing, they charged it to their parents. Ron took the refund for some plumbing materials to pay that bill. He did not want Mike Mansard, the owner of that restaurant, to think he couldn't pay his bills. And with a strange logic, he felt almost justified in using the money for the restaurant bill, because he had refused the temptation of taking money to buy Judy the expensive ring. In a way, it seemed to him that the money he was using was his. He was working so hard. His life seemed completely tied to the rec center: they owned each other in a way.

These things happen to people: you are sitting in an airplane on the way to a vacation, and the plane crashes into a mountain; you are skating on a pond and hit thin ice and fall through; you're walking through the skeleton of a house without your hard hat on and a beam falls and smashes your head open. These things happen to people every day. Bridges collapse, houses burn, cars collide, the heart attacks. Disasters. Surely those people sinking through ice, crashing in a plane, sliding off the road in a car, cried out with all their beings: No, God, *no!* It did them no good, and it would do Ron no good now, to cry or to wish he had done anything differently. For here he was, sitting by the fire with an empty brandy snifter in his hand, confronted with the truth.

He had taken over a hundred thousand dollars from the rec center fund. He had lied to Reynolds and Peter and Gary—poor loyal Gary, who had been so embarrassed by it all. The lie had seemed the right thing to say at the moment. It had saved them all a scene, and it had bought him time to think. Although there really was not all that much to think out. It was as clear to Ron as a blueprint, he could see it all at once. He did not have the money. He would not be able to give them back the money, not in the morning, not ever; he had no money left. Looking back, he could see he had been stupid, but it was too late now to think of that, and it was foolish to waste energy on self-reproof. It was done now, like a fallen plane.

There was one option open to him still, he supposed. He could admit that he'd taken the money, and could not repay it; he could declare bankruptcy, sell this house, and slowly, over the years, pay back what he owed. That way he would be at least morally in the right. But it would cause his children and wife such disgrace and anguish—he couldn't even imagine what it might do to Judy. She had been through bankruptcy once in her life, she should not have to go through it again. She should not have to lose her house, her life, she should not have to watch her daughter be refused the college she'd chosen because of money. If he told the committee he had no money, but would sell the house and slowly pay them back, he knew the inevitable outcome: people in town would be dismayed and angry, they would turn against the Bennetts, and Ron wouldn't have a chance of getting another house to build. In short, they would all be ruined. The three people he loved most in the world would be ruined because of him, because of his stupidity. If he alone were to bear the consequences, he would gladly do so, but he could not bring himself to pull this catastrophe down on the heads of those he loved—not if he had any choice left open to prevent it.

Ron rose and walked through the house to his study. Here he kept the household bills and warranties, the children's health records, all the information needed to run a house. He sat down at his desk and pulled out the file marked Insurance. If he were to die now in some sort of accident, his insurance company would pay his wife the full premium: two hundred and fifty thousand dollars. That would cover the money he owed the rec center, and leave Judy relatively well off, although sooner or later she would have to get a job or remarry. It would see Cynthia through college. If Judy were widowed, Ron had no doubt that Gary, who was their lawyer as well as their friend, would do everything in his power to protect her. Gary would handle Judy's financial affairs, and he would see to it that no nasty rumors got about. Whatever security was left to this family, then, was contained in this file folder. It was their salvation. Ron put the folder back in his desk and shut the drawer, then sat a moment looking at the polished burled walnut wood of the desk. He ran his hands over the smooth surface, appreciating its cool, solid perfection. Wood grains, he thought, were like snowflakes: similar, but surely never exactly alike, like lives.

He turned off the light in the study and went as quietly as possible up the carpeted front stairs. In the master bedroom, Judy lay curled on their king-sized bed, the brown afghan pulled up over her. Ron smiled when he saw her there, still dressed, even wearing her shoes. He knew what she had planned, to wake up at nine-thirty to find out whether or not Johnny had come home. But he reached over and switched off the alarm. She was in a deep sleep, and he did not want to awaken her. He just wanted to look at her again, this woman he had lived with for over twenty-five years. She did not look much older than when he had first met her. She still wore her hair in a braid, she was still slim and supple, and except for a few lines around her eyes, her face was unmarked by signs of stress or worry. He had given her a good life. They had given each other good lives. Now she lay there, safe in her sleep, trusting him to close up the house for the night. Trusting him. She had never failed him, and he would not fail her now.

When they had first moved into this house fifteen years ago, Judy had spent the winter months studying gardening books and drawing up sketches of how the flowers should be planted at each side of the house. She plotted wind and drainage conditions, sun positions, the weeks each flower would bloom, the heights and colors each flower would attain. All that first spring and summer she worked at her planting, and to Ron's eye the result was marvelous. But the second summer, when the first perennials began to bloom, he came home from work one evening to find her in the garden, furiously digging out a bed of marigolds she had planted the week before.

"What in the world are you doing?" he had asked.

"I'm taking these damned things out," she said. "They ruin the effect. They look . . . too common."

"I think they're pretty. A pretty color," Ron offered.

"Oh, yes, they're a pretty color by themselves, but with the other flowers—they ruin the overall effect. I want it to be *perfect*."

She had kept on digging, until she'd gotten all the marigolds out and replaced them with a border of sweet alyssum.

Ron had been slightly amused by this, but as the years passed he had grown to admire his wife for her persistent efforts toward perfection. It seemed to him that the unspoken motto of her life was that *this was her life*, and she would live it well, or not at all. He had no doubt now as he stood watching her that she would approve of his decision, if she could know of it, and that, if she were in his place, she would make the same choice.

He went back down the stairs and into the kitchen. The fire was dying out; he scattered the last glowing embers about with the poker, then drew the screen. He took his brandy glass to the sink and rinsed it and the other three and stacked them in the dishwasher, then sponged off the counter top and checked to see that the cork had been put back firmly in the brandy bottle. He put the untouched raspberry pie back in the refrigerator. Then he walked through all the downstairs rooms of his house, quietly, just looking.

Back in the kitchen, he scrawled a note on the chalkboard that hung by the telephone: "Had to go to the office for a while. Will be home soon. Love, R." He put on his coat and hat and gloves, like any man afraid of catching cold, and went out into the night.

The rain was coming down heavily now, and the air had grown bitter; he hurried toward the garage. Once inside his car, he sat awhile, considering the possibilities. It was not often, he supposed, that human beings got to choose just where in the world to die. But it was important that he choose carefully. He did not want to be only maimed or injured. The roads into the mountains would be the most logical places for an accident, but he had no reason to be going into the mountains. He did not like the idea of having the accident right in Londonton—it might make people have sad memories, or become superstitious—but in order to appear realistic, it had to be somewhere near his home or office. It seemed the best place was the bridge that passed over the Blue River.

He backed the car out of the garage. When he turned out of his driveway, the car slid on a wet patch, and he laughed at the irony of it: wouldn't it be terrible if he had an accident before he arrived at his destination?

He drove slowly down Slope Road, past the Vandersons', past the Moyers'. Goodbye. The houses he passed were clearly occupied by people getting ready for bed, for the downstairs windows were dark, while on the second stories one or two lights still shone; as he passed one house, the light went out. It was just a little after ten o'clock on Sunday night. Ron imagined all the people shuffling around in their robes, completing familiar tasks before tucking themselves into the gentle blanket of sleep. Death was like sleep, it was said; he was not afraid of death. He was only afraid, now, of somehow bungling this one last task left to him, and so he set himself to gather all his competence toward it.

"When all is said and done, I've lived a good enough life. I've been a good enough man," he said aloud, feeling the need to say something conclusive.

Then he just concentrated on his task. He turned off Slope Road, drove down the hill past the college, and entered the square. Here the lights were bright, and cars were parked along the curb; moviegoers at the last show, students at the Pub. At the end of the square the Congregational Church loomed up, white and narrow. He paused to look at it one last time, thinking as he had thought so many times before what a grand and gracious piece of architecture it was.

But it wouldn't do to hesitate too long, so he turned right and drove down Main Street, past all the Colonial houses, until finally the Blue River was in sight. The street was still fairly well lighted, and the blacktop glistened brightly in the rain. The wipers of his car went rhythmically back and forth, but the rain was coming down hard now, and sticking to the windshield. Automatically he turned on his defroster, as if safe driving were a real concern.

The bridge over the Blue River was modern, steel-supported for safety, but there was a spot just before it where, if a man accelerated, and jerked the wheel to the right, and held his breath and aimed, a car could fly off the road and hit the ground, then bounce and plunge straight down into the depths of the river. At this spot the river was not deep enough to cover a car, but it was night, and black, and raining, so it would be morning before anyone spotted the trunk of the Mercedes sticking up, like a bright yellow upended barge. And even later when those attempting rescue discovered that the front driver's section of the car had been smashed in, and washed over by the rushing river all through the night.

PART THREE

Saturday morning
September 4, 1982

All summer long Leigh had devoted herself to her flowers. In the early spring she had had a man come with a Rototiller to plow up and fertilize her back yard until all the rich black soil lay exposed, a patch of farmland in the middle of town. Then, working with great care, she divided the back yard into precise rows, and she planted zinnias, dahlias, begonias, gloriosa daisies, snapdragons, calendula, petunias, and marigolds. She spent most of her summer evenings sitting on her back patio with a drink in her hand, reading a book and looking up from time to time to study the garden in the summer light—listening to the gentle *shoose-shoose* of the sprinkler, watching the water rain down on the ripening leaves. It was the sweetest summer she could remember, full of dreams of blossomings, and at the end of the summer she had an acre of flowers blooming in every imaginable shade of yellow.

The first Saturday in September, when all the flowers were at their finest, she rose at five-thirty, when the sun was just lighting the sky. She put on her usual gardening outfit—blue jeans, a baggy T-shirt, sneakers—and went out into her back yard. With exquisite patience, she cut down all the yellow flowers. She put them in boxes and baskets. At seven-thirty Patricia Taylor arrived to help her. They loaded their cars with the flowers and drove to the church. Inside the sanctuary, they arranged the flowers in bowls and set them in all the windowsills. They tied the flowers into bouquets and garlands and draped them along the ends of the pews and along the walnut balustrades leading to the chancel. They brought in two long walnut tables and placed them at the front of the church on either side of the main aisle, and arranged the flowers so that they covered the tables completely, rising up in sprays and spires, cascading down in leafy scallops almost to the floor, smothering the tabletops in layers of variegated golden leaves. It was an inordinate display, and the mixture of these common household flowers gave an air of gaiety to the white and gold church. The sun streaked through the high windows, lighting on the flowers, causing them to gleam with a buttery luster, and warming the air so that the entire sanctuary was filled with the mingled fragrance of all those flowers. Finally Leigh and Patricia's work was done.

They stood at the back of the sanctuary, admiring their handiwork. The church was dazzling with yellow flowers. They had done what they could do to surround their children with beauty, to festoon the hall of their celebration with fresh living gold, as if with promises, with hope.

The women went home then to array themselves for the wedding; it was to take place at ten-thirty that morning. As Leigh drove to her house she hummed and smiled, feeling grateful that the sky was a flawless brilliant blue. The temperature was climbing into the seventies; it would be a perfect day. And she felt so clever for having planned this garden last spring and for having planted it in the early summer. She had planted all those seeds like a good witch plotting destiny. For after Michael and Mandy had begun living together, Leigh had realized that they really were *good* together, good for each other, and she began to hope that it would last, this lucky love they had found. She and the Taylors had made an agreement with the children in the fall: if you live together and make good grades in school and show us that you're responsible, you can get married next fall. Now "next fall" was here and the children were getting their wish—their wedding—and everyone was happy.

How the world had changed, Leigh thought, that parents—and one of them a minister at that—would join together to postpone a marriage, to force their children to do what not so long ago would be considered "living in sin." But really, Leigh decided, marriage was such a feudal concept, all tied up with keeping control of wealth, power, and the proper bloodlines. It was so outdated. It all came down now to the individual in this singular century, and individuals were choosing to marry or not with one goal in mind: their own happiness. Of course what many were finding out was that over the long term, marriage does not provide happiness, and it certainly doesn't assure it. After all Leigh had been through and seen, she would not have minded if her daughter had never married. She might even have been relieved, although she would like to have grandchildren. But marriage was no longer a prerequisite even for that. There was something still seductive about the idea of family, complete with mommy, daddy, and children, but the truth was, Leigh thought, that that happy traditional family was as rare as a happy marriage. And if happiness were the measure, what family after all could be considered happier than the one created by herself and Mandy?

The two of them had lived very pleasantly together for eighteen years. She had helped Mandy become a fine woman, and Mandy had enriched her life. Certainly there had been tough times, angry words, but fewer, Leigh was sure, than if Mandy's father had remained in the household. No, Leigh had not grown all those flowers and decorated the church so gloriously because her daughter was doing the proper deed, or even because she hoped to embellish the marriage with the luck of longevity. It was simply that this was the last occasion Leigh knew she could orchestrate in any way for her daughter. After all the years of helping her dress and do her hair, of painting her room and sewing her curtains, of driving her to stores to help her find the right clothes, of providing the brightest, smoothest, most beneficial life for her one lovely child, Leigh wanted to give this final gift. It was such a milestone for them. Now Mandy was on her own—or, more exactly, on her own with Michael. It was Leigh who now would be really on her own.

She parked the car and went into the house through the kitchen. It was nine-thirty. There were signs that Mandy had risen and eaten breakfast, and Leigh heard her moving upstairs in the bathroom. She poured herself a cup of coffee and sat down at the kitchen table, looking out at the back yard. The yard looked strange now, slightly bare with all the yellow blossoms gone, but Leigh had foreseen this and planted enough other colors—reds, whites, violets—so that she was not faced with a totally stripped landscape. She stretched in the morning sun, luxuriating in the knowledge of a monumental task accomplished and a celebration ahead. She would not have even a moment to feel bereft—not that she should feel that anyway, for Mandy had been living apart from her for over a year now—because tomorrow she had to finish boxing up her valuables and packing up her possessions. Leigh was renting her house to a visiting professor and his family for a year, and she was going to spend the next twelve months of her life in Europe. She would spend the first six months in Paris, and the next six in Florence. She had already made the arrangements, written to friends, made plans to spend Christmas in Geneva with an old lover. It was the life she had longed to lead since she was a child, and at last she was going to lead it. Better late than never, she thought, and in fact, better late than early. Because this trip brought to her middle-aged body and soul the sensation of youthful adventure. She felt she was younger, freer, more fortunate than her own daughter. All summer long she had tended her garden and dreamed of the future, gorging herself on this last great domestic deed as if on homemade bread, knowing she was about to leave it all to taste the exotic.

She rose, stretched again, and went upstairs. Mandy was just coming out of the bathroom, and she looked shining and elaborate, with makeup painstakingly applied and her hair brushed to a sheen. She was wearing only a white slip.

"Flowerface," Leigh said, and moved to kiss her daughter on the cheek.

Mandy flinched back a bit from her mother's kiss. "Mom!" she said. "You'll streak my makeup! And look at you. It's after nine-thirty and you're still in *jeans*."

"Ah," Leigh said, "but you should see the church! Don't worry, baby, I'll be ready." She went into the bathroom and shut the door.

Mandy wandered into her bedroom and stood in the center of it, looking around. She was completely ready except for putting on the wedding gown and veil, and she had forty-five minutes to wait before it was time to go to the church. She knew that any moment now her father and his wife would arrive, and so would her two best friends from college and her best friend from high school, who were going to be bridesmaids. They would all go to the church together. In a minute or two, the house would be filled with noise and movement. But for this one moment it was silent, except for the noise of her mother's shower, and time retreated from her politely, like a docile servant bowing and backing out of the room, leaving her to her privacy.

This was what she had wanted, this vivid honest moment of separation, when she could stand in the middle of her childhood room as if still in the middle of her childhood, and wholeheartedly give it up with open hands. She had been happy here, in this house, in her childhood, but she had been a *child*; she would always be a child here. She was grateful for the ritual of marriage for providing that necessary sense that something was being officially and irrevocably renounced, and something else taken up. She needed the ritual of marriage.

She sank down on her bed and began drawing her hose up her legs. She moved slowly, smoothing the delicate silken material against her. She had only recently bought a garter belt, since she had grown up in a panty-hose world, and she liked the way she looked in just her bra and panties and garter belt and hose—erotic, exotic, a bit tarty, in fact. She had read enough propaganda in the literature her mother and female teachers foisted off on her to understand that in this particular culture and time women were raised to be self-critical, even self-deprecating, to think of themselves as fat. In one feminist article she had read that in a survey taken of hundreds of women of all ages, weights, and body types, 98 percent of them thought of their bodies as badly flawed in some way. *They all need a lover like Michael*, Mandy had thought, for over the past year she had lived with Michael she had developed a new appreciation of her own body, so that when she looked in the mirror she smiled and thought: Well, I'm not half bad.

So much in the world depended on vision. In fact, it seemed to Mandy that one's whole life depended on three things: luck, courage, and vision. She could still remember how it was when she was a small child, when her ignorance of the simplest things made the world seem blurry at the edges. It was as if she had always moved through a fog. The people she knew well and trusted were seen and felt as *people*: her mother, father, best friends, her teachers after a few weeks. But all other people appeared to her as objects, startling physical masses, who loomed up suddenly next to her in that fog, exuding their own personalities in the same way chairs exuded wood.

She could remember one boy in the third grade especially. His name was Billy, and he was handsome and smart and sophisticated and popular. Of course he must have worn clothes which had colors, but Mandy could never think of him as, say, a boy in a brown sweater. He was so bright and significant that he frightened Mandy, and when he approached her she saw him as a shiny metallic object, very cold and definite, like a spoon. It seemed to her that when he was near her he curved away from her, like a turned spoon curving naturally away; she could feel glitter, polish, and chill emanate from him.

Much later she met his younger sister, who said, "Oh, *you're* Mandy Findly! My brother Bill had a crush on you all through third grade. He used to come home and be *sick* because you would never speak to him." Billy and his family moved away shortly after that, so Mandy never got to know him, and while she was pleased to hear from his sister that Billy had liked her, she was also disturbed that her vision of him had been so wrong, that he had liked her, when she had felt he hadn't. But that was how it was when you were young, people just rose up in front of you, or came at you, like cars or dogs or walls or trees, and there was nothing you could do about it: you were held helpless in your vision, a prisoner of sensation.

She wanted to sculpt this, in fact had begun a piece, her biggest attempt yet, a blunted figure rising up, towering, a faceless apparition in heavy clay, which tilted treacherously forward. How could she shape it so that others seeing it would know that if you tried to touch this figure, if you threatened it, it would vanish? Her mother, and most older people, Mandy thought, led such elaborate and complicated lives, as peopled by their fears of possible problems as her childhood had been peopled by ghosts. They seemed to believe that if a person did the right things—went to high school, college, got the right job, married the right person at the right time—you could escape dark hazards, like a carefully driven car keeping cautiously to a path, not touching the barriers which edged the way. But then, it was true, few people had had the luck she had—and luck was as important, more important, perhaps, than vision. It was sheer, beautiful, generous luck, as bountiful as the sun, which had brought her and Michael together, just as it was luck which had brought her so early to her choice of work. She had her visions. Her mind was filled with them, a bizarre, demanding muddle of reality and dream, voices and fragrances which transformed themselves into shapes and colors, emotions which metamorphosed into objects. She could re-create her visions with her sculpting. And she could do this because of Michael, because of Michael.

She thought of him as being as necessary as the air she breathed or the ground which held her up, as comforting as a bed of tousled blankets, as refreshing as night rain on bare skin—if she wanted to, she could envision Michael as many things. But she knew that what he really was, was simply Michael: a tall handsome young man who for some mysterious reason needed her as much as she needed him.

They had lived together for almost a year now and she had become familiar with all the intimate details of his living, as he had with hers. He was a kind, gentle creature, who had long ago refused the powers of his intelligence in the way a person might refuse a dubious gift from a wizard. Michael liked the real stuff of every day; it had much more meaning, more reality to him than it did to Mandy. He made the coffee and breakfast in the morning, because it mattered to him that the coffee be brewed just right. For her part, Mandy would have made do with tepid tea or even a Diet Pepsi. He had bought a pickup truck to carry his tools in—he had gotten a job with a painter —and he liked his tools. He liked walking slowly through a hardware store, comparing saws and drills and blades. He washed and waxed his truck often. Sometimes Mandy would come back late at night from working at the college studio to find him sitting in front of the television, drinking beer, eating pretzels. "You're a stereotype, you know that, don't you?" she asked, teasing. "You're really nothing but a beer advertisement!" She only criticized him because she thought she should; she had been raised to think that sitting around watching TV and drinking beer was bad.

"If you've got the time, I've got the beer," Michael would say, and pull her down on the couch with him, and she would be engulfed in his slow, aromatic, masculine presence, as in a fragrance. Michael always lived in the present. He was not plagued or blessed by visions or memories which took him away from the here and now, and so when he focused on her, she was overpowered by his intensity, his unhurried concentration.

For his part, he did not seem awed by her art or intelligence, only pleased. He loved her, therefore he believed in her and would do everything in his power to help her, to sustain her while she worked. It didn't bother him to clean house or do the dishes or the cooking; these were tasks which satisfied him in the same way that mowing a lawn satisfied him. They were deeds that could be completed within a short period of time, so that he could see the results, and he liked the easy movements required of his hands and body. He did not seem interested in analyzing their love for each other or in exploring the cause of their lucky happiness. Their love simply existed for him as steadfastly as a tree or a building; it just *was*. Mandy knew that if she stopped working at her sculpting, that would be okay with him, and if she worked at it obsessively and became rich and famous, that would be okay, too, and if she dropped out or became a nurse, that would be okay. She supposed she could worry if she wanted to, about the future— was their marriage, their love, based entirely on sex? Would he, in ten or twenty years, grow tired of her? She of him? She did not think so. It seemed to her they had mated for life, in the mute, absolute way of animals; it was not just sex, but it was an even more physical thing that had happened to them. They were two masses fused together and held there by the force of the world, shuddering into each other, irrevocably locked.

That was luck. Mandy saw herself as a woman who had been given unusual vision, unusual luck, and she felt sure that she only needed courage now, to grab hold of all she had, to say: I love him, and I can do these things. She was grateful to her parents and to Michael's parents for allowing them to make this choice.

She knew this must be hard for them. Her own mother was one of the most intelligent, perceptive women she knew. Yet several days ago, when Mandy had been getting ready for a wedding shower, Leigh had walked into the room while Mandy was fastening her hose onto her new white garter belt.

"Hi, Mom," Mandy said. "Don't I look quaint?" For she thought she did, in that lacy old-fashioned contraption.

Leigh had stared at her daughter, who was wearing only a bra, panties, hose, and the garter belt. "I would hardly call your appearance *quaint*," she said, and walked out of the room without telling Mandy what she had come in for.

Mandy had crossed her room to look at herself in the mirror, then grinned. No, she did not look quaint. She did not look childish. She looked like a woman who had been caressed and loved by a man until her flesh shone. Without meaning to, she had embarrassed her mother with her sensuality. Yet she was glad, after all, for her mother's having seen her this way; it would make things even more definite between them. Mandy was no longer a child. She was a woman.

She was almost a married woman. Mandy trembled, and forced herself into the present. It was after ten o'clock. People would be gathering at the church. Michael was at his house, putting on his tux. She could hear people coming into the house downstairs, voices, laughter, calls. Suddenly she burst into tears—why was it said that way, that she burst into tears? It was rather that suddenly the tears burst from her, out of her eyes, down her face, streaking her perfect makeup. The morning sun poured through the windows, shaped by her frilly curtains, and made her childhood room seem a vessel of light. *She had been happy here*. Mandy walked around the room, touching the bed, her stuffed animals, her dresser, her desk, even each one of the walls, weeping and touching. If she could have, she would have taken that entire childhood room into her arms. Marriage was irrevocable, it was different from just living together, it was a shining sword which cut her off from her childhood and her mother, it was an act which rent every bit as much as it joined.

"Oh, Mandy, little honey," Leigh said. She came into the room and put her arms around her daughter and pulled her to her, not minding that Mandy might get makeup all over her silk dress.

"Mom," Mandy said, "I really do love you. I really do love this house."

"I really love you," Leigh said. "I always will. Come on, let's put your dress on and go in the bathroom. I've brought some flowers up. I'll weave them into your hair. We've got to leave for the church pretty soon."

Mandy got a handkerchief and blew her nose, then smiled at her mother. But as Leigh helped slide the heavy white lace and satin wedding gown over her, and fussed around fastening and fixing it, Mandy began to cry again, softly. This is the last time, she was thinking, that my mother, who has tended to me all my life, will dress me and take care of me.

Leigh led Mandy into the bathroom and waited while she repaired her makeup. She brushed her daughter's long hair and carefully wound tiny yellow roses into it. "Hold your head still!" she snapped. But she smiled. She was envisioning the future. Someday, not soon, but someday years away, Mandy and Michael would have children. Then Leigh would come back into her daughter's life, to help, to plump up the pillows and rub her back and brush her hair so she'd look pretty for Michael, to take the baby from its crib and change its diaper and bring it to Mandy to feed.

The church was beginning to fill with wedding guests. People were, in fact, crammed into the pews. Everyone in Londonton, it seemed, knew Mandy and Leigh or Michael and the Taylors. And everyone was in the mood for a celebration.

The women wore hats adorned with ribbons or flowers and dresses with lace or ruffles or some sort of frill, and the men had gotten out their best suits or blazers. The September sun blazed bright and hot. It was a ripe day, life and time at a glorious peak. As soon as a cluster of people entered the sanctuary, they stopped and looked around, startled, amazed at the abundance of flowers. Their spirits lifted and they laughed, as if they had been somehow pleasantly tricked. When they finally settled into pews, they were too happy to keep still; they turned their heads and waved and nodded at friends and whispered among themselves so that their hushed laughter and conversation drifted through the sanctuary air like streamers, airy banners, spirits in effervescence.

Suzanna Blair sat on the bride's side near the front of the church. Mandy had baby-sat for Seth and Priscilla several years ago. In fact, Mandy had been their favorite baby-sitter for a long while, and so Suzanna had dressed her children up in their Sunday best and brought them to the wedding. Priscilla sat next to her, carefully arranging the pink folds of her frilly skirt so that they covered as much area around her as possible, and Seth sat on the other side of Priscilla, eyeing her operation, trying to decide whether to tease her or not. Obviously he remembered his mother's warnings about the necessity of good behavior at this occasion, because he finally looked away from Priscilla and occupied himself by attempting to count the people in the church.

Madeline sat on the other side of Suzanna. Just this was their triumph. As Suzanna looked around the sanctuary at the elaborate and ingenuous flower arrangements, the pews packed with happy guests, the sun streaming through the windows, she felt a twinge of envy. She would have liked to have this. She would have liked to marry Madeline, to announce to the community her love and enduring commitment to this woman; to have their union blessed by God and man;

to provide her hometown with a cause for celebration, to stand in this holy place and affirm their love through ritual and ceremony. On the other hand, and she smiled to herself, the image of herself and Madeline proceeding in state down the aisle in matching wedding gowns was ludicrous. No, *this* good old ceremony would not do, and Suzanna wished Mandy and Michael nothing but good. And she was, when all was said and done, content, even amazed, with the way things had worked out for herself.

A year ago, she and Madeline had spent weeks discussing just how it would be if they ever could move in together, and then Suzanna would spend hours alone in her bedroom, or if the children were around, hiding in the bathroom, crying. For it all seemed so impossible. She and Madeline could compromise like a pair of saints about arrangements of furniture and schedules; those were only superficial issues. But no matter how they might manage to work out their living together, it could never happen, because of Tom. If he suspected Suzanna of being a lesbian, then he could take the children from her, he could cause her no end of publicity and pain. Suzanna had talked with three different lawyers, and they all said the same thing: in this state the judges would rule against a lesbian mother every time, no matter what the sins of the father were.

Suzanna began to dream of Tom's death, to long for it, because it seemed finally the only solution. But even as she longed for his death, she was ashamed of herself, because he was a good human being, she didn't really wish him ill . . . still, if only he would just disappear! For weeks it seemed that her mind chased after itself like a rat caught in some bizarre and cruel maze. She could not stop her thoughts, but she could not find the way out. She was miserable. Christmas came and went, and New Year's Eve. She and Madeline received separate invitations to parties with the message "Please feel free to bring a friend" handwritten on the invitations. They laughed with each other about what a commotion it would cause if they actually did "bring a friend," if they did show up together. But in the end, they refused all invitations and stayed at Suzanna's to see the new year in by themselves.

It was what they would have chosen, actually, those quiet moments by the fire with champagne and music. Neither woman cared much for parties. Still they were acutely aware of the limitations of their situation that night. And New Year's Day, when Madeline dressed up to go to a brunch that was being given by the head of her department, a party which she thought she really should attend even if briefly, Suzanna felt everything inside her go wild with despair. She might as well be living in Russia, she thought, or Poland, she might as well be living in some kind of institution! She charged around the house, doing laundry, snapping at the children, feeling all wrought up and crazed, until suddenly she felt something flash within her.

She bundled up the children, threw them in the car with sacks of new Christmas toys and candy to entertain them, and drove three hours to Lowell, where Tom and his new wife, Tracy, lived. She liked pretty, tiny Tracy, who was so young, and who seemed to want to do the right thing even though she was never sure just what that was. When Suzanna arrived unannounced on their doorstep at five o'clock New Year's Day, Tom and Tracy were still in their robes, and Tom hadn't shaved. It was clear that he'd spent the day nursing a hangover; he had that grizzled, withered look about him. But he greeted Suzanna and the children quite cheerfully, given the situation.

"What a surprise," he said. "Come in, come in. Happy New Year, babies."

"Oh, goodness," said Tracy, appearing at Tom's side, looking wide-eyed and nervous. "Did I forget something?" She and Tom had had the children spend weekends there before, and it obviously took a great deal of effort on her part to have them. It was one thing to cater to her husband, another to a pair of energetic children.

"No, no," Suzanna said. "You didn't forget anything. I'm sorry to intrude on you this way—I should have called—I apologize—but I really need to talk to Tom about something. You—Tracy—you're welcome to join the discussion. There's no need to exclude you."

Tracy continued to look stunned and nervous, while Tom's tired face took on a wary, suspicious look, but they welcomed Suzanna and the children in. They settled Priscilla and Seth in front of the TV with sandwiches and milk and they gave Suzanna the tall scotch she asked for, then gathered in the living room, with the door to the den, where the TV and the children were shut, at Suzanna's request.

"Well, now," Tom said when they were seated. "What's this about?"

For a moment Suzanna was so terrified she couldn't speak. She was trembling from head to toe, and she was furious at herself for this schoolgirl terror which had overcome her. When she finally managed to speak, she heard her voice come out an octave higher than normal, squeaky and tight. She sounded like a mouse.

"Tom," she squeaked, "I have to talk with you about something. I have to get something clear with you. I can't go on with my life until you let me know what you're going to do about it."

"About what?" Tom asked, looking puzzled. Behind him, shy Tracy had gone white with apprehension.

"About—Tom—oh, *Lord.* Tom, Tom, I'm in love with a woman. I want to live with her. All of us, with the children. In a house. And I have to know what you're going to do about it." She stopped then, because fear had hit her in the stomach as surely as a physical blow, and her breath was knocked out of her.

She had played this scene through in her mind on the long drive over: Tom could react in so many ways, and it was certain that he would act dramatically. Would he be enraged, furious, shocked, disgusted? Would he rush to the rescue of his victimized children and play the heroic, good, *normal* father? Would he go very still and quiet and say with fierce elegance, "In that case, Suzanna, there's really very little for us to discuss. My lawyer will be contacting yours"? She could envision him ushering her out of his house with a flourish of righteous contempt.

But Tom only sat there in his blue-and-white-striped bathrobe, rubbing his hand over his stubby chin, shaking his head at her in amused wonder. Tracy, who had been just hovering, sat down with a plop on the sofa next to her husband and watched him.

"Well, well, well," Tom said slowly. "Who would ever have thought it. Little Suzanna. So you like women."

"Tom, I don't like women. I love a woman. One woman. A person."

"Well, well, well," Tom said again. "I'm sorry if I seem a little slow in the uptake, Suzanna, but you've got to admit I deserve a little time to work this one through." He was quiet a moment, then said, smiling triumphantly, "So all along you were a lesbian."

"I don't think that's quite fair," Suzanna said, but didn't see how she could go further. Did he really want her to review their past love life in front of his new, young, intimidated wife? That would be pointless and cruel. "I don't think I was a lesbian all along or that I am a lesbian now. I hate *labels*. I think I am just a woman, who once loved a man and lived with him and who now loves a woman and wants to live with her. But you've got some power over me, Tom, because of the children. And I need to know your feelings about it all—about the children."

"I'm not sure what you're saying," Tom said.

"What I'm saying," Suzanna said, and to her fury tears came to her eyes, she did feel so desperate, so caught, "is that you can cause me a lot of trouble if you want to. I suppose you have the power to ruin my life now. Oh, don't be so *dense*. Must I spell it out to you? Because of my—situation—you can legally gain custody of Priscilla and Seth. You can force me to give them up, to have them come live full-time with you."

"Oh, Suzanna, we would never do that!" Tracy said, eyes wide with earnestness.

The girl's outburst made Suzanna look at her, really look at her, and she saw Tracy sitting there in her slinky red lounging pajamas and realized that here was an ally. Tracy might look like a frail young thing, but she wasn't stupid, certainly not stupid enough to turn her little love nest into a family bulky with someone else's children. *Thank God for that much,* Suzanna thought, and began to relax a little.

"Do the children know about you and this other woman?" Tom asked.

"No," Suzanna said. "They know we are friends. Close friends. They know Madeline spends the nights with me sometimes. If we move in together—well, we can't move in together unless it's okay with you. I can't risk losing them if you're going to be terrible about it. I'll just have to not live with her. If we *do* move in together, well, I'll tell them that I love Madeline. That we care for each other. That I like having another adult around. But I don't think I need to go into any sexual details. They're still so young."

"You'll have to tell them sometime."

"Of course. I know that. But not quite yet, I don't think. Well, there's been no reason to tell them anything yet. And if you—"

"So what is it you want from me?" Tom asked. "My *blessing?*" His voice was light, sarcastic, but Suzanna knew well enough what a stinger he could have hiding there. How had it worked out, she wondered, that this vain cynic could sit in judgment on her life, could have her happiness at his mercy? She had to look away. It would not help for him to see the anger in her eyes.

"Your blessing would be nice, actually," she said softly. "I certainly have given you and Tracy whatever blessings I could. Where the children are concerned, I mean, and this is about the children. Tom, I'm doing everything in my power to be a good mother to Priscilla and Seth. They're turning into happy, nice, good people. I don't *do* anything in front of them, I never would. But it's so nice to have another adult in the house, to share things. It's lonely living alone, being responsible at night when the children are sick, or when I'm sick, and I'm happier, I'm a better person, knowing that there's one person in the world who cares for me, it—"

"Oh, Christ," Tom said. "Cut it out. There's no need to get maudlin. What do you think I am, some kind of monster?"

Suzanna began to sob. She covered her face with her hands and leaned forward so that her forehead touched her knees. She was furious at herself for this display of emotion, of weakness, and terrified that it was happening, that this torrent of tears should overtake her now, on enemy territory. But she had been so stiff with fear during the three-hour drive over, so afraid of this moment of confrontation.

"What is the matter with you?" Tom said, annoyed, upstaged, discomfited by her tears.

Suzanna could not lift her face to his. "Don't you see how it is for me?" She spoke through wet hands, and she wanted to say: Oh, Tom, you loved me enough once to marry me, can't you love me enough still to wish me happiness? "I could marry any kind of dreadful man this world could produce, and still keep custody of the children. But because I want to live with a woman . . ."

"My sister's gay," Tracy said. "She and her lover spent part of the Christmas holidays with us. We're not quite as medieval as you think."

This announcement did make Suzanna lift her head. She stared at Tracy in amazement. Then she smiled. How she had misjudged her ex-husband's new wife, with that ready bitterness that lay so close at hand, thinking that simply because the girl was young and pretty and went around in clothes that Suzanna could never again dream of wearing, she was also provincial and dense. There is a possibility, Suzanna thought, meeting Tracy's stare, that as the years go by we could all end up behaving civilly toward each other.

"Look," Tom said, "it's fine with me if you want to move in with a woman. I don't suppose she's terribly wealthy? It would be awfully nice to have the child-support payments reduced, and if you're going to have another income . . ."

Suzanna studied Tom a moment to see if he were blackmailing her. "Well," she said at last, "no, she's not wealthy. But she does work. It wouldn't be fair to expect her to pay any of the children's expenses, but, Tom, let me see how it works out. Perhaps if two of us live together, sharing the basic mortgage, utilities, that sort of thing, perhaps I could do with less from you."

That was the way it had ended, in agreement. Suzanna finished her scotch and they all talked politely about the weather and national news, careful not to mar this tenuous peace. Then Suzanna bundled the children back up and drove them home. Seth and Priscilla were confused by the quick trip to their father's, by the fact that they didn't stay long and that this time Mommy went and talked, but in the way of all children who move through a world where so much is confusing and unexplained, they accepted it without much of a fuss. Suzanna put down the back seat so they could stretch their legs out in the hatchback, and covered them with a blanket she kept in the car, and the children slept for all three hours back. Suzanna was weak as she drove, and not quite happy, because she was so surprised. She had badly misjudged her ex-husband, it seemed. She had forgotten, or worse, had never realized, what capacities he had for generosity and tolerance. Perhaps he was nicer than she had ever thought, and she had just not allowed those qualities to develop in him. She drove wistfully through the winter's night, slightly hypnotized by the glare of snow and ice against her headlights, reflecting in a melancholy way on the lost opportunities in her life.

But when she drove into the driveway of her house and saw it lit up by the headlights of her car, and saw the kitchen window shining with light—Madeline had a key to the house, Madeline would be there now, worrying about Suzanna's disappearance—Suzanna's heart expanded with joy; she felt as buoyant inside as a helium balloon. She had done it! They could do it! What a way to start the new year!

After the first rush of exhilaration, Madeline and Suzanna had settled down to the serious business of working out a life together, and much of it was not fun. They looked at houses which had the luxury of large adjoining bedrooms, and they looked at houses which had small adjoining bedrooms, but they very quickly realized that even with their two incomes combined, they could not afford a very big house. The interest rates were too high, so high that they would end up paying more for a small house than Suzanna was paying now for the house she and Tom had bought in 1970 when the interest rates were relatively low. This was a pedestrian bit of knowledge, not in keeping with the dreams of love, but one they had to deal with.

They ended up having a small wing built onto Suzanna's house. This provided a downstairs bedroom and study for Madeline, with a tiny circular wrought-iron staircase leading up into a corner of Suzanna's bedroom. It was an attractive addition, but an expensive one, costing almost as much as the equity in the main house itself. The builders began in early spring as soon as the weather was good, and Suzanna often came home from school and sat with her children drinking lemonade, watching the walls go up. She wished that Ron Bennett were still alive, because she thought that if he had done the work, this addition would have been much nicer. And she didn't care for the builder she hired; he was taciturn, abrupt, and condescending, a gruff chauvinist. Still, when the work was done and the builders were gone, Suzanna and Madeline painted and wallpapered the rooms, and made this new addition *theirs*, part of their life together. Suzanna would tuck the children in bed on the second floor, then go into her bedroom, which with the addition of the spiral staircase was now expansive with happy possibilities: Madeline coming up the stairs, Suzanna going down.

Before the construction of the new addition, Suzanna had sat Priscilla and Seth down in the living room, planning to have a long and serious discussion with them. She was ready for any questions. She explained gently, precisely, that Madeline was going to be living with them permanently, that the new parts of the house would be Madeline's rooms. Madeline was her best friend, Suzanna told them, and she would help Suzanna do the housework and cooking and even help drive the children here and there or read them books if they wanted. Madeline would help pay the bills, which would be a big help to Mommy. In short, Madeline would make Mommy happier. Suzanna hoped they could all live together happily.

"Okay, Mom," Priscilla said. "Can we go play now?"

Suzanna smiled. Children, their minds! "Don't you have any questions?"

The children both looked puzzled and bored. "Nope," Seth said, and wriggled.

So she let them run off. She stayed on guard, apprehensive, the next few weeks, for any sign from the children that they were disturbed by the new arrangements. She waited for them to come home from school with tears in their eyes and stories of nasty comments made by schoolmates. She prepared herself for a crisis, but none occurred. It seemed very strange.

It was May when the moving van bringing Madeline's furniture and boxes of books and possessions pulled up in front of Suzanna's house. The weather was spring-like and mild, and neighbors were jogging or strolling around. Suzanna waited until some of the older ones came by, looking with frank curiosity at the van. Then, unable to bear the suspense any longer, she charged out of the house and into the street to confront one of the couples, a pleasant older married man and wife who took their constitutionals every evening when the weather permitted.

"Hello!" Suzanna called.

"Hello, dear," they said, "are you moving?"

"No, no. I'm having a friend move in. Madeline Meade. She teaches psychology at Southmark College. That's why I had the addition built on. We're good friends, and it will be so much easier having another adult in the house."

"How nice for you, dear," they said. "We worry about you sometimes, you know, living all alone like that without a husband for protection."

They all talked a bit more about the weather, the children, the news, and then Madeline came out of the house, wiping her hands on her jeans, and walked out to the road to shake hands with the old couple and say hello. When everyone parted, Suzanna said to Madeline, "Why, it's amazing. They seem to think this is perfectly fine. They didn't raise an eyebrow. Do you suppose they wonder about our sex life?"

"I don't know why they should," Madeline said. "We don't wonder about theirs."

After Madeline moved in, there was a period of about two weeks when both women felt the town buzz slightly, as if a low-voltage electric shock had been passed around. When Suzanna pushed her shopping cart down the aisles of the Price Chopper, acquaintances who had formerly only said hello now stopped her for a long sociable chat, and Suzanna felt that they were looking her over, bright-eyed, searching her out for some sign. Once she had come upon Pam Moyer in the hardware store and Pam had smiled hello, then blushed scarlet. Ursula Aranguren reported that several people at the college who knew Suzanna slightly had bothered to ask if she supposed that Suzanna was a homosexual.

"I just told them that if you were anything, you were bisexual, since you have children," Ursula said.

This conversation had occurred over drinks at a local restaurant; Ursula, Madeline, and Suzanna were having dinner together.

"But I don't understand," Suzanna said. "I thought there would be so much more of a to-do about it all."

"Your timing's all off for a to-do," said Ursula. "Madeline should have moved in in January when we were all so bored we would have chewed any bit of gossip we could find to the rind. Last fall was taken up with Ron's death and Johnny's disappearance, and now Johnny's come home and taken your limelight."

"Oh, don't talk that way, Ursula," Suzanna said. "The last thing we want is limelight. I've been sick with worry about what might happen."

"Well, I think you can stop worrying," Ursula said, looking around the restaurant. "I can assure you I'm much more interested in finding someone to liven up *my* sex life than I am in hearing about anyone else's."

But Suzanna still worried. When June came and she walked down the hall from her classroom to her daughter's classroom for the final parent-teacher conference of the year, her stomach cramped so she could hardly stand. She had mentioned her new living arrangements casually over the past few months to the other teachers as they sat sipping their Tabs in the teachers' lounge, and no one had said, "My God, Suzanna, does this mean you're a lesbian, unfit to teach children?" She thought that now and then when she entered the lounge, conversation among the other teachers stopped for a moment—but that always happened, because there were factions in the school, some teachers for certain school policies, some against; there was always some small squabble going on. She had not felt personally snubbed by the other teachers. But what if Priscilla's teacher had been noticing some personality change, or felt that Priscilla was unhappy, becoming maladjusted? But Priscilla's teacher gave Suzanna a glowing report: she was fine, cheerful, learning easily and well.

"I was afraid that she might be exhibiting some signs of—oh, I'm not sure what—unhappiness, I suppose," Suzanna said to the teacher. "I mean, since Madeline's moved in."

Martha Martin was in her fifties, and today she looked tired. "I don't see why she should," she said. "I think the important thing when someone new enters a household—man, woman, or child—is to discuss this change with the child and to be sure to continue to give the child the affection and attention he or she is used to. And clearly you've done that."

"Well, then," Suzanna said, "thank you." She rose and went to the door.

"Suzanna," Martha called, so that Suzanna turned back, "Priscilla is really all right. It's *all* all right." She smiled.

Perhaps it really was *all* all right, Suzanna thought now, for here she was, in her church, at a wedding, with her children on one side of her and her lover on the other. The summer had been a quiet one. She and Madeline had started a huge vegetable garden. Tom and Tracy had taken the children on a camping trip to Canada for a month. Without the usual contact of fellow teachers at the school or other parents to arrange activities for the children, Suzanna had become slightly lonely, as if a void were expanding around them. And she had thought: Ah, this is what it's going to be. Not a noisy reaction of angry people, but a simple falling away. We'll be snubbed. Even Madeline agreed that it did seem the town was drawing back a bit, studying the situation in its conservative way. But at the end of the summer the Vandersons had their annual all-day swimming and barbecue party, and the invitation that arrived in the mailbox was addressed to "Suzanna, Priscilla, and Seth Blair and Madeline Meade." They had all gone to the party and had a good time, talking easily with everyone.

And now they had received a similar invitation, addressed to them as a pair, from Leigh Findly, for Mandy's wedding, and here they sat.

We'll never have this, Suzanna thought, this public affirmation of our love, a wedding. But we are living together happily, accepted by the town. We will live out our lives here, the children will grow up, we'll go to parties, weddings, funerals, concerts, and plays here. We will, we *do* belong. It seemed to her that people were kinder than she had ever supposed, and now as the sanctuary glowed with flowers and music, Suzanna's emotions expanded accordingly.

The family provides the world for children, but the town provides the world for grownups, she was thinking. We are all living here like a group of relatives, second cousins twice removed, stepsisters, would-be spouses, misplaced aunts and uncles; we're incestuous, marrying and divorcing each other, meddling in each other's affairs, counting on each other when our cars or marriages break down, turning to each other for a good game of tennis, bridge, or sex. We pass the gossip around as greedily as children whispering the game at a birthday party, but we mean each other no harm.

Why, consider Johnny Bennett, she thought, for just then he entered the sanctuary, following his mother and sister to a pew on the groom's side. He ran off last year with Liza Howard, Suzanna thought, and jilted poor Sarah Stafford, and created a big scandal. Perhaps we all did talk about it a lot, for the truth is, it cheered us up considerably: the fact that Liza and Johnny, who live among us, who are part of us, could do such a thing made us feel capable of exciting things, too. Exciting sexual things. Lust and drama. Escape. We thrilled with it for days, imagining how it must have been. Of course we all felt sorry for Sarah, but not too sorry, after all. She just went off to Paris for the year, and the newspapers have been full of little tidbits about her social life, the parties she goes to, the gowns she wears. She's probably delighted she didn't marry Johnny, she'll probably come home married to a count.

Suzanna studied Johnny as he settled his mother into the pew and seated himself next to her. He certainly was handsome. Too handsome for his own good, probably; she was grateful her daughter was too young for his charms. She wondered who he would marry now. He seemed to have given his complete attention over to his mother since he returned home, but surely that couldn't last.

"You know," Madeline had said this morning as they lay in each other's arms, "probably half the people in this town—the female half—

are delighted that you and I have each other. That takes two women off the market."

"What a way to put it!" Suzanna had laughed.

"Well, it's true, you know," Madeline had said. "There are more single eligible women in this town than there are men. Especially now that Judy Bennett's widowed. And I heard that the Moyers are getting divorced."

"I heard that, too," Suzanna said. "I wonder why. They always seemed to be the perfect family."

"I wouldn't be surprised if it had something to do with the Bennetts," Madeline had said. "The Moyers were their closest friends, and tragedies have a way of reverberating among friends."

"That was such a sad time," Suzanna said, thinking of those bleak fall days after the police had found Ron Bennett's Mercedes in the river.

"I know," Madeline replied. "That's probably another reason why no one made a fuss about us. This town was so hard hit by Ron's death. I think it made us all feel mortal. In the face of that, any kind of love seems a blessing."

So there they sat, together at a wedding, a couple fairly much like any other. They would never hold hands in public or even kiss a quick goodbye if anyone else was around, but in a way this necessary restraint provided an elegance to their relationship, and an awareness of pleasures they might have otherwise missed. Just now Madeline leaned over to Suzanna and whispered, "Look at that hat." Suzanna looked at the hat—it was a turquoise affair with a plume, very ostentatious for Londonton—and Suzanna smiled, but she was smiling not so much at the hat as at the rush of pleasure she got when Madeline's breath and perfume drifted up against her skin.

Gary Moyer was one of the last guests to arrive at the wedding. The usher who greeted him at the door was a seventeen-year-old hulk named Carter Doullet, who was a friend of Michael Taylor's and a friend of Gary's own eighteen-year-old son Matthew.

"Hi, Mr. Moyer," Carter grinned, "your wife's already here. I think I can squeeze you in next to her."

"That won't be necessary, Carter," Gary said. "I'll just sit at the back by myself, thank you."

Carter look surprised. Gary realized that meant that Matthew wasn't telling his friends that his parents had separated. Gary settled himself into his pew, wondering if he should now worry about the implications of his son's secrecy. Of course the boy did not want his parents to separate, so he probably thought the less he talked about it, the less real it would be.

The church was absolutely packed, each pew stuffed with brightly dressed well-wishers. These people, Gary thought, these people. My friends and acquaintances, my clients and colleagues. He understood now why it was that Johnny Bennett had run away—because after living in a town for a long time, a man feels duty-bound to remain superficially as he always superficially has been. The clothes he wears, the jokes he makes, the restaurants he frequents, the people he sees, all become established to the point of routine. It is this that gives a town a secure and homey atmosphere. People assume they can rely on each other to remain predictable and the world in turn seems a safer place. But if a man wishes to change even the slightest thing—the way he wears his hair, the color of his shirts, his restaurant, his sport—the town is discomfited and must go through a series of minute readjustments. And a major change, a death, a divorce, a serious crime, rocks the town like an earthquake, causing each member of the community to feel the walls of his house shiver with the precariousness of life. It would be easier to move away to a new town, where a lover or a hairstyle is readily accepted as part of you, than to make a major change in your hometown.

Gary had felt in the past few weeks that he owed an explanation for his impending divorce to his barber, his mailman, even the men who collected his trash. Not that these people would ever presume to ask, but the question was in their eyes, in their demeanor. Some of it was idle or even prurient curiosity, but most of it, Gary was sure, was real concern. He had in fact revealed himself to an old man named Jake who was the custodian for the building where Gary had his law offices. Jake came in to clean one night and found Gary sleeping on the sofa. He stayed, perching on the edge of a chair, to discuss his own divorce, his own love life, this old man of sixty-four. When he left, Gary was comforted by Jake's words: "Ah, it happens to us all sooner or later, age catches up with us and we want something wonderful to happen just one more time before we die." But Gary felt guilty, for he knew that just as Jake had provided comfort for him, so he had provided discomfort for Jake, a chilly reminder of things going wrong in the world.

As it was, he could explain himself to the custodian whom he scarcely knew with more ease than he could to his friends, than he could to his wife. Where did it begin? He and Pam and the Bennetts had been friends for over twenty years, so that they felt like family to each other. They shared memories, hopes, old jokes, and the right to criticize each other, to bare their worst faults to each other and still expect respect. A sense of competition existed between them, and of course that pleasant sensation of mutual attraction. Like any other quartet of close friends, they admired and complimented each other, they indulged in flirtations that were real even though they were harmless and slight.

It was almost a year ago that Reynolds Houston called Gary with his suspicions about Ron. Gary's instinctive reaction had been anger at Reynolds: pathetic old dried-up busybody! Then he had seen the figures, and been even angrier: at Reynolds for discovering it all, at Ron for being such a damned fool, at himself for not taking precautions as a lawyer and a friend to safeguard the rec center money and Ron. When they had confronted Ron on that Sunday night last fall, Gary had been nearly dizzy with relief at Ron's easy explanation.

"Much ado about nothing," he said to Reynolds as they drove away from Ron's house that night.

"So it seems," Reynolds replied. "We'll see if it's so in the morning when Ron writes us a check."

Old maid, Gary had thought, old troublemaker. The men had finished the drive in silence, mutually irritated, Gary by Reynolds' cynicism, Reynolds by Gary's naïveté. They had just managed to say a civil good-night when Reynolds dropped Gary at his home.

"Just more boring rec center hassles," Gary had told Pam when he got home. Then he had settled down to watch some Sunday-night TV, and had been self-indulgent enough to feel slighted by the bowl of pretzels his wife set on the table next to him. The image of the raspberry pie that had been sitting on the counter in the Bennetts' kitchen haunted him. He had always admired Judy's flair for cooking; Pam did not like baking. She never made pies. Pam doesn't love me as much as

Judy loves Ron, Gary had thought, sulking. Then, quickly ashamed of his thoughts, he had reached out and taken Pam's hand and stroked it as they sat together watching TV.

What a *fool* he had been! He had believed Ron completely. He had sat there like an idiot, safe in his own home, coveting a piece of raspberry pie, instead of worrying about his friend. He had gone to bed, he had slept soundly. God, even now the remembrance made him squirm with shame. He had been so dense that he had slept soundly while his best friend committed suicide.

At five-fifteen on Monday morning, the phone rang. It was Mich Michadello, the local sheriff. Gary and Mich had gone to school together from kindergarten through ninth grade, when Gary had gone off to prep school. As children they had played cops and robbers, and now they were both in their late forties, and playing the game for real. They shared the same sense of values; they liked seeing criminals locked up; they enjoyed a sense of mutual admiration and companionship as they each worked at their own place in the system of providing law and order for their town. Several times a month they got together in a coffee shop to discuss current cases and to trade information. When Gary first heard Mich's voice, he assumed that was what he wanted; then he saw the time on the clock.

"What's happened?" he asked.

"It's Ron Bennett," Mich said. "He's been in an accident. His car went into Blue River right at the Main Street bridge. Do you think you can get down here right away?"

"Yes. I'll come right away," Gary said, and from that moment on he knew his life was changed. Now there was no doubt in his mind. He knew Ron had taken the money, and he knew Ron had committed suicide rather than bear the disgrace. Gary was sick at heart. He thought: If we had not confronted him with this information, he would still be alive.

It was still raining when he got to the bridge. It had been raining all night, and from the looks of the low gray sky it would keep on raining forever. The street and sidewalk were plastered with fallen leaves that glistened slickly in the dim light. The street was shining with water, and rivulets ran down the side of the road to gather in puddles at low spots or to gurgle down the drains. Three police cars were parked by the side of the bridge, their flashers spinning in senseless circles, the vivid streaks of light making the bleak morning sky seem even grayer. Will White's big black-and-yellow tow truck was parked up on one side of the grassy bank, and policemen in identical rain slickers stood near the truck, yelling at each other over the noise of the rain.

Gary looked down. The river was not blue today, but muddy gray, and turgid. It surged over and around Ron's yellow Mercedes as relentlessly and effortlessly as if it had always done so. Gary felt nausea rise in his throat. It could not be true; it was true. He swallowed and grabbed on to the bridge railing for support.

The metal was cold and wet. He began to shiver. My friend, he thought, how I have failed you.

"Christ," Will White said, so loudly that Gary could hear. "*You* tell *me* how. I can't see no way to get a truck down this bank. It's too damned steep."

Mich Michadello left the group of policemen and came walking through the muddy grass to join Gary at the bridge. His feet made squashing sounds as he approached; his slicker squeaked.

"You okay?" he asked.

"It's Ron's car all right," Gary said.

"We know," Mich replied. "He's already out, Gary. The ambulance left for the hospital about ten minutes ago. But he'd been dead for hours. Looks like the impact of the crash killed him. He didn't know a thing. At least it was quick."

"Shit," Gary said. "Christ."

"Listen," Mich said. "I have to talk to you. I'm trying to figure this thing out. We've never had an accident like this before, and we've got to find out what it is. We don't want this kind of thing happening again. But it's a real puzzle. The road is a straight flat stretch for a good three-quarters mile on either side. It was probably slick out last night because it was raining, but it wasn't that slippery. Unless Ron was speeding, he should have been able to stop the car if he went into a skid. There aren't any tire marks, but there wouldn't be with all this rain. It looks like he just drove off the road and into the river, like he aimed the car, and pressed on the gas. Otherwise the car should have stopped on the bank."

"What are you saying, Mich?"

"Well, I think you're about as close to Ron as anyone. I guess I just need to know if you think there's any reason why Ron Bennett would have committed suicide."

"God, Mich, you can answer that question as well as I can. Ron loved his family, he was a happy man, he was building the rec center —do you think he'd commit suicide in the middle of a project like that? *Christ.*"

"I had to ask," Mich said. "I thought it'd be better to ask you than to ask his wife."

Gary looked his old friend straight in the eye. "It's a terrible, terrible accident, Mich," he said. "It's a tragedy that's going to rock this town. Don't try to make it into anything else."

"I'm just doing my job," Mich said.

The two men stood there a moment, deadlocked in the rain. Then another policeman came muttering past them, "There's nothing more we can do in this damn rain," he said.

Mich sighed. "All right," he said to Gary. "It was an accident. Do me a favor. Come with me to tell his wife."

It had been a little after seven when the two men had arrived at Judy's house. She must have been sleeping soundly, because they had to knock and ring a long time before she appeared at the front door, and when she did, she seemed disoriented and slow. Her face had that blurry, saggy look that Pam's had after a long sleep. She was wearing plaid slacks and a yellow sweater, but they were creased and wrinkled as if she'd been sleeping in them, and her hair was coming loose from the braid. He had never seen her look quite so disheveled—so vulnerable.

"Gary? Mich?" she said, opening the door. She was quiet as they came into the hall, and then she said, "Johnny. It's Johnny, isn't it? Oh, Lord, how could I have slept? I set the alarm clock for nine-thirty, but Ron must have turned it off. Gary, tell me what happened. Is Johnny okay? Where did you find him?"

"Judy, let's go sit down—" Gary began.

"Tell me now," Judy said. "Where's Johnny?"

"It's not Johnny," Gary said. "It's Ron. He's been in a car accident. Judy, he's dead."

Judy's forehead wrinkled with her attempt to understand. She put one hand to her face and one hand on the wall behind her, for support. "I'm so confused," she said. "Wait a minute. I don't understand.

Is this Monday? Last night was Sunday? What do you mean, Ron's dead? How can he be dead? He was just here, in the family room—" She turned and walked down the hall to the family room, then just stood there, looking around. The room was empty, the fireplace grate cold and black, the windows blocks of chilly gray. "Please tell me what's happened," Judy said, not turning around.

"His car went off the road at the Main Street bridge," Mich said. "Sometime last night around midnight, as far as we can tell. It was slick out, and he might have been going unusually fast—"

"He was looking for Johnny," Judy said. She turned to face them. She had gone very white, but her eyes were dry. "Johnny hasn't been home since yesterday morning. He went to church with us, then he disappeared with that Howard woman. I wanted to call the police all day, but Ron wouldn't let me. We had dinner guests. Reynolds Houston was coming over to talk with Ron at eight, and I went upstairs to lie down for a while. I—I had had too much to drink, because I was so upset about Johnny. I don't drink much, and I guess it just put me to sleep. But I can't believe Ron would go off looking for Johnny without telling me. And I've been asleep all this time—and now you say Ron's dead? Oh, Gary," she said, putting both hands up to her mouth, "please help me."

He had helped her. He had spent the past eleven months of his life trying to help her. It seemed that he owed it to her for Ron's sake. There was so much that needed doing. He helped put out tracers for Johnny. He got Cynthia home from college. He helped with the funeral arrangements. And that very afternoon after Ron's death, he sat with Judy in the downstairs study, and they went through Ron's papers. He explained the financial situation to her, including Ron's embezzlement.

"We are ruined, then," Judy said quietly. "Ron has ruined us."

Gary looked at her, this pretty, slender woman, who had always been so good, and who now sat before him rigid and white with shock at what the world had brought.

"No," Gary said. "You are *not* ruined. I won't let you be ruined. There is no reason why anyone else should know about it. Only Peter, Reynolds, and I know, and I can deal with them. I think the important thing, Judy, is for us to reimburse the rec center from the insurance money. That would satisfy Reynolds."

"Damn Reynolds," Judy said.

"Well, it's not just him," Gary said. "He's on the board, but he represents the entire town, you know. Sooner or later it would have had to come out—when the building was not completed but the funds were gone. I think this way we can just put the money back and no one will know. And you'll have plenty of money left. You can pay off the mortgage on this house, you can still send Cynthia to college. You won't be rich, but you'll be all right."

"How could he have been so stupid," Judy said. "I always thought he was so competent. I always relied on him completely."

"Everyone makes mistakes," Gary said. "And, Judy, he did what he could to make it right. He killed himself, I'm sure of it. So that you'd have the insurance money. So that no one would know about his theft. He did it to protect you and the children."

"I don't believe that," Judy said. "I can't. I can't believe he took the money, I can't believe any of this. You're making him seem like some kind of—*crook*."

It took Gary a long time to convince Judy. At last he offered to bring Reynolds in with the figures to prove it to her, but at this, Judy stopped, defeated. She said she believed him. She had heard enough. She agreed to let Gary handle it all for her; he would get the insurance money, reimburse the rec center, discuss the matter with Reynolds, arrange for as much of it to be covered up as possible.

"Gary," she said one afternoon, "you understand that there is no way I can thank you."

"You don't have to thank me," Gary said. "I'm doing this because I love you, and because I loved Ron. I think this is what he would have wanted me to do."

"Do you?" she asked. "How lucky you are that you can think of him so clearly. I'm all muddled. He deserted me. He left me *stranded*. If it weren't for you . . ." Her voice dropped. "If it weren't for you, I'd be lost."

She turned away then. She had never once cried in front of him, or shown any violent emotion, and her composure tantalized him. He began to fantasize about embracing her as she finally collapsed, weeping in his arms, in much the same way that he fantasized seeing her naked body, which she covered so completely from his sight. He drove over to her house almost every day to be sure she was all right. She was always sitting in a chair, dressed simply, her hair brushed and plaited, her hands folded in her lap. She didn't watch television or read or listen to the radio; she just sat.

"I can't seem to go on from here," she told Gary when at last he presumed to question her. "My husband's dead, my son has vanished, my daughter is away. I am useless. I have no one to give to."

"But you're wrong," Gary said. "You have so much to give. Any man would love to live in a house kept by you, to eat your wonderful food, to share your life, Judy."

"Any man?" Judy asked. "Gary, what would I want with *any man?* And surely Johnny will be home soon . . ."

Gary tried to talk to Pam about Judy's plight, but Pam had become curiously cool toward Judy in the past year, unfairly, to Gary's mind, for now was the time that Judy needed friends the most.

"She's got money, she's got her health," Pam said. "She's a fortunate woman even though she's been widowed. I'm sorry, Gary, but I've lost patience with her. The world has too many problems that need solving. She should be out trying to help others instead of sitting at home indulging in her loss."

How harsh she has grown, Gary thought. It was the influence of all those feminist friends she ran with. He studied his wife—*looked* at her for the first time in years—and saw that she had changed. She was growing plump with middle age, and sloppy with her intellectual and social concerns. She was always rushing off to some meeting, or delivering dinners to shut-ins, or driving cancer patients to Southmark for their treatment, or canvassing for some election. He couldn't blame her; he was proud of her; their children were almost grown and didn't need her attention. She was doing what they talked about for years, helping her community. He admired her. But she seemed as appealing to him these days as one of the mediocre dinners she was always serving, which she pulled from the oven either burnt or half cooked and soggy. He took to driving out to Judy's house more and more often. They would sit outside in the early evening just quietly watching spring come. Sometimes they didn't even talk. Sometimes Judy would serve him some dessert: strawberry shortcake or rhubarb pie. "It is so lovely to have someone to cook for," she said to Gary. "I can't tell you how much it means to me to have you come out here. It gives me something to live for."

One night he arrived later than usual. He knocked, then let himself in the front door as he usually did. The scent of perfume wafted down the stairs, and Judy called, "Oh, Gary. I didn't think you were coming. I'll be right down. I've just gotten out of the bath."

He went up the stairs without thinking, and found her in her bedroom, tying the sash of her blue bathrobe. Her hair was not in its usual braid, but hung free, thick, glossy, all around her shoulders, down her back. He crossed the room, took her in his arms, and began to kiss her on her neck, her shoulders, down inside the damp V of the robe. He waited for her to pull him to her, to return the embrace, but she only rested her arms lightly on his chest, as if she meant to push him away but didn't have the energy.

"Are you angry?" he asked, puzzled.

"I'm frightened," she said.

He made love to her on the bed, untying her bathrobe and spreading it wide beneath her. She was so slim and firm, like a young girl, and so very quiet. She kept her face turned away through it all, so that the very old-fashioned thought—I am taking advantage of her—passed through Gary's mind. But when it was over, she buried her head in his chest and cried for the first time. "My God," she said, "I have been so lonely. I have been wanting you for so long."

This seemed miraculous to him; Pam hadn't wanted him at all recently. She was always busy, gone, or exhausted. In the course of their marriage they had weathered many times like this, when either he or she had been too wrapped up in a current crisis to give full attention to the other. But their unhappiness with each other recently had an air of finality about it. At last they fought, the night that Gary missed his son's band concert because he had been visiting Judy.

"His last band concert of high school," Pam shouted. "He played a solo!" She had been waiting up for him, lying in wait for him. She had sent their son to spend the night at a friend's house; the other children were at college. The two of them were alone.

"I'm sorry. I've told you, I'm sorry," Gary said. He hated being put in the wrong like this, and worse, he hated Pam when she was righteous.

Now she stalked about the living room, her face grim. She had her period, and they both knew that always made her bitchy, but Gary was losing sympathy with this complaint. He was familiar enough with Judy by now to know that she was never bitchy during her period.

"Are you having an affair with Judy?" Pam asked.

"Of course not!" Gary lied, indignant that she would suspect him.

"Then I do not understand," Pam said. "Why do you have to go out there so often? *Every day.*"

"She's lonely. You never go to see her."

"I used to go see her all the time last fall. It's spring now. She's been widowed for months. I have tried my best to get her involved in outside activities, the church, some charities, anything, but she prefers to sit out there pining, and you are just helping her indulge herself by going out there all the time. She's got to enter the real world, Gary. Ron kept her so protected, as if she were some fragile, sensitive creature, and now you're doing it."

"Maybe some people are more fragile and sensitive than others," Gary said.

"You *are* having an affair with her."

"I am merely trying to point out that not everyone can just *buck up* like you do, not everyone can be a . . . a *bustler.*"

"A bustler," Pam said, and was silent. She sat down in a chair and was quiet. When she raised her head, her eyes were full of tears. "Gary," she said, "let's go away. Let's go to Jamaica or Nantucket—anywhere. Let's spend three weeks together and get to know each other again. I'll stop *bustling,* and you stop nursing, and we'll spend some time enjoying each other. Let's do go off together, please."

Gary looked at this woman, who had borne his children and shared his life for twenty-four years, and a cold wind passed over him. She sensed this just by the look on his face; they knew each other that well.

"Well," she said, rising. "I see. No, I don't suppose you do want to go off with me for a few weeks." She crossed the room then, and stood behind the chair where Gary sat. She rested her hand gently on his shoulder. "Well," she said lightly, "do me a favor at least. Don't go off with anyone else."

"I won't."

"We've been through worse than this, I suppose," she said. "We'll survive this, too."

She went to bed then, but Gary did not feel cheered or pleased by her words. She was such a hearty *survivor,* he thought with distaste. All the qualities he had once loved her for—her optimism, patience, goodwill, courage—now seemed reflected to him in another light, so that she seemed to him pushy, gross, and tough. She would be able to take care of herself, she would pull through anything. But Judy did not have such endurance; she was truly delicate. Ron had known this, and had given up his life for her. She was the sort of woman that men had to protect, even in this liberal and feminist age.

At the beginning of the summer they finally managed to get in contact with Johnny. They had known for months that he was safe, because he had sent postcards. The first one arrived about a month after Johnny's disappearance. It read: "Dear Mom and Dad, This is just to let you know I'm okay. I'm sorry if I've worried you. I just had to get away. I know it's hard to understand but maybe I can explain it to you someday. I'm with Liza Howard, so I don't have to worry about money. I'll be in touch and I'll let you know my address as soon as we get settled down somewhere. Hope you're okay. Love, Johnny." The next few that followed were in the same serious, concerned tone, although no address was given. And then the postcards came less often and in a more flippant tone: "Hi, M&D, Just wanted to let you know I'm still alive, happy as a clam in Margarita Land. Haven't even had a case of dysentery yet. Hope you're all okay, Love, Johnny."

When two postcards arrived within one month, both of them showing pictures of Acapulco and bearing Mexican postmarks, Gary contacted the American Embassy. After several queries, he located a hotel manager in Acapulco who told Gary during a long-distance phone call that Johnny and Liza had stayed there for two weeks but were no longer staying there.

"If you see them again," Gary told the man, "please ask him to call home. It's an emergency."

At the end of May, Johnny called. Gary had been sitting on Judy's bed. They had just finished making love, and Judy had gone downstairs to get the cocktails they had started and abandoned earlier in the evening. Gary was smiling at Judy's modesty; she pulled on her robe each time she got out of bed, even if it was just to go to the bathroom or down the stairs of her own house to get drinks. She had just entered the bedroom again, drinks in hand, when the phone rang. She handed Gary his drink, sat down on the side of the bed, and answered the phone.

"Johnny," she said, "oh, thank God you've finally called. We've been trying and trying to reach you. Johnny, you've got to come home. Your father's dead."

The next afternoon, the last day in May, Gary drove to Hartford to meet Johnny's plane. Judy didn't want to make the hour-long drive; she told Gary that she had to get Johnny's room ready, but Gary understood that it was herself she had to get ready. Johnny had put her through so much—worry, fear, anger, disappointment—and Gary felt he could make things easier for her by explaining some of this to Johnny.

Johnny was easy to pick out in the lines of passengers descending from the plane. Everyone else looked mortal; he looked like a tall tanned blond god. Gary couldn't help thinking: So that's what eight months with Liza Howard does for a man. In the car on the drive home, Gary tried to get more details from him, but Johnny only talked about places: hotels, beaches, casinos, Mexican resorts.

"Is Liza coming back to Londonton?" Gary asked.

"I don't know," Johnny said. "I doubt if she will for a long time, if ever. In fact, she's written her lawyer to have him put the Howard place up for sale. This is not her favorite spot in the world, you know, and if she did come back, people would only snub her."

"Well, you two did a pretty terrible thing, you know. To your mother. To Sarah Stafford."

"I'm sorry about that. I'm sorry about Sarah. But I'm sure she's okay. We didn't exactly share a great love."

"But you were engaged. And your mother—"

"I know. I feel worse about her. But Christ, Mr. Moyer, how was I to know my father would have a car accident that night? Would you tell me about it?" he added in a softer voice.

Gary told him about the accident and the funeral, and the reaction of the town. He did not tell him about the embezzled money, because he and Judy had agreed that neither child needed to know such a terrible secret. When they entered Londonton, Gary drove over to the rec center, which was finished now, and which sprawled like a glass-and-concrete giant along the Blue River.

"Look," Gary said. "I wanted you to see this first thing."

Over the wide double doors at the front of the center were large, bright red plastic letters: The Ron Bennett Memorial Recreation Center.

"Already people are calling it the Ben-Cen for short," Gary said. He was slightly surprised when Johnny began to cry. He was also deeply touched. "A lot of people loved and respected your father," he said.

"My father was a *fool*," Johnny replied. "All he did his whole life was work. He and my poor mother. They lived such boring, trivial lives! They never did anything but work. They never danced all night or gambled or went scuba diving. The best they could do was take an occasional trip to Bermuda or Nantucket. They never even went to Europe! They never went to Marrakesh."

Gary stared at the young man, stunned. Finally he said, "I'm not sure I see that the value of a man's life is gauged by the choice of his vacation spots. I'm afraid your months with Liza Howard have done you a lot of harm, Johnny. You've lost the values your parents raised you to have, and taken up ones that are frivolous, wasteful."

"Yeah, well, at least they are *my* values," Johnny said. "For eight months of my life I got to live as I wanted to, by what *I* thought was right. Now I'm trapped here again. I'm going to have to stick around and take care of Mother."

Gary had drawn himself up at these words, offended. You little shit, he wanted to say. Instead he said, "If you're worried about having to stay around to take care of your mother, you can be relieved. I intend to marry your mother as soon as my divorce from Pam comes through. This is private information, however. I don't want it gossiped about."

Johnny, blowing his nose in a wheat-colored linen handkerchief, had looked sideways at Gary; he seemed to leer. "Everyone's been busy while I've been gone," he said.

"Your mother still needs your support," Gary said. "I hope you won't take that sarcastic tone with her." He started up the car and drove away from the rec center.

"Don't worry," Johnny said, and sagged against the car door, resting his head on the window frame. "I love my mother. I'll be as good as I can be. I can see her in a different way than I did before, but I still love her."

Now they were all together in this church. Johnny sat on one side of his mother, and Cynthia on the other: the perfect children framing the perfect mother. Thank God the kids were almost grown and the insurance money would cover Cynthia's college tuition for the next two years, Gary thought. Pam was not being nasty about the divorce—and she easily could be, she could sue Judy as a corespondent and cause a scandal—but the price of her compliance was high. She wanted a lot of alimony, and a lot of child support, and the house as well. It was a good thing Judy owned her house clear and free now. It was a good house. Gary had always liked it. He could foresee how the next six months to a year would be difficult, as the town sorted out its feelings about this new separation and entanglement. He and Judy would have a private wedding; they would live quietly for the first few months. Then, he knew, invitations would begin to come, and before long, he would be sitting at one end of the table in Judy's elegant dining room, sharing dinner with a dozen good friends, eating Judy's delicious food, and after a while their marriage would seem as natural and acceptable as the one that was taking place right now.

"The church looks beautiful, doesn't it, Mom?" Cynthia Bennett asked.

"Actually, darling, I think it looks rather tacky," Judy replied. "All these homegrown flowers strewn about. It's overdone. Almost cheap."

"Oh, *Mother*," Cynthia whispered, and with as much petulance as she dared display in such a public place, she drew herself up and looked away from her mother.

Cynthia's jealous, Judy thought to herself. She could understand that. She could remember a wedding which had taken place during her high school days and which had filled her with envy for that one day. Sonja Wallace had gotten married in the middle of her senior year, and all the girls had admired her so, and envied her wedding showers, lacy trousseau, and early admission into adulthood. But Sonja had gotten married because she was pregnant, and she hadn't been able to go on to college like everyone else.

In fact, after the wedding no one had seen Sonja or thought very much about her at all. But *the wedding*: well, it was an event, wasn't it, and Judy had envied Sonja that one day and could understand Cynthia's envy now. Cynthia and Mandy were the same age, and here

Mandy was, Queen for a Day, marrying a boy who, in his own way, was almost as handsome as Johnny.

But he was so young, Michael Taylor, a year younger than Mandy, just *eighteen*—oh, they were fools, the parents, letting these children marry at this age. It was all so *inappropriate*. She didn't really approve. But when the wedding invitation had arrived, she had known she must go. If she didn't, people would think it was that she was too embarrassed and resentful because Johnny's wedding had fallen through. No, she had to make a public showing, after all these months of crisis. She had to go with her head held high, with her two children at her side, presenting a united front. To do anything else would be to admit to failure, and she would not do that, for she could not see how she had failed.

She had *not* failed, her psychiatrist told her. She had *not* failed, Gary told her. Yet in these past months the suggestion that she had in some way failed rang through her daily thoughts like the refrain of some catchy tune that her mind wouldn't stop replaying. How could she not have failed: her husband had embezzled money, then committed suicide, if Gary were to be believed, and her perfect son, her darling, had run off with that woman and left Judy to face the Staffords and the town alone. She *must* have failed to have the two men in her life treat her in such a way—and yet, what was it she had done? How exactly had she failed? What was it she should have done differently?

Now, for example, she could, with only a slight tilt of her head, study her daughter Cynthia, who sat next to her in the pew, gazing with foolish rapture at all the flowers. Judy had given birth to this girl, and had done everything in her power to help her grow into a lovely woman, yet here she sat, a lump, overweight, with bad skin and an unbecoming hairstyle, if you could call the simple hanging down of hair around one's face a style. When Judy questioned Cynthia about her appearance, her daughter said that she was too busy with her studies to spend much time on her looks. "Oh, sweetie, even in this liberated age, a woman's looks are at least as important as her mind," Judy had said to Cynthia, gently attempting to win her over. But Cynthia had only turned away. She was always turning away. Yet she came home dutifully enough, for Ron's funeral, for the various vacations, and although she could never be as lovely as Mandy, who had such undeserved beauty, she still was retrievable if she would only *try*, Judy thought. If she would only lose weight, have her hair fixed in a feather cut, wear contact lenses instead of those dreadful thick glasses which hid her pretty eyes . . . It made Judy twitch with impatience to see her daughter; she looked like such a grind. It really was not necessary. Was it Judy's fault?

This was the question foremost in her mind: was her daughter's almost aggressive unattractiveness somehow a sign of failure on her own part? Judy could not see how it could be. She had devoted her life to making her home and family enviably attractive. She had surely taught her daughter how to face the world. And yet look at her, and at Johnny, who had run away, and at Ron.

Perhaps, Judy had almost concluded, it was simply that the number of people in the world who were willing to put forth the effort to live life decently was exceptionally limited, and perhaps one was just born with this strength of character, like a chromosome, or one was not, and no amount of parental guidance could change things. Oh, she didn't really know, and the thinking made her tired, and she didn't want to be sitting here at this wedding now, where people could see her and Cynthia and pass judgment on them. And if anyone dared to express any more *pity* toward her—well, the thought nearly made her weep.

It had taken her a long time to come to the realization of Ron's death. So much cruel news had come at once that bitter day last October that for weeks her main sensation had been one of unreality. It really was bizarre that one night she would go to bed the mother of a perfect son, the wife of a perfect man, and wake up the next day deserted by one and widowed and shamed by the other. She had called her psychiatrist in Southmark immediately. When she said, "I do not think I can bear this," he had prescribed the necessary drugs that kept her from feeling anything much at all for many days.

All the doctors she went to, her internist, her gynecologist, were sympathetic, and now she had a cache of wonder drugs that would see her through the next ten years. Getting through the funeral had been easy, even in its own way pleasurable, for she had an instinct for such occasions. She remembered Jackie Kennedy holding her head high behind her black veil, walking all that way behind a riderless horse, and she held that image of proud widowhood in her mind as a model. At Ron's funeral she had held her head high and received condolences with dignity and dry eyes. The pills helped her, of course. She probably could not have cried if she had wanted to. She was so anesthetized that at certain points during the day the grief of other people, the rush of tears, the contorted faces, seemed puzzling to her, even rather absurd, and sometimes embarrassing—so much emotion! She found herself smiling in response. That was the effect of the drugs, but still the funeral had been the easiest thing, because it was acceptable and universal. It would happen to everyone in this town at one time or another. That Ron had died in a car accident when he was still so young was tragic, but it was not curious; it did not reflect upon her.

Johnny's leaving did. This she found harder to bear than Ron's death. It had been the cruelest thing a person had ever done to her, and she would never forgive him. All that rainy October day while she and the town were absorbing the news of Ron's death, Gary and others were making calls, trying to trace Johnny. At three o'clock in the afternoon, they had a phone call from a man named Lewis Pinter, who was a professor of English at the college in Londonton. He was not a close friend of the Bennetts, but he had lived in Londonton for years and attended the First Congregational Church of Londonton. That afternoon he had returned from a conference in Baltimore, and while he was at the Hartford airport, he had seen Johnny and Liza at the American Airlines ticket counter. He hadn't spoken to them—he had been in a hurry to get home, and they had been too occupied with each other to notice him—but he was sure it was they.

Judy had been relieved: Johnny was alive. She had also been sickened, because he had run off with Liza Howard. Gary had driven over to tell her what he had heard, and Judy had just sat in her chair in her kitchen, looking at him. "I can't think of a thing to say," she said.

"At least he's alive," Gary replied. "He's a fool, but he's alive." Then he had asked Judy if he could have access to Ron's study; he wanted to check Ron's private papers.

"Surely we don't have to go through all these things now," Judy said.

"I'm afraid we do," Gary replied. "There's a reason for it—there's a problem, Judy. I think I can help you, I think I can figure it out, but I need to see Ron's private papers. I am his lawyer, you know. Please trust me."

She had trusted him. She had taken Gary into Ron's study and sat in a wing chair silently, her hands folded in her lap for—how long?—hours, while Gary went through Ron's papers. Finally he had turned and explained it all to her, all that had happened last night, all that he had discovered today. Ron had embezzled one hundred thousand dollars from the rec center trust fund. Gary had already gone over the records and accounts in Ron's office, and there was no money in any of the accounts there. It was as clear as day what had happened: Ron had taken the money, and when found out, he had chosen this way to keep his name from scandal, to pay the committee back, and to still in some way provide for his family.

Finally Judy had risen and turned from her chair slowly, searching. She was so stunned by all the horrors of the day that she was not even certain where the door leading from the study was; she was nearly blinded. She had gone upstairs to her bathroom and taken another pill.

Day after day Gary had been there, spending hours in Ron's study, sorting through papers, calling Judy in the evening to tell her what queries had been sent around to locate Johnny, and sometimes just coming out to have a drink, to sit with her, to be sure she was all right. How wonderful he had been, and how different from Pam. Judy hated it when Pam came out with Gary, because then the atmosphere changed entirely.

"Look," Pam would say, walking across the room and gesturing as she spoke so that her coffee sloshed from the cup onto the saucer, "you've got to make some plans. It's been three weeks now and I don't think you've gone out of the house. You can't just *sit* here for the rest of your life. The church auxiliary is planning its Christmas bazaar now, and we need committee heads desperately, and the League of Women Voters is—"

"Pam," Judy said firmly, "I don't want to help anyone. I don't want to see anyone in this town. I can't bear all their drippy, smarmy pity."

"Oh!" Pam said, then, only slightly daunted. "Well, then, why not take a trip? It would do you good to get away from here. There's certainly no reason for you to stay. Cynthia's off at college, and who knows when Johnny's going to show up again. Surely you've always wanted to travel somewhere, off to visit old friends or to see Europe . . ."

"I don't want to travel. I don't want to go anywhere. I just want to stay here and have my privacy," Judy said.

"But can't you see that's bad for you?" Pam said. "It's not healthy to spend all your time grieving."

But Judy was not spending all her time grieving. She did not mind that others, looking on, thought that was the activity of her life; it was the proper thing for a woman in her position to do. But long ago —long ago, when she was a teen-ager, losing an entire way of life because of her parents' foolishness—she had learned absolutely the futility of grief. It was a useless emotion, accomplishing nothing, changing nothing. She knew her life had been changed completely; she did not want it to be so, but there was nothing she could do to make it otherwise. Yet she did not see that she should have to give up everything, her entire style of living, and she refused to be drawn into the peppy circle of valiant widowed and divorced women who began to cluster around her in the weeks that followed Ron's death. How she despised those women with their mawkish cheer, inviting her to movies, bridge parties, dinner parties, tea parties; how she hated them for their attempts to include her in their pathetic little group. She would not join them, she would not take up macrame or aerobic dancing or charity or paddle tennis. She would not join this disenfranchised, second-class, manless world. She would not wear her inferiority like some bright badge. She would rather die. She would rather sit in her house, where she remained inviolate and superior. She would rather wait.

It was not that she had actively planned to seduce Gary Moyer away from Pam; never that. It was simply that she had waited. The day that Gary told her about Ron's death, and later about Ron's difficulties with the rec center money, he had told her that he would take care of her, and she had taken him at his word. She had spent her entire adult life constructing her world so that she would receive envy from the people she lived among, not pity. When she left her house to go to the grocery store or the lawyer's or the post office, people could not seem to pass her on the street without expressing their pity. Even if they did not speak, it was in their eyes. She hated all that pity, it fell on her like a blow. She was all right on the inside, she was a fine quiet void on the inside, blank and still, smoothed out by pills. But all that pity coming toward her hit her, shocked her, ate into her. She hated it. She preferred to stay at home. She preferred to wait.

Each morning after life was back to normal—after the funeral, and Cynthia's return to college, when the phone calls and drop-ins from well-meaning acquaintances had died down—Judy would rise, shower, and dress in something nice, something expensive, a cashmere sweater or a suede skirt. She would fix herself a proper breakfast, complete with cloth napkins and a tea cozy over the teapot, and she'd clean up the dishes. Then she'd just sit in her living room, admiring her furniture. Sometimes she would clean house; sometimes she dozed sitting up. Her waiting had a secretive and industrious function. She was like a woman growing a baby inside her, who appears to be doing nothing on the surface, or like a spider silently creating the chemicals that will become the filaments of a web.

And in time Gary had become her lover, and now he was filing for divorce from Pam so that he could marry her. It would not be too much longer before her life would reach some kind of attractive normality again. She had always liked Gary, and she was pleased that he was a lawyer. That was definitely a step up from a contractor. She liked his suits. He went all the way to Boston to buy them. They would have a good life together, an elegant life. She would always be grateful to him, because he had saved her—saved her in so many ways —from disaster. And he would always be grateful to her because he liked being a hero. That was why he had chosen the law, to enforce the execution of justice in the world, and now he could do it personally, which was more satisfying because it was so clear-cut. He was saving her life.

They had discussed Pam, of course, and agreed that although their divorce might cause her some temporary anger and discomfort, ultimately it would make her happy, too. Now that her children were growing up, Pam seemed to find the outside world more interesting than her home, and with Gary out of the way, she would be free to do whatever she wanted. She was that kind of woman. Now Judy looked across the aisle and up a few rows at Pam, who sat chatting to her children as they waited for the wedding to begin. It seemed to Judy that a shade of unhappiness lay beneath Pam's eyes, like a pale bruise. Of course this would be a difficult morning for her. She would be forced to remember her wedding to Gary as she sat here anticipating Mandy's wedding to Michael. She did not have another wedding of her own to dream toward, but then, Judy thought, Pam was not the sort who needed weddings or even dreams. She would be all right.

It was Johnny who worried Judy the most now. She would never understand why he had run off with Liza Howard, and she knew in her heart she would never forgive him. But that did not mean that she wanted him to be unhappy for the rest of his life. He was still her son. She had devoted her life to the raising of her children; she had done everything in her power to help them grow into well-adjusted, successful people. If he failed to become what she hoped, then all those years —all her life!—would have been a waste. And that would be intolerable.

No one ever told the truth about motherhood, Judy thought. The first year of Johnny's life had been difficult and demanding. She had been exhausted with the tending and washing and feeding and carrying, but in spite of the hard work it had seemed a reasonable task. But when Johnny began to walk, and at eighteen months was reeling through the house, creating chaos with his every step, drinking Ivory soap from under the sink, pulling dishes off the table, plugging the toilet with tissue, climbing up in the cupboard to find and eat the aspirin, Judy realized that she, like all new mothers, had underestimated her job. What she had to do with one individual in the space of a few short years was nothing short of what the force of evolution did with a species over billions of years: she had to transform this wild, uncivilized animal into a functioning human being.

It had puzzled Judy that no one had ever told her about this side of motherhood, for the violence, the vigilance, the forceful channeling away from beasthood was certainly as much part of her daily life as was the cuddling and rocking and stroking. Johnny was not even hyperactive. He was simply a healthy, strong, curious child. He would have happily broken every dish and glass in the house for the sheer joy of throwing, hearing china crash, watching things spatter. He did not know the value of things. When placed in a room with another child his age, it seemed to him a perfectly natural act to hit that child over the head with a plastic hammer. Children were brutes by nature, and the job of the mother was to transform them into human beings.

When Johnny was three, Judy had taken him to the public library for an afternoon's Children's Hour. All the children were asked to sit on little swatches of rug in a cluster in front of a smiling librarian. The mothers were given small wooden chairs to sit on at the back of the room, where they could observe their children but not interact. Judy watched, holding her breath, while Johnny sat through an entire story; at home she read to him often, but he tended to become restless quickly, and would slide off her lap and start tossing his toys about. Then the librarian played a singing game with them called "Where is Thumbkin?" The children put their hands behind their backs, and following the librarian's lead, brought out their fists with the appropriate finger sticking up at the right spot in the song. It was at the fourth finger—"Where is Ring Man?"—that Johnny brought out his hands with his ring fingers sticking crookedly up. Judy watched, and as she did, she felt tears streak her face. She was so relieved, so grateful. Her child was beginning to play the games of others. He was entering into the civilized world rather than disrupting it. He was going to be okay.

That was the turning point. She had told herself she would remember this moment always, and she was right. As the years passed and new challenges arose, she knew she could meet them because of that first small success. She did not demand unusual accomplishments from her children. She gave them piano lessons and skating lessons, but did not wish that they would excel, win medals, take part in competitions, that sort of thing. In fact, she shied away from children and parents who were competitive in sports or academics; they seemed so intense, almost vulgar, so blatantly *attempting* things, going about their learning so earnestly. No, she wished overall, unobtrusive, serene success for her children. And they had been good children, they had made her so very proud of them—until Liza Howard came along.

"I don't think I'll ever be able to understand why you ran off like that," she had said to Johnny the day he came back. They were sitting formally in the living room; Judy was wearing a blue checked shirtwaist. Gary had discreetly dropped Johnny at the door and left the two of them alone. Johnny was so handsome, tanned, filled-out, manly-looking, that Judy wanted to embrace him with joy: *my handsome son.* But she was so furious at him for what he had done that she also wanted to slap him, to rail and curse at him. These two violent emotions seemed to cancel each other out, and of course she had taken some Valium so as not to make too much of a scene, so that she sat in a blue velvet wing chair, cool and quiet, staring at her son as if he were some sort of specimen, a human curiosity, which actually he was to her.

"I don't think I'll ever be able to explain it to you," Johnny replied.

"Don't you feel obligated even to try?" Judy asked. *How could you have done this to me?* she wanted to shriek.

"Oh, *Mom*," Johnny said impatiently. "I'm twenty-four years old. I'm a grownup."

"I know," Judy said. "I'm well aware of your age. I'm also well aware that you were engaged to Sarah Stafford. You had commitments here. And you just walked out, without a word."

"I'm sorry, Mom, I really am," Johnny said, but as he spoke, Judy could see that he was not sorry. He was glad. He was strong and proud from his rebellion; he was like some fancy stud horse who had jumped the fences and galloped away. Now, captured and brought back home, he could not help tossing his head in admiration of himself. And of course it was sex at the source; after all her devoted work, bestiality had triumphed again.

"You could have called," Judy said. "You could have done that much."

"If I had called, you would have convinced me to come home," Johnny said. "You would have been angry. I was too happy. Mom, I've always been so *good* all my life . . ."

"You make 'good' sound distasteful," Judy said.

"Well, I suppose it is distasteful to me," Johnny said. "Being *good* the way I was, well, it was almost the same thing as being *dead.*"

"I don't think your father would think so," Judy snapped, and there she had him. It only remained for her to remind him at a later point in their discussion that Ron had gone out looking for Johnny the night he died. If he had not had to go out in his car on that rainy night . . .

So her son was hers again. He behaved civilly. He took a job at a local men's clothing shop, an exclusive shop that catered to wealthy clientele, and he spent the summer selling cotton slacks with whales or ducks on them to potbellied men from Connecticut. He gave his mother half his salary for rent and food, and put the other half in the bank. Or so he said. It seemed to Judy recently that he was spending a good bit of his money on alcohol. He always smelled like gin these days, or like the mints he sucked to hide the gin. He did not go out to drink. He did not go out at all. He stayed home watching television with his mother, or playing card games with her, or simply sitting outside on a summer night, staring. She knew he was not happy, and she was afraid that he was becoming an alcoholic, and she was not sure, after all, just what kind of victory she had won.

Carlos was a phony, Judy thought now, seeing him enter the church with Ursula. He could no more read palms than fly to the moon. He had promised her that nothing bad would happen to her again, and instead her entire life had been ruined. She had lost her husband, she had lost her son, and if her daughter was going to turn out like this, so unappealing and obsessed with books, then she might as well lose her daughter, too.

It made her feel very cold inside to know this. She thought that if she did not have her Valium and her alcohol to act as buffers, the coldness of all this knowledge would sear through her body like dry ice.

But she did have her drugs, and she did have Gary. Because of his efforts, the rec center had been named after Ron, and, in a way, that honor publicly canceled out the dishonor of Johnny's sordid episode. Because of Gary, she would soon have a center to her life again. She thought it was stupid of Johnny to scorn Gary, to hold the man in contempt because he was divorcing his wife to marry her. Couldn't the boy see that Gary was giving him his freedom? Gary was handling the dissolution of Ron's contracting firm; Johnny would never have the interest to carry on his father's business. When Gary and Judy married, she would no longer need Johnny for an escort, for company, or for financial reasons, and perhaps then she could let him go off again. Perhaps then she could let him go off again to be whatever it was he wanted, even if that thing was a bum, a playboy, a man who lived off a woman.

One day late in May she had casually looked out her bedroom window, and there Johnny had been, below, in the garden. Thinking he was completely unobserved, he had stood above a grouping of bearded iris. Tall-stemmed, elegant, delicately petaled, with a strip of fur at their mouths, the flowers stood, dazzling in their full bloom. As Judy watched, Johnny knelt down so that both knees were pressed firmly into the dirt, and he leaned forward and gently took a ruffled, flaring, peach-colored iris in both his hands, as a man might cradle a lover's face. He bent down and kissed the long fragile petals; he slowly licked his tongue down into the flower's core. Judy had shivered, watching him. She had never seen such reverence expressed before. Then her son let go of the flower and bent even further forward, so that his head was pushed onto his knees. He wrapped his arms around his head and his back shook. He was crying.

Judy turned away, unable to see any more. Could he love that terrible woman so much? In this case, love must surely mean only lust. She had spent her life protecting him from tempting dangers, from touching fire, from walking off high places into air; it is a mother's job to say no. When he was a little boy, he had sobbed because she would not let him play with a strange and to her mind dangerous-looking dog. Surely this fierce sorrow of his was no deeper or more serious than that childish grief. He had never liked to be deprived.

And she had never meant to cause him such pain. He was her son.

But what would it look like to the town if she let him go off again? Good Lord, what if they came back together, the two of them, and lived in the Howard house? Surely they would not disgrace her so. She felt very strongly the need for Johnny to remain in her house, at her side, as if his presence were proof that he had not meant to run away, to disgrace her, that he really did love his mother and meant to live by the values she had worked to instill in him. And if this were all only superficially true, perhaps with time it would become wholly so; these things did happen. Surely with time this bizarre passion of Johnny's would fade, and she would be proven right.

Now Leigh Findly came down the aisle on the arm of an usher and was seated in the front row with people whom Judy assumed were Leigh's parents and relatives. Judy wondered if Leigh had any idea how she did not deserve her good fortune. She had not even tried to keep her marriage together. She had not tried to please her husband, and she had not tried to live a moral, normal life. Everyone in London-ton knew that Leigh had had many lovers; over the past ten years at least six different men had lived with Leigh for several months. What an environment for a girl to grow up in! And yet here they all were, and Mandy was getting married to a minister's son, and Leigh sat in the front pew, an object of admiration. *You do not deserve this!* Judy wanted to yell. She wanted to stand up, to explode upward into a giant fiery message: *You do not deserve this, and I do!*

But she would not explode, she never had before, and she would not now. She would sit here, in this church, with her unsatisfactory children at her side, and she would look serene. Perhaps people admired Leigh, but surely they must also admire Judy, for carrying on so well in the face of adversity. Judy admired herself. She had spent more time in introspection this past year than ever, and she still liked herself. She was tired of self-analysis, though. She wanted just to get on with life. She wished she could thin her daughter down and dress her up and plan a wedding for her. She wished Johnny would settle down and find a decent girl and marry her and have children. But at the very least she had Gary, who would soon be her husband, and who would soon give her a normal life again. She thought she had weathered circumstances very well, and so she held her head high, and looked around her. The wedding was about to begin. From where she sat, she could see Patricia Taylor, dressed in flowered silk, a rich peach color. *Such a frilly dress makes Patricia look her age*, Judy thought.

Johnny Bennett had a letter in the breast pocket of his suit. He brought his hand up to his breast now and then to touch the letter, because it comforted him. But he could not touch it too often, for he might arouse his mother's suspicions; she was sitting next to him, and he felt her vigilance.

He had received the letter only yesterday, but he had read it over so many times that he had the words committed to heart. Still he could not be parted from the letter, because it was from Liza, and carried with it her fragrance, her touch . . . and because he was not sure what this letter meant. People gathered in the church around him, but he was unaware of them. He was as inwardly focused on the letter as a man straining to hear a sweet and perplexing sound. The letter said:

Darling Johnny,
I just returned today from a marvelous long cruise around the Caribbean islands with the Martins and the LaVeques and some other people, and I found your pile of letters waiting for me at the hotel. I'm

sorry to have made you so angry by not answering all your letters—
but you see, I wasn't receiving them, because I was out at sea. We had
such a beautiful cruise. The nights were warm and gentle, you
remember how they can be, so soft, moist, aromatic . . . It seemed the
moon was always full, and it shone down on the water in such a long
enchanting stripe that I yearned to dive overboard into the water so
that I could come up with my skin dripping with phosphorescence. But
I was always too lazy and dazed to try. I spent most of the time just
lying in the sun. We were all wicked and casual and went around
naked, so I have the loveliest tan; I'm golden brown all over, every
inch of me. The crew spoiled us. We didn't have to lift a finger, we
were kept in constant supply of those exotic rum and fruit drinks you
love so much. I think I was slightly drunk the entire time—so it's a
good thing I didn't dive overboard at night.

We found ourselves "discovering" tiny unspoiled islands as we
sailed. I think that from the sky this part of the world must resemble a
case in Tiffany's, for the islands are so green and lush, bordered by
smooth golden beaches, they must look like rough-cut emeralds set in
14-carat gold, nestled in a glittering display on rippling blue waves of
silk. Every time we found one of these islands, we had to dock and
explore. We were like children on a fantasy treasure hunt. At night we
built huge bonfires on the beach and ate fresh lobster or casseroles of
red snapper cooked in tomatoes, peppers, onions, and wine—the chef
on the yacht was an artist. Now and then we would stop at a large
island—Montserrat, Antigua—where the Martins or the LaVeques had
friends with large houses, and we would stay ashore for a while, playing tennis all day and dancing all night.

So you see, my love, I have been too busy to miss you. Johnny, I
would be a fool to waste a moment in missing you. I'm a fool to waste
the time it's taking me to write you this letter. But for the sake of
whatever we had together, whatever in the world it was (and it was
sweet, I admit), I will take the time to answer all your letters. And
with this, darling, our correspondence must stop. You made a choice
when you boarded that plane to go home to Mother, and no, I'm not
angry with you for it, though I don't admire you, either, but I have a
right to my choices, too. Still, I will answer your questions.

No, I am not "being faithful" to you. Why do you even bother to
ask? I never promised you that I would be and I can't imagine why I

should be—Johnny, honey, you are gone. Yes, I do think we "had something special": we had eight months together of luxury and ease and splendid sex and pleasure. We had eight months together of happiness, and that is rare. But I'd rather spend the night with a live man than with the warmest of memories, and no matter what we had, all we have now is memories. And oh, no, Johnny, I won't come back to Londonton, and I won't marry you. My God, you can be silly sometimes. Oh, Johnny, you don't understand a thing. You assume that because Londonton welcomed you back with open arms they'll do the same for me. You don't understand the nature of that place. You were accepted back in the fold because you belong. *You were born and raised in Londonton, your mother still lives there, your father built homes there, they know you. No matter what you do, no matter how far you stray, you will always remain one of them. But no matter what I do, darling—if I were anointed a saint—I couldn't become one of them, thank God. I will never be accepted there. Probably you'll never understand this, because you are an insider, and I am an outsider, and insiders rarely have the ability to see the whole picture clearly. And part of the power of the prejudice you are immersed in is its subtlety. And no, Johnny, it has nothing to do with time, or even birth. If I had been born and raised in Londonton, I would still be an outsider. I do not fit there, and I do not want to. I have fought all my life and will continue to fight against living a life in such busy, blind complacency.*

It touched me that you said in your last letter that you'd leave Londonton if I wished, that we would marry and live anywhere I chose. But that wouldn't work, either, would it? For your mother would always be able to lure you home—no, really, think seriously about this a moment. What would you do, for example, if your sister had some sort of crisis? Or if your mother had another one? You are the man in the family now. You'd have to go home, you know you would. No place we could move to would be far enough away from Londonton, no place in the world.

You wrote so many sweet, sad, romantic letters—my wastebasket here in the hotel is full of them. And you should throw this letter away when you've finished it, and go on to other things, for it is over between us, my love. Oh, Johnny, all the things you said were so foolish: of course you'll fall in love again. Open your eyes, look around you. Londonton is full of pretty women and girls, and they'd all get in bed with you in an instant. You will forget me sooner than you can imagine.

One last question I should answer before I close. You ask me repeatedly in your letters if I love you, if I ever loved you. Why, Johnny, how can you ask? Of course I loved you. I loved your body, your laugh, your skin, your tongue—but oh, I remember that in one of your letters you asked if I loved you instead of just your body. I thought only silly women asked questions like that. I would never have noticed you if it were not for your body, your gorgeous smile, your long slim legs. Let's not get into a discussion of whether or not I'd love you if you were crippled, deformed, ill, and maimed, that's for kids in high school. I cannot separate who you are from how you look, and you can decide for yourself if the fault lies in my imagination or your personality. I do think you are generous, kind, gentle, sometimes clever and witty. You have a marvelous tantalizing charm, oh, sweetie, sweetie, of course I loved you. You are a truly beautiful boy.

But you aren't very interesting, you know. You haven't really gone anywhere or done anything. You don't have any power or competence, that is, without your beauty. You are generous only to those from whom you want something, and oblivious to everyone else in the world. Your vision is limited—a Londonton inheritance, I assume. You are spoiled. When the shell of your body which has protected you so completely begins to wither, I cannot imagine how you will weather the world—but then you don't have to worry about that for years. You have the kind of looks that will keep you appearing twenty until you're almost fifty.

Have I said enough? Have I made myself clear? Would you like it summarized? Yes, I did love you, but no, I don't now. No, I won't marry you, or ever return to Londonton. No, I am not being faithful. When I finish this letter, I'll shower, put on my white silk dress, and meet a new lover in the hotel bar. You and I are finished, Johnny, just like in the song. It was great fun, but it was just one of those things.

Am I being cruel? Perhaps—so here's a weapon for you. Remember that I am eleven years older than you are, and that women age faster than men. When you are thirty-five, I'll be forty-six. Johnny, when you say you love me, you mean you love my body. We can never pretend that our relationship was built on intellectual compatibility or "mutual interests." Let's not kid ourselves. Let's say goodbye for good *while it's still all so fresh and sweet. I swear I'll never write another letter to you in Londonton, and I'll never read another that you send me here. It's really over for us, darling.*

On the other hand, if you were to walk into the hotel someday soon, I'm not sure what I might do. . . .

Love, Liza

Johnny kept feeling in the breast pocket of his suit to be sure the letter was still there. The organ music had begun, but he didn't hear it, he was so involved with his own thoughts. Was she insulting him, trying to get rid of him, teasing him with this letter? Or was she luring him? After all those months of living with her, he still found her mysterious, he still could not figure her out. And never mind what *she* intended; what did *he* want? He could hardly leave his mother and this town again. He had had his fling, and now it was time to settle down, wasn't it? He loved this town and the people in it, and he had a duty to his mother. . . . Still he sat mesmerized by Liza's final words. She had conjured up for him a vision: he would walk into the hotel unannounced, unexpected. Liza would be standing there with her back to him, her arms lifted as she slid a hibiscus into her hair, and she would slowly turn, arms still upraised, and see him. They would both smile. This illusion was so enchanting that as Johnny sat in the church next to his mother, surrounded by his community, he was really a million miles away.

Reynolds had spent the past eight months in Seattle. He had returned home only three days ago, and found the invitation to Michael and Mandy's wedding in his mail. So he had put on a good suit and silk tie and come. Now he sat in the sanctuary, looking around him with admiration. He had missed this building, and he was glad to be back, and glad for the wedding which caused him to return to the church when it was in a state of such adornment. The very air seemed opulent with promise.

In Seattle, Reynolds had become acquainted with a couple whom Peter Taylor had suggested he look up if he wanted company. Mark Frazier was a history professor at Seattle University. He was a handsome young man with an impeccable memory and a love for debate, and he and Reynolds enjoyed each other immensely. They spent hours in sportive argument. Mark's wife, Lilia, was just as attractive. She taught physics at the same university and was obviously an intelligent woman. And she was beautiful, in a lithe and clever way. She was sixteen years older than her husband, however, and this was obvious: she *looked* sixteen years older than Mark. But Mark seemed absolutely entranced by his wife, and as much as Reynolds enjoyed his intellectual discussions with Mark, he also enjoyed just watching the Fraziers, observing them, trying to see just how she worked her spell, for it seemed to him an unusual thing that a man should love a woman so much older than himself.

One evening when he arrived at the Fraziers', he noticed a tension in the air. Not wishing to be intrusive, he said nothing, though the atmosphere grew blacker as the evening progressed.

Suddenly Lilia said, "Mark. We're being awfully inhospitable to Reynolds. If you won't tell him why you're such a grouch tonight, I will."

It turned out that Mark was in a snit because a mutual friend had asked Lilia how she liked a new and expensive restaurant. Lilia had not told Mark that she had been to that restaurant, and she still refused to tell him whom she dined with, even whether she had been with a man or a woman. As Reynolds sat sipping his martini, the Fraziers argued. Mark thought Lilia should tell him whom she had been with, and why; Lilia refused. Mark accused Lilia of being unfaithful; Lilia said that was ridiculous, she had only had dinner with someone. Then why wouldn't she tell him about it? Mark asked. Because she didn't want to, she replied.

"Oh, this is intolerable!" Mark yelled at last, and left the room.

Reynolds leaned toward Lilia. "He's very upset, you know," he said.

"He'll recover," she replied.

"Who in the world *were* you dining with?" Reynolds asked.

"Can you keep a secret?" Lilia said, smiling her beautiful smile.

"Of course," Reynolds said, indignant and eager.

"Good," Lilia said. "So can I." She rose then, to refresh her drink.

Reynolds was piqued and intrigued by her answer, and he finally left without eating dinner, for he could tell the Fraziers wanted their privacy. So that is how she keeps him interested, Reynolds thought, and later that night as he sat on the balcony of his rented apartment, looking out at the clear summer sky, he experienced a minor revelation about the importance of mystery. God remains mysterious in the first place because He/She/It is too complicated to be easily understood, and secondly because God likes to be pursued. In the pursuit comes not only the answer but the pleasure. Reynolds did not feel ashamed to interpret truths about God from the lives of ordinary people; he was beginning to see that the lives of ordinary people were full of all sorts of extraordinary matters.

When he had learned about Ron Bennett's death that Monday morning last October, he had been plunged swiftly and terribly into self-hatred and remorse. If it had not been for Peter Taylor, he might never have emerged. It was all so much and so sudden. The Monday evening after Ron's death, Gary had asked him to come to his house, and Peter was there, too. Gary had explained what he thought had happened—Ron had had a car accident. There was no money in any of his accounts to reimburse the rec center fund, but the money would be reimbursed when the insurance came through. He asked the two men if they would agree to keep Ron's embezzlement secret, in order to spare Ron's family any more grief. Of course Peter and Reynolds had agreed to this strange little pact; they would keep Ron's secret. It seemed the least they could do. Gary and Reynolds never did discuss with each other the nature of their relationship in this matter; they did not say to each other that they held themselves responsible for Ron's death. It seemed too delicate and terrible to discuss. Reynolds simply went home, intending to continue as he was. But he was plunged into a bleakness that went past the intellectual despair he had been living with. He felt guilty and disturbed. His spirit was twisted in upon itself; he was sick with confusion.

He thought he had been doing the right thing—he had tried to stop a man from stealing money from a community. But somehow he had done the wrong thing. He had caused a man to take his own life. He had not meant to do this, but it had happened. Of course Gary and Peter had been there, too, but it had been Reynolds who had discovered the situation and who had pushed to have it stopped. Should he therefore shoulder a certain percentage of the blame? Did that mean he had to feel only partially bad? He felt totally wretched, as if he were diseased inside.

He really was ill, and he took a leave of absence from the college in Londonton and went to Seattle as he had planned. But the physical distance did not provide relief. He continued to feel sick, cramped and battered with guilt and anger. At last, in desperation, he wrote Peter Taylor one of the most intimate letters of his life, explaining his misery, asking for help. Probably he could not have said any of these things in person, but over the months he and Peter established a lengthy correspondence, in which Reynolds played the Devil's advocate and Peter played God's.

"I do not hate you for what you did, and God does not hate you for it," Peter wrote. "Nor, do I believe, does God hate Ron."

"But I hate God," Reynolds replied. "And I hate myself."

"Yes, I understand that," Peter wrote back. "But I believe that what you call hate is really an energy within you that is equal to the energy of the earth that crushes coal into diamonds. If you do not give up, that energy will condense the blackness in your heart into a nugget of great light and illumination, which is love."

"But a man has died because of my pride and righteousness," Reynolds wrote.

"Do you really think it is so simple?" Peter replied. "Can you really believe that Ron was so simple?"

"I never should have brought the matter of his embezzlement to light," Reynolds wrote. "It was unchristian of me. Uncharitable. Arrogant."

In reply, Peter sent Reynolds a passage quoted from St. Matthew:

"Moreover if thy brother shall trespass against thee, go and tell him his fault between thee and him alone: if he shall hear thee, thou has gained thy brother.

"But if he will not hear thee, then take with thee one or two more, that in the mouth of two or three witnesses every word may be established.

"And if he shall neglect to hear them, tell it unto the church; but if he neglect to hear the church, let him be unto thee as an heathen man and a publican.

"Verily I say unto you, Whatsoever ye shall bind on earth shall be bound in heaven: and whatsoever ye shall loose on earth shall be

loosed in heaven. Again I say unto you, That if two of you shall agree
on earth as touching anything that they shall ask, it shall be done for
them of my Father which is in heaven.

"For where two or three are gathered together in my name, there
am I in the midst of them."

"But the four of us—Gary, Ron, you, and I—were not gathered
together in God's name," Reynolds wrote.

"Perhaps we are now," Peter replied. "This event has changed us
all."

"But it did not happen to change us all," Reynolds wrote.

"How can you know?" Peter asked. "It is arrogant to think we
know the one clear cause of anything. The result in this case is that
one of us has died, and the rest of us are suffering. I believe we will all
be redeemed."

Certainly Reynolds felt bound now to Londonton, and in a
strange way to Peter Taylor, and the Bennetts and Moyers, and the
rest of the congregation of the church. He could not see what he could
do directly that would make a difference, and he thought perhaps that
was the point, or was at least acceptable. He would return, pay taxes,
teach students, lead committees, greet his neighbors on the street when
he passed them.

He called Peter his first evening home, to tell him that he had returned and would take up his regular teaching duties. "I'm grateful to
you for your help. For your letters," Reynolds said. "I can never express
my gratitude sufficiently."

"And I'm grateful to you," Peter said. "You provoked my thoughts.
You should have been here—I gave the most wonderful sermons! I am
grateful to you." When Reynolds was silent, Peter said, "Reynolds, I
meant that."

Now Reynolds thought that he would live out his life happily
enough, doing what he enjoyed. He would teach; he would take part
in community activities. He would read, search, and pray; he did not
think now that he would find all the answers to his questions or even
be a perfect man, but he believed that in the quest he would find re-
demption. In any case, at the very least, it would provide him with intellectual pleasure, and he need never worry that this puzzle would dis-
appoint him by proving too easily solved. He felt that he had entered a
black night of the soul, and with the grace of God and the help of

Peter Taylor, he had emerged from it. He did not feel that he had escaped it forever; rather it seemed he would all his life hover just above it, aware of its closeness, and staying safe from its grim grasp only by constant exertion and vigilance. There were times when the knowledge of this black nihilistic presence filled him with terror; he would roam his apartment, unable to sleep. But there were also times when that knowledge filled him with the exhilarating boldness and zeal of a warrior or explorer venturing forth on dangerous waters, searching for new land.

Now he sat in church smiling a small smile. If there were times when a man stood burning in terror and loneliness, fearing the black void, there were also times when a man could sit in comfort and warmth, surrounded by light. If he had a home, it was this church; if he had a family, it was this congregation. They would go about their complicated lives, providing him with the most amazing metaphors and messages; he appreciated their human beauty, but even more he was grateful for the ambiguity of their living. Oh, he knew he was a cold man, seeing human beings as metaphors, but then he knew that there are as many ways to see people as there are people to see. Perhaps these people really were metaphors; who knew God's design? And in whose intelligence does the ultimate sight reside?

Wilbur thought about salt a lot. Sometimes he'd catch himself running his tongue over the roof of his mouth, imagining the gritty white crystals there, and his mouth would fill with saliva. Pretzels, nuts, bacon, pizza. Before his heart attack, he used to sprinkle his popcorn with so much salt that after eating his lips would be tender, slightly blistered from the tasty abrasion. But now he was on a low-salt diet, and he often thought that if he were given the choice between knowing the answers to the nature of the universe and being free to eat corn on the cob slathered in butter and salt, he'd choose the corn without hesitation.

He was tired all the time. He had recovered from his heart attack, and his life was fairly normal once again, but he was tired all the time. His doctor told him that was to be expected because he had had a heart attack, but Wilbur's theory was that his body was weak because it was deprived of salt. How could something so basic be bad? At last he understood the serious nature of Norma's complaints all those years when she had been dieting. Life was just not as enjoyable when eating was limited.

He'd gotten so cranky when he first went on the low-salt diet that Norma, in sympathy, threw out all the salt in the house and vowed she wouldn't use it either. She fixed him fresh vegetables and fruits, vanilla puddings. She made her own salt-free bread and served it to him with honey for a treat. They kept no salt shaker on the table, and when they sat down to a meal, Norma ate exactly what Wilbur ate, with the same seasonings. It helped him stay on his diet, and he appreciated this. But last week he had discovered that she had little caches of goodies hidden all over the house: he'd found a package of pretzels among the guest towels and a jar of salted cashews among the vacuum-cleaner bags. He'd nearly burst into tears at the sight. "It's so unfair!" he said aloud, and sat down on the bed, trembling with anger.

He had thought that over the months his craving for salt would diminish, that his body would get used to the blandness of his diet. Instead, the craving grew, so that it went everywhere with him and shadowed his every thought. When he read a newspaper account of a criminal who had been sent to prison for life, Wilbur thought: Well, that man doesn't know how lucky he is; he'll be locked up, but they won't deprive him of salt. A television commercial for pizza or hot dogs could drive him into a day-long depression, but in spite of that, he had taken up a perverse new practice: he sat around for hours at a time looking at Norma's women's magazines. He didn't read the articles or stories; he read the recipes. He looked at the ads showing smiling women holding out sandwiches made of corned beef and cheese with pickles on the side or canapé crackers with anchovies curled in the middle, and he'd run his tongue around his mouth and fantasize the taste of all those salty pungent foods. Afterward he'd be filled with melancholy. In his better moments he reminded himself of Norma long ago when Queen Elizabeth was crowned. Norma would sit and study the glossy pictures of the coronation in magazines, and sigh and sigh, completely entranced, but afterward, when cooking dinner for her husband and little sons, she'd be in a bitter mood; she'd grumble around the kitchen muttering, "I'll bet *Queen Elizabeth* doesn't have to force *her* children to eat their vegetables." Wilbur guessed it was just part of human nature to long for what you knew you could never have.

His doctor had told him that he had to cut out smoking, drinking, and eating salt.

"I haven't smoked for years, and I seldom drink; couldn't I have a little salt?" Wilbur had asked.

"You can have all the salt you want," the doctor replied, "but it will kill you."

"I shouldn't have heart trouble," Wilbur complained. "I'm not overweight, I don't smoke, and I've been walking regularly ever since my bladder operation."

"Yes, and I have patients who are dying of emphysema who have never smoked a cigarette in their lives," the doctor answered. "You don't always get the disease you deserve."

Wilbur had spent a month in the hospital, and two months in bed at home. During that period, he had been too weak to miss salt, too weak and too grateful each day to wake up alive. As the months passed and his life got back to a semblance of normality, however, he found himself much more depressed by his new situation than he thought he should be. Sometimes he cried for no reason at all. Then he'd think, well, he had plenty of reason, he was old and his health was fragile, and he couldn't have salt, and he couldn't have sex.

The doctor had told him after his six-month checkup that he could resume sexual activities as long as he was sensible about it. That night he and Norma had lain naked together—oh, how sweet it was to press his naked body against hers, to run his hands over her warm skin. The fatness of her hips and stomach and breasts was so sexy: so much healthy flesh! They caressed each other tenderly, old lovers that they were, caught up in the moment, glad for each other's life. Wilbur's penis, which for six months had been humbled and ignored, rose up like a phoenix reborn, and he and Norma had smiled at each other triumphantly, delighted at the virile return of this old friend's powers. But when he was inside Norma, clenching her against him, gratefully lost in the physical delirium of sexual pleasure, something happened. His body betrayed him. He was distracted from the joy in his loins by a sensation of pain in his chest. For one brief moment, he thought that Norma was squeezing his chest too hard with her arms, but he quickly realized this was not the case. She did not have the strength to lock him in such a crushing grip.

He collapsed against her, crying out, and quickly rolled off of her and lay whimpering against the pillow, his hands at his throat, for he felt he was being strangled. The pain passed fairly quickly as he lay quietly on the bed, and the terrifying pressure in his chest was soon replaced by a bleak misery. Angina. He had been warned about this; the doctor said it would happen if he overexerted himself. He was supposed to exercise moderately each day: *moderately* was the key word. Apparently sex, even easy tender sex between two people who were more like friends than lovers, was not a moderate activity. He would have to cut it out, at least for a while, or risk the chance of another heart attack.

No salt, no sex. It really did not seem fair that the joys of both the top and the bottom of his body should be lost. His mouth, his penis, organs of tangy, greedy gladness, were now relegated to functions of bland maintenance. It made him mad and sorry for himself.

He was ashamed of himself for this petulance. At least he was alive. Ron Bennett was dead. When Norma told him about Ron's death, three weeks after it had happened, when Wilbur had been pronounced in good shape and she thought he could take the news without too much stress on his heart, Wilbur had been stunned. Blown away, as the young kids said, by the news. Blown away into other spaces of the mind, vast gray areas where he roamed in confusion, searching through the fog of wonder for one solid grit of truth. It seemed to him that a mistake of enormous proportion had been made in his favor: the Angel of Death had been hovering over Londonton, and had accidentally swept up into her arms the wrong man. *He* should have died, not Ron Bennett.

Wilbur did not believe for a minute that Ron's death had been accidental. Ron was an excellent driver, and the strip of road he'd been traveling on was so flat that a rolling ball couldn't gain the momentum to cross that stretch of pavement and drop down that embankment, let alone a heavy car with brakes. He felt certain that Ron had committed suicide, but he could not figure out just why. Norma, who sat by his bed each day, giving him each ounce of Londonton gossip she could think of as if she thought it were some kind of medicine, the more for him the better, reported that the majority of Londonton assumed that Ron had been on his way to a clandestine liaison that night; what else would he be doing driving around by himself that time on a Sunday night? There were no meetings going on then, he hadn't been to the movies, he had finished a routine conference about the rec center with Gary Moyer and Reynolds Houston at his own house earlier that evening—this bit of factual information they had gotten from Gary, who reported that they had gotten together at eight that evening to go over some rec center details. So he hadn't been out because of his work, and Judy hadn't been with him, so it couldn't have been a social engagement. Gary Moyer had advanced the theory that Ron had been out looking for Johnny, who hadn't come home all day, but the townspeople didn't believe that. Johnny was not an adolescent just learning to drive; he was a grown man, entitled to stay out late. The people of Londonton surreptitiously concluded that Ron must have been having an affair with someone, and that he had been in such a state, such a hurry to get to her, that in his blind passion he had driven off the road.

Wilbur tended to agree with part of this. He didn't tell Norma, but he knew better than anyone else that it probably was true that Ron had been having an affair. Still he knew from all the conversations he'd had with Ron that Ron's affairs were of the body, not of the heart. He could not imagine Ron so overcome with desire that he would drive off the road.

As he lay in his hospital bed, Wilbur had plenty of time to think about Ron, and he finally concluded that Ron must have been having an affair and his lover had threatened to tell Judy, or had pressured Ron to divorce Judy and marry her, and Ron, whose obsession in life was the happiness and respectability of his wife and family, had driven off the bridge in desperation, trusting that his mistress would not be cruel enough to cause trouble when he was dead. It was not a totally satisfactory conclusion, but it was finally the one he settled on. Everyone in Londonton waited in their various social clusters for this mistress of Ron's to announce herself in some way; to be overcome with grief at the funeral, or not to appear at all. People longed to know who she was: A married woman perhaps? Or a divorced woman like Leigh Findly? Of course *not* Leigh Findly, she was too flaky; Ron was too conservative. On the other hand, they say opposites attract, and Leigh was a pretty woman. The town buzzed and watched. The fact that Judy Bennett hid herself away in her house for the first few months after Ron's death strengthened their belief that Ron had had a mistress. Many people called to invite Judy over for dinner, but she refused every time. Poor woman, she was undoubtedly so embarrassed.

Wilbur didn't worry much about Judy Bennett, for he didn't know her very well, but he did miss Ron. He mourned him. He realized that he had come to think of Ron as almost another son; he certainly had gotten on better with Ron than with his own sons. Both sons had flown in from their various homes off in other places of the United States in order to be at Wilbur's side for a few days after the heart attack, and Wilbur had been glad to see them, but he wished he could have seen Ron, too.

The knowledge came to him as he lay in his hospital bed waiting for his body to recover that he would have liked to give his peoms to Ron when he died. Ron wasn't particularly the sort to like poetry, but they had spent so much time talking together, more time than Wilbur ever spent with his sons, that he thought Ron might see the poems as just another way of continuing that conversation. Now Ron was dead, and Wilbur didn't know what to do about his poems. Phrases and images occurred to him from time to time as he lay there staring at the ceiling, and when he could sit up in bed, he attempted to write these things down, but it was too exhausting. Humph, Wilbur had thought, it's a fine state a man's in when just thinking up a line of poetry is too exhausting!

He had told Norma about the poems the first day after his heart attack; it had seemed an urgent matter then. "They're up in the attic in my old fishing-tackle box," he told her. "If I die, I want you to read them, then you can do whatever you like with them. They're probably no good. I don't know why I wrote them."

"So that's what you were doing up there," Norma said. "I was beginning to wonder. Poems, huh? My, my. Wilbur, you'd better get well and live a long life. I think there's no end to the things you want to get up to."

There was no end to the things he wanted to get up to, but Wilbur was afraid that in spite of his desires, his energy was failing him. He tried walking short distances every day during the summer, tried to build up his energy level, but it didn't seem to work. He was always so tired. It was as if his body had always operated off of two powerful motors and now one of them had shut down. He didn't have the endurance or the stamina. And his mind was playing tricks on him, though he'd never tell Norma; he didn't want to worry her. One moment he'd be sitting on the back porch with her, drinking lemonade and watching her weed her flower garden, and suddenly he'd be back in his dry-cleaning shop when he had just opened the business. He could see skinny, lank-haired Gretchen Hardt in her blue flowered shirt pressing the cleaned clothes with a flatiron. He'd blink his eyes, and Gretchen would disappear; he'd find himself in the shop as it was when he sold it a few years ago. He'd be standing by a big drum of Du Pont Val-Clean, the fluorocarbon chemicals they used to clean the clothes now, and Amy Vaden would be laying the clothes out on the hydraulically operated press and pushing two buttons to get the work done. "It's amazing how technology has changed things," Wilbur would say.

"What?" Norma would ask, and he would find himself staring at his wife, back on his porch on a summer day.

These flashes of vivid memory were not unpleasant. Still he hoped he'd die before he somehow got lost in them and ended up scaring Norma by mentally living in the vast reaches of his mind. She'd think he'd gone mad.

No, it was necessary to hang on to his sanity, his sense of reality, for all it was worth. It was necessary not to eat salt, not to have sex, to drink only one cup of coffee a day, and to get moderate exercise. Living could be an effort and a bore, he was discovering, and he knew he was losing his sense of humor, or at least it seemed now that when he made a joke it always had a sardonic cast to it, and this shamed him. He was alive. He still had Norma and two sons living and five grandchildren. He still had friends and a whole world to watch.

Days like today, of course, made it all seem worthwhile. If death was the price of life, he'd gladly pay it, to earn such a day. The sunlight flashed and glittered through the windows with such brightness that it seemed it must be made of angels' wings, and the opulent beauty of all the flowers made his soul expand. The matter of the earth was miraculous. He and Norma had arrived early, so that he could take his time getting settled in the pew. They sat toward the back so that Norma could get a good long look at everyone as they entered and went down the aisle. Wilbur enjoyed looking at the people, too: how wonderful they all looked, dressed up in their fancy best, smug as flowers, pleased as youngsters on a holiday. Wilbur forgot to think of salt. He stopped turning inward and was satisfied to sit and gaze and reflect on this portion of mankind with whom he had spent his life. It surprised and strangely depressed him that after all they had been through, the Bennett family looked exactly as they had a year ago. Judy had not gained or lost weight or gotten one gray hair. She seemed untouched by the tragedy of her life, and Wilbur wondered if what was superficial was also real, or whether she was just very crafty at deception. He was glad to see that Reynolds Houston was back; he'd missed his presence. He didn't know Reynolds well, and seldom talked with him, except briefly at coffee hour, and yet he felt the town needed Reynolds, who seemed to move through their lives like a headmaster passing quietly through a schoolroom, causing everyone automatically to correct his posture or his thoughts. They might not like him, but they were better people because of him.

"Look," Norma whispered to Wilbur now, "Pam and Gary Moyer aren't sitting together. Do you suppose they're having trouble? Actually, I've heard rumors that they're getting separated."

"Well," Wilbur said, "they're certainly separated here and now."

"Oh, dear," Norma said. "I wonder what's happened. Poor people."

Poor people? Wilbur thought, looking at Pam and Gary. No, not really, he replied to himself: they are only in their forties, they are young, and they can eat salt and have sex. Their lives are full.

"Hats are coming back," Norma whispered.

"Who?" Wilbur asked.

"*Hats*," Norma said. "Women are starting to wear hats again. I'm so glad I've saved all mine, up in the attic. I think I'll go dig them out this afternoon. I hope I saved the one with pheasant feathers."

Wilbur smiled and patted his wife's hand. *Hats*, he thought, and he was pleased at the thought of Norma's pleasure.

The organ music swelled. Peter Taylor walked in, regal in his black robes and white stole, followed by Michael and his best man, his brother Will. The congregation whispered in anticipation, then were still, as they turned to watch Mandy Findly walk down the aisle. Wilbur felt lifted up on a wave of music. He was overcome with joy; he wanted to laugh out loud; for one moment he seemed to rise above the congregation, to hover there looking down; and he was exhilarated by this illusion. He grabbed up a program that had been left in the pew rack from last Sunday, and took a pen from his pocket, and quickly wrote a poem. He wrote:

Mirrors reflect the sun's light so that the warming glow
Is magnified, expanded. Prisms refract that light
Into a dazzle past our one sun's art. This is right.
Even God needs humans if He wants a brilliant show.

Just so, yellow roses shimmer in a crystal bowl.
My friends glitter in this church, a varied, lovely crowd
That gladdens me. If I were brave, I would shout out loud
To all who gather here: I love you, body and soul.

Then he folded the program, put it in his pocket, and turned his
attention to the wedding. He hardly knew where to look, everyone was
so beautiful.

I've got the best seat in the house, Peter Taylor thought, though he
wasn't sitting down. He had just entered the sanctuary and from where
he stood he could see everyone clearly: the jubilant congregation, his
wife, Patricia, in the first row in a beautiful dress that made her look
too young to be the mother of a groom, and, coming up to stand in
front of him, his sons.

Will was fourteen now, and in the past year he had suddenly,
thank God, started growing, so fast that they hadn't been able to keep
him in clothes or shoes that fit. He was wearing a rented black tux and
he looked handsome and almost manly, as long as he kept his mouth
closed over his braces. Also his crutches kept him from moving toward
the center of the church with the appropriate grace and solemnity.
He'd practiced furiously, but he just hadn't had enough time to get
used to them. A month ago he had gone to the new skating rink for a
roller disco party, and in a fit of abandon while showing off for his
new girlfriend, Will had leaped, twirled, and crashed to the floor,
breaking his right leg. Peter wasn't there to see it happen; he had been
called to the hospital during the evening. When he arrived to find his
son in the emergency room, the ambulance attendants and the cluster
of friends who had followed Will to the hospital had informed Peter
that Will's major worry was that now he wouldn't get to be best man
for his brother's wedding. "I'll kill myself if I can't be his best man, I'll
really kill myself!" Will had sobbed, crying like a child. After his leg

was set and he was settled in his hospital bed, they had called Michael in Northampton. Peter had listened casually as Will, trying to seem cool, told Michael what had happened.

"But listen, Michael," Will said, "I still want to be your best man. They said I'll be on crutches by then—would you still let me be best man if I'm on crutches?"

Peter couldn't hear what Michael answered, but he saw the look of relief and joy pass over his younger son's face. When he hung up the phone, Will told him that Michael had promised he could still be best man, and that furthermore, if Will wasn't able to walk by September 4, they'd just put off the wedding until he was able to walk. Will had been delighted, but Peter had been stunned. Since when had his sons developed such devotion to each other? All this intense love his children were involved in amazed him.

Look what love had done for Michael. In the past year he had moved to Northampton with Mandy, gotten straight A's in all his high school courses, graduated from high school, and at the same time made a good living. He had worked after school from three till eight at night five days a week and all day Saturday for a man named Lars Larsen, who ran his own wallpapering and painting business. Lars liked Michael's work so much that he gave him three raises in the space of eleven months, and Michael learned a lot of useful information as well. This morning, when Michael came down for breakfast after spending the night in his old bedroom, he suggested that he come up some Sunday and redo the bedroom for them.

"I could turn it into a beautiful guest room for you," he had said. "You pick out the paper, Mom, and I'll paint the ceiling and woodwork and paper the walls. Of course, I'll have to do some sanding and wallboard compounding on the wall where I nailed so many posters and models and junk. I was checking it this morning, there are some bad holes in the plaster that could become a problem if they aren't taken care of."

"Why, that would be lovely, Michael," Patricia had said. "How nice of you." But her eyes met Peter's across the table and she telegraphed him a silent message: *guest* room. Our son wants to turn his bedroom into a *guest* room.

As if sensing this, Michael had said, "Well, then Mandy and I could come up and stay with you a lot. Course, you'd have to get another bed. You could buy a bed with the money you'd be saving on having me do the work. I wouldn't want you to pay me."

All these calculations, Peter thought. All this energy, all these plans. Short-range plans; Michael still did not intend to go to college, and he had even refused Lars's offer to become a junior partner in the business, because he wanted to try his hand at other things. He still thought he might like to be a landscape contractor. He was not doing any of the things Peter had hoped his first son might do, yet Peter had to admit he was growing proud of the boy. Michael had become competent, and certainly more sensitive—a year ago he never would have noticed that his mother was hiding a sadness behind her smile. Much of this was probably Mandy's doing, or at least the consequence of living with Mandy for a year. Peter liked Mandy; in fact, he thought Michael was a lucky man.

Now Michael stood before him, his thick black hair brushed till it shone, his powerful body nearly bursting from the seams of his rented tux. The processional had started, the ushers were bringing the bridesmaids down the aisle, and the young people all looked lovely, but Peter could not keep his eyes off his first son, who seemed to be the handsomest person he'd ever seen. The church was packed with people, for not only did most of the Londonton friends come for the wedding, but so did an entire contingent of Northampton friends—men and women who called Michael "Mike."

Peter's daughter Lucy came down the aisle now, scattering yellow rose petals for the bride to walk on. Small breasts budded under the yellow lace of her dress. Even his little girl was growing up. Lucy was smiling, embarrassed and pleased to have so many people watching her, and then she looked right at Peter and flashed a grin. *My children*, Peter thought, and a knowledge clenched inside him, taking his breath away. Patricia and I gave these children life, Peter thought, we did our best to keep them safe, to encourage them in their growing, and we have loved them. In turn, they survived this love and the knowledge of our fierce expectations. He did not suppose that this relationship was very much different from the one between God and man.

Mandy came down the aisle now on her father's arm; yellow roses were twined in her hair. She looked beautiful. As she passed each pew, little joyous exclamations rose into the air like bright balloons: "Ah!" people said, seeing her pass. Then she stood before Peter, and smiled up into Michael's eyes. For one brief moment, Peter felt buoyant with optimism, drunk with sunshine, Mendelssohn, and hope. Then the organ music stopped and the church was quiet. Mandy and Michael looked at him, trusting him to know, for these few moments at least, just what to do. He smiled back at them, as a father, as a minister, as a fellow human being who loved them in their young beauty. He said:

"Dearly Beloved, We are gathered here today in the sight of God and man."